By SHELTER SOMERSET

NOVELS
Between Two Worlds
Between Two Promises

On the Trail to Moonlight Gulch

Published by DREAMSPINNER PRESS
http://www.dreamspinnerpress.com

SHELTER SOMERSET

# On the Trail to
# MOONLIGHT GULCH

*Dreamspinner Press*

Published by
Dreamspinner Press
382 NE 191st Street #88329
Miami, FL 33179-3899, USA
http://www.dreamspinnerpress.com/

On the Trail to Moonlight Gulch
Copyright © 2012 by Shelter Somerset

Cover Art by Anne Cain    annecain.art@gmail.com
Cover Design by Mara McKennen

ISBN: 978-1-61372-446-0

Printed in the United States of America
First Edition
April 2012

eBook edition available
eBook ISBN: 978-1-61372-447-7

To Marco

# ACKNOWLEDGMENTS

I WOULD like to thank the Chicago History Museum for its prodigious aggregation of data on every conceivable topic from Chicago's early Swedish migration to the imperceptible gay scene of the Gilded Age. I would also like to acknowledge the South Dakota State Historical Society for its wealth of information on frontier life in the Black Hills during the Gold Rush years.

# AUTHOR'S NOTE

*MATRIMONIAL NEWS* was an authentic weekly matchmaker periodical published in San Francisco and Kansas City from the 1860s to its demise in the 1890s. We can assume of the thousands of respondents from around the world who answered the frontiersmen's calls for companionship, some might have been lonely homosexual men hiding their true identities, like this novel's protagonist, Torsten Pilkvist. The personal advertisements illustrated in the novel are fictitious, but they represent a typical approach used by the men and women who advertised.

# CHAPTER ONE

LOVE smacked Torsten Pilkvist in the face like a sack of flour. He knew the moment Joseph van Werckhoven stepped off the hansom cab. Normally, Torsten paid scarce attention to the boarders his parents took in for ten dollars a week at their six-bedroom row house in the North Side of Chicago. But this time, Tory, watching from one of the guest room windows upstairs, could barely peel his eyes off the stranger from New York City.

Mr. van Werckhoven had traveled to Chicago to oversee the opening of his family's downtown drugstore. According to the telegram from Tory's second cousin in Brooklyn, a long-time housekeeper for the van Werckhovens, the store would be the family's first outside of New York. The Pilkvists had prepared for the gentleman with far more effort than for any other guest that Tory could remember. Fortunately for Tory, Chicago had grown so rapidly the past few years that local inns, already bulging with lodgers, could hold few newcomers. The well-to-do Mr. van Werckhoven had limited options of places to stay.

Fifteen years after the Great Fire of '71, Chicago had mushroomed to more than one million residents, surpassing Philadelphia and Brooklyn to become the nation's second-largest city. Buildings rivaling cathedrals were being constructed downtown. Some people were calling them "skyscrapers." Only five years old when the fire had spread across the city, Tory remembered little of the calamity. But he would never forget the anguished faces of the adults. Even in his neighborhood of River North, which the flames had spared, residents, including his parents, wore their somber expressions as tangibly as their derbies and bonnets. Perhaps that was why Tory had developed a profound fear of fire.

Yet the enthusiasm to rebuild soon eclipsed the city's despair. Survivors had said the fervor for renewal overtook the city almost as quickly as the fire had. Resurrected into action, residents and ambitious newcomers alike lifted the city from the smoldering ashes. The building frenzy continued unabated and seemed to grow with intensity each passing year. Joseph van Werckhoven, like hundreds of thousands like him, had ventured to Chicago to capitalize on that unstoppable growth. Peering at him while he paid the coachman, Tory was delighted he had.

The New Yorker nodded to the coachman and, with a crocodile valise clasped in each hand, ascended the marble steps. Tory dashed to the upstairs landing to gaze through the balusters while his mother greeted the debonair stranger at the door. The setting sun hadn't played tricks on Tory's eyes while he'd gazed from the window. The newcomer radiated masculine good looks. Taller than average, he stood above Tory's five-foot-one mother by at least eight inches.

"Good afternoon. I'm Joseph van Werckhoven." He slipped off his gloves and top hat and bowed his head.

"Ja, of course, we expect you. Please come in. I am Anna Pilkvist." She opened the heavy oak door wider and gestured for him to enter fully.

A typical flush heated Tory's cheeks when his mother greeted their new boarder. Her thick Swedish accent, sticking to her lips like molasses, was not always easy for outsiders to understand. Mr. van Werckhoven, obviously a gentleman, seemed unfazed. He nodded in acknowledgment of her kind words and mentioned how fortuitous that Heloise had recommended their home to his family.

"It will be so much nicer staying in a pleasant home than a stuffy hotel," he said.

"So glad Heloise write us about you," Mrs. Pilkvist said, looking up at the guest through batting eyelashes. "Heloise say only wonderful things about your family."

Mr. van Werckhoven set his luggage on the mahogany floor and gazed about the narrow entrance foyer, his expression cheerful and earnest. "I must say, Heloise failed to do your home justice in her descriptions. It's quite lovely."

From Tory's crouched position, he detected a pink hue germinating over his mother's pale cheeks. He wondered if she might not be playing coy. She smoothed the front of her bustled skirt and blushed some more. Laying the gentleman's frock and hat on the sideboard, she called for Tory using what he surreptitiously referred to as her "party" voice.

Tory jumped to his feet, checked his reflection in the hallway mirror, and patted his hair to make sure the pomade still kept the unruly waves in check. His heart pounding, he descended the stairs, careful not to appear overzealous.

"We run bakery next to house," Mrs. Pilkvist was telling the new boarder as Tory made his way downstairs, his sweaty hand dragging along the wooden handrail. "My husband there now working."

"Heloise mentioned your bakery." Mr. van Werckhoven raised his nose elegantly and inhaled. "I think I can smell it now."

"Folks come from as far away as Hyde Park and Douglas for our tasty lussebulle and tartas." She giggled. "You come at good time. Supper will be ready in about an hour, and afterward you can try some of our treats. We like to have cakes with tea and coffee for our guests in the parlor." She turned to Tory, standing on the bottom step. "Torsten, come meet our new boarder, Mr. Joseph van Werckhoven. This is man Heloise write us about. Mr. van Werckhoven, this is my Torsten."

It was as if the soles of Tory's gaiters were nailed to the wooden step. He could barely compel himself to move forward and accept Mr. van Werckhoven's outstretched hand. The guest stepped closer. Tory, trying his best not to ogle the man's shimmering cocoa-colored eyes, finally shook his hand. He hoped that the stranger would not notice his sweaty grip.

The man's touch sent a tremor along Tory's arm. Alarmed by the sensation, he let his hand drop by his side like a dead weight.

"It's a pleasure meeting you." Joseph's smile revealed a large set of even white teeth.

"Heloise tell me all about how nice your home is in New York City," Mrs. Pilkvist said. "She say it's like a palace. I hope that you will find ours to your liking."

"Heloise flatters us," Joseph said. "But there's nothing more splendid than a well-suited home for one's family, regardless of size."

"Ours suits us good," Mrs. Pilkvist said. "We bought it five years ago. We used to stay in small flat above bakery. We rent it to young couple now. Then we see the new row houses be built, so we buy one from bank. At first we think it too big for our family, especially since Tory's two sisters each had one foot down the aisle, but Mr. Pilkvist come up with idea to take in boarders. Chicago growing so fast, we think to make money off it."

Joseph chuckled. "It does seem the entire world is moving to Chicago. The train here was packed full, and with the most interesting types of people. My father and I hope to achieve as much success here in Chicago as your family has."

"Ja, your store will do good." Mrs. Pilkvist giggled and blushed. "I have no doubt."

"I'll make sure to toast all of our prosperous futures at supper," Joseph said. "You still live here with your parents, Torsten?"

For a moment, Tory had no idea the stranger had addressed him. So mesmerized he was by the man's dignified manner and looks that every sound seemed absorbed by the papered walls. His chestnut pompadour flipped stylishly over the top of his head, and the thick, curly mustache, precisely waxed, accentuated his soft lips. His shoulders, broad and sturdy, held aloft his lean body like a statue. And the lavender cologne rose from under the banded collar of his Coulter shirt as if he'd stepped from a garden. When Joseph repeated himself, Tory shook to attention. "Yes, I do still live here."

"Then you'll be taking supper with us?"

"We all usually eat with the boarders," Tory said. "Except Pappa. He's often busy in the bakery."

"Good, then you can tell me about your wonderful city. I'm eager to learn more."

"We have three other boarders who come from elsewhere too," Mrs. Pilkvist said. "They maybe tell you what they discovered about Chicago."

Joseph eyed Torsten. "I'd much rather learn from a native."

Tory's mother lifted her eyes to the high ceiling. "I never quite think of it that way. Tory is only one among us who is born here. Even his sisters all born in Sweden, although just babies when we come to America." She looked back to the guest. "In the meantime, Mr. van Werckhoven, we show you upstairs where you stay. Torsten, follow me with Mr. van Werckhoven's things."

"Yes, Mamma." Tory reached for Joseph's valises, but Joseph kept him from lifting the larger one by laying his hand on top of his. Another tremor traipsed along Tory's arm.

"Please, let me get that," Joseph said. Their faces were close enough Tory could smell the mint on his breath.

Tory slid his hand from under Joseph's. With the smaller valise clasped in his shaky hand, he followed his mother and the newcomer upstairs.

THE supper table vibrated with chatter. After three days without a fourth boarder, everyone appreciated the fresh energy. The usual boarders (Miss Clair Schuster, a young woman about Tory's age from Wisconsin; Mr. Anthony Dunlop, a standoffish and painfully bashful thirty-five-year-old engineer from Scotland; and Mr. Abner T. Raincliff, a middle-aged banker from Indiana) sat in their proper seats around the table, riveted on the newcomer. His wealth and standing had not eluded them. Mr. Dunlop seemed even shyer in his presence, and Mr. Raincliff harbored a cutting envy in his blue eyes.

Yet Clair Schuster's ogling upset Tory the most. She had begun flirting with him the moment they'd met in the parlor. He'd been embarrassed for Clair when she'd asked about Joseph's marital status. With a slight flush, Joseph had replied to her naïve question that, even at twenty-six, he was still searching for "the right person."

Joseph seemed to take little notice of Clair Schuster's coquettish head-tilting and impish giggles. Tory wanted to fling a spoonful of his mashed potatoes at her. She had lodged with them for five weeks, waiting for a vacancy at one of the women's hotels. She worked as an assembler at an agricultural implements factory downtown. Tory wanted her gone once and for all.

"I've never been to New York City," she said in her infuriating crooning manner. "Is it as big as they say? Bigger than Chicago?"

"Yes, it is a bit bigger," Joseph said with a paternal air. "But the buildings seem taller here. I have a feeling once this new steel frame construction takes off back east, New York, perhaps even Boston, will catch up in no time."

"The building where I work on Polk Street is eleven stories," Mr. Raincliff said boastfully. "If you go to the top floor you can almost see clear down to the stockyards."

"Nothing that big in Sweden," Tory's father said from the head of the table, where he was already working on his second helping of roast beef. His duties in the bakery were yet unfinished, but he had told Tory and his mother he wanted to dine with their latest guest. Joseph van Werckhoven was the most distinguished boarder to stay under their roof, and he refused to forego a meal with him his first night.

He appeared as charmed by Mr. van Werckhoven's presence as everyone else, which meant a lot to Tory. His father, often unfairly judgmental, could cause Tory embarrassment with his abrupt manner. "Of course," he went on, "Mrs. Pilkvist and me haven't returned to Sweden since we left over twenty years ago. But the Swedes swarming into Chicago today say little has changed there."

"I read in the papers about the famine a few years ago," Joseph said, his mouth downturned with genuine empathy. "Hit Finland too, I believe."

"Ja," Mrs. Pilkvist said, shaking her head. "That's why so many come here. From Finland, Norway… all over Scandinavia."

"It's good they have a place like America to come to," Mr. Raincliff said in his gruff yet jovial voice.

"We are fortunate," Mr. Pilkvist said.

"That reminds me." Joseph raised his glass of merlot. The crystal glinted in the candlelit chandelier above the table. "I vowed earlier to toast all of our prosperities." He raised his glass higher. "To Chicago and the United States." He peered at Tory. "And to new friends."

"Hear, hear," the diners said in unison and clinked their glasses.

Only the Scottish man, Mr. Dunlop, remained quiet. He had barely raised his wine glass. He rarely partook in the conversations at the supper table unless directly addressed, and even then he responded with one or two words. As an engineer working for one of the larger architectural firms in town, Tory thought he should have much to share about the new construction projects taking place, a frequent subject at the supper table. But he almost never communicated his thoughts.

In the company of a man like Joseph van Werckhoven, broad-shouldered and confident, Tory understood why the man from Scotland might find his words all the more restricted. Even his father seemed smitten by the New Yorker's charm.

"Maybe Miss Schuster show you the city," Mr. Pilkvist said, biting into a biscuit. "She's here in Chicago long enough to know her way about. Ja, Miss Schuster?"

"I would love to show Mr. van Werckhoven around." Clair's gray eyes shone as brightly as the new electrical streetlights downtown.

"A nice young lady for an escort would be first-rate," Mr. Pilkvist highlighted.

Torsten's face burned. He resented his parents forcing Clair onto the newcomer. She acted as simpleminded as a small-town girl could get. About the most intelligent sentence he'd ever heard the girl from Kenosha utter was speculation about how long it would be before every house in the United States got a telephone. A gentleman with the breeding of Joseph required a proper guide, one who knew the city as well as only a local could. Besides, Joseph himself had mentioned he wanted a native's view.

"You can go tomorrow," Tory's father said. "It would be good to go Saturday, before you have to focus so much on your work. Ja, Mr. van Werckhoven?"

"That would be fine," Joseph said, nodding toward Clair politely. But the tightness around Joseph's curly mustache betrayed his true thoughts, Tory believed. Or was Tory staking too much on implausible dreams? He was certain Joseph's expression lacked sincerity.

Clair's gray eyes fell to her roast beef and potatoes. "Tomorrow? But I have to work tomorrow," she mumbled toward her plate. "Mr. Deering makes us work Saturdays, sometimes even for a full day." Subsequently she brightened and flashed Joseph a smile. "I can show you around Sunday. Not even Mr. Deering expects anyone to work Sundays."

Despite the shyness he felt in Joseph's presence, Tory realized he had but one chance to cut Clair off. "I can show you around tomorrow," he said, his voice high. He cleared his throat and spoke deeper. "That is, if you prefer to see the sights on a Saturday, when most things will be open, rather than Sunday, when everything will be closed."

"Well?" Joseph flushed. "I suppose… hmm. I hadn't thought of that. Maybe you're right. Saturday might be best. I mean, if you think there'll be more things to do."

Mrs. Pilkvist dabbed the corners of her mouth with a cloth napkin. "Maybe Saturday better for seeing things," she said, nodding reflectively. "More places open."

"Are you sure?" Mr. Pilkvist inserted. "Sunday people aren't so pushy and you can take time strolling the avenues without getting trampled."

Mrs. Pilkvist giggled. "Young folks don't mind a little hustle and bustle, Gustaf."

"I suppose it might be nicer for you to see the city tomorrow rather than on Sunday," Clair said into her lap.

Tory smiled. "Then it's settled?"

Joseph stared directly into Tory's eyes from across the table. They held each other's gaze for what seemed an eternity. "It's settled," he said with a wide grin. "If you're sure you don't mind."

"Of course I don't mind."

"I'll look forward to it, then," Joseph said.

Tory barely heard the rest of the suppertime conversation. His mind cleaved to one thought: he and Joseph van Werckhoven, strolling together along the streets of Chicago.

UPSTAIRS lying in his bed after everyone had taken coffee and cake in the parlor, Tory continued to daydream about the newcomer. What would spending Saturday with Joseph be like? What should they do? Where should they go? And what about those stares he had given Tory at the supper table and later in the parlor? What had they meant? Could it be possible that Joseph was like him?

Tory had come across clandestine mentions of same-sex love while studying literature and the ancient Greeks at school. Men like Plato, Herodotus, and Walt Whitman wrote about their attractions to other men. Reading between the lines, he had instinctively known that they were referring to him. Some new type of doctors had even said it was a natural occurrence in nature, including in humans. They'd said that some American Indian tribes practiced it as part of their culture. Was it something Joseph van Werckhoven practiced too?

Tory had had encounters with boarders in the past. His first foray with a man had occurred with a boarder a month after Tory had turned sixteen. A twenty-five-year-old Michigan man settling in Chicago had asked Tory to help run his bath. Eventually he suggested Tory strip and get into the tub with him. Overcome with physical yearning, Tory had obliged him, although nothing had occurred between them afterward. The man had moved on five days later as if nothing had ever happened.

Nearly a year later, Tory had another one-time encounter with a boarder who had played footsy with him under the supper table. That night when Tory had carried tea to his room, as the man had requested, the thirty-year-old businessman from Ohio had commanded him, point blank like a bank robber, to shut the door and lock it.

And there were two times at the cabaret on 35th Street where men like him went searching for affection. Each a one-time affair, amounting to nothing more than two men seeking physical pleasure. Tory had always hungered for more.

Walt Whitman, his favorite poet, best delineated Tory's romantic notions. He had read the venerable poet's work so often he could recite many passages word for word. They flowed through his veins as easily as his blood.

When his father had found his edition of *Leaves of Grass* in his bedroom two springs ago, he had called it "Amerikanskt skräp"— American trash—and confiscated it. Luckily for Tory, his father had wasted no time incinerating it. If he had thumbed through it, he might have noticed the dog-eared pages where Tory had read the more erotic passages over and over.

He recalled one such passage now.

> *Whose happiest days were far away*
> *through fields, in woods, on hills, he and*
> *another wandering hand in hand, they*
> *twain apart from other men;*
>
> *Who oft as he sauntered the streets curved*
> *with his arm the shoulder of his friend,*
> *while the arm of his friend rested upon*
> *him also.*

Might Saturday be that way with Joseph? Strolling the streets of Chicago, arm in arm?

He'd never had a special friend like the one described by Whitman. Now that he was burgeoning into a full-grown man (nineteen years old as of February), he yearned to stand on his own two feet and search for true love. His two elder sisters had found love. Why couldn't he?

Rolling to his side, he pictured Joseph in the room down the hall. He wondered what he might be thinking at that moment, what he might be doing. He dozed, giddy with anticipation for tomorrow.

# CHAPTER TWO

TULIPS lined the median of the sun-soaked street. Passing cable cars rang their strident warning bells as they streamed down the tracks alongside stagecoaches and horsemen. Steam engines that powered the never-ending building spree screamed. Vendors shouted, policemen whistled, strollers laughed, pushed, grunted. Life coursed through Chicago's streets like the frothy rapids of mountainous rivers Tory had read about in dime novels.

The temperature was cool, a typical late March in Chicago. But the sun on Tory's grinning face warmed him. The dusting of snow from last week had already melted into a faraway memory. An expanding contentment nudged the residual anxiety from Tory. He felt alive, more a part of the city than he'd ever experienced. Walking alongside the dashing Joseph van Werckhoven pumped new life into him.

That morning, Tory had dressed with the utmost care. He'd washed his face and neck, not forgetting the backs of his ears. He'd waxed his hair with pomade and sponged limewater from his scent box on his chest and underarms before buttoning his shirt. When he'd come downstairs, his mother had commented that he looked and smelled more fit for a church service than a Saturday tour of the city. Joseph looked equally dapper. His mustache, freshly waxed, curled over his upper lip like a fancy scroll; his burgundy ascot anchored his oval face. Tory expected nothing less from the elegant man from New York City.

"There are many tall buildings, aren't there?" Joseph said as they meandered side by side down State Street. He peered at the recent construction. "Where will they find room to fit them all? I can't imagine them getting any taller."

"There's talk of adding land along the shore of Lake Michigan," Tory said. "I'm not quite sure how they'd go about doing it."

"In New York City," Joseph said, "they've built artificial islands."

"Are you from New York originally?"

"My family's lived there since before the Republic was formed."

"That's a long time. My parents have only been in America since the 1860s."

"Your family appears to be doing quite well for itself."

"Mamma always says my sisters and me take everything for granted."

"Will I have the pleasure of meeting your sisters? Do they still live in Chicago?"

"One's married in Washington, DC, and the other lives in Springfield," Tory said. "She's married to a teacher. They run a school together. I'm the only one left at home."

"You don't mind living with your parents?"

"No, not really. There aren't that many places available in the city right now, anyway. And my parents need help to run the bakery and boarding house."

"What about the apartment above your bakery?" Joseph raised his eyebrows. "Can't you move in there? It would give you some privacy, at least, away from all those boarders."

"We rent it to a couple from Peoria."

"Can't you ask them to leave?"

Tory enjoyed the tender yet masculine tone to Joseph's voice. His intelligence flowed unabashedly, without the weight of seriousness. "I suppose we could ask them," Tory said. "I never really thought much about it. Do you think I should move in?"

Joseph tilted his head toward the buildings silhouetted against the powder-blue sky. "Perhaps I should."

"You?"

"If Father wants me to stay here for an extended period, I suppose I'll have to find a place. If it's as difficult to find housing here like you and everyone say, I might not have any other choice."

Tory's heart quickened. Saliva evaporated from his mouth. "You... you think you'll get to stay? For an extended period?"

"I don't know." Joseph kept his mouth taut, his head held upright. "I'll have to wait and see. It'll be nice to have someplace, just in case. I like the room I have now, but a man needs privacy, don't you think? And I do like your neighborhood."

"I'm sure arrangements can be made for you to stay in the apartment," Tory said.

"Do you think the couple you rent it to would be ready to leave?"

Tory tried to ease the excitement in his voice. "I'm sure they are. They've lived there almost two years. I don't talk to them much, but they must be on a wait list for someplace. Maybe they're having a place built. The apartment really isn't so bad. It has a kitchen, and two bedrooms, and plenty of sunlight. And Pappa even installed a water closet, although it's very small."

"I'll keep it in mind," Joseph said in a sober and reflective tone. "Depends on how well things go here, of course."

"I can't imagine they won't," Tory said.

"Look here." Joseph stopped before a construction site. "They're preparing the foundation for one of those steel-framed buildings. It's for a new hotel. See what that sign says? 'The Heathcliff House: Ten Stories of Magnificence.'"

They watched the workmen strategically lay dynamite sticks into holes drilled into the dirt. They then rushed into a hut near Tory and Joseph. A man shouted something. Seconds later, a chain of implosions ripped a hole in the earth. The street rocked. Yet scant debris spread beyond the construction zone.

The blast had frightened Tory. Fire, even the fleeting kind that came from explosives, terrified him. He had not wanted to show that fear to Joseph. While the men had prepared the dynamite, he'd willed himself to keep from grimacing, dreading the inevitable. Even after the dust from the implosion had settled, his body shuddered with horror. He breathed in relief that Joseph hadn't noticed.

"That was something, wasn't it?" Joseph said as they continued walking down State Street.

"Yes," Tory said. "My parents are proud that a Swede invented dynamite."

"Such a simple concept," Joseph commented. "The ideas of great thinkers always seem so obvious once they come up with them."

They walked along, shoulder to shoulder, while Tory pointed out interesting sights and mentioned what he knew about the growing city.

Joseph seemed to adhere to his every word. They browsed the goods in a department store as large as one city block and as tall as six stories. Tory mentioned Marshall Field & Company was one of the largest stores in the world.

"I'm so glad that I have the chance to tour with a native," Joseph said once they returned to the street. "I did want to thank you for saving me."

"Saving you?"

"From Miss Schuster," Joseph said. "Not that I would have minded her company, but I fear she might not have known the little things that make touring interesting, like all that you told me about the department store and the buildings and other things."

A tinge of sympathy had poked Tory that morning watching Clair Schuster mope at the breakfast table and later slump out the door to her factory job, knowing that she was unhappy she couldn't spend the day with Joseph. But now he wondered if she had said something in retaliation to Joseph for his choosing to tour the city with him on Saturday rather than with her on Sunday. Although improperly forthright at times, she did not strike him as the sort of woman who sought vengeance. But one never knew.

"Did she do or say something to upset you?"

Joseph snorted. "No, nothing like that."

Relief softened the strain in Torsten's limbs. "A lot of women like her have moved to the city. They're as common as bees in summer."

"She's not quite my type," Joseph said.

What was his type? In the parlor yesterday, Joseph had mentioned he was single and hadn't met "the right person." But did that mean he wasn't dating anyone? "Do you have a girl back in New York?" Tory dared to ask.

Joseph, his firm mouth offset by his well-groomed mustache, waited a moment before answering. "No, I can't say that I do," he said flatly. "What about you? Surely you must have one, or maybe two or three stashed around Chicago somewhere?"

"Not me." Tory shook his head.

"But I find that hard to believe."

Torsten flushed. Had that been a cryptic response? He sensed something. Something emerging between the two of them. What had Joseph van Werckhoven alluded to when he expressed disbelief that Tory courted no women? What did he mask behind that grin?

Joseph held that same mischievous smile for another block. Sounds of traffic and people and the smells of smoke and food receded into the background as they walked. For a moment, the only reality for Tory consisted of him and his new friend. The city faded to a mere backdrop to their private world, a distant array of colors, smells, noises.

Had Tory really understood Joseph? Many times Tory had come across men who spoke in puzzling tongues. About the only men who made their intentions clear were the ones who ventured to the South Side cabaret. Joseph, too refined, would never behave so brutishly. Yet Tory wouldn't have minded a soft touch from him, a simple gesture of friendship.

Joseph might as well have read Tory's mind. A tingling burn raced down Tory's arm when Joseph placed his hand on his shoulder. He could feel the transference of heat even through his wool frock.

"Oh, look," Joseph said, pointing across an intersection to a street sign on a building. "Van Buren Street. That's where the family's drugstore will go. I believe that's it there, inside the lobby of that new building. Father said it would be a tall one."

"What do you say." Tory followed Joseph's gaze upward along the twelve-story building, his eyes squinting into the sun. The exterior of the building appeared on the verge of completion. Except for on the lobby level, workers had yet to install the windows.

"Come," Joseph said. "Let's get a peek inside."

They crossed the street, dodging carriages and pedestrians. The lobby was an empty shell. A few workmen were installing what looked like a reception counter. Joseph pointed out the two elevators, although after inspecting them they concluded no one had wired them yet. Next, Joseph escorted Tory through wide doors where the drugstore would be. Interior work for the store would begin Monday morning, Joseph said. He'd oversee the effort, which was what had lured him to Chicago. In the back, away from the windows, where the light grew dimmer, Joseph again placed his hand on Tory's shoulder.

"What do you say, Torsten? Do you like the store? Keep in mind it's still under construction. Use your imagination."

Tory swallowed hard, trying to ignore the quiver Joseph's touch gave him. "Such a big place." He steadied his voice. "I think you have a fine location. I'm sure everything'll look wonderful once it's done."

"It's much larger than I imagined," Joseph said in a hushed voice, as if he were thinking of nothing but success and magnificence. "This might be our largest store yet. Father made a grand find. No reason why this one shouldn't be the best one yet. Yes, I can indeed imagine myself staying in Chicago for an extended period, perhaps indefinitely. Won't that be grand, Torsten?"

A ruckus outside startled the two men, and their mutual smiles faded in a flash. Tory and Joseph hurried to the front. Outside, a hansom cab had collided with a vegetable cart. The cart owner, standing among his scattered melons and tomatoes, spit curses in Italian while the cab driver hurled back insults of his own. Tory understood enough Swedish to flush over the cabby's words.

Leaving behind one of the ugly sides to a fast-growing city, Tory led Joseph back onto the street, farther along Van Buren, toward the Chicago River, where he had read in the *Chicago Tribune* about a carnival on Taylor Street. He guided Joseph through a maze of people and vendor carts until they came to a large red-and-white big top.

The after work crowd from surrounding factories and offices filled the many kiosks at the carnival. The smells of hotdogs, pretzels, and roasted corn made Tory's stomach rumble. He suggested they get something to eat. They bought a bag of peanut brittle from a vendor wearing a clown outfit and sat on a bench to people-watch. Organ music grinded in the background.

"What a wonderful and unexpected treat," Joseph said, laughing. "I haven't attended a carnival since I was a boy. It reminds me of Coney Island."

"Once the weather warms, it'll be much nicer."

"It's perfect the way it is." Joseph gazed at Tory. Tory flushed. Their hands brushed each other as they shared the bag of peanut brittle. But Joseph appeared unfazed.

Flocks of pigeons gathered by their feet. Tory tossed them pieces of brittle. Joseph seemed amused. To Tory, their moment together was worth all the peanut brittle in the world.

Joseph spotted a game called Pitch Out, and, tossing the remaining crumbs in his hand onto the ground where the pigeons swarmed them, he encouraged Tory to follow him.

"Step up, step up," the vendor cried. "Get a baseball in the hole, win a stuffed animal. Five cents for five tries. Step up."

"I'll have a go at it." Joseph handed the vendor a nickel.

The first four throws came close to entering the hole cut in the catcher's glove, but on his fifth and final throw, the baseball entered the hole squarely. Joseph and Tory cheered. The vendor tossed Joseph a stuffed bear. With a grin, Joseph handed the prize to Tory. "For being such a grand host," he said.

Tory simpered. Cradling the bear, he held his tongue about his prized baseball skills. Tory, who played baseball with his chums at least once a week, most likely would have made each of the five throws. He valued Joseph's kindness more than his own ego.

"There's my favorite ride." Tory pointed to the mine train rising in the distance on the edge of the river. "I had no idea they had one of those. I rode my first one last year in Wicker Park."

"Well, then, come on." Joseph grabbed Tory's arm and ushered him along. After waiting in line for ten minutes, they paid the attendant four cents and climbed inside the car. A steam-powered pulley lifted them along the wooden track. From the top, the sprawl of the city astonished them. They both took off their derbies. Tory covered the stuffed bear with his hat and latched onto his elbows in anticipation of the freefall. In an instant, gravity raced them down the first and largest drop. Wind whipped at their faces. They rolled over two bunny hops until reaching a slow stop.

"I have to say," Joseph said as they climbed out of the car, "I hadn't expected this much fun when I set off for Chicago Thursday night. I thought it would all be dull work."

Tory's heart kindled while he absorbed Joseph's soft gaze. The nippy air seemed insignificant against the warm thoughtfulness flowing through him. They explored more of the carnival, and with a gentle tug, Tory suggested they best return home, since he knew his mother was preparing a special goose for supper.

As they headed home, Tory used the bustle of pedestrians as an excuse to brush against Joseph. The more he bumped into him, the more Joseph seemed to reciprocate by leaning closer. Eventually, he and Tory walked up Market Street with their arms hooked around each other's like old chums.

Like the two friends depicted in Walt Whitman's poem.

# Chapter
# THREE

LONG after the last lantern in the house had been extinguished, Tory sat by the open window in his bedroom and stared at the glowing, pulsating city. He barely noticed the chilly air or the waxing moon that cast deep shadows along the alley. Doubt, mixed with exhilaration, stirred him. Had he read Joseph correctly? Had he only imagined that Joseph was interested in more than friendship?

Joseph, thoughtful and debonair, a man of fine breeding, had expressed his words and gestures in the most solicitous manner all day. Tory judged him to be sincere. Joseph had been trying to communicate something to Tory. Even when they had first met yesterday afternoon and stood in the entrance foyer with Tory's mother cooing and blushing, unspoken words had ebbed and flowed between them.

A few hours ago, he and Joseph had barely the chance to speak to one another in the parlor (the other boarders and his mother dominated the conversation), yet their glances from across the room expressed those same tacit thoughts, Tory believed. Upstairs, before saying a final goodnight, they had hesitated on the landing, grinning at each other under the glow of the gas lanterns Mrs. Pilkvist hadn't yet had the chance to snuff out. Their bedroom doors had shut slowly, quietly, with dull thuds, almost as if neither had wanted to leave the other's company.

Two pigeons cooed under the eave of the row house across the back alley. Their nestling against the chill brought a smile to Tory's face. He didn't mind the pigeons that seemed to have descended onto the city the past several years as feverishly as the people had. Others always kicked at them, cursed them. Some even shot at them. Tory liked that they were around.

As a boy, he remembered seeing a pigeon struck by a carriage while another pigeon flew to its side. It circled the dead pigeon, gently pecked at it, looked lost and even sad. It was then Tory remembered what he had read in an ornithology textbook at school. Many pigeons mated for life. Tory realized the two birds had been partners, and the one left behind was mourning the loss of its lifemate.

From that moment on, Tory looked on the pigeons as soul mates rather than pests. Kindred spirits, he considered them. They desired love and commitment as adamantly as Tory. Many times he fed them behind the bakery with stale bread he'd concealed in his pockets, away from his father's reprimanding ice-blue eyes. Mr. Pilkvist, like most everyone else, viewed the pigeons as nuisances. Tory wished he had a handful of crumbs to toss to the nuzzling birds now.

"Hello there," he whispered to them, leaning farther out the window. "I wish I had something to give you. Wait for me behind the bakery tomorrow and I'll have a treat for you." He chuckled. "Take care of one another. Look out for those speeding carriages and nasty boys with shotguns."

"Torsten, is that you?"

Startled, Tory peered down the side of the row house toward where the voice had come from. Joseph van Werckhoven's head hung out the window of the room down the hall.

"Joseph?"

Joseph tittered. "I suppose we're both unable to sleep. How about we have a chat in your room?"

Tory swallowed. "All right."

"See you in a moment." Joseph's head disappeared from view.

Tory slid the windowpane shut with a thud and stooped down to glance at his reflection in the oval mirror above his dressing table. Still dressed in his day clothes, he supposed he looked presentable. His heart raced at the thought of having Joseph van Werckhoven in his bedroom. What would they talk about? How should he behave?

Joseph didn't bother to knock. He poked his head into the room, eyebrows arched high above his brown eyes. Seeing Tory staring at him, he entered fully and gently shut the door behind him.

"Why can't you sleep?" he asked with a hint of playfulness to his northeast accent.

"I don't know. It's one of those nights, I suppose." But Tory understood perfectly why he had been unable to sleep. His beating heart, catching breath, the daydreams that ransacked his brain… those had all forced him to remain wide awake.

"Yes, it does seem to be one of those nights," Joseph said, stepping closer. Like Tory, he was still dressed in his day clothes, but he had left his ascot and coat in his room. His shirt, unfastened at the throat, accentuated his long neck and lean physique. He appeared not to have even lain down to rest, for his shirt and breeches remained unwrinkled. Had he paced his room, his head heavy with daydreams, like Tory?

"Almost a full moon, I believe," Joseph said. "Perhaps that's why we're so restless. They say a full moon can play tricks on people's minds and make us act in bizarre ways."

"Do you think that's what's happening to us?" Tory asked, genuinely interested. He already looked to Joseph for answers to life's oddities. Was that how love worked?

A flash of red streaked across Joseph's pale cheeks. "I'm not sure. I suppose. Actually, I feel rather… well, in complete control of my faculties."

Tory edged closer. He wanted to oust whatever awkwardness lurked between them in the ensuing silence. He shuffled to his bed and invited Joseph to sit. "My room is a bit small." He snickered self-effacingly, gesturing with his hand at his simple furnishings. "I'm sure it's nothing like what you must be used to."

Joseph peered around. "It's a nice room, a perfect fit." He gazed at Tory from where he sat on the edge of the bed. His brown eyes glistened in the glow of the two wall lanterns above the headboard. "I still live with my parents too, Torsten. My father puts most of his money back into his stores. Don't think I live like a king."

Tory lowered his head. Had he come across as a sycophant?

"Although I would like a place of my own," Joseph said. "If all goes well here, I could get a place in Chicago, like we spoke about. Perhaps even stay in the apartment above the bakery, for a while, anyway."

Tory sat next to him, almost without thought, as if someone had kicked the back of his knees and he had no choice but to buckle. "I'm sure everything will work out," he said, trying to sound casual. "Almost everyone who moves to Chicago has good fortune. I don't want you to go back to New York—" He stopped himself and turned his burning face away from Joseph's gaze. "I mean, I'm sure you won't have to go back."

"Would you like it if I could stay?" Joseph asked softly.

"Well, yes," Tory said. "I would like it. Why wouldn't I?"

"We've become fast friends, haven't we?"

A tingle fluttered along Tory's limbs. He wanted to respond, but his words lodged heavy in his dry mouth. Could Joseph, sitting so close, hear, and perhaps even see, his racing heart?

"I hope your parents won't mind you're staying up late with one of the boarders," Joseph said, flashing Tory a toothy smile.

"Their bedroom is downstairs," Tory said. "The walls are thick. The other boarders shouldn't hear. I don't recall anyone ever complaining about noise."

More throbbing silence hovered around them. The stillness of the house seemed eerily electrified. Neither man looked at the other. Tory rested his eyes on the New Yorker's hands, gripping his knees. He sensed an involuntary shuddering in those slender fingers. Blood and warmth coursed through the visible veins. The drumming blood exposed something else too. Was it craving? His hands seemed to yearn to rise, perhaps to touch the heat pulsating in Tory's cheeks.

He wouldn't have minded such an advance. Tory had experienced them from men before, even from boarders like Joseph. Those times had been strange and emotionless. What he felt with Joseph was different. His physical yearnings combined with something profoundly emotional. He feared he might faint when Joseph finally released his knee and reached out to him. His palm rested just below Tory's shoulder.

"I hope you don't mind my saying," Joseph said, "but I've grown fond of you, Torsten Pilkvist."

Tory licked his dry lips. "I've grown fond of you too, Joseph van Werckhoven."

Dreamlike, they gazed wordlessly into each other's eyes. Tory swallowed the phlegm that wedged in the back of his throat. Was it real? Tory hardly believed it. But it *was* real. He hadn't imagined it all this time. The chocolate brown of Joseph's irises concealed no pretense.

Doubt drifted away and out the window. Wonder stymied Tory's senses. Only smell seemed to linger. Joseph's lavender cologne wrapped around him in a gentle mist. Tory closed his eyes, allowed the pull of Joseph's breath to bait him.

Their lips touched.

Electric shocks rendered Tory both rigid and elastic. For what seemed an eternity, they kissed. When they drew apart, a string of saliva connected their lips. A tear trickled down Joseph's flushed cheek. He stood before Tory, mouth agape, his eyes wide and crazed.

"I'm sorry," he said, shaking. "I… I don't know what came over me. Please… please, forgive me."

"There's nothing to forgive," Tory whispered.

Below Joseph's button-fly, there was no denying his wanting.

Tory reached for him. "Please," he said, "I don't mind, really."

In an instant, Joseph leaned into Tory to exchange more kisses. They melded their lips onto each other's more firmly. Tongues pried into their watering mouths. Arms wrapped tightly around their waists.

They disrobed each other, fumbling to unfasten shirts, climb out of breeches, nearly tearing off undergarments, all the while wanting to keep their lips locked. Tory trembled; he worried he might faint. Joseph steadied him. Explosions erupted inside Tory's burning chest.

Joseph pushed Tory back onto the bed, where they explored each other's bodies with hands and tongues, wrapping themselves in each other. With mounting need, Tory positioned himself on the edge of the bed with his legs spread and gestured for Joseph to stand before him. Joseph seemed to need few words to understand the gesture. His face aflame, Joseph let a stream of drool fall into his palm, and he lubricated himself. Eyes shut, he pressed into Tory. A moan escaped from between Tory's wet lips. He relaxed and Joseph leaned in harder, gazing deep into Tory's eyes. His mustache, smelling of pomade, brushed the side of Tory's swiveling head. Their hands clasped. Tory clenched down, encouraging Joseph to move faster, to lower his weight on him.

Joseph took Tory's lopping tongue into his mouth. Sensations Tory had never experienced with a man—with anyone—filled him with blinding desire, love, fear.

Swallowing back a groan, Joseph collapsed on top of him. He lay still for several minutes. Only his heavy breath evinced life burned within him. Tory clutched him to make sure he stayed in place. Slowly, Joseph lifted his head off Tory's shoulder. A smile grew along Joseph's lips, turning into a full grin under his mustache. Joseph's grin vibrated into laughter. Tory, too, began to laugh. And with Tory's rising and quaking chest, Joseph laughed all the harder.

"Shhh," Joseph said. "We don't want anyone to hear us."

"I know how to keep you quiet." Tory pushed Joseph's head down, and Joseph's mouth instinctively engulfed him like a warm bath. A minute later, Tory jerked up. A yelp like the cluck of a dying bird broke from his lips.

Joseph wiped his mouth and smiled at him. "I have never done that before," he said.

"I just wanted to be closer to you."

Joseph replied with many light kisses on Tory's mouth.

Still naked, Joseph went to the window and stared out. From the bed, Tory admired his new lover's body. Tall, lean, firm. The light of the blue moon, no longer visible as it settled to the west, highlighted his pointy shoulders and enshrouded him in a surreal glow. Affection surged in Tory's veins. He actually had found love. Like his sisters.

Rattling in the hallway startled them. They remained frozen. Someone was using the water closet down the hall. From the floundering footsteps, Tory deduced they belonged to Clair Schuster. She often used the water closet at the first hint of morning twilight, before anyone arose.

Joseph tiptoed to the door and pressed his ear against it. Backing away, he gestured that whoever it was had returned to his or her room. After dressing, he bent over Tory and kissed him on the lips, his pompadour falling over his forehead. Just before opening the door, he whispered, "I will see you in a few hours, my love," and with a wink, he slinked out of the room.

# Chapter
# FOUR

"Build up the fire before it die down."

Tory obeyed his father's choppy English and tossed an armful of logs into the hearth, recoiling as he always did to avoid getting too close to the lashing flames. The writhing fire appeared more like an octopus with fiery tentacles. He feared that if he got too close, the flames would pull him into what he viewed as a conflagration. Rationally he knew the hearth fire could not reach him, yet the fear seized him each time he stoked the fire.

He drew his hands back and returned to the counter where he had been kneading dough for a limpa bread. Across from him, his father rolled out rectangles of dough for the kanelbulle. The raw odors of yeast, cinnamon, and the wood fire permeated the kitchen.

"You and our new boarder have become fast friends," his father said after a prolonged silence.

"Yes, Joseph's a nice man," Tory said.

"Joseph? You do not call him Mr. van Werckhoven? Ah, you *are* on friendly terms with him, I was not imagining things."

"Don't you want me to be polite to the boarders?"

"Ja, of course. But you and him, you sometimes walk around yoked together like two carriage horses. He only here not even a week."

"I'm acting hospitable."

"Hospitable? You are more. You have made him your brother." Mr. Pilkvist wiped his perspiring brow with the back of his stubby white hand. "You having only two sisters, I can see why you might take to him. But remember, Mr. van Werckhoven will leave here in a few weeks and go back to New York City. You shouldn't get so attached to the boarders. They come and go."

His father's counsel brought out the anxieties that had pestered Tory lately. Would Joseph have to return to New York City despite his talk of wanting to remain in Chicago? What if Joseph's father wanted him back in New York to help run the family business? Tory's father expected the same from him. It was reasonable for fathers to want their enterprising sons close by.

Tory had wanted to discuss his concerns with Joseph whenever they were alone together, either in his bedroom late at night after their lovemaking or while strolling the neighborhood before supper. But he had stifled himself for fear of appearing too desperate. Tory did not wish to risk chasing Joseph away.

"He said he wants to stay," Tory said, reassuring himself. "He might even want to rent the apartment above the bakery." He glanced at the ceiling. The young couple from Peoria prattled about upstairs. Was there a way to get rid of them?

Mr. Pilkvist snickered. "The Wentworths are good tenants. Besides, a man of Mr. van Werckhoven's means won't want to stay in that nest." He peered at Tory through the pots and pans hanging from steel hooks above the counter. "Han är aristokrat."

"You can't say such things about Joseph." Tory grimaced. "He's not an aristocrat. He's a gentleman."

"He still not of our same class."

"Oh, Pappa." Tory took out his frustrations on the limpa dough, punching and dropping it on the floured countertop. "That's old-world talk. His family works as hard for their money as we do."

"His money is older than ours, that is big difference. He only condescend us while he stay here."

"Pappa, you're wrong."

"I am not so sure I am wrong. Best thing for you is to learn some people should not mix. Getting close to him is like throwing yeast into boiling water."

After setting the limpa dough into a bowl to rise, Tory marched for the door.

"Where you run off to now?"

"I'm going to play some ball at the park," Tory said gruffly. "I need some air."

"Don't get so dirty you need a bath," his father called after him. "We save hot water for the boarders."

Tory raced upstairs, grabbed his mitt, and descended the steps by twos. Outside, the chill air tempered his anger. His father and his irksome talk. He found fault with everything. He placed everyone into categories like mere insects cataloged in some entomological registry. Mr. Pilkvist never could get past such old-world notions. Especially in a city like Chicago, fledgling and vibrant, where everyone came from every part of the world, hardworking and eager, the idea of abiding by an archaic class system seemed ridiculous. Joseph van Werckhoven stood farther apart from snooty aristocratism than anyone Tory knew. Even if his family had lived in America since before the Revolution.

Never once had he uttered a single word that had made Tory wince with aversion. Ever since their first night making love, he had never expressed anything other than the utmost sincerity and respect.

An aristocrat? Joseph? The idea made him snicker.

Tory's father hadn't bad-mouthed a good honest boarder—he had disgraced Tory's beau.

Walking along the sidewalk to the baseball park, he realized he could never defend Joseph to his father the way he would like. If he stood up for him too adamantly, deeper suspicions would arise. Best to the play it safe, in any case. He already suspected his father questioned his sexuality. Three years ago, in a moment of heated exchange, his father had let loose a string of Swedish curses followed by the accusation that Tory was "like Tchaikovsky." And of course he had confiscated Tory's volume of Whitman's *Leaves of Grass*. Tory did not want to cause difficulties for Joseph during his stay with them. Especially if he might move into the apartment above the bakery.

His thoughts led to Clair Schuster. Had he put on airs with her like his father accused Joseph of doing? Perhaps he had been too harsh with her. Nothing wrong with coming from a small town and working in a factory. His own parents had come from an impoverished village in central Sweden. He had never intended to act snooty with her. She merely bothered him. He'd find a way to make up for his surliness before she left for the women's hotel. Now that he and Joseph were courting, she no longer posed a threat.

When he arrived at the park, he was glad to see a baseball game about to start. Tory loved baseball, one of the few pastimes that provided him a release of energy and frustration. His natural bent for quickness had earned him the nickname "Locomotive" from his comrades. They always seemed impressed at the speed with which he'd take the bases.

His friends, happy to see Tory, greeted him with robust hellos. They formed two teams, six men on each, no catcher, shortstop, or center fielder this time. Tory played third base. He always strove to play as well as his hero, Ned Williamson, third baseman for the Cubs. For nine innings, nothing but the game concerned Tory, along with the passion to win and the enjoyment he got from the handshakes, back slaps, and friendly cheer. Two hours later, with the sun setting over the row houses and factories, he returned home, flushed and lightheaded from exercise, eager to see Joseph once he returned from overseeing the construction of the drugstore.

Clair Schuster's voice flowed from the parlor when he stepped inside. She suddenly quieted when she took notice of him gazing at her from the foyer threshold. She was taking afternoon tea with Tory's mother and father. Odd his father should be there. He almost never bothered with tea when work dictated he stay in the bakery. Embarrassed by his scruffy appearance, Tory made to head upstairs, but the alarmed expressions on their faces rooted his feet to the floor.

Clair set her teacup on the side table with a clank of the spoon and raced past him up the stairs faster than a housecat. The swishing of her bustled skirt faded, followed by the bang of the bedroom door. Looking after her with narrowed eyes, Tory feared the worst. Questioning words rushed to his throat when he gazed back at his parents and saw that his mother had turned away with quivering shoulders. His father, still dressed in his baker's smock, stood and peered at him, his eyebrows knitted.

"Torsten," his father said, his voice coarse and stern, "we have just found out something we do not like to hear."

The cold air from playing ball still lodged heavy in his lungs. With one hand over his rapping heart, Tory whispered, "What is it?"

"It's about Mr. van Werckhoven," his father said through tight lips.

Tory's eyes, moist with apprehension, implored him to continue.

"Actually, it's about you and him," Mr. Pilkvist said. "We hear that the two of you spend hours together in your bedroom behind closed doors when the rest of us are asleep. Tell me, is this true?"

Baffled, Tory peered at his mother. Her head, still downcast and her cheeks red as rubies, shook like a fashion doll's.

"Please don't be angry with them, Gustaf," she said to the Oriental rug. "They are young men. I'm sure they were playing cards or chess."

"Var tyst, Anna. I will handle this." After shushing his wife, Mr. Pilkvist laid scrutinizing eyes on his only son. "Tell me, Torsten, are you gambling and drinking in this house with the boarders?"

"No, Pappa, you know I don't do that."

"Then what do you two do concealed in your bedroom in the middle of the night? Is it games you play, like your mamma say? If so, then they should be taken to the parlor."

"Games? No...." Tory dared to push his father. "What worries you, Pappa?"

Mr. Pilkvist waited an agonizing moment before responding. "I sense something wrong with all this. I don't know, but all this stops now, here, today, for good. You will not permit Mr. van Werckhoven into your bedroom tonight, and as of tomorrow, he no longer a boarder in our house."

"But Pappa, you can't. You can't toss him onto the street. So few rooms are available in the city—"

"When he return from his duties at his store this evening, I will tell him he must leave tomorrow. I know this will reach New York and come to look bad on us and Heloise, but as head of this household, I must do what best for family."

"I won't let you."

"You won't let me? Did you not hear when I say I am master of this house?"

Tory chewed on his fury. "Is it that Clair? Is she the one who turned you against Joseph?"

"This has nothing to do with Miss Schuster."

Fuming, Tory rushed upstairs and slammed his bedroom door shut behind him. He hurried to change his clothes, unconcerned if he left his breeches and shirt on the floor the way his mother disliked.

Rage blinded him. A few moments later, dressed in proper street attire and a frock coat, he opened the door to find a startled Clair Schuster standing before him, her hand raised as if she were about to knock.

"Please, please, I didn't mean to cause trouble." Her red eyes met his. "I only mentioned Mr. van Werckhoven spending time in your room because I was confused. Why does he spend so much time with you and not me? Do you know? Why?"

Furious, Tory wanted to slap her, toss her to the floor like he had his soiled clothes. He pursed his lips, able to think only of cruel curses to spew at her. Decorum cleaved his tongue to the roof of his mouth.

"I didn't mean to hurt anyone," Clair went on. Fresh tears streamed from her bloodshot eyes. She wrung her hands, her fingernails chipped and dirtied from her factory job. "I mentioned it to your parents to ask them why he spent so much time in your room, that's all. I was so confused. I didn't imagine they'd get so angry and force Mr. van Werckhoven onto the street. Try to convince your parents to let him stay. Please, try."

To think he had wanted to act kinder to her. That he had harbored regret for the way he had treated her. All the while she had plotted her betrayal of him and Joseph. The meddlesome girl from Kenosha had sat in her room listening to them from the start. Irked with jealousy, she'd finally unleashed her bitter vengeance by revealing his and Joseph's secret meetings in his bedroom. And now she pretended innocence. He refused to fall for her false sweet demeanor.

Biting his lower lip, he scooted by her and dashed downstairs. He heard the anguished call of his mother as he hustled outside down the marble front steps, followed by his father shouting at her, "Var tyst!"

He paid the hansom driver twenty-three cents and stood on the corner of State and Van Buren, gazing at the building that housed the van Werckhovens' drugstore. He had come to see Joseph on a rescue mission. But to rescue him from what? His father's wrath? The relentless clutches of Clair Schuster? Or the humiliation of having been found out?

To what depth did Clair and his parents understand their relationship? Tory did not care. He and Joseph van Werckhoven loved each other. Nothing wielded enough power to wedge a barrier between them now. Not confusion, not jealousy, not resentment. Destiny demanded they remain together.

Straightening his spine, Tory waited for a break in traffic before marching across the street. He entered by the lobby, where busy laborers raising the interior kept him from fully entering the drugstore. He saw Joseph turn his way and flash him a wide smile.

"Tory." Joseph, wiping his hands on his smock, sidestepped the combo machines and wood planks on the floor and scurried over. "What are you doing here?"

"I was curious how things were coming along." He glanced around, forcing a grin. "I can see a lot has come together in just a few days."

"We've been working diligently, that's for sure. Come in and have a peek." Joseph escorted Tory inside the door. "How do you like the shelves? The carpenters have done a wonderful job, don't you think? They've got most of them in place. You can see the electrical workers have gotten the lighting installed. See how the lights will allow us to work late if needed?"

Tory's smile expressed his marvel. He noticed the muss of Joseph's russet hair, his smock covered in sawdust and paint, the smudge of grime below his right eye. Joseph had toiled as hard as his laborers. Mr. Pilkvist had been wrong about him. No aristocrat would dirty his own hands when a team could do the work for him. A new wave of happiness, respect, and awe covered Tory. His smile, losing its tenuousness, taxed his cheek muscles.

Still, he must warn Joseph about the altercation he'd had with his parents and Miss Schuster. Returning to the row house would be difficult for them. Nevertheless, Joseph must know in advance what to expect. Tory decided to wait until Joseph finished showing him around the store.

The unwitting Joseph took him by the elbow and guided him farther into the construction. Workers, too focused on their chores, merely glanced at them. They stopped in a corner at the far end where columns and beams formed a rectangular division.

"Remember when we stood here last Saturday?" Joseph said, his voice full of pride and anticipation. "The pharmacy will go here. We're about a third of the way done."

"A perfect location," Tory said. "You can see out over everything."

"All our stores in New York are laid out in the same fashion. Father insists they keep the same interior design. He says it gives the store a unique imprint. By next week, we should have the shelves complete and the cabinets and the druggist table set up."

"I can't wait to see everything put together."

Enchanted by Joseph's enthusiasm, Tory followed him to the front of the store. Pedestrians passed by the windows, unaware or disinterested in the burgeoning dreams of the two young lovers inside.

"The counter supports are already in place," Joseph said, running his fingers along the freshly sanded wood. "All we need is the top. The carpenters are working on that right now." He nodded toward two men hand-sawing an elongated flat board. "We're using only the highest grade of Michigan pine."

"Everything looks wonderful," Tory said. "Your first store in Chicago. It's actually going to happen."

"Come with me, Tory." Joseph grabbed Tory by his arm. "Come see what I've discovered."

Before Tory formed any words, Joseph steered him into the lobby and inside one of the electric elevators. Wordless, Tory gazed around him. "I've never ridden in one of these before," he said.

"They just got the elevator moving this morning," Joseph said. "The electricians finished wiring the entire building a few days ago."

He shut the screen and pulled back a lever. The floor vibrated, followed by a sudden jerk, and next Tory felt an upward movement, a sensation not unlike riding the mine train. The stir both exhilarated and frightened him. Instinctively, he clutched Joseph's arm.

Joseph chuckled. "Don't worry," he said. "I felt the same way my first time riding in the elevators in New York. But I've never ridden one that goes as high as twelve stories. I've gone up and down on this one a dozen times already. It's quite something, isn't it?"

"Like flying without your feet leaving the ground."

Joseph threw his head back and laughed. "I love how you see things, Tory. I really do." He turned to kiss him on the lips. A prolonged kiss, but light and gentle, a kiss expressing hopes and dreams. His curly mustache tickled Tory. Tory rested his hand on

Joseph's shoulder and held him in place, wanting a deeper kiss. Joseph obliged.

Still overwhelmed with the frankness of their affection, Tory chuckled when Joseph pulled away from his mouth and gazed into his eyes. When he had first seen those cocoa-colored eyes of Joseph's almost a week ago, he had never imagined he'd have the chance to see them up close so often. Their relationship had sprouted as fast as the elevator climbed the building.

For a moment, he forgot what had driven him to rush to Joseph's drugstore. His parents and Clair Schuster faded like a meaningless delusion. Dilemmas no longer existed. Only discovery, newness, joy persisted.

Two minutes later, they reached the twelfth floor. Alone at the top of the world, a sense of privacy like he'd never known besieged Tory. Joseph pushed the lever into the lock position and opened the screen. A wide empty space opened before them. Grinning in wonder, Tory sauntered to the center. Wind gusted from the windows still without glass panes. The dull howl seemed to materialize from every corner. Tory joined Joseph in wandering about the barren space.

"An insurance company is moving into this floor," Joseph said. "And an accounting firm just below, and an export company below that. I'm unsure about the others. Our store is considered the anchor."

Tory remained speechless. Loving words did not always come easy to him. His bashful nature often paralyzed his tongue. But when had he ever needed to express the lofty emotions circulating through him now? He slipped off his white glove and held onto Joseph's hand, rough from his stint with manual labor. Another rush of pride rose inside him.

"Come and look out." Joseph led Tory to the row of windowless sockets. "This is what I wanted to share with you, my love. Do you see?"

Tory looked out. Sounds from the beating street below seemed distant, yet distinct and within reach. Faint lights emerged against the dusk. He had never stood so high, both literally and figuratively. Looking down at the bustle of the city with its glowing streetlamps, Tory wondered if he were not dreaming.

"Isn't it amazing?" Joseph said, his pompadour blowing in the breeze.

"Yes, it truly is."

"They were supposed to install the windows last week," Joseph said. "But union issues have stalled work. I'm sure they won't let it go undone too much longer." Joseph's arm tightened around Tory. All Tory's worries flew out the window. His father's fury stood like a mere bump in their path. His wrath had perhaps spurred forward everything Tory had wanted from the first moment he had spied Joseph van Werckhoven descending from the hansom cab Friday afternoon.

He and Joseph could get their own place. Even move back to New York City, if that was what events dictated, once Joseph had finished overseeing the building of the drugstore. They could stay in a room somewhere until then. Possibilities stretched endlessly, like the sprawl of the city below them. Two young lovers could surmount any obstacles.

"I can see the Chicago River," Joseph said. "Look! I believe I can even see out west to the prairie." He giggled and pointed southeast. "Is that Indiana over there?"

Tory chuckled. "No, I don't think we can see that far. But I can see the lake."

Joseph leaned farther out the window, his hand firm on Tory's back. "Yes, you're right. I can see it."

His head full of lofty notions, Tory left Joseph by the window and wandered the expansive space some more. Riding on a cloud, he rubbed his bare hand along the cement and steel beams that held the monolithic structure together.

"Wouldn't it be grand to live this high?" Joseph said from the window, where he still leaned out.

"Yes, it would," Tory said. A simple statement, but one that held mounds of meaning for him. Could he and Joseph live together, in a relationship that transcended time, high above the judgmental eyes of society?

From the corner of his eye, Tory glimpsed Joseph sitting on the window sill and spreading his arms wide.

"I'm on top of the world," Joseph said, as if for the both of them.

Tory glanced up to send him a smile, but Joseph had disappeared. Just like that. In an instant. He peered about the empty space. The wind howled around the support beams and stirred the debris in the corners.

Tory blinked, rubbed his eyes, shook his head. How could he have vanished like that? Where did he walk off to?

Was he some kind of a prankster or illusionist?

"Joseph?"

In a trance, Tory edged to the window where Joseph had been sitting. He thought he detected the building wobbling. Or was it his legs? Unable to process what he thought he had seen, he placed a shaky hand on the sill and allowed his eyes to move down toward the lighted sidewalk.

Laborers from inside the drugstore had gathered around something. A mob of curious onlookers surrounded them. A brief part in the crowd revealed what Tory couldn't grasp but on some unspeakable level had understood all along.

Joseph's body lay sprawled on the sidewalk face up, a dark spot growing by his head.

# CHAPTER
# FIVE

MRS. PILKVIST, sitting in her favorite armchair in the parlor, cried into her embroidered handkerchief. Tory merely stared, eyes wide and stinging with dryness. The undertaker had laid out Joseph's casket away from the windows, which Mrs. Pilkvist had draped in black fabric, as she had the two mirrors in the room and even her shiny silver tea service. A combination of gas and electric lighting cast flickering orange orbs about the dim room. Tory stood in the far corner, away from the two dozen or so mourners who had called to pay respects to someone they'd barely known. None of it seemed real to him. Even while the undertaker had prepared Joseph's body for the wake behind the parlor doors, a potent emptiness had gripped Tory.

Clair carried on as badly as his mother. She kneeled at the open coffin by Joseph's head and dabbed at her eyes, a pointy finger poking under her handkerchief. Her knees must have been adhered to the prayer kneeler, for she remained there a good half hour. The seething hatred that Tory had harbored for her had vanished. He no longer blamed her for Joseph's death.

He no longer felt anything. The dizzy confusion and despair that had whirled around his mind yesterday while he stumbled down the twelve flights of stairs (after dozens of frantic failed attempts to get the elevator to work) to find his beloved dead on the sidewalk had left him. He was too numb to feel anything other than stunned nothingness.

The other two boarders, the Scottish man Mr. Dunlop and Mr. Raincliff from Indiana, also attended the wake, their faces drawn and uncertain. And there were the laborers hired to raise the interior of the van Werckhovens' drugstore. In under a week, they had already grown to respect their overseer. "A man none too averse to gettin' his mitts dirty," one of the men had said in a heavy Irish drawl. Death jarred all of them, yet few had had the pleasure to truly know the New Yorker.

Mr. Pilkvist came in from the bakery and set a large tray of pastries on the coffee table next to the ceramic coffeepot. Tory barely compelled himself to gaze through the steam rising from the hot water bath in which his mother had set the pot. Beyond the mist lay the body of Joseph van Werckhoven, a man whose eyes he had never seen before a week ago.

Now he grieved for him as if he were his widower.

Too numb to cry like the women, Tory stood and watched the goings-on as he would a stage play. Even a few of the rugged workmen shed a straggling tear or two from red downcast eyes. But not him. No, for Tory, the stubborn tears failed to come.

Objects, fluctuations in shadows, subtle sounds of conversation or sobs—they were mere echoes from faraway places. Nothing remained tangible to him. The wake went on and on, an endless chain of nothingness, until the last of the laborers left for home while muttering about what would become of the new store, and Mrs. Pilkvist cried into the last of her clean hankies.

The next day, Tory traveled in the hansom with his parents, tailing the wagon driven by the railroad agents transporting Joseph's body to the train depot. Earlier that morning, Tory had overhead his father telling his mother that he had sent a telegram to Joseph's family in New York informing them of the calamity. Only a slight wonder about what they might think had skimmed across his mind. None of it was happening.

Clair Schuster had expressed distress that her factory job would not permit her time off for a final farewell. Mrs. Pilkvist's sobs had increased since yesterday. She insisted they had failed their handsome and promising boarder. He had arrived in Chicago a lively, energetic man, and a week later they were sending him home in a pine box.

At the station, Tory watched, numb and wordless, as the porters lifted the casket from the wagon onto the baggage car that would carry Joseph's body back to New York City. By tomorrow afternoon, his family would be receiving the casket along with his personal belongings at Grand Central Depot.

No one had mentioned the quarrel from Thursday. Resentments still simmered, but what did any of it matter now? Only the slightest regret for having threatened to oust Joseph eked from his father's crystal-blue eyes. No one had asked why Tory had gone to see Joseph or why Joseph had taken him to the top floor. It would've made sense that Joseph might want to show off the building in which his family was leasing space. The event had happened, unraveling like an abrasive burlap sack.

The porters slid the casket against the far wall of the car, silent and reverent. With a rumbling and final thud, they secured the door shut. It was then that Tory noticed a transformation in himself. His soundless shock was mutating into something new. His throat caught and his eyes burned. Sheer sorrow welled up inside him. He bit down on his anguish. His father, especially, would deplore such an outpouring of grief from his son. Surely his father already suspected that he and Joseph had become lovers.

When they returned home from the train depot, Tory descended from the hired hansom and scurried off without uttering a word. He did not want his parents to detect the tears that singed his eyes. Away from the spread of the city, he came to the Chicago River, half a mile from his home, and stood along the bank. With a sudden tremble, he fell to his knees and sobbed into his palms.

The cold breeze coming from the north chilled the tears dribbling through his fingers. Released of the pressure that had been building inside him since that horrible Thursday evening, he slowly raised his face and stood gazing into the water. The river, too murky for him to see his reflection, drifted past with muddy indifference. Downriver, grain elevators and factories mushroomed around Chicago's downtown. Already a dozen bridges crossed the river from the near west side. North of the city, the sprawl had leaped west across the river and out of sight, beyond West Town. The Chicago and Milwaukee Railroad tracks paralleled the river along the west bank and veered sharply westward, heading off to a world only glimpsed in dime novels and travel guides. He remembered seeing farms dot the horizon as a boy, where his eyes now traced the tracks. One of his favorite lines from Walt Whitman weaved through his mind:

> *But I do not undertake to define thee, hardly to comprehend thee,*
> *I but thee name, thee prophesy, as now,*
> *I merely thee ejaculate!*

He supposed it was impossible to find that kind of love again. Wasn't that why men like Whitman wrote poetry, because of love's utter unattainability? Tory's kind of love existed only in romantic fiction and within the confines of idyllic and cloaked verses. Death's snatch had made sure of that.

Why did Joseph allow it to happen? And so soon after their meeting? Their love had only begun to bloom. Another shudder of sobs overtook Tory. His shoulders grew heavy and tossed him forward, as if the city behind him had knocked him down. Weakened, he wiped his throbbing eyes with the back of his hand and inhaled the nippy air, thick with smoke from the factories abutting the coal yards upriver on Goose Island.

Through his damp eyelashes, he watched the red sun set over the western sprawl of the city, a ball of fire descending into oozing expanse. The river transformed to a brownish red, like molten lava. He stepped back. Even the illusion of fire upset him.

He turned his back to the river and faced the heaving city. He could hear its incessant growling. A conglomeration of horses' hooves, steam engines, trains, hammers, saws, thumping, grinding, churning, and wielding. The buildings, like a collage of steeples and prisms, stretched upward and outward. He had always observed the ever-expanding city with a spirit of awe. The buildings now transformed into Cyclopes, lurking man-eating giants seeking to devour whatever lay in their paths.

As the days passed, Tory's melancholy gripped him like the mitts of the city. His mother, who usually pestered him to do one thing or another, left him be. She seemed to sense his need to languish alone with his grief. His father, less empathetic, grew restless with his gloominess.

"Stop this sulking," Mr. Pilkvist said one night two weeks after they had seen Joseph's body off at the train depot. They were in the bakery preparing for Easter, and the kitchen, a mess, like always before a holiday, smoldered with activity. Flour dusted his father's face, white like a ghost. "You only knew the man a week. He couldn't have been more than an acquaintance to you."

"Pappa, please, I don't wish to discuss it."

"Sometimes I don't understand you, Torsten. You become too attached to people and things, like those silly pigeons. I saw you yesterday, feeding them. I told you, I don't want those pests coming around here. And I see you sometimes clinging to that stuffed bear. Where did you get that silly thing?"

The one item left from Joseph van Werckhoven's short juncture in Tory's life—the stuffed bear he'd won playing Pitch Out at the carnival on Taylor Street. Joseph had given it to Tory as a gesture to salute their burgeoning friendship, yet it had far greater implications. Tory had suspected that even then. Only later that same night, after Joseph had stepped into his room, had Joseph proven him right. Clinging to the bear whenever he moped in his bedroom, Tory almost heard the merry sounds from their antics at the carnival. Had all that actually happened only three weeks ago? A few times, he had even carried the prized bear with him to the breakfast table, forgetting he still clung to it until his mother commented on it.

"It's a toy bear, Pappa. There's nothing for you to worry over."

"A boy your age shouldn't want toys."

"I'm not a boy, Pappa."

"Then why do you act like one? I fear I lose you to the clouds one day." His father kneaded into the vetebröd dough. "You always off in daydreams."

"You know how the springtime sometimes affects me."

Mr. Pilkvist revealed a rare smile. "Ah, I do remember springtime from my youth. When I your age, I must admit, I'd get lightheaded too. I would stroll along the Osterdal River and make necklaces out of the yellow daffodils growing along the bank. And in the woods, my brother and me, we pick lingonberries for your grandmother to make jam, but most times they'd be eaten before we carry them home." He chuckled. "She yell at us, but we know she smile inside. Then, after I meet your mother, we would pick berries together. That is how we first court. We walk for hours in the cool woods and use picking berries for excuse to talk and be together."

He fell into silent rumination. But his father's distant memories failed to move Tory. His own life stretched ahead of him, as empty as his father's reminiscences. His father's past meant little to him at that moment. It only reinforced his loss. A loss no one would ever understand. He clenched the gooey dough with white knuckles while the loneliness engulfed him.

Snapping to, Mr. Pilkvist sharpened his expression to its usual solemnity. "Listen to what I say, Torsten. Keep your feet planted on the ground, ja?"

Tory placed the dough for bullarna in a large bowl to rise and shuffled over to the cooled semlorna, which he topped with powdered sugar. He stored the last of the semlorna in the display case and draped his smock over the counter. "Unless you need me for more chores," he said to his father, "I'd like to turn in for the night."

Mr. Pilkvist sighed. "Ja, you can go. But I will need you bright and early tomorrow for the rush of customers. They will be demanding and impatient for Easter week."

Stoop-shouldered, Tory slumped upstairs to his bedroom like he had for the past fortnight. There, he lay on his bed, cradling the stuffed bear with the short curly wool against his cheek. No more tears came. Tapped dry, he sighed. In the course of days, the calamity of Joseph's death hardened into ugly acceptance.

The house harbored an eerie emptiness. Clair Schuster had left a week ago for the women's hotel. Mr. Abner T. Raincliff had departed two days before. Although three new boarders had already claimed the vacated rooms, including the one once occupied by Joseph, they all worked long hours for the same accounting firm and rarely made an appearance at the house except at the breakfast table. Mrs. Pilkvist had a difficult time concealing her angst that they rarely took supper or cake and coffee in the parlor with them. Tory could have cared less.

Only the Scottish boarder, Mr. Dunlop, remained, quiet enough that Tory seldom remembered him. Yet the past few days, Tory suspected Mr. Dunlop was eyeing him from under his brow whenever taking a meal together or passing each other in the hallways. Was that how chronically shy men found their way out of their shells? With furtive glances? Encased in his own sorrows, Tory cared little for Mr. Dunlop's hidden issues.

Clinging to his bear, he stared out the window. Workers dressed in their black leather aprons, boys no older than fourteen, were lighting the gas lanterns along the visible stretch of Dearborn. Only downtown glowed with the electric streetlights. Soon, the entire city would be ablaze with electricity, Tory speculated, but unaccompanied by the usual enthusiasm he experienced whenever he contemplated the city's rousing future.

He was about to prepare for bed when he heard a light tap on his door. Curious, he set his bear atop his pillow and opened the door a crack. Mr. Dunlop stood on the other side, his brown eyes wide with self-consciousness, a soft mustache of perspiration above his thin upper lip.

"Yes?" Tory asked, perplexed. "May I help you with something? Do you need anything?"

Mr. Dunlop, shoulders against his ears, said in a hushed thick Scottish accent, "I... I wanted to... to express my condolences for... for the loss of Mr. van Werckhoven." And with those words, he turned and disappeared before Tory could fully open the door and respond. Fast and quiet, the boarder concealed himself behind his door to his room down the hall.

Tory stared after him. Had it taken two whole weeks of mental torture for him to muster the courage to utter those simple words? The depth of his and Joseph's relationship perhaps had not been lost on the man from Scotland. The quiet ones seemed to possess the keenest insight.

Tory, heavy-lipped and pondering, sat on the edge of his bed. A minor ease lifted his malaise. What had forced it? Someone appreciating the magnitude of his loss? Mr. Dunlop's sympathies might have only nudged aside his grief, yet it was a beginning.

# CHAPTER
## SIX

THE crack of the bat striking the baseball resounded in Tory's ears. He had hit the ball dead center on the barrel of the Louisville Slugger, and he knew the moment it connected with the ash wood that he had hit a two-run homer. He tore past the bases with his standard lightning speed, almost passing the runner in front of him. The cheers of his comrades followed him around the diamond like music.

His teammates greeted him at home plate with back slaps and applause. Tory basked in their praise. Their weekly baseball games had become scarcer now that his friends were married with babies. Since Tory was the only one among them single, they often tried to set him up with their sisters and cousins and the flood of newly arrived girls from rural parts of the Midwest. His mother still dreamed he'd meet a nice Swedish girl. Tory held no interest in girls of any nationality. The more he refused his friends' attempts to play matchmaker, the more they lost interest in him. Their adult lives took them down different paths.

His time with his chums was contracting, much like the vacant land surrounding the ballpark. Their schooldays long past, their favorite pastime lacked the force to unite them. As they played, Tory divined that this might be one of his last ball games with his friends.

At least for the moment, the heat of competition elbowed aside the differences in their lifestyles. They played the remaining five innings, after which Tory said farewell and headed home for his Saturday afternoon bath.

A month had passed since Joseph's death. Time had softened the pain, but it still lingered like an itchy scab on an old wound. He swore at times he still smelled Joseph's lavender cologne, but then he noticed the spring flowers popping out in planter boxes hanging from the windows of the row houses. Joseph had lived with the Pilkvists for too short a time to have left remnants of himself behind. Other than the stuffed bear, nothing physical remained of the New Yorker ever having entered Tory's life. The thought both comforted and troubled him.

The sharp sting of regret and grief pierced his mind. He realized his time with Joseph was a once in a lifetime love. Joseph's ghastly fall had taken part of Tory down with him, along with his hopes and dreams.

But the harsh truth made his fate tolerable. He accepted his destiny. No changing the course of the future—he would live the life of a bachelor.

Somber thoughts followed him into the tub. Refreshed and clean after his bath, he longed to immerse himself in the company of others. Being around his baseball friends in the warm spring air had made him crave more of the camaraderie that sometimes chased away his glumness.

He splashed limewater on his chest, dressed in a crisp white shirt, gray pinstripe suit, blue cravat, and felt derby, and then jumped on the electric streetcar to go from State Street to the 35th Street cabaret secretly known as a watering hole for men like him. Love was not his aim—he knew that was far from his grasp at a place like the cabaret. He wanted only company, affection, the fleeting kind that might lessen his grief and loneliness, like the way some used alcohol.

The instant Tory stepped inside the cabaret, the usual stares burned holes into him. He disliked the scene, yet he knew of no other place like it in Chicago. Many of the young men, both Negroes and whites, came for "business." They congregated at the bar and the small standing tables, some selling, others buying. The regulars recognized him as one who seldom interacted with the locals, especially those known as "renters." A few of the renters dressed as women, which Tory found both entertaining and distasteful. The older men from out of town ogled him. They often mistook him for a renter. He avoided eye contact to communicate his disinterest.

A player piano rolled out tunes in the corner. Some of his favorites, "Oh, Dem Old Golden Slippers" and "American Patrol," lightened his mood. The cabaret, less crowded than usual for a Monday evening, ebbed and flowed with a sluggish apathy. Since it was the day after Easter, most of the regulars who often stopped by after work for drinks had likely remained at home with their wives and children. Not many out-of-towners had scheduled trips away from their families during the holiday.

The two bouncers appeared more relaxed than usual. Tory never learned if they were like the men who patronized the cabaret. They seemed disinterested in the goings-on, their eyes always narrowed with vigilance.

A boy of about fifteen, the cabaret owners' youngest son, served drinks behind the bar. With a thin cigar clenched between yellowing crooked teeth, he poured and poured, his face lined with labor. The slightest spill of the liquor and his father, Mr. Levitzki, the stony-faced proprietor with the cannon-like voice, who roamed the cabaret like a grizzly bear, would slap the back of his head. The father's temper was enough for Tory to want to leave the place, but there was no establishment as safe when looking for companionship.

Tory found an empty bench against the far wall. He kept his derby on, for it gave him the extra furtiveness he liked while at the cabaret. With his hands balled in his lap, he peered around under the short brim, taking note of anyone who resembled a gentleman. Weekdays were often more rowdy than weekends. During the week, drunken construction and railroad workers would come in to make "dates" with some of the younger men. The owners tolerated the flood of teamsters until their pockets came up empty. Afterward, Mr. Levitzki would give a subtle sign—two fingers tickling under his chin—and the bouncers would dispatch to their duties and herd the rowdies like cattle and toss them out the door.

Tonight, the holiday kept most of the heavy drinkers away. Tory enjoyed the dim calmness. Disorderly crowds and obnoxious noise were not what he searched for. Light from the setting sun oozed through the stained glass above the bar. A reddish blue hue, mixed with the pipe and cigar smoke, floated around the establishment. A Negro boy in women's clothing swaggered by him. The bustle on his skirt protruded clownishly. Not even a stage actress would paint herself with so much makeup, Tory imagined. His contemptuous smirk brought a grunt from the faux woman, and he strutted off.

Some of the patrons held hands and nuzzled while sipping their drinks. Mostly they were renters and buyers. Another couple danced cheek to cheek to the high-pitched music streaming from the player piano. Tory watched, fascinated, as a couple kissed passionately in a dark corner. Even to him, overt displays of romantic affection between men in public seemed shocking.

A man walked into the bar. From across the dimly lit cabaret, Tory saw that he held his breath when he glanced around. He appeared as out of place as Tory felt, but his Panama skimmer and bamboo walking stick gave him a debonair quality. Clearly an out-of-towner on Chicago business. Men like him filled Chicago during the week, working all day, playing all night, looking for brief companionship. Tory watched as the two renters who had been sitting at the bar, including the Negro with the caricature-like bustle, circled him. They could spot an out-of-towner with money like an alley cat sniffing out fish carcasses. The competing boys grimaced at each other, their eyebrows arched high. The white boy nudged out his shoulder, indicating he was willing to fight. The renter in women's clothing appeared ready to counter, but then his painted face fell. Slump-shouldered, he trudged back to the bar.

As if relishing his victory, the white boy grinned and rubbed against the man, flirting like the coquettish females in burlesque shows. Curious, Tory took mental notes of the out-of-towner's reaction to the renter. Were his initial perceptions of the dark-featured man with rounded spectacles accurate? The man's gaze remained fixed on the dartboard along the far wall. Suddenly the man turned to the boy. His lips moved. A second later, the boy's smile transformed into a scowl, and he stomped off to stand next to his companion by the bar. Inwardly, Tory smiled. He had been right. He was a gentleman. But a married gentleman, no doubt. And a nervous one, at that.

Such men, whether locals or out-of-towners, frequented the cabaret. A few of these older men had offered Tory jobs with their companies as messengers, copy boys, anything to keep him nearby. They sought only playthings. Tory desired to be more than an older man's trinket.

The weighty realization that Joseph van Werckhoven would no longer grace his sight crushed him. The bachelorhood that he had solemnly accepted imposed on his destiny. He could not fathom feigning devotion to a wife, like most of the men who frequented the cabaret. Fleeting encounters hardly substituted for a loving and devoted lifemate.

The cabaret grew darker. An image of Joseph sprawled on the sidewalk shook him, and before he even comprehended the sad metamorphosis that had gripped him, he flung himself off the bench and raced for the door.

Outside, he breathed. He thought he had left behind the loneliness and desperation inside the cabaret until he noticed the man in the skimmer following him onto the street. He wanted to rush away. Pedestrians descending from the streetcar pushed him back.

The man laid a gloveless hand on Tory's arm. "Why did you run?" he said in a gentle voice.

Tory tensed. He remained still, like a rabbit near a fox. Passersby pushed and shoved.

The man smiled warmly. "I noticed you in the cabaret. I wanted to speak to you, but you ran out before I could." He chuckled. "I can understand your leaving. I don't much like those places either. But sometimes, when… when a man seeks companionship, there's nowhere else to go."

Where had Tory heard his accent before? He spoke like Tory's brother-in-law from Maryland, who practiced law in the nation's capital.

"Would you like to go for a walk?" the man said. "Just to talk?"

Tory understood what the man wanted. Didn't Tory want it too? Without answering, Tory moved with the flow of people on the sidewalk. The man walked alongside him, wordless, for many paces. The out-of-towner seemed to know his way around the streets. Perhaps he traveled to Chicago often for business. How might Tory shake him?

With Joseph, life had evolved into a dream. But this man, like the two boarders Tory had been with, like the others he'd met at the cabaret, had never sought a lasting relationship with other men. He had a wife. Tory knew for sure now by the ring displayed on his finger. His face showed he was about thirty. He most likely had a handful of children.

They stopped at a traffic signal.

"My name is Calvin. Calvin McGregor." He held out his hand. Tory ignored it. "I'm from Ellicott City, Maryland. I'm a salesman for a fabric manufacturer there. We make sails and tents and other things of that sort."

Tory kept quiet.

"Are you from Chicago? You don't need to answer. I can tell you are. Chicagoans have a unique quality about them. Nothing seems to faze you." The man chortled. "I do believe I could have horns growing out of my head and you'd still not flinch."

Tory could not help but inwardly grin at his comment. He'd often heard the same appraisal of Chicagoans. Changes came so quickly to them that few cared about the many differences that surrounded them. People came from literally every corner of the world and each of the states. None were outsiders because they all were. A city with a tough temperament, he'd heard some proclaim.

"What is it you do here…?" The man was fishing for his name.

Warming to him despite his better judgment, Tory muttered, "Torsten," but he held back providing his family name.

"Torsten. That's a good name. Do you attend school in Chicago, Torsten?"

"No," Tory said, his mouth firm. "I work for my family."

"A family business. A good thing. So much more secure. I have four daughters, so I won't be able to hope for a son following in my footsteps, will I? I suppose perhaps I could interest one of their future husbands to go into the fabric business with me. Do you think?"

Tory noted an East Coast habit: phrasing an opinion in the form of a question. Joseph had spoken in that fashion. Emptiness bit into his gut. He should have known better than to venture into the cabaret seeking strangers. Such men only exacerbated his heartache and lonesomeness. An evening out had not soothed the pain the way he had hoped.

"I'm here in Chicago digging for clients," the man went on. "Chicago is the fastest-growing city in the country—in the world. So much opportunity is here. My wife isn't happy I scheduled my trip over Easter. She's more into fussing over the children and the holidays than I am."

They stopped at another intersection. The crowd, thinner than usual due to the holiday, pushed against the crosswalk.

"I'm staying at a nearby hotel," the man went on. "I was lucky to get a room. Often when I'm in Chicago I have to find lodging at a boarding house. I suppose it might have something to do with the holiday. Fewer people travel away from home."

They waited for the policeman to blow the whistle, indicating they could cross.

"Would you like to have a drink up in my hotel room to get away from these grimy streets?" Calvin McGregor asked. "My eyes are burning from all this dust and smoke. And the crowd can be overwhelming."

On the other side of the street, Tory slowed his pace and glanced at the man. Life seemed odd to him. Odd, and painfully short. Disregarding any other thoughts, he followed the man down a side street and into a hotel lobby.


"I HOPE I didn't hurt you."

Tory was dressing slowly but purposefully. He and Calvin McGregor had finished what Tory classified as sex: quick and passionless. Empty. The Marylander was obviously inexperienced with men. Tory had had to instruct him. Even after that, he'd pinched and grabbed like a clumsy, unsure oaf. Yet he had been driven to completion.

"No, you didn't hurt me," Tory said, his eyes on buttoning his shirt.

"Can we see each other again?" the man said. "Perhaps tomorrow for supper? I leave on the Wednesday train. But I can arrange to come back to Chicago as often as I like. I head the factory's sales department."

"I may not be here," Tory said. He slipped on his pants, tucked in his shirt, and fastened the button fly.

Calvin McGregor sat up, alert. He reached for his spectacles from the side table and placed them over his nose. "But where will you be going? You live here, don't you?"

"Yes, but I'm thinking I might travel."

"Travel? Travel to where? Out east, perhaps? To Maryland?"

"I suppose I could. I have a sister who lives in Washington, DC." Tory cared little what he said to the man; he had no connection to him.

Ten minutes of heartless physical interlude had not united them in any way. Once he had disengaged himself from the man's clammy grip, they were no more linked than two strangers waiting for a streetcar.

"Your sister lives in Washington? What do you know? See, the moment I saw you, I knew we had much in common. Will you be staying with her for a lengthy period? It'll be perfect if you do. Ellicott City is only a short train ride from the nation's capital."

Tory was sitting on a ladder-back chair, lacing his boots. "Well, I… I was only thinking of visiting for a few weeks."

"When will you know for certain?" Calvin McGregor lowered his head, his brow furrowed. Gazing back at Tory, he said, "Do you think you'll come out for the summer?"

Tory stood, snapped on his suspenders, slipped on his jacket. "I'm not certain. I still have to think on it."

The man gathered the sheet around him and approached Tory. "Can we write? Can we somehow stay in touch? I can give you the address where I work."

A welling emptiness choked Tory. If only Joseph van Werckhoven were with him in a South Side hotel room, instead of Calvin McGregor. His experience with Joseph, no matter how short-lived, had spurred him into demanding more than cheap lovemaking with strangers. He dreamed of a husband. Yes, he dared to say it to himself. A husband. No matter how absurd it sounded to his and everyone else's ears.

"No," he snapped. He softened his tone. "No, I don't think that's a good idea. We mustn't write to each other."

He fumbled with his cravat, unconcerned if he tied it straight. Turning sharply from Calvin as he came closer, he put on his derby and said, "Good-bye. I wish you the best of luck in your fabric business," and he trotted out the door. He heard the man shouting for him down the cavernous concrete stairwell, but Tory ignored his call.

On the street, he ran, glancing back to make sure the man had not dressed and followed after him. The evening crowd had grown, pushing and nudging. Wishing to hide from the world and catch his breath a moment, he found refuge behind a stand selling dime novels, newspapers, and periodicals.

Wedged between the kiosk and a parked police wagon, he read the headlines from the *Chicago Tribune* and the *Daily News*. The country marveled at the overdue near-completion of a massive statue in New York's harbor; more labor disputes around the country had unions hankering for power; riots in central London had spread into the central part of England; another conference to establish disputed lands with the Plains Indians remained uncertain. None of that interested him. But a periodical grabbed his attention. He had seen one of his aunts reading it a few years before. She had stowed it under her skirt when he'd surprised her. Curious ever since, he took it off the rack and thumbed through it.

As he read the inside of the front cover, he learned that *Matrimonial News*, published in San Francisco, arranged matches between "refined ladies" and gentlemen living in the American West. Men and women submitted advertisements, and the magazine's editors forwarded the responses to the interested parties. Recipients decided whether to meet face-to-face. Tory considered the entire concept absurd. Flipping through the pages, he couldn't imagine meeting someone he had found in a periodical. What was the world coming to?

But hadn't he done something far worse? Hadn't he met a man in a cabaret and, without even courting him, lain with him naked in his hotel room? A married man with four daughters, no less? Well, at least he had seen him face to face. An advertisement was so... so impersonal.

Skimming down the advertisements, he snickered despite his scorn.

> Aged 26, height 5 feet 7 inches, blond hair and blue eyes; considered the most attractive of all my brothers; relatives say I am ideally suited to be a husband. The maiden must have substantial money.

Lively bachelor of 33, 5 feet 5 inches high, weighing 140 pounds, wanting to correspond with a marriageable young lady between ages 17 and 26; am strong in build and character; mostly American with some French and Norwegian. Lady should be temperate, calm, and like to cook.

A fine lady seeks man to love, be true to, cherish, honor, and obey. Will never grimace. Pretty and small in waist. No man under 5 feet 5 inches, and must be kind and giving.

Gentlemen, are you searching for an older woman? I am a widow, age 59, but don't feel or look a day over 40; 120 pounds, 4 feet 10 inches, brown hair and eyes, Irish/German; cute, kindly, good-hearted, many years of love yet to give; would like to meet someone likewise kindly with a generous disposition. Let's make a good home.

"Hey, laddy, you that naff statue they're building out in New York?"

Tory jerked up and stared into the narrowed eyes of the rotund vendor with the English accent. "Pardon me?" Tory said.

"That periodical ain't no Declaration of Independence for you to hold in your yobby hands. Buy it or bugger off."

"I'll buy it." Tory slapped five cents into the man's palm and stuffed the magazine under his jacket. Weaving through the crowd, he made his way to the streetcar for home.

BACK in his bedroom, Tory hungrily perused the periodical. Images of rugged, brawny bachelors living on the wild frontier filled his head. They must be so lonely, he imagined. So lonely and desperate for human affection. Much like him. And the women? Desperate for a husband or an excuse to leave their unhappy families, like Clair Schuster. Some were probably foreign women looking for an easy route to American citizenship. Or bored maidens seeking adventure.

Muffling his giggles so that his parents would not grow curious, he read more of the advertisements. Hundreds of them. Some short, others lengthy and long-winded enough to make him shake his head at the arrogance and lack of shame.

He tried to find those advertisements that might contain secret codes. Maybe some of the men sought male companionship. Maybe they had cryptic meanings for those discerning enough. But he'd never heard of such a gimmick. Did people do such things?

> Lonely fellow, long on love and short on stature, seeks someone to keep close to his heart....

"Someone"? Might that be a hint? Most of the other advertisements were specific. The women sought men; the men sought women. Was this man being purposefully vague? Did "someone" mean a man? It was a long shot the advertisement concealed a coded message.

He read more of the advertisements, monitoring them for secret meanings. Nothing really jumped out at him. But one in particular touched his heart. Despite the bachelor clearly mentioning he sought a woman, Tory kept coming back to it, rereading the short passage over and over.

> Softhearted, tall, good-looking bachelor, aged 38, looking to correspond with ladies between the ages of 19 and 35. I'm partial to blondes, but you can be of any nationality. Sturdiness and honesty are most important. City life not for me; I like quiet rustic living. Let's become friends.

Transfixed by the words, Tory could hardly take his eyes off the fine black print. He had no idea where in the western part of the United States the "softhearted" bachelor lived, but his musings carried him over the vast prairies west of Chicago, past Peoria, over Iowa, to Nebraska, and onward to the frontier, where wild animals and Indians still roamed, lurking behind mountains and in canyons.

A gentle implied honesty emanated from the man's reaching out for human companionship, accentuated with masculine determination. Tory, both aroused and intrigued, yearned to learn more about him. Where did he live? Where had he come from? He reread the earnest advertisement again and again, as if the more he read, the more he might unlock some special meaning concealed behind the words.

Animated in a way he hadn't experienced since meeting Joseph van Werckhoven, he sat at his desk by Edison lamp (the latest gadget given to him by his parents for his nineteenth birthday) and withdrew a sheet of paper from the top drawer. Did he dare do what traipsed in his mind? It would be cruel and improper, wouldn't it?

Yet unlike most those who frequented the cabaret on 35th Street, the men who had placed advertisements in *Matrimonial News* were bachelors, uninterested in renters, male or female. Writing to one of those men couldn't be horribly wrong. Living alone on the wild frontier, the man would appreciate someone taking the time to reach out to him. What if no one else bothered to write? As long as Tory kept his identity hidden, a mutual correspondence between two lonely souls would harm no one.

He twisted the lead from the fluted end of his pencil and placed the tip on the paper. He figured the best way to compose the letter was to write with little reflection. Let his heart flow and the words would follow.

With the pencil poised in his hand, he pictured the "tall, good-looking bachelor" with honed muscles living ruggedly on his homestead. Chopping wood, retrieving water from an old-fashioned well, trapping rabbits and possums or whatever frontiersmen trapped.

Tory gazed toward his bedroom door. Somewhere out there in the wilds of America's frontier, a real man needed love. Desperate to the point he'd taken out an advertisement.

A strong man, a man who had already stolen Tory's affections with one simple message....

# Chapter
# SEVEN

THE pot boiled over onto the cast-iron stovetop, hissing with steam. Franklin Ausmus cursed up a storm.

His mind was stuck on more than cooking his venison stew for lunch. He still worried over the silly personal advertisement he had placed in *Matrimonial News* three weeks ago. By now, the latest edition must've hit the kiosks across the country. Would anyone even bother to respond? He had been living in the Black Hills of Dakota Territory for nearly ten years, and the longing for companionship had begun to gnaw at him like a chigger bug. In a few more years women would most likely no longer find him a good catch—if they ever had.

He hadn't even set eyes on a decent woman in years. The ones he came across in Spiketrout were mostly "working women" catering to the men of the gold rush. Those who were God-fearing arrived in the Hills already married, usually to missionaries who wasted most of their time with the Indians, trying to civilize them. He only knew of one decent unmarried woman in town—a widow close to sixty. Spiketrout's marshal had whispered to him a few years back that nine out of ten women in the Black Hills worked as prostitutes.

He'd had his fill of those types. During the Civil War, commanding officers had brought prostitutes into the camps when the waiting for battle got so gruesomely tedious men in the same units were fighting each other to burn energy. Fearful of losing precious soldiers in careless duels, they paid "camp followers" in silver to entertain the troops. He didn't care for women like that, but even he had had needs. An enlistee in the Union Army, like most of the boys back home in eastern Tennessee, he'd had difficulty resisting the temptation more often than not.

And there was that crazy time in Richmond back in 1864. He was only sixteen at the time, with two years of fighting already under his belt. The city was crawling with soldiers, both Federal and Confederate. He had never witnessed so much carousing. As a country boy, the largest city he'd ever seen was Knoxville, nothing near as teeming as Richmond.

Residents fumed over the drunken antics of the soldiers who furloughed in the city during the year-long siege of Petersburg—and over the prostitutes, male and female, hawking their trade wherever they were appreciated. One time, a male renter had enticed Franklin down a secluded alley. Franklin had understood what the spicy boy, no older than he, had intended. He didn't dwell on it much at the time— nor did he now. War was a different animal. Comprised of different parts. Particular mores and ethics. No borders, no laws. Just war. Under the constant strain of fight or flight, soldiers searched for anything to alleviate the tension.

On the planet War, his fondling of the renter seemed as natural as when he and his girl back in Tennessee had kissed for the first time by the creek behind the schoolhouse. The boy in Richmond had unleashed something primitive within him. He recalled how the boars on his family's hog farm would sometimes mount the beta males in a show of dominance. Some boars seemed to prefer them over the females. Their troublesome antics worried the hog farmers, who often had to force copulation, a not-so-pleasant task. In that instant in the alley, Franklin had understood the power they might have felt, the drive for domination. The stress of battle had been released in a way he'd never imagined.

His cheeks heated as he remembered his escapades in the South's capital. He realized he was getting a little aroused thinking of how he had pushed against the renter's backside, pressing him into the brick wall of the tavern in the alley. A beer in one hand, and in the other… well…. He had been drunk. From what he'd noticed, the boy had had an abundance to drink himself, and plenty of money stuffed in his pockets. Apparently Franklin hadn't been his only client.

"Why aren't you fighting in the war?" Franklin had asked him afterward, while the renter counted his remuneration.

"I am." The boy had fanned his greenbacks before Franklin's bleary eyes and grinned. "I'm helping, you can be sure of that." And he'd raced down the alley, most likely straight back to work.

Not too long after that, a lucky shot from a falling Confederate landed Franklin in an Army hospital in Maryland for a good month. He hadn't even heard the gunshot blast. His comrades said the shot had come from the forest partition between rival camps. His unit had scouted out the woods and found a dead Confederate, his musket still smoking. Someone had blown off half of his head, they said. He had likely fired off a ball as a last hurrah, striking Franklin Ausmus in the process. A blistering exclamation point at the end of his farewell proclamation. Franklin had predicted nothing good would come from the grove of river birch and pignut hickories. But one good thing came from his injury: his foray as a soldier had ended.

Yet war waged on for him on other fronts. When he returned home to Tennessee, he experienced the first pinch of rejection. Soldiers' lives were in a constant forward march. So were the lives of those left behind. While he had fought for the Union, his girl had taken up with another man—a Confederate soldier with a far less gruesome injury than Franklin's. Last he heard she had married the Confederate veteran, now a big gun hog dealer with stock in the railroads.

Her rebuff forced him to demand something more from people. He would not give himself to anyone out of desperation. He longed for something deeper than a bride and a balloon-framed house. He'd rather live alone than cling to a frivolous marriage that exuded loneliness.

But years of high expectations had alienated him from many. His only constant companion the past ten years was Wicasha, a Lakota Indian he'd met while working in the quartz mine north of Deadwood back in '75. He lived beyond the hillocks in a camp in an area even Franklin had never ventured into. Besides Wicasha, nine years ago Franklin had befriended a yellow retriever he'd named Ash because she'd survived a small forest fire. A loyal companion for four years, she had died from tumors that had devoured her body. Franklin couldn't withstand the anguish of losing a beloved hound again.

The years had piled up, each one lonelier than the preceding. Finally, he'd come across that silly magazine at the mercantile in Spiketrout. His advertisement was a last-ditch effort at true companionship. Like a fish net tossed into a lake, perhaps it might catch something worthwhile. Still, lingering doubts circled him.

The periodical listed no rules regarding who could answer. The editors merely forwarded the letters of those who bothered to write.

What if some crazy woman replied? At least it would be nice to correspond with a woman of a gentler disposition than he'd become accustomed to in the Black Hills. A simple penmate might pass the lonelier hours, at least. He didn't have to meet anyone eye to eye.

He wondered if he should have come out clean straightaway about his deformity. Not too many women wanted a lame man like him. But there lay the glory of letter writing. He could keep the sides of himself he disliked concealed.

He wasn't a gambling man. Yet placing the advertisement was a game of chance. Risk-taking amused Franklin when the odds tilted in favor of the players. What were his chances of actually meeting a fine lady who might one day become his bride?

Steam from the pot of stew irritated his face. The moisture clung to his whiskers, which he needed to shave. Perhaps he'd go into town after lunch for a bath and trim. Of course, he knew he was fooling himself. The real reason he wanted to go into town was to check with the postal office to see if he'd received any responses to his advertisement. He reckoned it might be too soon for anyone to have replied, but no harm to look.

"Ausmus!"

He jerked up. That wretched man was pestering him again. He recognized his irritating accent. He wiped his hand on his buckskin trousers and glanced out the window. Some men had no understanding of the word "vamoose."

He strapped on his holster, in case the man wanted more trouble, and stepped outside his cabin. "What're you doing back here? I told you last month to keep off my land."

"I was hoping you changed your mind about selling," the man said in his French drawl.

"Won't happen, Bilodeaux. Been here near ten years, before all these deadbeats came barreling through the Black Hills looking for more and more gold. If you want gold, go find it, just not on my property."

"You have a natural creek pool." From his mount atop his gray stallion, the French Canadian pointed his white-gloved finger toward a grove of ponderosa that concealed the creek running through Franklin's land. "Everyone knows there are gold deposits that fill the pool. Lots of it. Everywhere else, the placer gold has dried up."

"It don't make me no nevermind."

"You are a selfish man, Ausmus."

"Selfish for doing what I want with my own legal property?"

"Only a fool could resist panning for such easy-gotten gold."

"Only a fool would, if you ask me."

"I will not give up on you, Ausmus."

"I keep telling you, I won't change my stance."

"Every man has a price."

"You think you're Napoleon, Bilodeaux?" In fact, Bilodeaux, short like Napoleon, carried airs the way the French general was said to have done during his charges throughout Europe. His eyes, sharp blue, intelligent, and penetrating, absorbed everything around him. His full lips were always puckered as if he wanted to spit. But Franklin harbored no fear of the man. Like the mosquitoes that attacked the Hills in midsummer, Bilodeaux was a mere pesky annoyance.

Yet lately, Bilodeaux's encroaching had increased, along with the fast depletion of the easily gotten placer gold. In the past, when gold had come easier, Bilodeaux and Franklin had butted heads over his land only once or twice a year, when they ran into each other in town. Already this spring, the bandit had trespassed on his property twice. The warming weather had made it easy. Were his incursions going to increase in frequency?

Franklin had decided years ago, when he'd first settled on his homestead in 1876, not to pan for the gold. Not everyone understood. Sometimes even he didn't. But he had made an unbreakable promise to himself. The gold would stay put. No one, not even cotton-picking Bilodeaux, could force him to change his mind.

A sturdy gust came down off the mountains surrounding the homestead. Smoke from the chimney swept over the mounted Bilodeaux. His form wavered. Franklin resisted the urge to pull out his sidearm and shoot the bastard.

"Listen, Bilodeaux," he said between clenched teeth as the smoke cleared, "this is my land, legal by law and decree. I was here after the government kicked out the Indians. I got the deed to prove it. You have no rightful business coming around here. I'm tired of telling you."

Bilodeaux's gaze from his high mount, menacing and persistent, cut through Franklin. "Laws never meant much in the Hills, Ausmus," he said. "I am speaking not solely for myself, but on behalf of the entire community. The Black Hills are growing up around you. The frontier is officially closed. You cannot hold out the people much longer. Gold is in that creek pool that sits on your property. The people have a right to it and all the wealth it can bring them."

"The people have only one right, and that's to mind their own businesses," Franklin said, stepping forward to emphasize his point, his hand braced close to his sidearm. "And unless you're interested in joining Napoleon in his grave, I suggest you mind your own business by removing yourself off my property, once and for good."

Bilodeaux drew in his heavy lips. He stared down hard at Franklin. "I am not finished with this, Ausmus. There are still matters that need settled. You will hear from me again. Be sure of it. À bientôt." He turned his gray stallion and rode off down the trail leading into Spiketrout, leaving behind a plume of dust.

Franklin stared after his adversary long after the hurried gallop of the horse's hooves faded. He shivered from his latest encounter with him. But not due to fear. Disgust sent a cold spasm through Franklin's limbs.

Frustrated, he traipsed back inside the hot cabin.

"What does that fool want this time?"

Franklin stirred the pot of venison stew. His Lakota friend, Wicasha, had already served himself and was eating at the table.

"Same thing he's been after since the pacer gold started drying up," Franklin murmured. He plated himself some stew and sat down across from the tall Lakota, who had been paying one of his welcomed visits. "No wonder three wives left him. That man is surlier than a badger cornered in a woodpile."

"He's nasty, no doubt."

"I hate to say it," Franklin said, shaking his head, "but I might have to place barbwire around my land to keep that ruffian out. Never foresaw I'd have to resort to it, but if that Bilodeaux don't stop coming around here making threats, might have to get some."

"Barbwire won't keep him out," Wicasha said as he chewed the potatoes and venison.

"At least I'll be making myself clear."

"If you ask me, next time shoot him for trespassing."

"I only wish it was that easy, Wicasha." Franklin spooned hot stew into his mouth, chewed, and swallowed. "He's got a lot of the law on his side. If he dies, no telling who else might be hankering for the gold. More than just him think they have a right to my land and whatever they find on it. A lot of deadbeats in Spiketrout."

"Maybe we should pray he dies like Napoleon."

Steam from his stew washed over Franklin's face. "Consumption would be too good for him. Let's pray that he dies like Custer."

PINE mist sparkled in the rising sun like a million shards of diamonds. Deep-blue spruce and pines surrounded the gulch with their usual brilliance. The caterpillar-like buds of the aspens had begun to open, the unfolding leaves green and tender. Rays of sun warmed his face where he sat at a roughhewn plank table he'd crafted from the local pine. Refreshed from a restful sleep, Franklin, still in his union suit, ate his breakfast of scrambled eggs, jerky, and fried potatoes away from the heat of the cabin. With the magpies and canyon wrens yapping in the aspens on the slopes, he chewed slowly. No need to rush. Quiet and peace trickled down from the granite peaks. He relished life on his homestead, a paradise he called Moonlight Gulch.

Gazing at the periwinkle sky, he concluded he had found Zion, with or without someone to share it. With the sun shifting higher over the peaks, he reckoned life could be a lot worse. He would never forget how he'd first come across his land. After he left the quartz mine in '76, he'd set out on horseback to find a spot to call home. He'd wandered the Hills for weeks, camping, biding his time, waiting for a place to holler his name. One night, sitting by his campfire, the nickering of distant horses traveling among the thick aspens and pines grabbed his attention. Although the federal government had officially opened the Black Hills to white settlers by then, he still feared the Sioux or a rogue cavalryman. He'd dismantled his camp and followed an old Indian trail lit by the full moon deep into a gulch. Shortly, he came into a clearing. The moonlight slicing through the pines and aspens danced off what he thought was flat-lying granite. Closing in, he realized it was a slow-moving creek. Soon, he heard the lush valley call his name. He was home. And he hadn't looked back since.

The call of an osprey forced him back to the present. A full day loomed ahead. He carried his empty plate into the cabin and dressed. After slopping the hogs, milking his one dairy cow, feeding the horses, cow, and mule, he hitched his mare, Lulu, to the wagon. The morning warranted a trip into Spiketrout to run some errands—and to check the mail at the postal office. He hadn't gotten around to it yesterday. Bilodeaux's unexpected visit had set him on edge, and he had wanted to stay close to the homestead to keep an eye on things. Today, he was more relaxed. Wicasha, who had wandered back to the homestead from his camp with the sunrise, had said he'd watch things.

Midmorning sun hung from the sturdy aspen and spruce branches and warmed his back as he made his way along the nine-mile makeshift trail into Spiketrout. A steep rock face soared above him to his right, the meandering creek for about two miles to his left. The familiar cool draft from the five-foot waterfall greeted him before the trail veered sharply right. As he left behind the rock face and the rush of the waterfall, the gulch opened into a sun-splashed dell. Blue pasqueflowers bloomed in tall clusters in sunny spots. Golden butterflies, newly emerged from their cocoons, danced above the yellow buds of the larkspur. Alfalfa—the same patch from which Franklin gathered the propagation for his crop field—filled the dell with lavender sprouts.

Lulu followed the trail onto a forested ridge. The trail, grooved from ten years of Franklin's wagon wheels rolling over it, climbed the longest of about four inclines. The mare snorted as she pressed her ears into the upslope. Cries of hawks trickled down from the lush mountainside.

The trail leveled off in a wide alder grove. For half a mile, Lulu followed a family of mule deer, before the mother and her two yearlings disappeared into the cluster of alders.

Franklin wondered what type of woman would want to live in such rustic environs. Few women—the sort that he envisioned—sought a secluded, rustic lifestyle. Were the ones who read those matchmaker periodicals savvy enough to understand the type of men who advertised in them? The closer he came to Spiketrout, the more his mouth drained of spit.

As much as his friendship with Wicasha had strengthened during the years, he didn't feel comfortable enough to tell him about placing the advertisement with *Matrimonial News*. Late last night, after their usual good-natured bantering, Wicasha had hiked back to his camp without Franklin uttering a word about his plans. Wicasha harbored a keen inquisitive streak, one Franklin believed best left unstirred. He worried that James Carson, Spiketrout's postmaster, might have questions. The last time Franklin had business at the postal office, he'd sent his advertisement to *Matrimonial News*. Postmaster Carson had barely glanced at the envelope before he'd stuffed it in the slot that read "U.P. West/San Fran." Franklin prayed Jim retained his professionalism once Franklin started receiving mail from mysterious women—*if* he received any.

Two hours and many doubts later, the dusty, decaying town of Spiketrout appeared. The town, both quiet and rowdy, always struck him as odd. Spiketrout, like Deadwood (a town four times larger and ten times as raucous), clung to its bygone gold rush days but always seemed on the verge of waking from a drowsy hangover. The population had declined from three thousand at the height of the gold rush to just under eight hundred today. Only one drinking hole remained—the Gold Dust Inn.

Franklin parked the wagon alongside the barbershop, where he figured he'd get cleaned up before heading to the postal office to check his mail. A trim, shave, and quick kettle bath later (all for thirty-five cents), he crossed the street to see Postmaster Carson. Hot blood seared his cheeks when he thought of how silly his pursuit of a mail-order bride might look to others. He tried to will down his flush before stepping inside the postal office.

Jim Carson flashed him his typical friendly smile when he entered. "Hi, Frank. How you been?"

"Things are good, Jim," Franklin said. "What about you?"

"Can't complain. Things back at the homestead going all right?"

"Spring's keeping me busy," Franklin said. "Still got lots of mending work, and the planting's coming along."

"I know what that's like," Jim said.

Franklin, holding his Stetson in front of his pants flap, detected a slight tremor to his hat.

"You here looking for your mail, I reckon," Jim said. "I got a bunch for you."

Franklin's heart quickened. He gulped, trying to maintain his composure. Jim dug behind him and slapped a bundle bound with twine onto the countertop. From his frozen position, Franklin noted three pieces of mail, two more than usual. He rarely heard from his folks back in Tennessee. When they did correspond, they usually waited until July, when the hog farm quieted long enough for his mother to compose a lengthy letter. No one else he knew would be writing him.

"Here you go," Jim said, sliding the bundle closer to the edge of the counter.

Squaring his shoulders, Franklin placed his Stetson on his head and snatched the mail. Avoiding eye contact with the postmaster, he stuffed the bundle in the side pocket of his buckskin jacket and thanked Jim for his service.

"See you in a few weeks, Frank. Good luck."

Good luck? What had he meant by that? Postmaster Jim had never bid farewell to Franklin with a "good luck." Had he?

Had Jim known all along about Franklin's silly scheme? The notion that anyone might sent a chill up his back. His folly was embarrassing enough without the entire Dakota Territory finding out.

Nonetheless, once outside, Franklin could hardly wait to sort the mail to see who had written. He found a secluded bench on the edge of town, across from the Chinese laundry (he made a mental note to bring his clothes for a wet wash next time) and away from pestering eyes. With a quick scan to make sure no one spied him, he withdrew the bundle of mail from his jacket and untied it, sorting it over the bench. One letter was from the Department of the Army. The second was from the company that had sold him his windmill, most likely another bill. Grimacing, he tucked those away in his jacket for later. The last unmarked envelope, heavy and thick, was postmarked from San Francisco. Respondents to his advertisement in *Matrimonial News*.

His heart beat so fast he grew dizzy. Why was he anxious to read mere letters? From women he'd never had contact with before? But that was the hot spice in the stew. Inhaling the crisp mountain air, he opened the envelope and gazed at the four letters from inside, numbered so that the publisher knew whom to forward the letters to, unsure which one to open first. One letter had no actual name for the return address other than initials. He decided to save that one for last and secured it under his thigh.

The first letter he read came from a twenty-three-year-old Cincinnati woman who lived with her parents. Her family owned a butcher shop. They had something in common, Franklin thought. His family ran a hog farm. She had recently graduated from finishing school in Lexington, Kentucky, and hoped to go off for two years in Europe, "perhaps on my honeymoon." Sounded a little too sophisticated for Franklin's tastes. Educated, yet her words came across as childlike, unsure, hackneyed. He took an immediate disliking to her. He set that letter aside and opened the next.

The second letter was from a seventeen-year-old from Rotterdam, New York. She talked about how she disliked working in a ticket booth at the canal, the town in which she lived was too wet, and the house for her family of ten was far too small. Franklin shook his head. Too negative.

The third letter—written with such a fancy script Franklin had to hold the pages in different positions to comprehend the curly words—bored him to tears before he reached the third of seven pages. From what he could decipher, the twenty-nine-year-old St. Louis native currently resided in Kansas City where she worked for a steamer company. She was elusive about her job duties. Franklin had worked for a steamer along the Mississippi long enough to know for what purpose steamer companies usually employed women. "Another prostitute," Franklin muttered, and he tore the letter to pieces and let the wind carry them across the street to the Chinese laundry.

Sighing, he gazed down Main Street to where the spruce-covered gulch sandwiched the town. So far, the letters came from women seeking a means to escape their lowly lives. Franklin did not wish to be a mere island of security for desperate maidens. He began to worry he'd wasted his thirty-five cents to place the advertisement.

He studied the fourth and final letter, the one with mere initials for a name on the envelope. "Well," he said to himself, prying open the letter with his thumbnail, "this one couldn't be any worse than the others."

*April 26, 1886*

*Dear Sir,*

*I hope my letter reaches you in good health. I read your advertisement in* Matrimonial News, *and your words touched me deeply. I like that you are softhearted. That is a good trait for a man. Despite what others may say, kindness in a man is not a sign of weakness but shows his true strength. I have turned nineteen as of two months ago to the day I write this letter, and I am of Swedish extraction, as both my parents are from the Old Country. I have the blond hair that you stated in your advertisement you prefer. My weight is perfectly suited to my height of five feet five. I live in Chicago, where I work at my family's bakery. Chicago is growing fast; the words to describe Chicago's growth do not come easily for such a short passage. Since you dislike the bustle of cities, you probably will prefer that I leave Chicago to your imagination.*

*Until recently, I never envisioned life in the West, but your advertisement stoked my curiosity. Perhaps a land where grass is more common than dirt and concrete would be something to behold. I sometimes wander to the river near my home, where the prairie grass still grows in a thin yet dense strip along the bank, and I stare for long hours out west. When I was only seven years of age, I used to see the prairie, but now development expands far beyond my eyes, and where I used to play along the river are now factories, buildings, and even a hospital. The city is splendid in its way, and I do find the mushrooming growth thrilling at times. But there are other things to see in this great land of ours, would you agree?*

*I have reread your advertisement many times since I first cast eyes upon it. Your words touch me deeper each time I read them, if you allow me to be bold enough to say. I would, indeed, like to become your friend. Perhaps as we get to know one another, I can tell you more about Chicago and my life here and you can tell me more about where you live. I do hope you will receive this letter with gladness in your heart and want to correspond with me. I will keep my letter short and look forward to reading your reply, should you feel I warrant one.*

*Yours,*

*T.P.*

*Chicago, Ill.*

He rested the letter in his lap. A soft breeze tickled his freshly trimmed mustache. The edges of the letter curled and seemed to sing to him. With his thumping heart, he reread the letter. Never had he devoured words so hungrily. Each word wafted off the white paper like the scent of limewater. He held the letter in his trembling hand as if it were fragile lace. After reading the letter for a fifth time, he tri-folded it the way it had come, as if to make sure he altered not a single word, and carefully replaced it in the envelope. Little doubt which of the four letters exuded the most sincerity and thoughtfulness.

The writer, who identified herself only as T.P., expressed her thoughts without complication. Even her handwriting contained little nonsense. Straightforward and lacking flourishes. Attributes Franklin valued in a woman—in anyone. He had never read anything from a woman who demonstrated such self-assuredness. The other letter-writers had either played coy or came across as self-serving and negative. This woman had addressed each of his points in the advertisement. He liked that. But he wondered why she refrained from giving her name. Perhaps she wanted to keep things anonymous until they had a chance to become better acquainted. A sensible woman, not prone to mawkish romantic notions. Another good trait.

He hadn't noticed until a woman passing him along the boardwalk nodded and smiled at him, but a grin stretched his mouth full to near his ears. The more he reflected on T.P.'s letter, the more he hankered to send her a reply.

Collecting himself, he pocketed the other two letters, which he planned to burn once he returned to the cabin. The letter from the woman calling herself "T.P." he took extra care to keep unwrinkled and separated from the others. He placed it in his breast pocket, close to his heart.

But rather than waste time going back and forth between his homestead and town, why not purchase lead pencils, tablets, and envelopes (items he needed anyway) at the mercantile and compose the letter right there in the seat of his wagon? That way, Jim could load the letter on the next stage to Cheyenne City, where the Union Pacific would speed it off to T.P.'s Chicago address at 12416 Chicago Avenue, saving him an extra trip.

Franklin returned from the mercantile with his purchases and propped himself on the wagon. Lulu nickered, curious what irregularity her master was up to. Placing the tip of the sharpened lead pencil to his tongue, he took extra care to conjure the right words. Something insisted that he be forthright with this woman. Although she had refrained from giving her name (which, on some level, he found appropriate), she had expressed herself plainspoken without haughtiness.

Watching a fluffy white cloud drifting over the surrounding granite peaks change from a footprint shape to something akin to puckered lips, Franklin sensed that he had stumbled upon someone unique. To correspond with her mandated special consideration.

# CHAPTER
# EIGHT

"WHAT are you doing out there, Torsten?" Tory's mother poked her head out of the dining room window, which overlooked Chicago Avenue.

"I'm cooling off a bit, Mamma," he said from where he sat on the front stoop. "It's warm inside."

Fanning herself with her hand, Mrs. Pilkvist moaned in agreement with her son. "Suddenly we have hot spring, ja? But I will need you soon to help with the furniture polishing. And your pappa will need you in the bakery before supper."

"Yes, Mamma. I'll be along in a minute."

Tory rested his chin on his balled hands, his elbows pressing into his thighs. He glanced up and down the street. What was keeping that dastardly postman? He wanted to catch him before he rang the cord. Ten days had passed since he'd sent out his letter to the bachelor in *Matrimonial News*. He needed to intercept the return letter before his mother or father laid their hands on it and asked him a barrage of questions. He had a hunch today a letter would arrive—if the man had bothered to reply.

His emotions oscillated between apprehension and hope. Was his loneliness so acute it had forced him to impersonate a woman? He wondered if he would have dared such eccentric action if Joseph van Werckhoven hadn't come into his life. Joseph had planted a seed deep inside him. The sturdy roots had sprouted into an eternal need for love.

Thomas Persson from the postal office turned the corner from Clark. Tory leaped to his feet. The postman limped down the sidewalk with his signature gait. From the neighborhood grapevine, Tory had learned the postman suffered from an old Civil War injury. Rumors circulated that enemy canister shots had blasted his left foot to bits.

"Hello, Mr. Persson." Tory met the postman a block from his home, too anxious to sit idle by his stoop and wait. "Do you have any mail for us I can take off your hands?"

"You're certainly eager to get your mail today, Torsten," Mr. Persson said with a broad smile. "Expecting something important, are we?"

"No, sir, I only wanted to lighten your load."

"That's awful kind of you. The new Montgomery Ward catalogs are out, and they sure are a haul." Mr. Persson dug inside his canvas sack and withdrew a bundle of letters, including the catalog, addressed to the Pilkvists. "Here you go."

"Thank you, sir." Unable to hold back a wide grin, Tory rushed back to the front stoop, where he shuffled through the mail. Only one letter was addressed to him—postmarked from Spiketrout, Dakota Territory. That must be from his *Matrimonial News* bachelor. Good news that he had responded so speedily.

Tory lifted the letter to his nose as if to discern more about the bachelor from the scent. He detected the musky fragrance of earth, exactly what he'd expect from a man who lived in the Wild West.

He left the remaining mail on the foyer sideboard and absconded to his bedroom. He stashed the letter in his desk drawer where it would remain until he completed his chores and supper. He did not want anything to interrupt his enjoyment of the letter. Free from obligations, he'd read in peace, devouring each word without interruption.

His mother eyed him with wonder while he diligently went about scrubbing and polishing the wood furniture with linseed and ashes from the hearth. Mr. Pilkvist also found his bouncy attitude curious. Tory kneaded dough for the kärleksmums, filled the almond tarts, and stacked wood for the fire as if his shoes were filled with helium.

At supper, the table conversation grew cumbersome. A whole new group of boarders had arrived during the past two weeks, and Tory had little in common with any of them. After the last morsel was eaten, he skipped dessert in the parlor and rushed upstairs, where, behind his locked door, he slit open the envelope. Before reading the letter, he scanned down to the bottom to read the signature: "Franklin A." He smiled. A sound, pleasant name. Steadying his breathing, he turned up his Edison lamp and flattened the three pages against the desk. He restarted the letter twice before he calmed enough that the words did not blur into a muddle.

*May 5, 1886*
*Dear T.P.,*

*I am pleased you responded to my advertisement. You sound like a practical, intelligent young lady. I would love to read more about your life in Chicago. Although I do prefer country life, I am entertained by the diverse regions of this great country God has generously graced us with. Do not hesitate to tell me more about your life in the wonderful city of Chicago.*

*I live in the Black Hills region of Dakota Territory. You might know something about it from reading newspapers regarding the Indian Wars. Do not fear. The wars with the Indians have ended (save for a few skirmishes), and peace covers the land. The Indians have been corralled in a reservation north of the Hills, and the ones who mix with the White man are of the civilized kind and respectable. Perhaps my one and only true friend is a Sioux Indian, Lakota to be exact, 100 percent purebred. (Although it's likely he must have a small amount of French in him based on the history of these parts.) I will reveal more about him later if you are inclined to wish to correspond with me further.*

*The Hills have grown much since I first settled on my homestead in 1876. The Gold Rush swept the Hills a few years before I arrived; I am happy to say most of the gold has dried up. I did not come here for easy loot. I came to earn my keep, and hope to find my way living idyllically in the rustic environs nestled among the granite-peaked mountains and the dark blue-green spruce and pine endowing the Black Hills with its name.*

*I found my way to Dakota to work in a quartz mine several years after I fought in the Civil War. With money saved after a year of hard labor, I found a parcel of good earth for my own subsistence. I have cultivated the land and built a self-sufficient homestead here. The cabin is small, but I can always build onto it if need be. A good-sized barn and a wondrous windmill that I purchased from a company near Chicago straddle my land. It seems many things come from Chicago these days, as I'm sure you are aware. Perhaps something even more extraordinary might come from Chicago, one day? I fortify my needs on my small homestead by selling eggs from my hens, vegetables from my crops, hams and bacon from the five to seven hogs I raise, and venison jerky that I cure from deer kill. People in the nearby town of*

*Spiketrout are always looking for foodstuffs. I must say that town cries out for a refined lady.*

*Civilization is never too far these days, even in the Black Hills. The Union Pacific shall commence train service into the Hills soon, now that the Indian Wars have settled. They say direct service from Chicago should reach us by next spring. In the meantime, travelers to the Hills usually come through Cheyenne City in Wyoming Territory via railroad, where they board the stage for Deadwood.*

*Before coming here, I worked at a lumberyard in Kentucky, then had the pleasure of spending a few years in your great state of Illinois. I worked for a steamer in Quincy. But the Panic of '73 left the steamer in a tight financial state of affairs, and I lost my job after two years. I decided that it wasn't such a bad station. I had always wanted more pasture for my ruminating soul. A friend of mine was fortunate to find me work in the quartz mines of Dakota. Yes, ten years is a long time to live as a bachelor nestled in the woods, but my time has been fruitful and pleasing to me. I respect your not wishing to reveal your name, but perhaps in one of your subsequent correspondence you can share it with me?*

*I hope Chicago is finding you well and that you are cheerful.*

*Your new friend,*

*Franklin A.*

*Spiketrout, D.T.*

*P.S. Happy Belated Birthday*

Tory did not exhale until he finished reading the last word. Overcome, he pressed the crisp pages to his heart. He was touched the man took care to respond to everything he had mentioned in his letter, including his birthday in February. Was it possible to fall for a man he had only known from one correspondence? The more he reread Franklin A.'s letter, the more the loneliness lifted from his soul. But also, the more it seemed to increase.

He imagined what Franklin must look like. He had said he was tall in his advertisement, but little else. Tory suspected he must be powerfully built if he ran a homestead single-handedly. Tory gazed at the letter, his breath catching. Franklin's handwriting was shaky, as if he were using the wrong hand to write, yet his words stood out bold and confident.

Perhaps he should wait a few days before responding. He did not wish to appear too eager. But Franklin had responded in quick fashion. He had been living without companionship in the Black Hills for ten years. How desperate must he be?

A jolt of jealousy raced along Tory's body. Had Franklin corresponded with others? He shook his head and chuckled. What difference did it make? He could never meet Franklin under any circumstances. Besides, Franklin deserved other correspondents. Actual women, no doubt.

After rereading the letter four more times, he took out his lead pencil and tablet from his desk drawer. Without further delay, he wrote the rugged man living in Dakota Territory a heartfelt reply.

*May 14, 1886*

*Dear Franklin,*

*I received your letter today with gladness in my heart. Your life in the Black Hills sounds more exciting than what I read in the silly Wild West dime novels I sometimes buy from the street vendors in Chicago. People say your part of the country has beauty matched only by the glory of California's mountain parks. I can imagine how awe-inspiring everything must be to behold.*

*How is the weather there this time of year? Springtime has arrived in Chicago. The weather is warm for May. We usually do not warm up until around mid-June. I expect the thermometer to fall any day. One of my former teachers informed me Lake Michigan affects Chicago's weather in unusual ways. It's more than a lake, however; it spreads as wide as the largest seas. I tried once to look across the other side to the state of Michigan; I saw only more water. Are there large bodies of water in Dakota Territory?*

*I have never traveled west of Madison, Wisconsin. But I have seen the eastern states. My sister lives in Washington, D.C. I had the great fortune to visit her a few summers back. The journey excited me, for I was able to see other states. My dream is to one day visit each of the thirty-eight states and their capitals. Do you think Dakota will ever be admitted to the union? From what I read, many people are moving there. Is it possible as many people are moving there as they are to Chicago? Sometimes I imagine Chicago will sink into the lake, so many have filled the city. I hope that you are not getting squeezed out like we are here.*

*My parents appreciate the influx of people. In addition to the bakery, my family runs a boarding house to profit from the overflow. My mother and father, poor peasants from the Old Country, are almost shaken by how their hard work brings them good money. In Sweden, they had very little even after relentless toil. Personally, I've never cared much for money. Perhaps that is because I've never worried over it to such an extent that it weighs on my mind. Nonetheless, your life in the woods is admirable, and I envy you.*

*One of my favorite poets, Walt Whitman, believes nature inspires the individual to greatness. Do you find that true? Here is a passage from one of his finer works:*

> Smile Oh voluptuous cool-breathed earth!
> Earth of the slumbering and liquid trees!
> Earth of departed sunset, earth of the mountains misty topped!
> Earth of the virtuous pour of the full moon tinged with blue!
> Earth of shine and dark tide of the river!
> Earth of the limpid gray of clouds brighter and clearer for me!
> Far sweeping earth, rich apple-blossomed earth!

*Whitman's words inspire me to discover wonder where I had once seen only open space. I suppose poetry can lead to passivity, and that is not good, for we need labor and industry to keep us alive and well. But allowing the soul to ruminate can be good also, do you agree?*

*Please write me soon, Franklin. I look forward to reading one of your fine letters. I sense that you are a gentleman, with sincere compassion.*

*Yours*

Tory paused. He pondered how to sign off. Franklin had requested his name. What should he write? He did not want to use an alias. He had misrepresented himself enough already. Besides, the postal office would want a name to match the person of residence. Postman Persson would be confused if Tory fabricated a name. Perhaps Franklin would mistake Torsten as a female name. Many people unfamiliar with Swedish names often did.

Before signing off, he considered doing away with Whitman's poem. Would Franklin find the passage offensive? He had left out the last line to refrain from coming across too forward: "Smile, for your lover comes." He snickered realizing how shocking that would be for Franklin. What would he think of his new "refined lady" from Chicago then?

Shaking his head, he turned back to his composition and decided to keep the poem. He signed off as "Torsten P.," matching how Franklin had signed his name, and set his pencil aside. With conviction, he sealed the letter in an envelope and delivered it to the postal office straightaway.

Ten days later, Tory intercepted another of Franklin's letters from Postman Persson.

*May 24, 1886*

*Dear Torsten,*

*I have just finished reading your letter and I was unable to keep from writing you right away. Your name is very pretty. It reminds me of my sister's—Gretchen. She was named after my great-grandmother, meaning "Little Pearl." I am told I am the namesake of Benjamin Franklin, our country's great philosopher. That is much to live up to, I must say. Does your name have a special meaning in Swedish?*

*Today the weather brings all of us in the Black Hills much-needed rain. My newly planted crops drink thirstily. The rains also give me more time to devote to sitting at an inn in Spiketrout and writing you. A fire rages next to me, and its warmth only eclipses what I feel from your latest correspondence. I cannot tell you how much joy it brings me to receive your response to my letter in such quick fashion.*

*I must confess your letters bring me into Spiketrout more often than usual. Once the weather warms, I typically venture into town once a fortnight. Now, I take to the trail into Spiketrout no less than once a week. I no longer worry what the postmaster here might think of my correspondence with an "unknown" lady from Chicago. I only look forward to reading your replies.*

*The passage from Walt Whitman nearly brought tears to my eyes. He expressed my true emotions with such clarity. Each morning I awake and step from my cabin and I behold the earth and sky and mountains that surround me. The mountains let out a sigh, and I can*

*smell their sweet breath. If you could only blanket yourself with such
beauty! I flush thinking I must have some cowboy poet deep inside me.*

*Since we are in the initial stages of a steady correspondence, I
feel I must confess to you something at this juncture. I hate to transform
my letter from ruminations of Whitman's gentle poetry and the beauty
of the Black Hills to something ugly, but I fear that I must.*

*As I once mentioned, I am a veteran of the Civil War. I enlisted at
the youthful age of fourteen along with many of my comrades in eastern
Tennessee. We stood loyal with the United States in that part of the
commonwealth. Strict abolitionists, we had fought to secede from
Tennessee but failed. Steadfast in our convictions, we joined the
Federal troops and headed to battlefields along the western front.
Under the command of the great and venerable General Ulysses S.
Grant, I saw sporadic fighting in western Tennessee during the Battle
of Fort Henry and on to the Battle of Fort Donelson, which both
quickly fell into Yankee hands. Most of us from eastern Tennessee were
glad to see it happen.*

*After combat in that theater, my regiment traveled eastward to
southern Virginia. We had no idea we would encounter the fiercest
fighting yet of our young age. The fighting raged incessantly. My
regiment soon learned we were still tenderfeet as soldiers. I lost many
a good comrade during those southern battles, which lasted nearly the
length of an entire year.*

*It was during the siege of Petersburg, a gruesome and endless
battle that raged near the South's capital, that I found a fate that I will
carry with me to my grave. One day during ferocious fighting, a musket
ball struck my right arm just below the shoulder. I had lost too much
blood for Army doctors to save it. They amputated above the elbow the
next evening. Although I lost my arm, I considered myself lucky to keep
my life, unlike many of my comrades during those bloody mêlées.*

*I hope I have not scared you away with my revelation or
disturbed you with horrific images of war's grim realities. Although
God made me right-handed at birth, as are most decent men, I've
learned how to use my left quite well over the years. Working at the
lumber yard and quartz mine, I proved as capable, if not more so, as
my comrades. I can chop wood, stir a pot, and even thread a needle.
And I can also hold onto a woman as gently as any two-armed beau.*

*Torsten, it's best to leave this letter at that. I will wait and read
your next reply, if you choose to write. If you decide you no longer wish*

*to correspond with me, do not lament. I understand a woman would
want a man who is not lame or disfigured.*

*May your life in Chicago forever treat you well.*
*Regards,*
*Franklin Ausmus*
*Spiketrout, D.T.*

Tory shielded the pages of Franklin's letter under the desk to
prevent the tears that trickled down his cheeks from smearing the
words. Both esteem and remorse touched his soul. Of course Franklin
having only one arm did not concern him. If anything, his disfigurement
endeared him to Tory more. A war veteran with a permanent injury
must crave love and affection more than anyone. He certainly deserved
as much.

The amputation of his right arm explained the shaky handwriting,
Tory thought, wiping a straggling tear. Adoration heated Tory's wetted
cheeks. Eagerly, he composed another letter, insisting in no way would
Franklin's affliction sway him from wanting to correspond.

Twenty-three days later, a reply arrived.

*June 17, 1886*
*Dear Torsten,*

*Do forgive me for failing to reply to your last letter in a more
timely fashion. I am so happy to read that you are not dissuaded by my
war injury. Reading your kindhearted reply made what I had to endure
here the past several days more tolerable.*

*That brings me to why I haven't written you as quickly as I would
have. I had wanted to write you several times, and you crossed my
mind often, but business demanded action. I've had some issues here at
my homestead. I will not burden you with some of the problems of life
in the Black Hills. I suppose all places have their drawbacks, including
Chicago. Word of the labor unrest in Chicago has reached the Black
Hills. I am saddened to have heard about the calamity. That someone
would use dynamite to cause such a brazen act of bloodshed bruises my
heart. I pray those who were killed will enter God's Kingdom. The
warmer weather brings out the savagery in men all over, so it seems.*

*In Spiketrout, we have ruthless men as well, and some women,
who have but one master: greed. They know nothing about decent*

*behavior and respect for private property. With the receding winter, their fingers have thawed, as has their self-indulgence, and they are apt to wrap their hands around my land. I mentioned previously about the Gold Rush of the Black Hills. Gold is still to be got, but the spots are drying up. That is why many hunger for my homestead.*

*I sit on what might be a healthy amount of placer gold. A creek pool on my land harbors much of the gold that man will often die and even kill for. Yet I have chosen not to pan for it. You might ask why. I suppose I have my reasons. I simply wish to keep things as they lay, as God intended. In truth, I have no desire for gold. Years ago I chose to leave the gold to the trout.*

*Men in the area, drunk for gold, know about my untapped creek. They want it for themselves. Unfortunately, one of the filchers—and I hesitate to allow you to read his name with your own eyes—Henri Bilodeaux, has enlisted a man of the cloth to use scripture to wrestle my land from me. Father Peter Fisk, the Catholic priest of Spiketrout, has said that God, and God Himself, insists I allow the prospecting of my creek so that the hungry and homeless can be fed and sheltered. He claims that "the meek shall inherit the earth." I had to laugh at him, although I felt badly for guffawing in the face of the clergy. But perhaps he had it coming.*

*Do you think of me as harsh, Torsten? Perhaps I am in the wrong? I've resided on this land for ten years; surely they should respect my civil liberties. I respect God's words and I keep in my cabin a cherished Bible given to me by my beloved mother the day I marched off to war. Although I do confess that no one has heard the step of my boots inside a church in many years, yet I believe in our Lord. I consider Nature to be my church.*

*The events with the nefarious Bilodeaux led me to a trip into Spiketrout at the bequest of the local marshal, another man who lacks in fortitude and decency. He has his good points, but his weaknesses far outweigh them. Unfortunately, he tends to bet his chips with the bandit, Bilodeaux. They often work side by side in dastardly endeavors. The good news is that I have extricated myself from both men's grips— at least for now. I am happy to say our correspondence may continue unimpeded. That is, if you wish it to.*

*I only fear now that you are displeased by my rancor with a preacher. Forgive me if I have offended you.*

*I hope that you and your family are found in peace and good health.*

*Regards,*

*Franklin*

*Spiketrout, D.T.*


No, Tory did not find fault with Franklin's actions. He understood them completely. Using an ethically questionable priest and a marshal to pry him from his land seemed unjust. The urgency of Franklin's script left an indelible imprint on Tory's heart. The man had suffered enough. Must he face the wrath of ruthless gold diggers? And that nefarious Henri Bilodeaux. Reading his name had chilled Tory's veins. He imagined what a cold-blooded bandit he must be, worse than the wicked characters he'd come across in dime novels. Worse, perhaps, than the German nationals who had lobbed dynamite at the Chicago police officers attempting to disperse a mob of labor protesters, the same ghastly affair that Franklin had referred to.

Again, Tory wasted no time in communicating his sympathies to Franklin.

# CHAPTER NINE

TORY took refuge in Franklin's correspondence. They ameliorated his loneliness. As the weeks passed, they exchanged more letters. The letters grew lengthier and lengthier. Tory lived his days and nights riding on a cloud. When not reading Franklin's latest correspondence, he reread the previous ones until the bulb in his Edison lamp flickered and weakened. He floated about the house, taking care of his chores with his head full of Franklin. His entire life that spring and summer passed immersed in Franklin Ausmus's world.

Every nine or ten days a new reply arrived. Immediately after reading one, Tory would compose a response. At that point in their correspondence, neither showed modesty by waiting a respectable period of time before responding. Other than that awful occasion when Franklin had encountered Henri Bilodeaux, each of their letters was dated the day they had received the previous one.

Tory learned more about Franklin's homestead and his companion, Wicasha, the Lakota Indian whom Franklin often referred to as his "good friend." At first, Tory shuddered to think that a white man might choose to befriend an Indian, but he found Franklin's manner of expressing his affection for Wicasha touching. Soon, Tory envisioned the Indian his friend also.

Moonlight Gulch became Tory's home. Like in any well-crafted account, he visualized himself surrounded by the same mountains and pines Franklin wrote about. Much affection and awe for his hallowed homestead flowed from Franklin's pencil. Other than Walt Whitman, Tory had never come across anyone who expressed a love of the earth like Franklin Ausmus.

In turn, Tory wrote Franklin details of his life in Chicago, his dreams, his hopes, his fears. He had wanted to mention Joseph but decided it was best to keep that part of his life secured inside his heart.

Guilt for masquerading as a woman irritated Tory at times, yet he allowed the excitement of Franklin's letters to reassure him that they were only corresponding as friends. Neither had declared a romantic affection for the other, although Franklin had alluded to wanting to "settle down with the right girl" more than once. Tory did not wish to carry his writing to such a grandiose level. What matter if "Torsten P." was a man? They had written each other kind, earnest letters, and that was what mattered, as far as Tory was concerned.

Tory was not always available to intercept the letters. Twice Mr. Persson rang the door chime sooner than scheduled, and Tory, each time occupied with a demanding chore, failed to free himself swiftly enough to reach the door. Fortunately, his mother had handed him the letters with no questions. Both times she had gazed at the envelopes with narrowed eyes, but she seemed too preoccupied with maintaining the boarders who came and went with the breeze to worry.

The warmer months swept a hectic pace to Tory's life on Chicago Avenue. Summer meant floors needed scrubbing, windows needed washing, furniture needed waxing. If his mother wasn't hollering for him to finish some task, his father demanded more of his time in the bakery. Although his father had hired a girl to help out on weekends, Tory, to his frustration, squandered more hours training her for the position than he ever had baking.

By midsummer, Tory's enthusiasm for Franklin's letters failed to wane. But they seemed to slow in frequency. Exactly two weeks had passed since he'd last received a response. There hadn't been such a long gap in their correspondence since Franklin's run-in with Henri Bilodeaux. One day while free from chores, Tory waited for Mr. Persson on the front stoop, eager to see if Franklin had sent another letter.

When Mr. Persson arrived that day, the postman said with a taut smile that he carried no letters for Tory. The next day, and the next, were more of the same. The following week, again, no correspondence. At one point, Postman Persson grew gruff with Tory. With a glower and a grizzled voice, he informed Tory that he should wait for the letters in the door slot, followed by the cord chime, and to stop bothering him.

Days turned into weeks. August passed. Tory worried something awful might have happened to Franklin. Had the wretched Henri

Bilodeaux raided his homestead and harmed Franklin in some way? How could Tory find out what had happened?

He was the first to race to the door whenever he heard Mr. Persson ring the cord, often brushing past his mother along the way. But no letter from Franklin came. By the second week of September, there was still no letter. Tory wracked his brain with worry and grief. Perhaps Franklin had grown tired of Tory's overly faithful writing or found a more likeable correspondent?

Surely others must have responded to Franklin's advertisement in *Matrimonial News*. Some small-town tart like Clair Schuster. Maybe Franklin's rejecting him was for the best. What had Tory to give him? Tory had misrepresented himself the entire time. He hung his head in shame and dejection.

But finally, Tory was unable to keep from pestering Mr. Persson. He approached the postman as he limped his way down Chicago Avenue, his canvas sack by his side. Tory took care to slow his pace so as not to appear frenzied like in previous weeks.

"Mr. Persson, may I ask you a question?"

"Yes, of course, Torsten." The postman retained a guarded voice.

"I've been getting letters, or at least I had, on a regular basis. You know because I have bothered you so much for them. But suddenly those letters have stopped coming. I'm surprised I haven't received any recently. Do you know anything about them? They are postmarked from Dakota Territory with the sender Franklin Ausmus."

Mr. Persson's face went white.

Tory knitted his eyebrows. "Tell me," he insisted. "What do you know about them?"

"I don't know anything," Mr. Persson said. But Tory detected a slight twitch in the postman's upper lip.

"Please, Mr. Persson. If you know what's happened, tell me."

Mr. Persson avoided Tory's gaze. Red streaks broke out along his neck and cheeks. "Your father insisted I burn any letter addressed to you from the Dakota Territory," he said in a rush, as if to get it out once and for all. "I'm sorry, Torsten. He gave me no choice. He was adamant. Said it was in your best interest."

Tory could barely form the indignant words that ricocheted inside his head. "You… you burned… Franklin's letters?"

"I'm sorry, Torsten. I truly am."

"You... you had no right. It's... it's against the law."

"I really do apologize. I did try to change your father's mind, but he insisted."

Tears boiled in Tory's eyes. "How many were there? How many did you destroy?"

The postman appeared flustered. He glanced toward the whitewashed sky from under his cap. "I... I don't know. I guess maybe four, five. I can't recall."

The street swayed. Tory hated everything and everyone on Chicago Avenue.

"Please don't say anything, Torsten," the postman said. "If the postal service finds out about this, I'll lose my job. Please don't tell them. I'm a veteran."

Tory glared at Mr. Persson. "Franklin's a veteran too." He scurried off to the bakery next to the house. Once inside, he shouted for his father. The new counter girl reported that he had gone in the house for a short rest.

When he failed to find his father inside the house, he shut himself in his bedroom and composed Franklin a brief letter, explaining why he had failed to reply in such a long time. The poor man must think Tory had rejected him. And yet Tory had thought Franklin had done the rejecting. Pencil clamped in hand, he nearly tore the paper while he scribbled an apology. With the letter sealed in an envelope and clenched in his fingers, he raced downstairs. Mr. Pilkvist, his face twisted, waited for him at the bottom.

Tory slowed. Inhaling, he descended the last few steps like a watchful fox, his hand loose on the handrail.

"What is this shouting, Torsten? I hear you near all the way to the mercantile."

The anger, like a steam engine, pressurized inside Torsten. "You had the postman discard my personal letters," he spewed at his father. "Why, Pappa? Why?"

"I do not like the tone you take, Torsten."

"Never mind my tone, Pappa. Why did you do it? Please, tell me. Why?"

"I not like you writing that person, whoever he is. Silly skräp, writing to strangers in far-off lands. There are more important things to do. You waste time and energy with such nonsense."

"It's my personal business. You had no right to interfere."

"I have the right to do as I see just in my own home," Mr. Pilkvist sputtered back. "I have a business here. I look after our welfare. First your silly nonsense with that boarder Joseph, and now—"

"Don't mention Joseph's name like that, Pappa. He wasn't just a boarder. You know nothing about him."

His father's eyes widened. "What is that in your hand?"

Tory's heart stopped. Before he could conceal the letter he had written Franklin behind his back, his father snatched it from him.

"No!" Tory grabbed for it, but Mr. Pilkvist held him back. "Please, Pappa," he shouted. "Give it to me. You have no right to read my private letters."

Mr. Pilkvist pivoted his shoulder, blocking the letter from Tory's reach while he tore open the envelope. Tory had no choice but to stand by and watch his father read. The farther his father's eyes traveled down the page, the redder his face became. Mr. Pilkvist's eyes narrowed into black dots, angry tears glassing over his blue irises. Grunting, he tore the letter into pieces and balled the scraps into a tight fist, which he shook at Tory.

"Why do you write this to some cowboy? Tell me now. Why do you write this?"

"He's not a cowboy."

Tory's mother shuffled into the entrance foyer, but she refrained from nearing them. "What's wrong?" she asked, her eyes darting from Tory to her husband.

"Nothing to concern you, Anna. This is between me and my son."

"But you speak so loudly."

"We are done here. It is all over with, once and for all." His father unleashed a barrage of Swedish expletives. In English, he said, "I will take this skräp to the incinerator where it belongs." He flexed his fist in Tory's flaming face. "And you, Tory, you no longer write such nonsense, understand? As of now, we put this behind us and get back to business. Right now, I need you in the bakery to help. Get your head out of the clouds and come with me. Come with me now!"

"No, Pappa. I won't. I won't come with you ever again."

"Torsten!" His mother scurried to the steps and reached for him, but he slipped from her slender fingers as he turned to dash back upstairs.

In his bedroom, Tory grabbed for his satchel. He tossed in whatever clothes fit without concern for wrinkles or snags. Through reddened eyes, he noticed his mother standing by the threshold.

"What are you doing, Torsten? Why are you packing?"

"I'm leaving, Mamma. I'm a man now. I'll be twenty next year. I can make my own way. I don't need either one of you anymore." He dug inside drawers, dressers, closets, throwing in anything he might need that would fit—socks, slippers, cologne box, comb.

He stopped long enough to fling his mother a steaming glower. "You're the one who told him about the letters, aren't you? Those two you intercepted. You told him about them."

"Tory, I only think of your best interest. You're my son—"

He rooted through his desk drawer for his tablets and pencils. And for Franklin's letters. He dug and dug. "Where are my letters from Franklin? I had many more in my drawer. Did you take them too? Did you?"

"No, Torsten. I not do that." Her cheeks colored a deep red.

"You're lying."

"Torsten—"

Tears blurred Tory's vision. "Why, Mamma? Why did you take them?"

She remained quiet, shaking. "I… I had to, Torsten," she finally said with a quavering voice. "When your father found out about the letters from that cowboy, I assumed you had more hidden away, so I find them before he do. I was trying to help you. I didn't read them. I didn't."

"Where are they?" Tory demanded.

Mrs. Pilkvist lowered her head. "I put them in the incinerator."

Red-hot flames flashed before Tory's eyes. "How dare you rummage through my things and destroy them."

Tory's father stood behind his wife, a grim look on his round face. "You do not use such insolent voice to your mamma, Tory. She do what is right. Like what I do with that book of poems that are filled with nonsense. Like what I will do with this letter." He raised his fist, where the torn bits from the letter Tory had written still protruded between his clenched fingers.

Chewing on the anger that burned his lips, Tory snapped his bag shut and put on his derby. "I'll never forgive either one of you for what you've done." With a cursory kiss on his mother's tear-moistened cheek, he nudged past them and fled downstairs.

"But where will you go?" his mother called after him through the balustrade. "What about us here? The business?" She pulled on her wetted face. "My children have all gone. They have all deserted me."

Tory stopped by the front door and scowled at his mother. "I'm sorry, Mamma, but I can no longer live in this house. Not after everything that's happened. If neither of you can respect my life, then I'll find a place where others will."

And with those words, Tory slammed the door shut behind him and was gone.

# CHAPTER
## TEN

THE Chicago and North-Western railcar rumbled along the tracks past the suburbs of Batavia and Dekalb. As the train left the sprawl of the city, the prairie opened like Lake Michigan to the east, empty and large, with sporadic dots of life. Farms and tiny balloon-framed houses scattered along the tracks. Small children raced along the train and gestured wildly. Some sat in trees and waved from branches. The engineer blasted the air horn. Gray smoke blew past the window from which Tory gazed out.

Immediately after rushing from home, he had drained his bank account of his last four hundred dollars and headed to the railroad depot on Wells Street. The thirty-five-dollar one-way fare to Omaha included supper.

In Omaha, he'd purchase another one-way ticket on the Union Pacific to Cheyenne City and then go onward to Deadwood via stagecoach, the way Franklin had mentioned people traveled to the Black Hills. Tory had never journeyed a long distance on a stagecoach, but he worried little about his discomfort. His only aim—to get away from his parents and Chicago, and to reach Franklin Ausmus.

He had no plans once he found Franklin. Yet he was driven to go to him. Even if he must remain clandestine. At the moment, Franklin Ausmus stood as the only person on earth with whom he felt a genuine and vital connection. In his mind, no other human being existed beyond him.

Staring out the window as the prairie grew wider, he imagined his mother wailing into her hands. His father certainly still fumed with resentment at Tory's abrupt departure. Mr. Pilkvist, always expecting Tory would remain at the bakery and master the trade, was probably beside himself with both anger and grief.

"I had to leave, Pappa, I had to," Tory whispered into the window, although even to his ears the words sounded like tin cans dropped on the thin red carpet of the coach car.

He had already told them once how he wanted to explore the country. He came from the new world, not the old, and no one could hold him back from satisfying his dreams. His real reason for leaving: to see a man whom he'd contacted via a matchmaker periodical. His venture might horrify his parents and his fellow passengers, but to Tory, westward expansion thrived solely for one purpose: so that he could meet his beloved.

He had left the stuffed bear Joseph van Werckhoven had given him on his bed. Tucked between his feather pillows, the bear, safe and sound from the perils of western travel, represented another life for him. A new world of unusual landscapes and realities awaited him in the far-flung distance, a mere train ride away—a world he'd only read about in newspapers and dime novels. A world inhabited by Franklin Ausmus. A man, in actuality, no more real to him than the romantic and fearless characters in the stories he'd read.

If he had one thing to dread, it was the uncertainty of whether Franklin would live up to his letters. Would Tory find a fragile, unkempt wild man living in the backcountry, unworthy of human companionship? Yet if anyone should be charged with misrepresentation, it should be Tory. Franklin knew "Torsten P." as an idealistic young female with a heart yearning for romance and adventure. If Franklin had misrepresented himself to Tory, then Tory deserved likewise.

The conductor patrolled the car, announcing the next stop. Tory craned his neck to get a better look. There was barely a town at all. The open landscape appeared so different from his North Side neighborhood. Apprehension gripped him. Should he debark and return to Chicago on the next eastbound train? Suddenly the romantic adventure he'd planned loomed menacing and uncertain now that Chicago was solidly behind him.

With a squaring of his shoulders, he closed his eyes and inhaled, imagining Franklin Ausmus at his cabin nestled among the mountains and high granite walls, the way he'd described it in his letters. What else might Franklin have revealed to him when Postman Persson had begun burning his letters? He opened his eyes. What right had anyone to interfere with his life? Postman Persson, his mother, his father. They had all conspired against him. He was glad he had left them behind.

While the other passengers debarked and new ones boarded, Tory took out his tablet and pencil and composed another letter to Franklin to replace the one his father had destroyed. He needed Franklin to understand that he had not rejected him. Anger for what his father had done coalesced into his fingers, and the lead point tore into the paper. Using a fresh sheet, he started again, but this time he hesitated. What good would it do to write him? His letter would only create more confusion for Franklin. He balled up the paper, tossed it into a receptacle in the vestibule, and headed for the dining car.

Glancing around, he saw no available seats. One middle-aged, well-dressed man sitting alone at a table must have noticed Tory's lost expression. He gestured for Tory to join him. Edging forward, Tory sat opposite the grinning man. They introduced themselves. The businessman, Abel Hendricks from Muskegon, Michigan, was traveling to Omaha to acquire lumber accounts.

"It's the place to be in my line of business," Mr. Hendricks said. Smoke from his cigar hovered above their heads. "They don't have much lumber out there, so we have to ship it to them. I'm hoping to stay ahead of the ball. Where are you going, Mr. Pilkvist?"

Tory hesitated. "I'm traveling to… to the Black Hills."

"Do you have business there?"

"No."

Mr. Hendricks laughed, his broad shoulders shaking like the cinched curtains on their window as the train passed a rock quarry. "Go west, young man. Isn't that what everyone says these days? Or is it already a cliché?"

Tory flushed and shrugged.

"Are you searching for gold?" Mr. Hendricks asked with a playful air.

Tory chuckled and shook his head. "I'm going for personal reasons."

A waiter took their order. After he left, Mr. Hendricks put a finger to his goatee. "Perhaps I should consider traveling to the Black Hills someday," he said. "I might be able to start a lumber company. I hear there's plenty of lumber there."

"I've never been, but I hear it's beautiful."

"Are you originally from Chicago?"

"Yes, born and raised."

"I grew up on a farm in Indiana," Mr. Hendricks went on. "I often miss the open country. But I couldn't possibly earn the kind of money I make now toiling the soil the way my family had. Poor Father worked himself into an early grave, and with very little to show for it. Of course, droughts were to blame for most of it."

A smile tickled Tory's face as Mr. Hendricks rambled on about one topic after another. He was glad when the waiter served their supper to break up the string of endless sentences. Tory ate his quail and string beans while Mr. Hendricks continued to chat about the developing prairie and how the trains had carried unimaginable industry and people to places no one had ever conceived of living. Tory allowed the food to warm him. Dabbing at his mouth, he peered out the window. They were crossing a wide, twisting river. Mr. Hendricks must have noticed his dazzled expression, for he suddenly ceased speaking.

"It's something, isn't it?" he said after a moment, chuckling. "Each time I pass over it I'm always impressed. The lifeline of America."

"Is it really the Mississippi?"

"None other."

"I never expected it to be so broad." Tory's nose was near flat against the glass. The river wound to the horizon like a colossal bronze ribbon. A few hundred yards from the bridge, a riverboat churned upriver.

"Nothing like the picture books, hmm?" the man said.

"No, it certainly isn't."

The conductor announced the next stop: Davenport. The two men finished their coffee and bid each other farewell.

Back at his seat, Tory again gazed out the window. The industrial town along the Mississippi seemed similar to Chicago, only on a much smaller scale. There was even a five-story building, from what he could see. But soon after the train lurched westward from the train depot, cornfield after cornfield rushed by.

His entire life, Tory had lived in the city. Such expanses of rural land filled him with awe, but also fear. Much of the world, far larger than his neighborhood of River North, lay untouched by his hands, unseen by his eyes. He had grown accustomed to the world coming to him—people from every continent moved to Chicago. To find himself carried into that world both delighted and troubled him.

What really waited beyond the cultivated farmland of the vast heartland? Was Franklin Ausmus a mere figment of his imagination, nothing but a fantasy concocted in his head from letters written by an invisible hand?

He was glad to see the lumber dealer approach him with a grin. Someone from his own world, a man grounded in the reality of day-to-day business. For a moment, uncertainty subsided.

"Ah, my young friend." The man, clutching his two satchels, greeted Tory with big yellow teeth. "Someone has taken my seat, I'm afraid."

"I'm sorry. Would you care to sit here?" Tory patted the empty seat next to him. "This seat is vacant."

"I think I will. Thank you." Abel Hendricks secured his luggage in the bin above and settled next to Tory with a sigh. "There's nothing like a comfortable train ride, is there?" he said, adjusting the legs of his breeches.

"It's my first real long one," Tory said. "I've only traveled as far as Washington to visit my sister."

"Oh my, then this must be a real treat for you. Long train journeys are full of so much more, well… romance and adventure. Especially those heading west. The landscape is unmatched."

"Have you been far west?"

"As far as Denver. You wouldn't believe the mountains." He shook his head. "So towering they cut the day's length by two hours."

"Really?"

"'Behold the rocky wall, that down its sloping sides, pours the swift rain-drops, blending, as they fall, in rushing river-tides.'"

Tory smiled at him. "Is that from a poem?" he asked.

"Oliver Wendell Holmes," Abel Hendricks said. "Are you an aficionado of poetry?"

"Yes, as a matter of fact, I am. My favorite is Walt Whitman."

The man lifted his eyes to the silk-lined ceiling and clasped his veiny, chubby hands in his lap. "Walt Whitman? Well, he is quite a poet. You have excellent taste. He's rather transcendental, don't you agree?"

"Oh, yes. He uses the most interesting similes and metaphors."

"Some say for things most of us would rather not speak about." Mr. Hendricks elbowed Tory lightly on his arm and chuckled.

This last exchange left the two men silent. Tory stared out the window at the setting sun. He wondered if the train might never stop chasing the red orb. Finally, the sun fell beyond the western horizon and darkness oozed into the car, turning the window into a mirror. Tory could see from Abel Hendricks's reflection that he'd fallen asleep. Soon Tory, too, nodded off to a jostling, dreamless sleep.

He awoke to feel something on his lap. The conductors had lighted the lanterns while he'd slept, and the dim glow revealed the hand of Abel Hendricks, still in a slumber, on Tory's right thigh. His heart somersaulted. Even more arresting, Tory had his usual middle-of-the-night arousal. No way had it come from the man's touch. The aching throb had occurred almost nightly since he'd turned twelve. What if the man awoke and believed Tory's erection was because of him? He slowly tried to ease himself from under Mr. Hendricks's hand, but the salesman stirred, and his hand nudged closer to Tory's swelling.

The businessman's lone visible eye opened. He was awake. But instead of removing his hand, he let it lay. To Tory's horror, Mr. Hendricks moved his hand closer until he completely enveloped Tory's bulge. No doubt the salesman was fully awake and wanted to fondle him right there on the train.

Almost as a punishment for losing Joseph, Tory had given himself to the fabric salesman from Maryland back in Chicago. In many ways, he blamed himself and his city for Joseph's death. Tory had fallen along with Joseph on that horrible afternoon. They had both landed in a dark hole, where despair and cold emptiness sealed their gloomy future. But now, hope beckoned. Each passing railroad tie pumped him with fresh optimism. Out there, Franklin Ausmus waited. Someone who unwittingly loved him.

Tory no longer sought to sacrifice himself upon the liturgical hill, like he had with Calvin McGregor in the hotel room on the South Side.

He must save himself for Franklin, and Franklin alone, even if his surrender was merely symbolic.

Tory wanted nothing intimate from Abel Hendricks. Sharing a meal, a seat, polite conversation—he fancied nothing more. Allowing no other thought, Tory jumped from his seat and darted for the water closet.

When Tory returned, Abel Hendricks had gone, along with his two satchels. The next morning, when they encountered each other in the dining car, the lumber salesman refrained from speaking to him or making any kind of eye contact. Just as well. Who needed a masher like him for a travel companion?

By midmorning, the train had rolled across the swift Missouri River into Omaha's West Lawn Station. Luckily, that was Mr. Abel Hendricks's last stop. Tory watched the middle-aged lumber dealer fumble with his luggage on the platform and, with only a cursory glance back at Tory, amble for his waiting stagecoach.

Another stage transported Tory and eight others to the Union Pacific Railroad depot four miles east of downtown, where he paid fifty-five dollars for a one-way fare to Cheyenne City, including stagecoach passage into Deadwood. Exhausted, he stretched supine across a bench with his head resting against his satchel. Two hours later, the conductor's call for all aboard roused him from his nap. Stepping onto the platform, he could see the engine's firebox, red-hot with coals. He shuddered, handed his ticket to the porter, and hurried aboard.

He found an empty row of seats and dropped himself into it. The Union Pacific carried a completely different group of passengers: authentic-looking frontiersmen, some wearing funny hats made out of animal skins with the tails still attached. The women dressed spicier, with ruby-red lips and long eyelashes batting at every man. The more decent folk—women traveling with children, families, men on business—huddled together in the middle car, although after his experience with Abel Hendricks, a salesman from the eastern shore of Lake Michigan, Tory wondered if perhaps the grungy prospectors and prostitutes might not make for better company.

Once the train got underway, Tory purchased a small lunch from the dining car (coffee, a ham and cheese sandwich, and pickle slices) and carried it back to his seat. The gruff patter of men's voices and chortling women entertained him while he ate. Worn out, he pushed aside the empty wrappers, laid his head against the seat, and gazed at the passing scenery of endless cornfields.

About one hundred miles west of Omaha, the landscape underwent an alien transformation. Tory had never seen anything like it. Gone were the verdant cornfields of the heartland. The earth lay arid, like a desert, and odd, isolated grassy uplifts appeared like forlorn goblins. Sagebrush rolled alongside the tracks. The Wild West erupted into his view, an authentic place outside of his imagination. He pressed his palms against the window and peered out.

Vast land stretched mile after mile, with few trees other than a narrow wind-blown strip abutting the Platte River, which paralleled the train tracks. No indication of human habitation other than far-reaching ranches where cattle grazed over tawny fields. A cowboy rode horseback while overseeing the cattle hoarded in a massive mud-covered pen, which Tory guessed were waiting to be corralled onto trains heading to the Chicago Stock Yards.

The train increased speed. Yellow and blue wildflowers carpeting the narrow strip of tawny grass along the river blurred into a haze of green. Afternoon came slowly heading west.

Nighttime eventually caught up with the train. After supper, Tory returned to his seat. He caught his reflection in the darkened window. He looked like a mere boy in ways, a boy rumbling off to meet a man who, in reality, knew nothing about him. The second night brought a nebulous comprehension of his journey, yet the darkness allowed his mind to settle. He drew the curtain and let his eyelids droop shut.

He dreamed of cowboys, Indians, bandits, carnivals. A one-armed homesteader waved to him along the tracks as the train passed. Tory hollered for the train to stop, pleading through the window for the man to wait for him. The engineer drove faster and faster. Black smoke concealed the sun. Wind rushed into his face as the train transformed into a mine car. He was sitting next to Joseph van Werckhoven. They were laughing and clutching each other's arms. A sense of lightness and gaiety replaced his fear. Then the car vanished from under him, and he was in a freefall. The wrenching fear returned. Below him, the street loomed closer and closer....

With a jolt, he awoke. For an instant, he grasped onto the armrest, fearful he was still falling. But it was the train that had jerked to a slow crawl. The train whistled. A conductor moving from car to car announced, "Cheyenne City." A robust man in his fifties stirred next to him. He must've gotten on while Tory had fallen into a deep sleep. Peering outside the curtain, Tory noticed the large town nearing, like a wooden cavalry under the mask of evening twilight. He checked his pocket watch. Six thirty. He'd slept on and off for the past eight hours.

Excitement and fear lurched in Tory's throat. He had never stepped foot outside the thirty-eight states. Although Wyoming Territory was poised to become a state, he still considered it a remote outpost, a rugged reminder of how the country stood before the growth of massive cities like Chicago and the western expansion of the railroads.

The western sky implied an earlier hour. He needed to set his watch back an hour to match Wyoming time. Out here, the sun worked differently from what his watch indicated. Everything seemed divergent and strange.

At the depot, Tory grabbed his satchel and debarked from the train with the flow of passengers. He lavished extra time on himself by washing in the depot's lavatory. He brushed his teeth, scrubbed his face, splashed limewater on his neck, and fixed his unruly hair.

Stepping outside, where the sun nudged above the flat highlands in the east, he peered up at the depot's lofty sandstone clock tower. That was when he noticed the time. The ticket agent in Omaha had said the stage for Deadwood would leave straight from the Cheyenne depot at six thirty sharp "without fail." It was twenty-five after.

He adjusted his eyes from the dust stirred by the carriages picking up and dropping off passengers, and peered around. The Cheyenne-Deadwood Stage, hitched to a six-horse team, was waiting by the western entrance. The final leg of his journey, and it was preparing to leave without him.

# CHAPTER ELEVEN

WITH his satchel bouncing against his side, Tory circumvented a jail wagon loaded with convicts and raced over to the stagecoach. Breathless, he approached a man who appeared to be the stage agent. "Is this the stage to Deadwood?"

The agent peered at him. "We... we... we almost l-l-l-left you behind. Y-y-you're late."

Tory was puzzled by the man's manner of speech. He had never come across anyone like him in Chicago. "I'm sorry, sir. I got held up inside the depot."

"N-n-no talking about getting held... held up around this stage. People riding s-s-stages don't like to hear such things. That's... that's number one on the list. Let m-m-me see your ticket."

Tory obliged him. Satisfied, the agent grabbed Tory's satchel and handed it to another worker, who was securing luggage on the back of the Concord. About six passengers sat on the roof of the stage. None of the workers seemed disturbed by their presence, so Tory assumed it was protocol.

The agent turned to another man, who Tory assumed was the driver. "This h-h-here's your l-l-last passenger."

The driver wide eyed Tory. "You're fairly late," he said. "I'll have to run down all the rules for riding the Concord. I just got done telling everyone else."

"I'm sorry, sir."

"Now listen good. Whatever you do," the driver said, "don't go mentioning stagecoach robberies or Indian uprisings while riding, even for laughs. If you do, I'll toss your little rump out the coach so fast you'd think you was a hawk flying through the sky. You understand, don't you?"

Swallowing hard, Tory nodded. So that was why the other agent had chastised him when Tory had mentioned being "held up." Boyhood stories of Cowboys and Indians sprouted into reality. They materialized as bona fide as the inhabitants of his neighborhood of River North.

"No cussing," the driver went on. "We got a lady and child passenger. No smoking cigars or pipes. You can chew tobacco, but use a spittoon—but only if no one inside the coach minds. There'll be no consumption of liquor whatsoever, no matter what. I'll know you're sipping even from my post outside, so don't even try. And if you're gonna sleep, which I reckon you got to for such a long journey, don't snore or lean on no one. It ain't none too polite."

"You don't need to worry about all that, sir," Tory said, his mouth dry. "I don't do any of those things."

"One other thing." The driver narrowed his brown eyes at Tory. "Keep your firearms on your person at all times. No drawing them out unless called for. I got a double-barrel shotgun and a .44 Smith & Wesson, and my partner riding shotgun got two sidearms and a state-of-the-art Winchester that can take down a buffalo if need be."

"But I don't have any guns," Tory said.

The driver's forehead corrugated with harsh wrinkles, his eyebrows raised near to the underside of his suede cowboy hat. "You don't got no firearms?"

"No, sir."

"You going into the Black Hills unarmed?"

Tory shrugged and flushed.

The driver shook his head and pulled on the end of his bushy mustache. "I'll be darned. You city folk sure do live dangerously, that's for sure. Now get a wiggle on so we can get this party rolling."

Climbing into the stage, Tory noticed what he feared were two gunshot holes on the side of the door. He worried he would never make it into Spiketrout alive. One good thing about arriving late—he secured a window seat. Fresh air from the open window would be welcome while squeezed in with seven other passengers.

Only two passengers, the woman with the child and a gentleman wearing a navy frock, returned his smile and nod. The others, greasy-faced, with razor stubble and soiled clothes, focused their bloodshot eyes on their battered boots.

For the first several miles, his fellow passengers rode solemn and quiet, and as deadpan as the eastern Wyoming landscape. No one read, for it would most likely have made them sick, as Tory discovered. The modern Concord stagecoach minimized the impact of the rough three-hundred-mile Cheyenne-Deadwood Trail; even so, the trail's unexpected jolts dropped Tory's stomach to his gaiters. He worried about the safety of the six men riding on top. Everyone else seemed to take it in stride. On the frontier, people seemed more hearty and individualistic. He did not want to appear too fresh out of the city.

He tucked his novel, *Adventures of Huckleberry Finn*, back inside his coat pocket, wishing to establish some connection with his fellow passengers. He was drawn to the one woman sitting across from him with the snoozing toddler in her lap. He cleared his throat and smiled at her. "How old is your child?" he asked, unsure if the child was a boy or a girl.

"He'll be three in December." The woman held the child tighter to her blouse.

"What's his name?"

"James Jr."

"He's a cute fellow. Where are you traveling?"

The woman studied Tory a moment with her blue eyes, apparently assessing whether his kindness preceded ill will. Then she grinned and gave a gentle tilt to her head. "We live in Ft. Laramie," she said. "I was visiting relatives in Cheyenne with my son."

"Have you traveled on this stage before?"

"Yes, many times. My husband works for a supply contractor in Ft. Laramie, and I travel frequently to visit family back home. Hopefully by this time next year we'll have train service in most of eastern Wyoming and we can leave these rickety stages behind."

Tory wanted to ask her if she'd ever encountered wild bandits or marauding Indians during her stage journeys, but he remembered the driver's dire warning. "They're building train routes all over, it seems," he said instead.

"Yes, I think they'll have them going clear up to Alaska one of these days. Where are you heading?"

"Spiketrout is my final destination."

"Are you a prospector?"

"No, ma'am." Tory tittered with laughter.

The woman shifted her dozing child on her lap. "Every time I take this coach it's full of prospectors heading to the Black Hills," she said, lowering her voice and nodding toward some of the other passengers. "It's the whole reason why the stage line is here. Started after the gold strike in '74. But the gold's running low, I hear."

One of the older scraggly prospectors lifted his head. His grizzled beard brushed against his lap when he fired gray eyes at Tory. "You going for gold?"

"No, sir," Tory said. "I have other business there."

"Most the placer gold is played out," the old man said. "There's some gold in the mountain rock if you willing to dig for it. I got a small mine near Lead I bought off some hard case for one thousand dollars. You ain't thinking of staking a claim near Lead, are you?"

"Like I said, I have other business in the Black Hills."

The old gentleman glanced out the window. "Everyone wants gold," he said, flashing Tory his sparkling eyes. His bushy silver eyebrows looked like caterpillars crawling across his forehead.

"I'm not interested in any gold," Tory said politely.

"You're not, huh?" The old prospector seemed to digest Tory's words, as if he found them alien. "Well, you might not be seeking gold, but you're searching for a treasure in some form or another. Everyone is."

"I suppose," Tory said, smiling with tight lips.

Yes, the old prospector, sage from many years observing human nature, perhaps had a point. Tory was a prospector of sorts. And he realized he was chasing after more than the old prospector. Tory longed to stake a claim, yet on something far more ethereal than hilly mines and muddy creeks.

The Civil War hero whom Tory had corresponded with throughout most the spring and summer stood as Tory's buried treasure. With each passing mile, Tory became more certain that Franklin had not misrepresented himself. But Tory had. How could he have been so deceitful, passing himself off as a woman? To a veteran? He had raised the hopes of a lonely man for his own selfish fantasies. And wasn't that all they were—fantasies?

He turned to the endless sea of grassland, hoping it might dull his guilt, when the woman seated across from him addressed him as if she had read his thoughts. "Are you meeting anyone in Spiketrout?" she asked.

Tory sat upright. "No," he said, his gaze falling to the roughhewn floor. "I don't know anyone in the Black Hills."

He had told her the blunt truth. Franklin Ausmus was no less a stranger than any of the passengers riding with him on the stagecoach. The realization sent a chill down his spine. For the first time since he'd set off on his journey, he understood how fantastic his scheme was. Franklin was not the one person in the world who adored him—Franklin had no idea Tory even existed.

Perhaps his father had been right. Tory had lived with his head in the clouds.

The more miles of trail the stagecoach swallowed, the more Tory realized he should never meet Franklin Ausmus face to face. But he was too close to turn back on his venture now. He really did wish to see the mountains of the Wild West. Franklin had described the Black Hills as another Switzerland. He might as well go into Spiketrout and see the sights, and afterward, like any tourist, return to his hometown—and beg his parents for forgiveness.

The woman turned her attention to her stirring child. Tory appreciated the respite in their conversation. He stared out the window, his private ambiguities churning along with the grinding of the wagon's rolling wheels.

THREE more passengers boarded the stage in Chugwater, filling the coach to capacity. One of the new passengers, a middle-aged man dressed like a lawyer, refused to relinquish his window seat after Tory climbed aboard from his rest break. Squeezing past him, Tory sat between the man and a cowboy who smelled like iodine. An extra passenger leaped onto the roof. Tory heard him clamber around until finally he settled into position.

The closer confines triggered more talk. One of the new passengers, a man in his sixties with bright brown eyes, told stories of his silver rush years in Colorado between spitting tobacco juice out the window. Everyone fixated on his tales, even Tory, who harbored no interest in scrounging for silver or gold.

"And the funny thing about it all, I weren't even looking for none," the man said of his silver days. "I was just wanting to plant my legs permanent on a homestead. It was like the silver came at me out the canyon like jumping mice." He scanned the wide-eyed faces of his fellow passengers. "But you best watch out what the earth spit up, you just might get more than you bargain for. I got silver happy, that's what I got, drunk with my easy-gotten riches. Started shooting at everything that moved in the woods. Even distrusted the chipmunks. Kicked up a row shooting everything that chirped under the duff. Thought the whole world was out to steal my claim. Yet in the end, I lost all I had in a faro game in Leadville." He shrugged. "But I'm hooked now. Can't get enough. Nothing I can do about it. Settling down on a homestead ain't enough. I wander all over the country chasing after the latest gold or silver strike, coppering my bets. Now I'm off for the Black Hills. A bit late, but I got nothing to lose. Nowhere else to go."

Tory listened to the man's haphazard adventures. He hoped his own fortunes came to him in a much different way. He did not want to find himself wandering the western landscape alone, "coppering his bets." How much of his hopes and dreams still rested upon the unseen shoulders of Franklin Ausmus?

The driver halted the horse team several times along the way for rests and to kick the mud that accumulated from the trail off the wheels. Evening twilight faded as the stage rolled into Ft. Laramie. The woman with the toddler said good-bye to Tory and wished him good luck in his Spiketrout business, "whatever it is." Tory, happy that the lawyer had also left, slid to the window and gulped in crisp air. Stars broke out in the eastern sky. A last fan of light swept over the western horizon.

Half an hour north of Lusk, the stage stopped at the Little Bear Inn. Worn out, Tory decided to stop overnight. He climbed out of the stage with two other passengers, including the driver and shotgun messenger, who changed places with their overnighting counterparts, and checked in.

The inn, crowded with gamblers and cancan girls serving frothy mugs and shot glasses, bustled with a dark energy. Tory had never witnessed such a display outside of the 35th Street cabaret. Sweet smoke hung thick. He took supper alone at a small table away from the action, grateful no one bothered him. The server girl, dressed in the deepest-cut blouse he'd ever seen (and uglier than a mastiff), provided him extra attention. He picked at his late-night meal and climbed upstairs for a bath and good sleep.

Unfortunately, before he reached the top step, the housekeeper informed him the inn had run out of hot water and rooms. Dirty and sweaty, he was forced to share a room with a grumpy soul around his age who had boarded the stage in Chugwater. He mentioned he came from Belgium, although he spoke so little that Tory had no way of detecting any accent. Tory wondered why he had stayed overnight after only an eight-hour journey from Chugwater. Perhaps the Belgian was unused to travel in the rugged frontier.

Although Tory took pride in his handling of the arduous journey (nearly two days without sleeping horizontally except for one short nap on the hardwood bench at the Union Pacific depot in Omaha), a soft bed pleased him—whether he must share it or not. Both men slept in their clothes and kept as far to their edges of the double bed as possible. After a surprisingly restful night, despite sleeping next to a stranger and the occasional disruption from the raucous crowd downstairs, Tory stirred first, dressed in fresh clothes, and took his breakfast alone before heading outside to await the next stage. Ahead of the sun rising fully above the horizon, the incoming stage, lighted by lanterns, appeared around a bend in the trail. The two drivers and their shotgun messengers swapped places. Following behind the Belgian, Tory guilefully snatched a window seat.

With a fresh team of horses, the Cheyenne driver steered the stage back on the trail. The rocking of the full Concord lulled Tory and most the other passengers into a snooze. Not too far down the trail, the sound of approaching horses jerked Tory upright. The other passengers also awoke with a start. Tory's Belgian roommate clutched the woman beside him. Three of the passengers, likely experienced stage travelers, reached for what were probably their firearms. Tory instinctively felt for his breast pocket, where he concealed his remaining three hundred dollars in a cowhide purse.

A group of horsemen sidled up to the coach. The driver halted the horse team. Tory craned his neck to see the goings-on. Above the horses' nervous squeals, the horsemen and the driver exchanged words. A moment later, the horsemen rode off in a plume of dust.

"Nothing to fuss about, folks," the shotgun messenger shouted back toward the passengers. "Just some hired men searching for two prospectors who went missing from their camp."

A sigh circulated inside the coach. Tory watched with fascination as the men removed their hands from inside their jackets where, he supposed, they carried their firearms. An old-timer with black eyes made the sign of the cross and suggested everyone join him in prayer for the lost prospectors, "most likely killed and eaten by Indians or gold-greedy deadbeats." The passengers obliged him. From under the brim of his derby, Tory glanced around at the downturned heads. Many of the passengers never lifted their heads or opened their eyes. With the jostling of the stage, they had already slumped back to sleep.

Unable to doze again, Tory kept his attention fixed out the window. The sun lifted higher over the grassy plains, casting long shadows from the isolated cottonwood trees. North of Mule Creek, he spied a dark mass in the midst of the grassland, black and strange, surrounded by the expanse of the American savanna. By early afternoon, the black island had transformed into a distant blurry wall. Ripples uplifted and jolted the stagecoach. The lead horses, pushing into the ascent, snorted and squealed. Suddenly, soaring pines, spruce, aspen, and birch trees appeared.

The trail cut a path through a small canyon. Emerald-blue hills peeked around the next sharp bend. The shotgun messenger shouted that they had just crossed into Dakota Territory. Tory leaned out the window and gazed at the granite peaks. His fellow passengers remained unfazed by the spectacular rising of the earth, so rich in green that the mountains appeared black. He realized then that the Black Hills had been aptly named.

But they were hardly hills. Some peaks soared close to what he guessed eight or nine thousand feet, the tallest natural structures ever to rise before his eyes, far taller than the office buildings of Chicago. The horse team led them higher into the mountains. He inhaled the sharp aroma of spruce and pine, a taste of damp sweetness on his tongue.

The trail revealed a treacherous side that came with the mountainous terrain. Old stagecoach wrecks rotted along the wayside. Harnesses and wheels lay abandoned. Flies swarmed the decomposed carcasses of horses, likely shot after breaking a leg. Or perhaps something worse had done them in. Had bandits shot them, looking to make off with everyone's loot?

Romantic and fearful notions filled Tory's head throughout the night. He chose to remain on the stage rather than stop over at another cheap trailside saloon. The dark confines, though disquieting (before nodding off, Tory had noticed the latest shotgun messenger standing with a lantern, showcasing heightened vigilance), lulled him into a deep sleep. He awoke by sunrise as the stage waggled into Ten Mile Station. A few miles north, the first hand-carved sign for Deadwood appeared. Soon, a cluster of tents emerged alongside the trail and off into the woods. Columns of smoke from fire pits blended to form an extensive cloud over the campsites. Men sat on stumps and stared into their fires. The thick smell of cooking meats, mixed with human and livestock waste, made Tory cough.

Before long, the trail widened into a road more like those found in Chicago. Brick and mortar two- and three-story structures lined the main thoroughfare and scaled the surrounding hills. The deep, lush gulch blocked much of the noontime sun. Streets fanned out from Main Street like piano keys. Felled lumber littered the sides of every block. The rancid stench of human and livestock waste and food of all sorts hit Tory in the face. At first glance, Deadwood seemed comprised of only saloons, brothels, and gambling halls. The teeming street seemed different from the crowds in Chicago. The people here looked harsher, less purposeful in their strides.

The stage pulled up to a transportation hub, and everyone filed out. Tory gathered his satchel from the shotgun messenger and asked him where the Deadwood-Spearfish stage left from. The man nodded across the street as he handed the other passengers their luggage. Tory maneuvered around the horse droppings for the stage that would take him into Spiketrout. From a second-floor window of a saloon, a painted woman whistled and flirted, motioning for Tory to come up and see her. A few cowboys on the street encouraged him to oblige. Flushing, he pretended not to hear.

The Deadwood-Spearfish driver told Tory he had a little more than an hour to kill. Tory wandered about a block down the street, his satchel clutched to his side. He glanced in the window of a shop and gave up trying to tame his wavy hair. He considered staying in Deadwood and doing his best to forget about the nonsense with Franklin Ausmus. But as he observed the rowdiness of the street, he fretted remaining in Deadwood any longer than he had to.

The smell of food set his stomach rumbling, yet he feared to enter the many inns lining Main Street that appeared loaded with drunks and prostitutes. Hankering for something to eat, he located a nearby drugstore. Joseph van Werckhoven popped into his mind when he stepped inside. Tory purchased two chocolate bars and paid the druggist. He nearly dropped his candy bars when he noticed a jar behind the counter that contained what looked like the severed head of a man floating in some yellow-green liquid. The druggist caught Tory's shocked gaze and chuckled, as if he was used to similar reactions from newcomers.

"That's the head of a redskin," he said, eyeing the freakish spectacle along with Tory. "Rumor is a prospector was camping out by his claim when a rogue Sioux came up from behind and tried to scalp him alive. The prospector, a wrestler from back east, knew how to defend himself. He flung the Indian to the ground, stabbed him with his bowie knife, and then decapitated the redskin on the spot. People saw him carry the head into town, holding it by its long black hair. No one thought it was real at first. He managed to sell it to an innkeeper, but after a few complaints from alarmed guests, the innkeeper sold it to me. I've had it for about five years now. No one knows the real story. Sure does stir up talk."

Tory didn't know what to think. He backed out of the store, his mouth and eyes agape, and walked into a gregarious pedestrian reeking of whiskey, who hugged him and patted his backside before continuing on his way. Still shaking from the image of the Indian head, Tory sat on the edge of the boardwalk and ate one of his chocolate bars. A stray dog, one of many of the same breed and identical auburn coloring wandering the streets, nudged its nose at Tory's hand. Tory broke off a small piece of chocolate and gave it to the dog. The dog rolled it in its mouth, spit it out, and trotted off down Main Street.

Observing the people on the street, he noted that Deadwood was as diverse as Chicago. Four men walking by were speaking Norwegian, he was sure. Two nearby spicy-looking women spoke Russian or possibly Polish. Across the street, a Chinese restaurant attracted an ample (and wild-looking) clientele. If he craned his neck, he could see the sign for a tavern serving Italian food. Another sign for a hostel was written entirely in German. Negro men carried on as openly as the whites. And Tory beheld a sight he'd never seen in his life—authentic Indians. Only two passed close enough for him to observe them. They wore western clothes, yet their unmistakable features mirrored the drawings and photographs he'd seen in books and periodicals.

Tory was relieved to board the stage with a group of smart-looking men and women about his age who said they were heading to the Spearfish Normal School to earn teaching certificates. Happy for the politer company, he braced himself for his final destination. So close to Spiketrout, he realized with a start he had planned little for his excursion. He had depleted so much energy focusing on Franklin Ausmus he'd forgotten to consider practicalities, like lodging. On some absurd level, he'd figured Franklin Ausmus might provide him shelter. But that could never be.

The jarring trip farther up the hills and through narrow gulches took another three hours. They arrived in Spiketrout with the afternoon sun resting above the pines and aspens atop the western slopes. Many of Spiketrout's buildings appeared uninhabitable, either boarded up—which vandals had clearly ignored—or leaning over as if they were falling asleep. The roof of one small structure had caved in and been left to rot. About a quarter the size of Deadwood, Spiketrout had only one visible inn—the Gold Dust Inn, which was marked as the staging station for the Deadwood-Spearfish line.

Tory was the sole passenger to debark in Spiketrout. He felt abandoned watching the stage carrying the students from the Normal School continue on to Spearfish without him. Alone, he looked up and down the dusty street, unsure where to go or what to do. A spicy-looking woman twirling a parasol stood outside the Gold Dust Inn. She seemed amicable despite her domineering stature. As he neared, the smell of her jasmine perfume overwhelmed him. Music from a player piano oozed onto the street.

"Excuse me, ma'am, do you know if this inn has any vacancies?" he asked.

The woman tilted her parasol away from her face. The afternoon sun revealed ruby lips, painted cheeks, and blue eye shadow clear to her eyebrows. Under the wisps of her thick eyelashes, she scanned Tory from his gaiters to his derby. "I'm the proprietress of the Gold Dust Inn. We got some rooms left. You looking to stay a while, honey?"

"I might need a place to stay for a few days. I'm new in town."

"I can see that, honey. You're about as wet behind the ears as I've seen around here. I saw you get off the stage. Most don't stop here for good no more, not since the gold's dried up. What brings a boy like you to Spiketrout? You're a little late for the gold rush."

"I'm not here for gold. I'm exploring, I suppose."

The woman threw her head back and laughed. Baubles hanging from her earlobes bounced and swayed. She twirled her parasol like a windmill in a storm. "I figure it's about time we started getting some tourists out here," she said.

"I'm not actually a tourist." Tory flushed. "At least I don't consider myself to be." He pondered how much to reveal about his travels. Perhaps she might be of some help to him. "Do you know the whereabouts of a Franklin Ausmus?"

"Frank?"

"I suppose so, ma'am. I believe he lives on a homestead outside of Spiketrout, but I'm unsure in which direction."

She pointed her long painted fingernail across the street, where a group of men were gathered outside a barbershop. "That's Frank right over there."

Tory nearly dropped his bag. He followed her gaze to the group of about four or five men. Composing himself, he studied the face of each man, wondering which one belonged to Franklin. When the one wearing a buckskin outfit turned fully toward Tory, he recognized the right sleeve rolled above where the elbow would be, the only one among them with one arm. He had not exaggerated the description of himself in his advertisement—*tall, good-looking.*

He looked exactly how Tory had pictured him. Dark-brown, wavy hair that matched the color of his horseshoe mustache fell from under a cowboy hat to his broad shoulders. Tight buckskin revealed a man accustomed to heavy labor. Qualms Tory had had earlier seemed to vanish. Franklin hadn't existed as a dream or a dime novel character. He was real. Flesh and blood.

"What do you want with Frank?" the proprietress asked.

"I know him in passing," Tory said, still gazing across the street. "I doubt he'd remember me."

"So you want a room, honey?" she asked after a pause.

"I'll check in later. Thank you for all your hospitality." Tory needed to get a closer look at Franklin before he left for his homestead. Clutching his satchel, he crossed the street without a backward glance at the painted woman and retreated behind a parked wagon, where he could watch Franklin undetected.

Franklin shook hands with one of the men and stepped inside a nearby mercantile. The weight of the surrounding gulch pressed on Tory's shoulders while he waited for Franklin to reemerge. A handful of minutes later, he came out carrying a crate marked "explosives." Tory marveled how he balanced the box with his one arm and stump. He carefully slid the crate into the back of a wagon, then crossed the street to the postal office. In short time, Franklin stepped back onto the boardwalk. Tory stooped lower and peered around the wagon to study his face. He looked dejected, sad. Next, Franklin walked back to the same wagon, tossed what looked like a Montgomery Ward catalog onto the bench, and headed straight for the Gold Dust Inn across the street. Tory followed him.

When Tory got to the inn, he stood by the door and gazed around. The inn, half-full of gamblers and carousers, reeked of tobacco smoke and alcohol. One of his favorite tunes rolled out of the player piano, "Oh, Dem Old Golden Slippers." A yellow cat brushed against his legs, stretched, then darted for the stairs. Looking up, Tory saw Franklin's reflection in the mirror above the bar. Tory had never seen anyone look so gloomy and angry at the same time. The bartender slid Franklin a mug of frothy beer.

What had made Franklin so angry in such quick fashion? He'd gone into the postal office a happy man and emerged desolate-looking. Suddenly, the answer grabbed Tory around his throat. Franklin had gone into the postal office to see if "Torsten P." from Chicago had sent him any letters. The poor man must still be hoping she'd written. What else could it be? He must be heartbroken thinking that she'd rejected him. What a mess Tory had made of things. Maybe he should have sent him a written explanation from the train.

He had never considered the impact his letters might have on Franklin when he'd first decided to write him. He had allowed his own selfish motives to blur reason. His self-interest had buoyed a lonely man's hopes for companionship and ground them into dust.

The painted proprietress stepped up beside him. "Well, why don't you go and talk with your long-lost friend, honey? He sure does look like he could use one."

"I can't, not yet." Cheeks burning, he dashed out the door and across the street, where he cursed himself for having misled Franklin all those months. Yet Tory's shame propelled him to long for Franklin all the more. He couldn't leave him. Not after such a long journey. Not now, when the veteran shouldered so much sorrow. He had to console him, without fretting about why.

With no eyes upon him, he climbed into the back of Franklin's wagon, careful to avoid the crate of dynamite, and hid under several burlap sacks. He rested his head on his satchel and waited for Franklin to come. It was the first time in a full day that he'd been able to lay supine, and the heat under the sacks tired him. As rhythms from the street faded into a monotonous hum, his dreams carried him adrift above the surrounding gulch.

# Chapter
# TWELVE

HE AWOKE to jostling and rocking. Rubbing his eyes, he realized the wagon was moving. Stealthily, he peeked out from under the burlap. Franklin was conveying him along a narrow trail surrounded by towering blue-green pines and spruce. A deep gulch veiled the trail in a dark shadow. He checked his pocket watch. He had slept a good hour.

From his concealment, he watched the gulch deepen. A sharp bend in the trail revealed a waterfall as tall as he was, gurgling with cooling froth. He resisted the urge to sit up to take in more of the scenery. He spied ravens clustered in the pines and aspens. The trail followed along the creek for another half hour all the way into a clearing. Soon after, the wagon turned sharply and stopped.

Tory ducked back under the sacks. He heard Franklin descend from the wagon and walk to the back. The horse nickered. Next, he heard Franklin pull the crate of explosives from the wagon. A low grunt followed by fading footsteps assured Tory Franklin had left. He waited a few minutes for the silence to seep in before folding back the burlap. Cool air refreshed him. The temperature was a good ten degrees cooler at Franklin's homestead than in Spiketrout.

Watchful, he raised his head to eye level above the side. The small homestead stole his breath. This was the paradise Franklin had described with so much passion in his letters. Difficult to believe he was seeing it with his own eyes—Moonlight Gulch.

Green mountains topped with granite fists soared on all sides. A sheer granite rock face towered from the creek to the horizon. Another smaller one extended along a small field of crops. What looked like string beans, potatoes, and leafy greens grew from the rich soil. Yellow alfalfa swayed in the breeze around the edge of the field. Tory noted that Franklin had worked the land with plow trails and irrigation ditches. Franklin's small barn rose near a henhouse and pigpen. Built into a hillside, a storage barn was barely noticeable. A windmill, the one Franklin had purchased from Chicago, worked steadily by a well. And anchored in the middle of it all was Franklin's small cabin, a column of smoke rising from the chimney.

Franklin stepped out of the barn. Tory hunkered down, his heart racing. He heard the clinking of leather and iron. Franklin was unhitching the horse. The sound of the horse's hooves abated as Franklin led it to the barn. Carefully, Tory raised his eyes above the side just enough to watch Franklin exit the barn, his shoulders still slumped, and slog inside the cabin.

With Franklin out of sight, Tory clutched his bag and climbed out of the wagon. He stole away behind the barn should Franklin unexpectedly emerge from the cabin and detect him. The smell of roasted venison set his stomach growling. He wondered if he could reach the storage barn. Potatoes, greens, or cured meats might be stored there. But the dash across the stump-covered grassy field would be too risky. He dodged inside the barn instead.

A dairy cow, a mule, and two horses greeted him. He gestured for them to keep quiet. They stirred a bit but eventually settled into their own world. For a moment, Tory inhaled the rich smell of livestock, enjoying his first genuine moment of privacy since he'd left his home on Chicago Avenue three days ago.

He edged about the barn, searching for food. An odd pile of barbwire lay in a corner. The crate of dynamite sat beside it. Then he remembered the one remaining chocolate bar he'd purchased in Deadwood from the druggist with the gruesome Indian head. He nearly ate it in one bite, the melting chocolate gooey and scrumptious.

In the barn's loft, strips of meat cured on wooden poles. Tory's mouth instantly watered. Still hungry, he dropped his bag, climbed the ladder, and pulled down one strip. Within seconds, he devoured it. Another strip went equally as quickly.

A sting of drowsiness weakened his legs. Too tired to worry about anything but lying down, he sprawled over a bed of hay and again floated off to sleep.

HE STIRRED, grumpy, swatting at his father's nudging. He wished he would leave him be. Just ten more minutes, he wanted to yell. But he wondered: How could his father be pestering him? He was not home in Chicago. His father was a thousand miles away. His eyes flashed open. A large Indian crouched over him, staring straight into his eyes. Tory shot upright. He shook his head, trying to rouse his senses. Like those in Deadwood, he wore Western clothes, but his burgundy skin, broad nose, and coal-black hair could only belong to an Indian.

Tory scurried backward against the wall. "Don't... don't you touch me," he said, wanting to inflict warning into his wavering voice.

The Indian held the wrapper from Tory's chocolate bar. He glanced at it with a wrinkled forehead then gazed back at Tory. "What're you doing in here?"

Tory imagined the most horrific scenario, like those he'd read in Wild West dime novels. Was the Indian going to scalp him? "Stay away from me," Tory said, kicking straw at him. "Stay away."

The Indian chucked the candy wrapper over his shoulder. "You're a chikala wasichu."

"W-what?"

"Tiny white man."

"I'm... I'm not tiny. I'm five feet five."

"You look like a chikala wasichu to me."

His near-perfect English bewildered Tory. "Leave me be, please."

The Indian narrowed his dark eyes, as black as onyx, and seemed to study him. He scanned Tory from his derby to the tips of his gaiters. "You have stylish clothes and wear fancy boots. You're not from here. You live in the big city."

"You don't know anything about me. Now, please, leave me alone."

"Why does a wealthy-looking city boy want to steal from a small homesteader?"

"I'm not wealthy, and I'm not stealing from anyone."

The Indian leaned in closer. His raw breath made Tory wince. "You have the whitest skin on a man I've seen in a long time. All the white people here are darkened by the sun, except the whores. You must come from a big city—unless you're a whore."

Tory grimaced. "I'm nothing of the sort."

Then a gruesome thought forced Tory to his haunches. Had the Indian done something horrible to Franklin? Why else would he be on his land? Unsure what else to do, he kicked and flailed his arms, terrified of what bloodcurdling fate had befallen the man he'd grown to love. But the Indian, with one hand, held him supine against the hay.

"You're a feisty one," he said evenly. "That's a lot of fight for one so small."

"I told you," Tory said between swings and kicks, "I'm not small. I'll fight you. I'll fight your entire tribe."

The Indian eased his pressure on Tory's midsection and laughed. "My tribe is long gone from these parts, chikala wasichu. But you're welcome to take them on."

Noticing a change in the Indian's demeanor, Tory stopped squirming and followed the Indian's dark eyes as he turned to gaze over his broad shoulder. Franklin Ausmus had climbed the ladder and was peeking into the loft at them.

"What in tarnation is going on here?"

"I found him sleeping," the Indian said. "Won't say much, Frank. Not sure what to make of him."

Hearing the Indian address Franklin by name, Tory sat up on his elbows. He'd forgotten about Franklin's good friend Wicasha, the Lakota Indian he often wrote about in his many correspondences. Relaxing at the realization, he no longer resisted Wicasha's grip.

"He's just a boy," Wicasha said, "but he's got a lot of fight in him."

"I'm… I'm not a boy," Tory said, softer. "I'm nineteen."

"Is he trying to steal from me?" Franklin asked Wicasha.

The Lakota glanced around. "Looks like he got into your jerky. He was probably hungry. Ate some chocolate too. He's got his luggage down there." He nodded toward the ground.

Franklin grimaced at Tory's satchel, then shifted his scrutinizing gaze at Tory. He screwed up his tanned face into sharp rivulets and stepped fully onto the loft. His hand went to his sidearm. "You a hired man of Bilodeaux?"

"Bilo—? No, no, never." Tory couldn't reveal what he knew from Franklin's letters. Although hearing Bilodeaux's name twisted his stomach, he had to play clueless. "I don't even know who that is," he said.

"You come here to spy?" Franklin's fingers twitched.

Sweat broke out over Tory's forehead. Despite the tense moment, Tory became mesmerized by Franklin's jade-colored eyes. Franklin had never mentioned his eye color in any of his letters, and Tory hadn't expected a pair so bright. "No, sir." He swallowed. "I have no intentions of doing anything of the sort."

"Then what business have you in my barn?"

"I... I... well, I was needing for a place to rest."

"On your way through the woods in your fancy boots and hat?" Franklin scrutinized him with contempt. "You just happen to be taking a stroll in the middle of the Black Hills, with your satchel in hand, and assumed my barn was an inn? You think we're fools?"

"No, sir, I do not."

Franklin lifted an eyebrow. "You one of those bankers from Spearfish or Deadwood come here on behalf of Bilodeaux?"

"I told you, I... I have no idea who this Bilodeaux is. I've never met a man with that name." He tried to maintain some truthfulness.

The Indian stood, towering over Tory, still sprawled on his back. Seeing how Franklin interacted so comfortably with the Indian, Tory suppressed the instinct to scurry from him. Surely if Franklin liked him, he must be a good man. But then, did Tory really even know Franklin? What kind of a man was he? Tory eyed the revolver inches from Franklin's hand.

"You have nothing to fear from me," Tory said.

Franklin shook his head. "I'm gonna have to barbwire the whole damn property, like I worried."

"You won't need barbwire because of me," Tory said. "I hadn't meant any harm. I was just tired... and hungry."

"You still haven't explained what you're doing here," Franklin said. "How did you come to be in my loft?"

Tory wracked his brain for a good story. He supposed he could reveal some of the truth. "I'm new in town," he said. "I only arrived this afternoon. I came all the way from... from the east. I was tired and wanted a place to lie down, so I climbed into your wagon and used the burlap sacks for blankets. When I awoke, I found myself on your homestead. I was hungry but didn't want to bother you, so I wandered into your barn to search for something to eat. It's the truth, honest. I planned on hiking back. I swear."

Franklin and Wicasha peered at each other. Then they studied Tory. Suspicious ripples curled along Franklin's forehead.

"He looks harmless to me, Frank. What do you say?"

Franklin waited a moment before responding to Wicasha. "I reckon he's telling the truth. Don't look like he can do much harm." Franklin reached out his hand to Tory. "Come on. Get yourself up from there. Might as well get something decent to eat other than jerky and candy."

TORY ate the hot venison stew as if he hadn't partaken food in days. The Indian had left for his home somewhere deep in the hills, leaving the two of them alone. Franklin, seated opposite him, stared at him with the same curious wrinkles on his forehead, his eyebrows knitted.

"I didn't get your name?" Franklin asked after a prolonged silence.

"Tor—" Tory's words skidded on his tongue and slammed into the back of his teeth. He couldn't give Franklin his real name. He had almost forgotten. He needed to practice more caution.

"Your name's Tor?" Franklin eyed him sideways through the steam rising from his plate.

"Yes, actually, it's Tory."

"Interesting name. I guess no stranger than mine. I'm named after Benjamin Franklin."

"I know." Tory nearly dropped his spoon. Franklin had mentioned his namesake in one of his letters. He must be vigilant not to divulge anything that he might know from them.

"How do you know who I'm named after?" Franklin again eyed him harshly. "I hadn't even told you my name yet."

Tory thought fast. "I heard the Indian call you Frank. I figured it must be short for Franklin. And who else would you be named after but Benjamin Franklin?"

Franklin seemed to soften as this possibility registered with him, and he went back to his eating.

"I'm sorry if I caused you any trouble," Tory said after several more silent spoonfuls of stew.

"You didn't cause much trouble. Just not common to get visitors around here unless they're after something."

"I'm not after anything. I don't want your possessions or anything like that."

"Best not."

Tory let his gaze rove around the cabin. It was smaller than he'd imagined. Only the barest necessities furnished the place, but they were all comfy-looking. The few possessions Franklin had seemed for functional purposes: cooking, hunting, fishing, trapping. Tory set his eyes back on Franklin. "I can leave after supper and be out of your way, if you like," he said.

"Leave how?" Franklin grunted. "You stowed away in my wagon."

"I can hike back to Spiketrout."

"It's over a two-hour hike even in the best cowhide boots. You wouldn't last a half hour in those fancy paper-thin city boots of yours." Franklin nodded out the window. "You'd be lucky to make it out of that gulch without blisters eating your feet like a swarm of mosquitoes."

Tory stared out the window to where the ponderosa abutted the creek. Somewhere beyond lay even wilder country than Moonlight Gulch. He cringed at the image Franklin had described. The thought of getting lost in the Black Hills terrified him. He thought about the two missing prospectors the horsemen along the Cheyenne-Deadwood trail had searched for and the severed Indian head in Deadwood. He had never considered how he'd make it back to Spiketrout when he'd stowed away in Franklin's wagon.

"I'll pay you for a ride back," he said.

"It'll be dark by the time we reach Spiketrout." Franklin stood and dumped his plate into a bin next to the stove. "You'll have to spend the night here. I can take you back in the morning."

Tory glanced around more openly. There looked to be no place to bed down. He was both excited and troubled. He had fooled the Civil War veteran long enough. Tory would spend one night. After that, bright and early next morning, he'd depart from his life once and for all, before his deception caused either of them any more heartache.

# Chapter
# THIRTEEN

FRANKLIN lay awake in his feather bed. The previous day had been rough. He had gone into town for a haircut, supplies (he'd ordered the dynamite on instinct thinking he might need it someday), and to see if his penmate from Chicago had sent him any new letters. How long had he waited for one of her replies? More than a month? No use hoping any longer. The dream of one day meeting the woman he had talked himself into believing he would marry had been dashed to the ground and grinded into the dirt.

He had received dozens of other responses to his advertisement in *Matrimonial News*, but none had touched him like hers. He had fallen in love with her way with words. Even her handwriting. He thought she had written something profound in her letters. The other letters he had thrown away. How had he allowed her to deceive him?

He'd kept writing her time and time again, hoping she'd reply. By the fourth letter, dejected and confused, he'd stopped. Why he still kept Torsten's letters in his old leather Army trunk, bound with twine, he didn't know. He could not force himself to toss them into the fire, although he had no real use for them. Perhaps he could read them later in life, remind himself what a fool she'd taken him for.

Sighing, he stared at the dark ceiling. She had been nothing but an illusion. She had teased him for her own feminine pleasure. She was no different than the women in the Black Hills. A mere flirt. Perhaps worse.

And then to come back to his homestead to find that young man stowed in his barn. At least his presence had taken his mind off his sorrows. Right now, the young man was nestled in the corner of the cabin on an old cot Franklin had used at the quartz mine. He sensed he was sound asleep. It was comforting knowing someone was close. Wicasha sometimes bunked at the homestead if he stayed late, especially in the winter months, when the sun descended early over the mountains and it was too dark for him to reach his camp in deep snow. Both appreciated each other's company, but they also valued their privacy.

Last night after supper, the young man had said he was from Chicago. It seemed like everyone was from there. Torsten was from Chicago. Franklin had read somewhere that more than one million people called Chicago home, and thousands more were pouring in each month. Not that many people existed in Dakota, Montana, and Wyoming Territories combined.

Outside he heard the nighttime winds rush off the mountains and rustle the branches of the aspens and pines. A comforting sound. A sound he had dreamed of sharing with Torsten someday. Night birds cackled in the distance. He understood, suddenly, why they were called mockingbirds.

He turned to his side. How could he have allowed himself to fall for someone whom he had never set eyes on? What a stupid idea to take out an advertisement in a matchmaker periodical. Love was nothing but an echo fading farther and farther from his ears. Self-loathing kneaded its way into Franklin's soul. He squeezed his eyes shut. Would the pain ever go away?

FRANKLIN awoke the next morning to the smell of frying bacon and brewing coffee. Groggy, he rubbed his belly and wobbled from behind the wooden partition that concealed his bed. Tory, dressed and refreshed-looking, was at the stove cooking breakfast. The sizzle of frying food set his stomach grumbling.

"Good morning," Tory said to him with a smile. "I hope you don't mind, but I took the liberty to make breakfast. It's the least I could do after you've put up with me."

Franklin scratched his head with a grunt. "Well, that's okay, I guess." Half asleep after a fitful night, he pulled on his boots and scuffled to the outhouse. After a short detour to the well to wash, he found breakfast waiting for him at the table. Tory grinned at him while he poured them each a cup of steaming coffee. The potatoes, scrambled eggs, and bacon looked and smelled tasty, he had to admit. He took a seat and sipped the black coffee, relishing the bitter hot liquid oozing down his throat.

"Good coffee," he said. "How'd you get it so smooth?"

"I put an egg in it. Learned it from my parents. It's Swedish."

Franklin shrugged. "Whatever works." He took a few bites of the hot breakfast. "So, you sleep all right?"

"Yes, thank you," Tory said. "The cot was very comfortable."

Franklin chuckled. "You're a flannel-mouthed liar. But thanks for not complaining."

"How can I complain after everything you've done for me?" Tory said. "I'm an intruder into your home, and you took me in like a gentleman. I'm in debt to you."

"I don't like anyone in debt to me."

"That's really just a figure of speech. But I am grateful."

"You never mentioned what brought you to Dakota," Franklin said. "You said last night you're not looking for any gold claims." The young man had remained oddly quiet last night, refusing to share much about himself. Franklin, uncomfortable eating meals with a stranger, wanted more information.

Tory shrugged. "I ached to see the West, I guess. I've read a lot about it."

"Is it what you expected?"

The young man seemed to avert his eyes. "Better, actually."

Several more silent bites later, Franklin said, "You sure don't ask a lot of questions. Not the curious type, huh? I guess I respect that. But I bet you're aching to learn what happened to my arm." Franklin lifted his right stump, covered loosely with the sleeve of his union suit. "Everyone does. Don't feel bad about wanting to know."

Tory flushed. "It's really none of my business."

"But you thought it was your business to hop in my wagon for a ride out to my homestead?" Franklin regretted his sarcasm when he took note of Tory's falling face. He chuckled to lighten the mood. "I lost it in the Civil War. Got it shot off. Actually, got my arm shot to pieces, had to have it cut off."

"I'm sorry," Tory said, his face puckering. "I hope it didn't hurt much."

Franklin wanted to tell Tory all the chloroform in the world wouldn't have salved his misery while doctors sawed into his arm. The amputation, and the phantom limb pains that had haunted him for months after, had hurt worse than the gunshot blast. Yet he held back, figuring to spare Tory the gory details. He thought it funny. He had never considered sparing another man's feelings before.

"I lived," he said.

"You must be glad the war is over," Tory said as he spooned eggs into his mouth. "I was born two years after everything ended. I learned a lot about it from history books."

"Those books can't tell you what it was actually like."

Tory lowered his eyes. "I'm sure they can't."

"I fought alongside many a brave boy from your home state," Franklin said, pursing his lips as he recalled the camaraderie between his infantry unit and the many Illinois regiments. Their units had teased each other for their strange manner of speaking, but they had fought shoulder to shoulder valiantly. He'd never forgotten the unity they'd forged—or those who'd never returned home.

"Our postman is a Civil War veteran," Tory said. "But I'm unsure which regiment he fought with."

They ate in silence. Franklin savored the hearty breakfast. But the young man's reserve still bothered him. "You'd think you knew me better than myself," he said under his breath, keeping his attention on his eggs and bacon.

"Pardon me?"

"Don't you want to at least know where I'm from?"

"Oh, yes. Umm… I was about to ask you."

"Grew up in eastern Tennessee. Knox County. On a hog farm. Taught me a lot about keeping livestock that enables me to sustain myself out here alone."

Tory glanced across the table. "Do you like living alone, Franklin?"

Franklin peered at the young man askance, unsure what to expect from him. He'd been so reserved that it seemed odd he would ask such an intimate question out of the blue. A curious fellow, he thought. Something about him was a bit different than most. An extra sparkle flickered in his eyes. Franklin turned away, afraid he might flush after realizing he had never seen such crystal-blue eyes.

He cleared his throat, lubricated with the grease from the tasty breakfast. "I like it fine," he said. "I get lonesome, of course. But who wouldn't?"

"You have a wonderful homestead. Anyone would be lucky to live here."

"Yeah, well...."

Strident shouting from somewhere outside forced Franklin to his feet. A wave of coffee splashed from his cup onto the table. Wicasha was shouting at someone near the creek. Franklin dashed outside.

By the time Franklin reached the creek, Wicasha was dragging a man away from the bank and onto the grass.

"Let me be!" The old-timer was struggling like a buck trapped in barbwire. "Let me be, you goddamn redskin. I'll have a posse out hunting for you if you don't let me be. We'll scalp you good."

"What's the fuss about now?" Franklin gazed at the squirming old man, scrawny with a silver beard snaking around his midsection.

"I caught him trying to pan your creek pool," Wicasha said. "It's that old penniless drunk we sometimes see in Spiketrout."

Franklin approached the old man and peered down at him. "What right do you have coming around here panning for gold on my property, Johnson?"

The old man, breathing heavy, peered at Franklin. "What difference is it to you, Ausmus? Everybody knows you don't pan for gold. I was taking what Mother Nature put on this here earth for man to get at. You're wasting it here. You're an abomination, Ausmus."

"I ought to kick you in your shriveled bones, old geezer." From the corner of his eye, Franklin noticed Tory standing off to the side. For some reason, Franklin tempered his tone. "Let him stand, Wicasha," he said through clenched teeth.

"I scouted him from clear over by the field as I was coming around the hillock," Wicasha explained. "He was already panning by the time I reached the creek." Wicasha held the man upright under his bony arms. He tried to stir loose, but Wicasha remained as solid as a granite spire.

"You're wasting good gold," the old man cried. Falling limp, he abandoned his struggle. He tumbled from Wicasha's weakened hold like a rotting scarecrow. "People are hungry and needing money." He sobbed. "You're sitting on tons of gold we could all use. It ain't fair. It ain't."

"It's my business what I got on my land and what I do with it." Franklin wiped spittle from his mustache and added, "I'm sick of telling you people. Now you got about thirty seconds to get off my property and stay off for good."

"He looks hungry," Tory said, stepping in closer. "Maybe he would want some breakfast before he leaves."

Franklin jerked around at Tory, surprised to hear his calm voice among the ruckus. "Don't feel sorry for him." He turned back to sneer at the old man. "He takes what money he gets and gambles and drinks it away. We're not responsible for that. I ain't the welfare board."

"I could use something for my growling stomach, now that you mention it," the old man said, his eyes wide like a deer's.

"Little leftovers won't harm anyone, would it?" Tory said.

Franklin rolled his eyes. "All right. Go grab him some of that breakfast you cooked. Give it to him in a sack to take with him." With Tory gone, Franklin hardened his voice. "Don't think us feeding you gives you the right to keep coming around here like a begging dog, old-timer."

"You're a cruel man, Ausmus," Johnson said.

"From my point of view, Johnson, a cruel man is one who trespasses and takes what don't belong to him."

A minute later, Tory returned with a small flour sack, a greasy stain forming at the bottom. "Here," he said, handing the old man the sack. "I put a spoon in it for you."

"I'm obliged to you, son." The wizened man snatched the sack from Tory and scurried to his feet. He seemed confused, uncertain what his next step should be.

Franklin leaned toward him. "Listen here, old man," he said. "If I had my way, I'd shoot you for trespassing. Best be grateful you got something to take back to Spiketrout. Now get along, before I change my mind."

Before the old-timer could run off, a rifle blast turned everyone on their heels. Dust kicked up near Johnson's feet, and soon they heard the steady gait of a horse. Bilodeaux, mounted high on his gray charger, trotted over to them, his rifle smoking.

"You better do what Ausmus tells you," Bilodeaux said to Johnson. "Next time, I will not deliberately miss. I will shoot you between the eyes."

Johnson gaped from one man to the other, the breakfast sack trembling in his hand. Finally, he rushed off down the trail faster than Franklin would have guessed the weathered old man could run.

"I got the feeling you weren't looking out for my best interest, Bilodeaux," Franklin said with a grimace.

"The old-timer might be a deadbeat and a sponge," Bilodeaux said, "but he is right about you looking down at Mother Nature. That gold in your creek is to be had by man. One of these days, Ausmus, one way or the other, I intend to get that gold."

"Head out of here, Bilodeaux, or I'll shoot *you* between the eyes."

"You got the whole town against you more and more, Ausmus. Spiketrout is dying, and you are sitting on about one hundred thousand greenbacks' worth."

"I mean what I say, Bilodeaux. Off my land."

Henri Bilodeaux grinned down at the trio. He circled the men, the stallion's slender legs high and showy. "Best look after your boy, Ausmus," he said, ogling Tory. "You do not want anything bad to come of him. Au revoir, mes copains."

Sweeping from his face the dust stirred by Bilodeaux's stallion, Franklin growled. His anger and frustration welled up inside him, and he had ample reason to unleash it: Bilodeaux, the old geezer, Tory, not to mention that coquette Torsten back in Chicago. He'd had enough of them all. People were nothing but pests. There was a good reason he'd sought the secluded backcountry for a homestead.

"Got too many damn trespassers on my property," he fumed. "Don't like it. Don't like it one bit." Snarling, he stomped off toward the cabin.

# CHAPTER
# FOURTEEN

THAT Bilodeaux character was something else, Tory mulled. What had he meant by saying he hoped nothing bad came of him? Had that been some kind of roundabout threat?

Tory had taken a disliking to him even before setting eyes upon his detestable grin. Franklin's letters had described enough of his nefarious nature to make Tory loathe him. He detested men like Bilodeaux. Always wanting something that others had but rarely working to achieve it on their own. Tory wished he knew a way to help Franklin rid himself of Bilodeaux for good. But how?

Tory felt bad that he had added to Franklin's woes. Not only had he intruded on his property like so many others, he had misled him with love letters. Realizing the best means to ease Franklin's troubles was to leave Moonlight Gulch as promised, he followed after him inside the cabin.

He heard Franklin moving behind the wooden partition where he kept his bed.

"Mr. Ausmus?" He peered around the partition. Franklin was sitting on his bed, his shoulder-length hair concealing his face. He held several papers limply in his hand.

Franklin jerked up. Without turning to look at Tory, he stuffed the papers inside his trunk and shut the lid with a thump. "What do you want?" he said under his breath, keeping his eyes averted.

Tory guessed what Franklin had been reading by the somber tone to his voice. The letters "Torsten P." had written—letters *he* had written. If only Tory could let him know the "fine lady" still cared. But if Franklin ever learned the truth about him, it would only compound his misery. Tory realized he had no means to undo the damage he'd caused.

"I've got my bag all packed," Tory said in a hushed voice. "I'm ready to go whenever you are. Or if you prefer, I can hike out as I suggested last night at supper. I don't want to burden you any further."

"You can't hike out of here, not in your getup. Where's Wicasha?"

"He said he was going to the barn to brush the horses."

"He can ride you out. Use the wagon. I got things to do here. Don't want to leave the place after what happened with Johnson, anyway."

Hanging his head low, Tory said, "I understand. I'll go ask Wicasha."

Tory glanced back at the cabin as he trudged to the barn. The column of smoke from the chimney made the cabin seem forlorn rather than inviting, as it had when he'd first popped his eyes above the side of the wagon yesterday.

"He's got a meaner bark than a bite," Wicasha said when Tory stepped inside the barn. "Don't feel badly about it."

"Would it be possible for you to give me a ride into Spiketrout?" Tory asked, unconcerned if he sounded blue. "Franklin said you can use the wagon."

Wicasha poised the curry brush over the gelding's mane and studied Tory a moment. With a chuckle, he continued brushing. "Sure, I'll give you a lift," he said.

"I'll give him a ride." Tory and Wicasha turned to Franklin standing in the doorway. "As long as you stick around here, Wicasha, and keep an eye on things. I decided I got some business in Spiketrout."

Tory's heart leaped. He relished the idea of spending added time with Franklin.


TORY had little to talk about with Franklin during the drive into Spiketrout. He already knew a great deal about Franklin, from his boyhood in eastern Tennessee to his stint in the Civil War. He had reread the letters detailing Franklin's world so many times he was certain he could recite them word for word, much like his favorite Walt Whitman poems. Some aspects of his life he wouldn't mind hearing firsthand, like how he'd first chanced upon his homestead and came to name it Moonlight Gulch.

Unlike the last time Tory had ridden the trail, he could enjoy the idyllic surroundings without sweating under heavy burlap. The more he saw of Franklin's home, the more he envied him. The richness of the forest seemed to echo off the mountains, as if the color exuded a life of its own, like the birds, trees, and flowers. Sun fell from the heavy branches like a shower of sparkling light. A dreamlike haze followed them along every bend and dip of the trail. Osprey called from overhead. Ravens seemed to pursue them from tree branch to tree branch. Porcupines and mule deer foraged on the forest's floor.

As they drove along the gulch, Tory watched Franklin from the corner of his eye. Tory marveled how his left arm, lightning-fast at times, did the work of two. Franklin maneuvered his stump like a counterbalance, sometimes using it like a blunt tool, expertly whipping it about.

Tory couldn't help but mention a thought that came to mind, a thought that he had once written in one of his letters, but then he had torn it to pieces, judging it too insensitive. Now, witnessing how comfortable Franklin was with his affliction, Tory saw no reason to hold back.

"They have attachments for people who've lost arms and legs," he said.

Franklin did not answer at first, his eyes fixed on the uneven trail. "I'm aware of those things."

"Why don't you get one?"

"I got one. It's in my war trunk back at the cabin. Army issued it to me after the war."

"Why don't you use it?"

"Gets in the way. I used to wear it when I went into town, mostly for appearances. But then I figured, who am I trying to impress in Spiketrout? There ain't no ladies there worth getting cleaned up for."

Tory reflected. He brooded over his alias, "Torsten P." Would the guilt ever quit biting him?

Lulu led them past the waterfall and around the first major bend. She snorted, flicking her ears at the flies gathering around her eyes. Golden sunrays draped from the aspen branches, their leaves shimmering like delicate hands carved from emerald stone.

"What are your plans in Spiketrout?" Franklin asked.

Tory hadn't really considered his plans. He had but one goal when he journeyed to the Black Hills, and that was to meet his long-time correspondent, Franklin Ausmus. He had accomplished that. He sat next to him in his wagon, a mere arm's length away.

"I'm really unsure," Tory said. "I suppose I'll look for work if I decide to stay."

"What did you do back in Chicago?"

"I helped in my parents' bakery. We also ran a boarding house."

"Explains your fine cooking."

Tory flushed. "Thank you. Do you think I might find something in town?"

"There're about three jobs in Spiketrout," Franklin said with a sarcastic inflection. "Prostitute. Gambler. Prospector. Some folks do all three. Somehow I can't picture you doing any of them."

"There's an inn in town. I could work there."

"That ain't really an inn," Franklin said. "Sure, they got rooms and a kitchen. But the Gold Dust is in business for one thing."

"Not much else I can do," Tory said, his head low, "other than go back to Chicago. I guess I really am nothing but a tourist."

"I know the lady who runs the Gold Dust," Franklin said, brightening his voice. "Madame Lafourchette. That's the name she goes by. Never learned her real name. Folks say she's from Poland, or her parents are. She's a good woman as far as they go around here, despite her keeping a stable of girls. She treats them good and fair. She doesn't take bark or bite from the men who carouse the place. She'd probably make a better boss than most in Spiketrout. I'll put a good word in for you, if you choose to stay, that is."

"That will be kind of you. Does she need any help?"

Franklin shrugged with a downturn of his mouth. "People in Spiketrout come and go, so she just might need someone in the kitchen."

The gulch opened into a dell bursting with purple and yellow wildflowers. Butterflies rested on golden alfalfa in grassy, sun-soaked gullies. A brown rabbit rustled in the duff, then scurried off once Lulu neared.

"I can understand why you've lived here for so long," Tory said. "It's beautiful, more than I imagined."

"What makes you think I been here long?"

"Well, by the look of your homestead, it's clear you've settled for quite some time." Tory had to exercise discretion. He remembered Franklin's earnest descriptions of his cherished parcel of earth. To make it seem he was unfamiliar, he asked Franklin how he had come upon it. He wanted to hear the story from his own mouth, to devour personally the passion in his voice.

"It's a long story," Franklin said. But he went ahead anyhow of how he'd wandered the Hills for weeks searching for the perfect tract of land to call home, until finally stumbling upon the moonlit gulch at the end of an old Indian trail. "That's when I knew I was home," Franklin said, grinning at the trees. "I decided to call my homestead Moonlight Gulch because of the moonlight dancing off the creek."

Tory, his hands balled in his lap, gazed at Franklin's profile while he described how he had found his homestead. His button nose, simple and soft, elicited a sweet contrast to his rugged features. His bushy horseshoe mustache seemed to swallow the entire lower half of his tanned face. The green fire in his eyes while he recounted his first encounter with his land nearly forced Tory to tears. He was grateful to share that moment in time with Franklin, no matter how brief.

They chatted about nature and life on the homestead the rest of the way into Spiketrout. Shortly the trail opened and Franklin steered Lulu onto dusty Main Street and parked next to the jailhouse. He set the brake, jumped out, and hitched Lulu to a post. Tory grabbed his satchel and followed.

"Make sure if you decide to nap in someone's wagon, you figure out who owns it first," Franklin told him. "They might not be so kindhearted."

"I'll remember that." Tory said, smiling. "You've been very generous. Thank you for everything."

"I got some things to talk over with the marshal," Franklin said. "If you choose to stay, you let Madame Lafourchette know I give you a good word."

Tory stared toward the Gold Dust Inn. His heart drummed against his chest. Franklin turned toward the jailhouse. Tory called after him.

"Do you come into town often?" he asked.

Spinning around on his boot heels, Franklin peered at him from under his Stetson. "I try to stay away as much as possible. I come in for my barbering, bartering and selling things, getting my mail. Usually not more than twice a month in the warm months. Why do you ask?"

"Just curious."

Franklin grunted and went about his business. Tory watched him disappear into the jailhouse. Clutching his bag, he inhaled and faced Madame Lafourchette's inn. Even at such an early hour, rollicking player piano music from inside seeped onto the street.

Had his traveling so far for a mere one-night stay with Franklin Ausmus been worth it? No, he decided with certainty. He wanted more. What waited for him back in Chicago other than the wrath of his parents and the miserable life of a lonely bachelor? He had unfinished business in Spiketrout. Franklin was still close by. An unquenched need nagged Tory. He couldn't leave. Not yet. Franklin had said he ventured into town a few times a month. Tory sighed. He supposed seeing him every few weeks was better than nothing.

Squaring his shoulders, he marched across the street. Three men who appeared to be arguing exited the inn as he approached the boardwalk. Two stumbled backward, as if inebriated. The other grabbed them by their shirts and crammed their noses within inches of his. One of the men spit tobacco juice into his assailant's face. The man was about to slug him when a fourth man came out of the inn and struck him on the back of his head with a newel post. He staggered back, releasing the other two. His face turned as red as a tomato and, he jerked around with a hauled-back fist, as if he were about to pitch a baseball, and cuffed the fourth man in the mouth. Blood and tobacco juice splattered over their shirts.

The other two seized the opportunity to jump the third man. A tangle of arms and legs spiraled in every direction. Madame Lafourchette rushed out of the inn with her parasol swinging. Using curses Tory had only heard from the mouths of drunken teamsters, she batted and kicked and punched.

"Get away from my inn, you deadbeats," she hollered. "Don't come back, you hear?"

One of the fighting men took a blow that knocked him into the street. Tory jumped sideways out of his trajectory. Shaking himself, the man scrambled to his feet and rejoined the fight.

"Stop that! Stop that!" Madame Lafourchette lurched for one of the men and dragged him clear down the boardwalk to the intersection.

She pushed him onto all fours and, with her steeple boot, kicked him into the street. He rubbed his rump and ran hollering toward the jailhouse.

Madame Lafourchette returned to the center of the ruckus and began striking the men in the head and shoulders with her parasol. Ear-curdling expletives spewed from between her cherry-red lips. More men poured out from the inn and joined the brawl. Tory was unable to count how many. Worried for his safety, he ducked behind a horse hitched to a wagon, but a man reeking of rum and urine came after him. Wobbly and bloodied, the man grabbed Tory by his jacket collar and thrust a fist into Tory's nose. Stunned, Tory fell backward into the horse. His satchel and derby slid under the wagon.

The man lunged for Tory again, but Tory rolled from his grasp just in time. The squealing horse landed a front hoof on the man's stomach. Growling in pain, the man stumbled blindly toward the boardwalk, where a boot met his forehead. He fell back onto the street and lay sprawled, motionless.

Numbing paralysis spread from Tory's nose to his ears. He checked for blood, but his fingertips came away clean. A heavy swirl of jasmine perfume revived Tory and made him cough. Leaning on his elbows, he watched in a daze as Madame Lafourchette crouched down to inspect him.

"You all right, honey?"

"Yes, I'm all right." Tory rubbed his nose.

The shouting increased. Madame Lafourchette wielded her parasol and let loose a new string of expletives in the faces of the brawlers. Tory heard Franklin's voice coming from down the street. He twisted around and saw him racing up the boardwalk with another lanky fellow. Franklin stopped before the spiral of fighters and glanced down at Tory. A fierce grimace ironed the fine lines around his eyes. Jumping into the fray, he became a one-armed fighting machine. He used his legs like a donkey. Tory wanted to race in and help, but he knew he was useless.

Madame Lafourchette's painted fingernails dug into the cheek of one of Franklin's muggers. Franklin kicked the man, and he doubled over. Franklin's companion (Tory noticed his marshal badge glinting in the sunlight) hauled two fighters upright by their collars, their feet dangling. The two men swung and kicked wildly at the air.

The marshal's robust voice crested above the shouts and curses. One by one, the men calmed. Madame Lafourchette held one man against the wall with her bustle. Most of the men were hunched over, clutching onto the side of the building, or lay flaccid on the ground.

"Who started all this nonsense?" the marshal demanded. The accusations began to fly as wildly as the fists had. The marshal insisted on quiet. "Help me with these roustabouts," he told a few of the men who were minding their own businesses. "Come on. We'll settle this back at the jailhouse."

"Don't let them come back here, Marshal," Madame Lafourchette hollered after them as he herded the men down the street.

Once they were corralled into the jailhouse, Franklin dropped to a squat by Tory's head. "Are you all right?"

"It's nothing, really," Tory said, touching his nose. "Someone just bruised my nose, that's all. It's odd. No one has ever struck me before."

Twirling her parasol, Madame Lafourchette looked down at them from the boardwalk. The exertion from the brawl had left the powder on her face splotchy, and the raspberry paint on her cheeks had bled. "I wish the gold hadn't dried up," she said, shaking her head. "When they had dust to spend, they weren't so quick to fighting. Now they all are like children without candy, always looking for a chance to throw a fit. It's a vicious circle, ain't it?"

Franklin glanced at her. "You might think about getting yourself some protection."

"Who do you think half those men were?" She guffawed and, swinging her wide hips, sauntered back into her establishment with the swirling parasol capturing the sunlight.

Franklin reached a hand to Tory and helped him to his feet, the second time in less than twenty-four hours he had done so. "You didn't get a job there yet, did you?"

"No, I never had a chance to go inside." Tory brushed the dirt from his clothes.

"I don't see you working at a place like that. And there's really nothing else left in town. You still wanting to stay?"

"I kinda had my mind set on it," Tory said.

Franklin shook his head and made a strange elongated grunt that came from the back of his throat. "Come on," he said, rolling his green eyes. "You best come back with me. I reckon I can put you to use on the homestead somehow. I can always use an extra hand."

Tory nearly toppled back to the ground. "You mean it?"

Franklin grabbed for Tory's bag and derby from under the wagon. He handed the derby to Tory. Scrunching his mustache at the satchel in his hand, he asked him, "What else you got in here?"

"Just some clothes, a few personal items."

"Fancy city clothes like you got on?"

Tory scanned the length of his body from his congress boots to his pinstripe pants, sack coat, tweed vest, and silk cravat, all disheveled and covered in dust and splatters of what looked like blood. "Yes," he said, his cheeks heating. "My clothes are about all the same."

"You best get something more suitable for ranch work. That fancy derby won't do you much good out in the field, either. You got money?"

Tory felt for the purse containing his last three hundred dollars in his breast pocket. Sighing with relief, he said, "Yes, I have money."

"Let's head over to the mercantile, then."

Half an hour later, they were riding back to Moonlight Gulch with Tory's new sturdy boots, wool socks, two pair of breeches, three flannel shirts, and an authentic rawhide Stetson rocking in the back inside brown paper. Franklin went down a list of what Tory should expect working on a subsistent homestead.

"This ain't Chicago with all your fancy things. No ice boxes, no electricity at Moonlight Gulch. And that's how I like it."

"I understand," Tory said, eager to prove himself to Franklin. "And I can sleep in the barn. I don't want to be a nuisance."

"Too late for that," Franklin said. "You can sleep on the cot in the cabin like before. No point letting you freeze. It gets cold at night in the mountains. You won't be any good to me if you're sick with pneumonia or dead."

And for the three dollars a week, plus room and board, that Franklin had said he would pay him in wages, Tory figured that was good enough. He tried his best to keep from grinning all the way back to Moonlight Gulch.

Seemed his trip to the Black Hills wasn't for naught, after all.

# CHAPTER FIFTEEN

THE happiest days of Tory's life passed at Moonlight Gulch. Though Franklin had kept his promise to work him hard, his first week by his side flowed as easily as the creek running through Franklin's land. He learned to slop the hogs and milk a cow, pump water into the sluice to water the crops, and snatch an egg from under a hen without getting pecked. Running a homestead, Tory discovered, was a never-ending task, much more tedious than the running of a boarding house and bakery. Yet Tory would not have traded his experiences for all the free time in the world.

The hardest task was censoring what he said around Franklin. He knew Franklin far better than Franklin would understand. The few times he had slipped, revealing information only Franklin would know, he wiggled his way out by blaming his knowledge on Wicasha, who popped in for occasional visits. Franklin seemed to accept Tory's explanations.

He felt bad for deceiving Franklin. He tried to atone by working extra hard. Franklin seemed to appreciate his diligence. Tory could not deny a genuine affection had developed between them. Franklin had taken a liking to him, he was certain.

That became clear one evening a week after Tory had first arrived at the homestead. They were idling in domestic comfort, away from the heat of the cabin while supper roasted in the oven, after toiling in the field side by side all day. Granite peaks were silhouetted against the indigo sky. The scent of wild honeysuckle wafted down from the forested ridges like sweet breath. By the added light of a torch, Tory rolled dough for kanelbulle at the plank table while Franklin, leaning against a tree stump, sewed a buckskin jacket. It was then that Franklin finally revealed his loneliness, previously disclosed only in his letters.

"It's nice to have someone around to talk with," he confessed. Tory detected a pink glow on his tanned face.

"That's understandable," Tory said in a casual tone. "You wouldn't be human if you didn't want company now and then."

"Wicasha's a good friend to have," Franklin went on, "but we have our separate lives."

Tory genuinely wanted to know more about Wicasha. Franklin had never gone into detail about the Lakota's life in any of his letters—at least not before Postman Persson began burning them.

"What's Wicasha's story?" Tory asked, lifting his eyes from the cinnamon rolls only long enough to gauge whether Franklin was ready to talk about him.

Franklin rested his sewing in his lap. Gazing at the lofty peaks, he seemed to reflect. "He's an outcast from his band," he said, turning back to his buckskin jacket. "He helped the cavalry scout out the Sioux back in the '70s."

"I thought he *was* Sioux?"

"He is. A Lakota, part of the Sioux Nation."

Tory's hands stiffened. "Then how did he come to fight against his own people?"

"It's a long story," Franklin said, "one even I don't fully know. But I do know Wicasha supported the United States like the Crow did."

"That must've been difficult for him."

"I reckon he's got his reasons. He's a good man. That's all that matters to me. What he did or why, that's all in the past. He's a decorated war veteran, even traveled to Washington to get a medal."

"No kidding?"

Franklin recounted how Wicasha had led scouting missions into Sioux land with thousands of Custer's troops at his back. He and other Crow soldiers easily blended into the natural surroundings and could track warrior bands with little detection. He was fluent in French, the language he learned from his father, who had been taught it as a boy by French fur traders, which enhanced his handiness in dealing with Sioux resisters. His understanding of the quirks of the Black Hills had earned him respect from soldiers and commanders alike.

The Lakota outcast lived deeper in the Hills than Franklin, inaccessible by wagon or even most animal stock. He had found the spot soon after he and Franklin had left the quartz mine, where they had become fast friends. He came across Franklin's homestead while wandering the Hills in search of what he had said was "Wakan Tanka"—God. Soon after, he settled nearby, beyond the hillocks. Wicasha was known by his fellow Lakota as "Chachola"—without friends.

Franklin called him by the basic Lakota word Wicasha, which simply meant "brave man."

"I guess it makes sense why you two would be friends," Tory said. "You're both decorated veterans and you both live apart from others."

Franklin smiled into the dancing torchlight. Chatter from the wrens and finches filled the short silence. "I guess you're right about that," he said.

"Weren't you afraid of any of the other Indians when you first moved out here?" Tory said. "They all can't be friendly like Wicasha."

"I never had much trouble with them." Franklin shook his head. "The federal government allotted the Black Hills to the local Sioux by treaty, but by the time I moved in, the settlers and gold prospectors had forced most of them out."

Gold. Seemed one couldn't talk about the Black Hills without mentioning gold. Tory knew Franklin sat on a fortune of it, yet he refrained from prospecting. Ever since reading his letter when Franklin had mentioned his troubles with Bilodeaux, Tory had wondered why.

"Did you ever consider prospecting?" he asked.

"I have no need for gold." Franklin's shoulders tightened as he worked the needle and thread with his one hand while balancing the jacket on his knees. "The boom didn't come until a few years after I got here. Custer and his men found the easy-gotten gold in the streams in Deadwood Gulch. When news broke out the gold was coming out of streams like bonytail biting on fishing hooks, the bevy marched in. Towns sprung up overnight. People like things that come simple and painless. I found out the easier things come, the greedier people get."

"You mean like that Frenchman?" Tory said, spreading cinnamon butter over the dough with a spatula while waving away two black flies.

"He's French Canadian. And yes, like him. He's been scheming to get his hands on whatever streams and creeks in the Hills haven't been tapped of gold. Dams the streams, takes in so much gold you'd think he'd be happy with what he got. But he wants more. Says it's for the good of the community, but he always pockets for himself what he gets."

"Won't the marshal help you?"

"Reinhardt's no use to me. He's more concerned about losing his hair than holding up the law. Besides, Bilodeaux's got him in his hip pocket."

Tory had started to take a liking to Franklin's southern twang. It sang to him like the rustle of the leaves in the lush forest. "Did you ever think about prospecting the gold anyway?" Tory asked.

"Nope, never," Franklin said, a frown stretching his mustache. "Nature's given me all I need right here without assaulting her for gold. I seen it turn decent men into scoundrels overnight. I'm comfortable with the way things are. I plan on dying here in my old age." He lowered his head. "Was planning on marrying, but I guess that won't be happening."

Tory grimaced. He still could not get past having caused Franklin emotional pain. If only he could atone for misleading Franklin. What would Franklin do if Tory ever revealed his true identity? He gazed toward the murky mountain peaks where the granite rock face edged closest to the creek. Dark clouds eased over the Hills from the west and obscured many of the higher peaks. A sign to keep his mouth shut, Tory figured. Franklin Ausmus would probably kill him if he ever learned the truth.

"What domestic bliss."

Tory and Franklin looked over to see Wicasha strolling toward the cabin. He was wearing that same odd grin on his face that Tory had noticed the past week. Apparently Franklin had taken note of it too.

"What's with you, Wicasha? You been smiling like a damn fool lately."

Wicasha snorted through his broad nose. "I'm not the one who's been smiling like a fool."

The silence that followed forced Tory to think. Franklin had been smiling a lot lately. He had no idea if Franklin smiled regularly, but he speculated it did not come easy to him. Unlike most of the weathered men of the Black Hills (many with brown-and-white road maps for faces), Franklin's face was devoid of laugh lines.

Tory wondered if Franklin enjoyed his new company more than he let on. Wicasha had a way of forcing issues to the surface. Tory was growing to like him more and more.

"I haven't been smiling any," Franklin said, turning his attention back to his sewing. "You come here just to make stupid comments?"

"No, I'm here like always to keep you company, but I see you don't need me for that much anymore."

Tory had never considered that he might have taken Wicasha's place. The two frontiersmen lived as loners and had become each other's only steady companion. He realized the Indian had visited less and less. He wanted to make it up to Wicasha. When Wicasha turned to leave, Tory called for him. Wicasha gazed at him, the torchlight throwing dark shadows around his eyes and mouth.

"Why don't you stay for supper?" Tory said. "There's a venison roast in the oven with potatoes and carrots and some wild mushrooms I found in the woods. And I'm making kanelbulle for dessert."

"You're making what?"

"Kanelbulle. Swedish cinnamon rolls."

Wicasha's taut mouth formed into a soft grin. He sat down next to Tory and watched him cut the rolled dough into two-inch portions.

"Swedish, huh?" he said, eyes wide.

"Ja," Tory said, chuckling. "Just like my pappa makes."

# CHAPTER
# SIXTEEN

"WOO-HOO!"

Wicasha dove into the creek pool with a splash, followed by Franklin. Small waves broke against the bank, where Tory stood looking on, unsure whether he should undress and join them. He desperately needed a bath. When he'd mentioned he was going to the creek to "freshen up" before starting supper, he hadn't expected Franklin to declare, "A peach of an idea," and dash to the natural pool along with Wicasha before Tory even had a chance to lift his feet.

Hidden behind a cluster of alder bushes, he gaped at Franklin and Wicasha's clothes strewn in a trail. Modesty most often circumvented Tory, but he felt bashful in front of Franklin. Realizing he had no way of avoiding it, he kicked off his boots, slipped off his work clothes and undergarments, and carefully draped them over a bush, all while keeping a close eye on Franklin and Wicasha. When their backs were turned, he ran for the pool and jumped in. Surfacing, he gulped a mouthful of air.

Several yards away, Franklin and Wicasha splashed and frolicked. The sun sparkled off the spraying water like it was quartz. Franklin ran naked to the cabin and returned a moment later, brandishing what looked like a cake of lye soap. Knee-deep in the creek, Franklin rubbed his body clean with the soap, stretching his legs, limber as a housecat with one arm. Within minutes, the water around his knees bubbled with soapy froth.

Tory could hardly peel his eyes off Franklin's glistening, sinewy body. Veins twined around the muscles on his forearm and calves. Water dripped from his horseshoe mustache and down his hardened chest and stomach. It was the first time Tory had seen his stump in the flesh, outside of a sleeve. He moved it as naturally as his left arm.

Sitting on a smoothed granite rock, Wicasha shouted for the soap. Franklin tossed it to him. Wicasha's thighs bulged as thick as pine trunks. But it was Franklin who captivated him. The missing arm failed to detract from his handsome looks. In a way, it accentuated his ruggedness. He had been wounded in battle, a brave warrior, with the stump more a testament to his courage than any government-issued ribbon or medal.

Tory tried to avert his eyes. Franklin dove into the pool to rinse off the lather. He surfaced, chuckling and guffawing, and blew the remaining bubbles toward the cornflower-blue sky. The smell of the lye, thick, like Tory's mother's chicken gravy, tickled Tory's nose.

Wicasha tossed the cake to Tory. He snatched it as it pierced the surface. A sting of lye splashed into his eye. With cupped hands, he rinsed water over his face until he could squint toward the sun. As he acclimated to the men's nudity, he felt less conspicuous about his own. He waded to the bank, where the water sloshed against his ankles, and lathered the cake over his body. He passed the cake from one slippery hand to the next. He took care to scrub between his toes and legs, under his arms, and to lather his hair.

He left the cake on the bank and dove deep to let the soap run off his body. Many feet below the creek pool's surface, the water turned cold. He opened his eyes and explored the deep pool formed by massive granite boulders that trapped the flow of the creek. He deduced the vortex created by the gentle run of the creek had, over time, trapped the gold deposits in the natural pool that everyone was after.

He let his fingers run along the sandy bottom. Tory had no idea what gold looked like in natural form. He sifted more of the silky sediment, uncertain. The sun penetrated the shallow areas and highlighted yellow flecks and rocks he speculated might be gold. Tory had never cared for gold or riches, anyway. He let the sand drift between his fingers and then he rushed to the surface.

He hoisted himself onto one of the smaller granite rocks and dangled his feet in the water, his back to the men. From the corner of his eye, he thought he caught Franklin and Wicasha staring at him. But he no longer cared. The longer he stayed in the creek, the more natural his nudity seemed. Sunrays warmed his shoulders and back. Minnows nibbled on his toes.

Franklin swam over to the far bank as effortlessly as if he had two arms. He reached for a low-hanging branch of a mulberry tree and pulled off ripened berries. "Good," he said, eating a handful. Tory and Wicasha swam over. The mulberries left a sour taste on Tory's tongue, but were still good enough to eat mouthfuls.

Tory floated on his back, the sun bright and warm on his face and belly. The sour taste of the mulberries lingered on his lips. He licked his fingertips with loud sucking sounds.

Suddenly, he felt himself heaved into the air and flying across the pool. He hit the water's surface and struggled to regain orientation. Grasping for air, he coughed water and gazed around, dumbstruck. Wicasha and Franklin were laughing good-naturedly. Franklin fingered Wicasha as the culprit. The Lakota shouted in some Indian language and slapped the water as he laughed.

Frank patted the man's back and laughed from deep in his gut. "I don't find honest bucks like him too often. Watch out you don't chuck him onto a rock and split his head open."

"He's sturdy for a city boy," Wicasha said. "Take more than me to hurt him."

His face heating, Tory joined their laughter. But he kept his distance for a good few minutes until his excitement eased.

"Hey, look." Tory, eager to distract their attention, pointed down the creek about fifty yards, where a yearling lapped water.

The men, hunkered down to their necks, followed his gaze.

"Hope he grows big and strong to make me a nice stew and good sturdy outfit someday," Franklin said, chortling.

The yearling, noticing the men, froze a moment, then, with lightning-fast speed, darted into the grove of ponderosa pine. The yearling's exit seemed to signify for Franklin that he too needed to get back to business. With one final dunk of his head, he strolled out of the pool like Poseidon from the sea, his long sleek hair clinging to his strong back. Rivulets flowing down to the small of his back and over his rump sent trembles through Tory. Franklin's lanky body bent gracefully as he scooped up his clothes and headed for the cabin.

"I think I'll stay in the water a while longer," Tory told Wicasha, who by that time had followed Franklin out of the water and was standing on the bank, clutching his clothes. Tory was unsure what to make of the glance the naked Lakota shot him from over his broad shoulder when he turned to leave. Why did he always have that odd grin on his face? Wicasha's shoulders shook as he made his way to the cabin.


FLAMES from the bonfire reached near to the stars. Tory watched, amused, as Wicasha played "Old Black Joe" on harmonica with startling skill and Franklin danced around the fire. Tory kept his distance. The huge bonfire with lashing flames and loud snaps frightened him. He cowered in a chair by the front door. Away from the strong blaze, he studied the flames play off Franklin's shirtless and perspiring torso. He seemed surreal in the conflagration. The music took Tory, and before he had even a chance to ponder, he was clapping his hands and stomping his feet in front of his chair. Franklin approached him. Embarrassed, Tory stopped, breathless.

"Why aren't you stomping with us by the fire?" Franklin asked.

"It's a bit hot," Tory said.

"Nothing like working up a good sweat," Franklin said.

"Yes, but I think I'll just stay here where it's cooler."

"You have a fear of fire?"

Was he that easy to read? He worried he might have mentioned his fear of fire in one of his letters to Franklin, but he failed to recall. He did not want any more coincidences between him and "Torsten." Grateful for the darkness that concealed the flush that burned his cheeks, he said, "I suppose I'd rather live without a fire so big."

Franklin chuckled. "All right, then." And he went back to join Wicasha.

Wicasha continued blowing on the harmonica while he and Franklin cavorted around the fire. "Little Brown Jug" flowed from Wicasha's broad lips as easily as the breeze that kissed the red-hot flames. Tory again stomped his foot and clapped his hands to the quick rounded rhythm. Even the hogs seemed to enjoy themselves. He heard them snorting and rustling about their pen with extra volume.

Music and laughter flowed for another hour until the waxing moon rolled above the eastern peaks and the stars dimmed. Franklin, exhausted, slumped near Tory against a tree stump.

"I'm plum tuckered out," he said. "You played those reeds extra nice tonight, Wicasha."

"You look rode hard." Wicasha stuffed the harmonica in his pocket and chuckled.

"I'll be sleeping as sound as a bear in January tonight. Almost feel like going for another dip."

"I think I'll head back," Wicasha said. "You boys have a good night."

Wicasha's departure left a piercing quiet over the gulch. Franklin suggested they go for one more quick swim to wash off the sweat. Half an hour later, dried and dressed in clean undergarments, Tory and Franklin rested by the creek with the moon hanging directly above.

"Nice this time of year, isn't it?" Franklin said, his voice low and deferential. "The creek's a perfect temperature; the air is soft."

"Sure is nice," Tory said.

"Always liked laying here at night, with the moon reflecting off the creek, the fish jumping," Franklin said. "I remember first time I laid here and heard the trout snapping. I went down to check, and one jumped so high it bit me on the nose." He chuckled. "Then I thought, maybe he was giving me a kiss, welcoming me home."

"Yes, I remember."

"You remember?" Franklin shot him an inquisitive look. "How do you remember?"

Tory's breathing stopped. He had to watch himself. Relaxing moments like this often knocked him off his guard. He'd remembered reading one of Franklin's letters in which he'd written about the trout kissing him "like a long-lost cousin."

"You been talking with Wicasha again," Franklin said, yet his tone was casual, unconcerned. He fixed his gaze on the moon's gray light slicing through the canopy of the trees.

"Oh, yes." Tory exhaled, relieved. "He tells me many things about your life here, like how once that fish kissed your nose."

The ensuing silence soothed Tory's nerves. The gentle ping of the running creek made him smile. Both stared toward the moon. No awkwardness lingered in the stillness. They were now at that junction in their relationship when quiet between friends failed to bother them, Tory was certain.

"Autumn will be here soon." Franklin's husky voice reached Tory's ears as exquisitely as the slow brush of the breeze. "I can hear it coming."

"You can hear the arrival of autumn?"

"Listen closely."

Tory cocked his head upward, trying to pick up on Franklin's meaning. Night birds sang as usual; the leaves rattled in the breezes coming off the mountains; the creek gurgled slowly; some hidden rodents foraged under the duff. He thought he heard even the "kissing trout" jumping for insects. All typical sounds for Moonlight Gulch. Then, yes, he was certain. He could hear it.

"I think I know what you mean," he said, lifting his head higher. "The sounds, they seem… crisper. The leaves rattle more pronounced in the breeze, as if they're harder, drying up. And the rodents are foraging more earnestly, as if stockpiling for winter."

"Yes, exactly," Franklin said with a merry lilt to his voice. "You do hear it, then."

Proud of himself, Tory rested his head back against the soft pine-covered earth. A few more minutes of silence had passed when one of Walt Whitman's poems floated through Tory's mind as softly as the curl of the thin black cloud above him.

"The sounds of autumn remind me of a poem by Walt Whitman," Tory said. "You like Walt Whitman?"

Franklin tittered. "Sure I like Walt. Even met him once."

Tory propped himself up on his elbow and peered at Franklin under the blue mist of the moon. He had never mentioned that in any of his letters—at least not the ones Tory had received. "You did? When?"

"During the war. In a veteran's hospital in Maryland. When I lost my arm, he was there helping care for the injured. I liked him. Nice old guy."

"He's my favorite poet," Tory said, gazing into the star-loaded sky.

"I don't reckon I got a favorite poet," Franklin said, "but there's some in the Black Hills, although probably not of Whitman's caliber. They're just cowboy poets."

"I like cowboy poets," Tory said, his voice high with sincerity. "Whitman is a cowboy poet of sorts. Would you like to hear one of my favorite poems of his?"

"Sure. Go ahead."

With the back of his head resting on his woven fingers, he gazed at the expanse of the Milky Way and recited word for word as best he could a poem he'd carried in his memory from the first time he'd read it, ending with:

*In the stillness in the autumn moonbeams his face was*
*inclined toward me,*
*And his arm lay lightly around my breast.*
*And that night I was happy.*

Only in the thick silence of night and heavy breath that followed his reciting of the poem did Tory fear he had crossed a line with Franklin. Where was he? So far away he seemed, with his face still turned toward the starry sky. Franklin did not stir from his supine position. The cool air from the mountains swept the hair from his forehead. The moon, the same moon described by Whitman, reflected in his green eyes. What must he be thinking? Had Tory's reciting of the poem unsettled him?

Finally, Franklin, with a slow and deliberate movement, turned his head toward Tory. "That's perfect," he said in a near-whisper. "How fitting for where we are right now."

"Yes, I know." Tory swallowed, unable to meet his glowing eyes. "I thought it was too."

Franklin turned back to the moon and stars. "Very romantic."

Tory let the silence linger a moment, then he said, matching Franklin's reverential tone, "Do you like romantic things, Franklin?"

"Yes," he said matter-of-factly. "I do like romantic things. You wouldn't believe it by looking at me, but I do have a bit of a sentimental poet in me, I reckon."

Of course Tory knew that Franklin had a poet inside him. He had perceived it from the first time he'd read his advertisement in *Matrimonial News*. Franklin was more than "softhearted." He exhibited the kind of strength that came only from gentleness. Tender masculinity pulsed in his veins and compacted in his bones. Like a shepherd who watches over his flock with stalwart, brutish conviction, yet capable of showing the most doting affection. That was all inside Franklin Ausmus.

A shudder rushed through Tory's limbs. Franklin's body, so close, so warm, so within hand's reach, like the lover in Whitman's poem, infused him with a quaking happiness that he had not known since Joseph had leaned in to kiss him for the first time.

But wasn't it all a mere quixotic fantasy? Franklin was as untouchable, as unreachable, as the stars above them. Moisture evaporated from Tory's mouth. He raised his head off his hands to swallow. With the sudden rush of a breeze off the mountains, a pang of regret swept over him.

# Chapter
# SEVENTEEN

FRANKLIN was milking the dairy cow when he heard Tory's shouts. Nearly upsetting the bucket, he raced from the barn. Outside, he twisted around to locate the direction of the commotion.

Another holler. Tory was calling for help. Franklin followed his screams into a shallow ravine alongside the Spiketrout trail. He found Tory staring down at something, his expression one of disbelief.

"What is it?" Franklin scurried down the slope to get a closer look. Halting behind Tory, he nearly gasped. The body of the old-timer Wicasha had caught panning for gold in the creek lay face up, a bullet hole right in between his shaggy silver eyebrows.

"It's that old man," Tory said. "I was searching for mushrooms and berries when I found him. What do you think happened?"

Franklin scouted around the area. Fallen leaves and twigs crunched and snapped under his boots. He noticed a sharp glint in the duff from the sun cutting through the aspens and pines. Dropping to his haunches, he examined the object closer.

"Anything?" Tory asked.

"Most likely the bullet casing that felled Johnson." Franklin blew off the duff and lifted the casing to eye level. "Looks like it could've come from anybody's rifle around here." He stood and dropped the spent shell in his front shirt pocket. "You hear any shots recently?"

"No." Tory was still gaping at the body of Johnson.

"Neither did I." Franklin stepped onto the trail and peered down as far as he could see. He walked back to Tory's side. "We know he wasn't shot earlier than around five o'clock yesterday. We would've seen him laying here on our way back from town, especially from high atop the wagon. Let me get a look at him."

Franklin squatted by the old man's emaciated body. He rolled him just enough to view the back of his head. No exit wound. Centipedes scurried over his neck. Tory stood and looked away. Franklin placed his palm on Johnson's forehead above the bullet wound. "His body's cooled. Not too stiff. Hard to tell. Could've been shot last night."

"Maybe he was shot somewhere else and dumped here."

Franklin liked Tory's quick thinking. "That could be. And whoever did it wanted us to find the body. He sure didn't try to hide it."

"Why would anyone want to do that?"

Franklin shook his head. "Not sure. You never know what motivates people in the Hills these days. Whoever did him in probably planted the spent shell too, so we'd think he was shot here."

"What should we do with him?"

"We better get the marshal in on this. Not that he's proved much help in the past, but little else we can do."

Those out on Spiketrout's Main Street hooted and hollered when they recognized the body of the old-timer sprawled in the back of Franklin's wagon. They swarmed around when Franklin came to a halt beside the jailhouse. Soon, many from the Gold Dust Inn and the other shops spilled outside to see the commotion.

Henri Bilodeaux, one of the curious bystanders, locked his arms across his chest and looked down his nose at the animated crowd. Franklin noted that he wore a strange, subtle grin, more arrogant than usual.

Marshal Reinhardt, a thin man of about six foot with long blond hair that flowed in thin strings from under his cowboy hat, sauntered down the street from the barbershop, his freshly shaven face glistening in the morning sun. Hands on his hips, he stood next to Bilodeaux, whose eyes came to just above the marshal's badge.

"Bilodeaux's got something planned, I can smell it," Franklin whispered to Tory. "You keep back behind me. Let me do the talking."

"What's all this uproar about?" the marshal boomed in his deep baritone. The scent of menthol rose off his pink face.

With his one arm, Franklin parted the mob. "I found him on my homestead along the trail," he said. "Someone shot him point-blank between the eyes."

The onlookers hissed and howled. Marshal Reinhardt silenced them. Lifting his oval head, he inspected the corpse with a deliberate scan.

Franklin reached into his front shirt pocket. "I found this near his body," he said, dropping the shell into the marshal's large hand. "I figure it's from the rifle that felled him."

Marshal Reinhardt studied the casing a moment, then peered again at the victim. He swatted the old man's boot. "Why would anyone want to beef Johnson?" he said, pocketing the bullet shell. "He's a deadbeat, but nothing worth shooting over."

Bilodeaux stepped forward. "If I might add my two bits worth, Marshal, I might be able to shed light on this. I was out at the Ausmus homestead not two weeks ago when I came across an altercation between Johnson and Frank Ausmus."

"He was on my land panning for gold," Franklin cut in. He could feel the spittle forming on the sides of his mustache, as it usually did when a fury built inside him. "I told him to move off my property."

"I also heard a few threats fly by," Bilodeaux said. "Something along the lines that he would shoot Johnson if he ever caught him on his property again."

"You're twisting his words," Tory shouted. "He was only saying what any man would."

Franklin stymied Tory with his one arm raised in front of him. Without even looking at him, he said, "He's right, Bilodeaux. I have a right to protect my land from intruders and raiders like you. He and Wicasha will back me."

Bilodeaux laughed. "Who will believe anything your Indian friend says, Ausmus? Or that boy, for that matter? Where did you get him, anyway?" Bilodeaux eyed Tory in such a way that Franklin instinctively stepped in between them. He noted that the last time they had met, Bilodeaux had locked threatening eyes on Tory. Like a fox on a rabbit.

"I heard Ausmus caused a disturbance in front of the Gold Dust Inn a few weeks back," a middle-aged man with several days' beard on his greasy face said. "He was fighting some ruffians on behalf of that young fellow there."

"That's right," another said. "I saw it with my own two eyes from the barbershop. He was throwing a hard fist and kicking at a lot of people."

"Every man within fifty yards was in that brawl," Franklin scoffed. "I came in long after it started. I was with the marshal. He'll vouch for me."

"He's right," the marshal said, although Franklin detected a trace of reluctance in his voice.

"Besides," Franklin said, "all that's got nothing to do with this man in my wagon here. Now I brought him into town for you, Marshal, to do your marshaling. If I had murdered him, wouldn't I just as well have buried him and never mention it? It's not like anyone would've missed the old goat."

"He's right," some in the crowd agreed, heads bobbing like ducks.

"He's got a point, Marshal," one said. "If he done beefed Johnson in cold blood, then why did he cart his body to town for all to see?"

"It is part of his scheme," Bilodeaux said. For the first time, Franklin noticed his haughty grin fade. Worry lines appeared on the bridge of his nose.

"The only man with a scheme here, Bilodeaux, is you," Franklin fired back. "Why don't you stop your lying to the marshal and everyone else? We all know you been trying to get your hands on the gold in my creek."

"It's true," the lone woman in the crowd said. The sound of the familiar feminine voice eased Franklin's mind for a moment. It belonged to Madame Lafourchette. Other than Tory, she was the sole reliable bystander in a mob of drunken and capricious gamblers and deadbeats.

"Bilodeaux's been hankering for Frank's placer gold since it started to dry up everywhere else," she went on. The air was thick with her jasmine perfume, a pleasant change from the heavy body odor of the men. "I can see a rat engaging in dirty tricks when I see one."

"You best mind your business." Bilodeaux flashed her a shaky smirk. "A woman who makes her living in your fashion can hardly speak of dirty tricks."

The crowd erupted into laughter. Marshal Reinhardt quieted them with a shout of "hush up" as loud as a shotgun blast. Instantly, everyone quieted, save for a few rolling snickers.

"I think the best thing for me to do is take you into jail, Ausmus. Let's see what a good jury has to say about this. I can't be the sole one who makes that choice in a town of laws."

"You can't do that," Tory cried, stepping forward.

Franklin nudged him aside. "Marshal, if anyone should be locked up and put before a jury, it should be Bilodeaux. You have no right to hold me."

"I have all the rights in the world," the marshal said, yanking on his badge from his starched shirt. "I was given that right by the people of Spiketrout who voted me into office."

Many in the crowd shouted in agreement.

"What about the casing Frank gave you?" Madame Lafourchette said. She edged her way closer to the marshal with the sharp point of her parasol parting the men. "Why would he give you the casing if he shot Johnson himself? That don't make no sense to me, Marshal."

"Yeah," someone in the crowd shouted. "Why would he do that if he beefed Johnson?"

"It is just all part of his ploy to deceive," Bilodeaux said, maintaining his composure, although Franklin noticed him twitching with increasing irritation.

Deputy Ray Ostrem, the marshal's right-hand man, raced down the street with a cloud of dirt on his heels. "What's going on? What's going on?"

"We got ourselves a murder investigation, Ray," the marshal said. He grabbed for Frank's sidearm from his holster and tossed the revolver to Ostrem, who always obeyed Reinhardt like any well-trained hound. "You'll get your gun back once all this settles, Ausmus—if a jury decides such." He handed the deputy the spent shell casing and whispered something into his ear. The deputy nodded and headed back down the street.

When the marshal reached for Franklin with his clawlike hands and began dragging him inside the jailhouse, the crowd whirled in a fury. The marshal raised his lanky arm to hold everyone back. In the midst of the uproar, he commanded that Johnson's body be taken off the wagon and delivered to the town's mortician. "It's starting to cause a stink," he said with a grimace. Five eager men dragged Johnson's withered, limp frame from the wagon with a dull thud once it hit the dusty street.

Franklin resisted the marshal's spindly fingers, but with only one arm, he had little chance against the towering Reinhardt. Tory pushed and even kicked at some of the men who followed them inside. Franklin, for a moment, almost worried more for Tory, who had been left in the hands of the ravenous town folk.

Marshal Reinhardt shoved at the crowd. He ordered Tory to stay put. Franklin was about to shout for him to find Wicasha, but the crowd pushed in on him, and all he could utter was a muffled grunt. The rank bodies of gamblers and drunks overwhelmed him. Never once did the marshal ease his clutches until he tossed Franklin into the jail cell. He slammed the iron bar door shut behind him with a resonant clank and twist of the key.

# CHAPTER
# EIGHTEEN

*I HAVE to get Wicasha*, Tory thought. He jumped onto Franklin's wagon and drove Lulu as fast as he could down the trail to Moonlight Gulch. He hoped Wicasha would be there. He had no idea where on the other side of the hillocks the Lakota lived.

He set the wagon's brake as the sun began to turn away from the homestead. He stabled Lulu in the barn and looked around for Wicasha. Down by the creek, out in the field, in the storage barn, he shouted for Wicasha using the full force of his voice. Wicasha was nowhere. Tory had no choice but to search for him at his campsite. Where else could he be? He knew of no other person who might help Franklin. It seemed the entire town was against him. Gold had turned them all into savages.

On the other side of the first hillock, he shouted for Wicasha. He heard no reply other than his own echo. Yelping osprey and screaming ravens mocked him. He figured there must be a trail from the many times Wicasha had traipsed back and forth between his camp and Franklin's cabin. He followed what he thought was a narrow groove of earth covered in matted grass. Droppings along the trail indicated animals used this path. Certainly Wicasha would too.

Travel was cumbersome. He fell, tripped, scrambled on his hands and knees to hurry himself along. Sweat burned his eyes. He came to a strange series of granite rock spires and columns anchored by gnarly alders. He squeezed through the mazelike impasse and on the other side discovered a muddy meadow. The mudflat stretched to each side of the dense forest. The negligible trail faded completely. Footprints were scattered about the muddy bank, but he had no way of knowing which set to follow or who they belonged to.

He followed along the edge of the mudflat until he came to a large rock outcropping. He scaled to the top and, with his hand shielding his eyes from the sun, scanned the horizon. Down into the rift, he saw no sign of a camp. He wished he'd remembered to grab Franklin's field glasses from the cabin before heading out.

"Wicasha!" Tory's lonely cry repeated off the mountain peaks.

He tried to use common sense to judge which way he should go. The ravens' screaming annoyed him. He was about to curse them in a birch tree when he remembered a war story Wicasha had told him while they had sat outside the cabin one night darning undergarments and whittling spoons from fallen branches. He had mentioned something about following ravens during his days scouting for the U.S. Army. The ravens, he had explained, always congregated wherever they found "action." Indians and early pioneers, he had said, including Lewis and Clark, sometimes used them as guides.

Tory instantly looked to the rowdy ravens with a new sense of respect. He watched them flutter from branch to branch in the birches and aspens. He called to them, encouraging them to fly. He grabbed a handful of pebbles and chucked them at the trees. The ravens screamed and fluttered into the washed-out sky. He followed them, scrambling over hills and down ravines, traipsing over chinks and crevices in the hilly terrain, always working his way toward wherever the ravens flew. If he lost sight of them, he'd listen in for their loud clatter coming from the top reaches of the trees and call to them to move on.

A flock of ravens fluttering in a tree lured him to a steep woody decline. Tory detected a cooling in the temperature near where he stood. Looking down, he saw through the trees a small stream meandering along like a gray ribbon. He knew that Wicasha would have to live near a stream or a creek. No one could survive without water. Leaving behind the ravens, he hiked along the high bank for what seemed miles, ensuring that he paralleled the stream. Finally, in a small valley framed by birch and spruce, he saw a column of smoke drifting from a campfire.

Five minutes later, breathless and perspiring, he found Wicasha cooking over a fire pit. Despite the urgency, he glanced around the camp. Wicasha still lived in a teepee. He had no livestock from what Tory could see. He remembered Franklin telling him that Wicasha kept his mottled gelding at his homestead, where Franklin stabled him at no charge. Wicasha gazed at him. Wrinkles marred his forehead and questions poured from his shiny black eyes. What a sight Tory must look with his muddied clothes, standing in the middle of his secluded camp.

"It's Franklin," Tory said, panting. "The marshal of Spiketrout arrested him... for murdering that old man we found at the homestead. This morning I... I found him dead. We took the body to the marshal, and now he and half the town think Franklin did it."

Wicasha did not waste any time. He doused the fire with a vat of water and, after the hiss of steam, they ran off over the hillocks toward the homestead.

"You best stay put," Wicasha said after he had led his saddled horse from the barn. "I'll go see how things are with Frank, and you look after things here. If you think anyone is coming, grab the guns from the cabin. But let them shoot first before you go and blow their heads off."

"But I want to go with you," Tory said. "Franklin might need me."

"He needs you more here." Wicasha hopped on the horse. "He'll be happy that you're watching the place."

Tory conceded Wicasha was probably right. As his shoulders drooped, he watched Wicasha tug the mottled steed sharply to his right and disappear in a cloud of dust down the trail to Spiketrout.


TORY paced inside the cabin. No matter what chores he did to kill time, he could not focus. He had deserted supper. For whom had he been making it? The cow had not liked Tory's unsteady hands, so milking had proved futile. The hens had not laid any eggs since the morning. A while ago, dejected and antsy, he'd quit tending to the wash. Each time he had set the water to boil outside over the fire, he'd upturned the kettle while flinching back from the flames and hissing steam. Even Wicasha's warning of intruders hadn't caused him much pause. His mind had fastened on one man—Franklin Ausmus.

His pocket watch showed that a good six hours had passed since Wicasha had left for Spiketrout. From a quick glance out the window, he saw that dusk was settling over the Hills. Would Wicasha be able to convince the marshal to free Franklin from jail? How seriously would he and the town folks take an Indian?

He was about to try to eat when he heard galloping hooves approach the cabin. Alert for intruders like Wicasha had warned, he grabbed for a fully loaded rifle and peered out the window. Franklin and Wicasha had given him shooting lessons with rifles and pistols, and he had grown fairly good at knocking the tin cans off the tree stumps from several yards away, but he feared shooting a living creature, even raiders. He sighed in relief when he recognized the stalwart Wicasha trotting in on his gelding. Laying aside the rifle, he rushed outside.

"What's happened?"

"The marshal's determined to keep Frank locked up until they can throw together a jury," Wicasha said after he'd climbed down from the horse. "With the way that town is all heated, there's nothing much to change anyone's mind. The few on his side with reason are outnumbered."

"A trial?" Tory's mouth went dry. "That's ridiculous. They have nothing on him. I wish I had never found that body."

"Don't blame yourself," Wicasha said. "Bilodeaux would've found one way or the other to get Frank blamed for Johnson's murder."

"I've got to go to him," Tory said, his mind numb from the turn of events. "I've got to help Franklin."

Standing by his steed, reins in hand, Wicasha locked black eyes on Tory. "There's nothing you can do for him now," he said. "If you ride into town, all you'll do is stir trouble. That's why I came back. The best thing for now is to let things simmer down. Besides, it's nearly dark, and you can't ride that trail alone at night."

How lightning fast things had turned around. Tory had experienced that horrible jolt when he'd gone to the twelfth floor with Joseph van Werckhoven. One minute they were both eager and full of life, the next, Tory had stood, helpless and numb with disbelief, by the glassless window gazing down at Joseph's sprawled body on Van Buren Street.

He shivered, remembering the decapitated head of the Indian in the drugstore back in Deadwood. The druggist had said a prospector had killed the Indian for trying to take his claim. Would Bilodeaux and the marshal prove equally ruthless and bloodthirsty?

"Why, Wicasha? Why doesn't he just pan the gold?"

In his usual manner, Wicasha waited a good few moments before responding. "He just don't want it," he said with a shrug. "To some people, gold is like whiskey. You either want it or you don't. If you don't, the thirst against it is as powerful as the thirst for it. I've seen people vomit after just one shot of whiskey. Others can't stop even after twenty. I guess Frank is that way with gold. He just doesn't want it. It makes him sick. For Frank, it's probably more the principle of the thing. He's not about to give in to Bilodeaux. Frank can be a stubborn man."

Tory had heard of the expression "drunk with gold." Perhaps there were those who, like Wicasha had said, just couldn't help themselves. Franklin was sturdy enough to resist. The thought made him yearn to help Franklin all the more.

"Has he ever considered charging a fee to let others pan for what gold might be in his creek?" Tory said, desperate for a solution. "Maybe then Bilodeaux and the others would get off his back."

Wicasha shook his head, his black hair brushing against his shoulders. "You got a good business sense, misu, but Franklin doesn't want strangers on his land. He moved here to get away from folks." He seemed to read Tory's body language. "Don't worry," he said with a chuckle. "Frank no longer sees you as an intruder. I think he stopped seeing you that way the day we found you in the barn."

Tory's cheeks heated against the evening chill. "You think so?"

"Yep," Wicasha said. "I think so."

The sun eased below the western peaks and the sky grew dim. Wicasha said he needed to turn in for the night. He agreed to Tory's request that he remain at the homestead but said he wanted to stay outside under the stars. Remembering the sight of Wicasha's camp with its primitive teepee and fire pit, Tory figured the Indian preferred the outdoors.

With Wicasha asleep outside the cabin in a bedroll, Tory chose to sleep on the feather bed rather than on the cot. He felt closer to Franklin that way. He could smell his musk enmeshed in the sheets. He laid awake most the night, staring at the dark ceiling, worried what Franklin must be enduring alone in a dungy jail cell.

# CHAPTER
# NINETEEN

WIND plucked the twigs of the aspens abutting the back of the jailhouse like the strings of a banjo. If Franklin weren't locked in a wretched cell, the cascading sound might have lulled him to sleep. Moonlight sliced through the barred window facing west. Judging from the shadows cast by the iron bars, he reckoned it was near two in the morning.

The town was hardly quiet, however. The Gold Dust Inn pulsed at full swing. He imagined most of the drunkards were already collecting a pool on what his fate would be—hanging or acquittal?

Deputy Ostrem was snoring and wheezing in the front office. If Franklin pressed his forehead tight against the bars, he'd get a glimpse of the deputy's booted feet kicked up on the desk. Sitting upright on the thin cot, he glanced around. Urine and vomit stains covered a large portion of the floor, a clear snub of the bucket in the corner. Former inmates had carved their initials and the dates of their incarcerations above the cot ("JJ, '74"; "CP, '77"; "JHB, '82"), along with meaty expletives expressing discontent with confinement.

He'd kicked off his boots. Might as well get comfortable. He was alone, at least. The other three cots remained unused, the bedcovers pulled clear to where the marshal or Ostrem should've placed pillows. And the second cell remained empty. He wondered when the deputy would be called to load the cells with brawlers following a night of heavy drinking.

He was surprised again that his thoughts should fall back to Tory. He never did get his last name. He wondered what his ancestry was suddenly, as his mind's eye scanned down over Tory's yellow hair and blue eyes and smooth skin that had bronzed rather quickly under the Dakota sun. Hadn't he mentioned something about his Swedish parents? *Must be a lot of Swedes in Chicago*, he mused, remembering with a wince that his former penmate, Torsten, was also of Swedish extraction.

Nearly two weeks had gone by without the image he had created of her pestering him. The same span of time in which Tory had worked as his hired hand. Other than a random pinching memory, he had swept her from his mind. He had expected to hanker for the woman much longer, considering the pain she'd dumped on him. He hadn't even reread any of her letters, not since the day Old Man Johnson had encroached on his land. He again wondered if he had written something awful that had made her stop writing. Maybe she really couldn't handle his having only one arm or that he'd cursed a priest. What did he care?

Tory had kept him busy enough that the Chicago woman rarely entered his mind. The young man was a handful. That was why she had escaped from his thoughts. He was too occupied making sure Tory did what was proper and right on his homestead. He had to teach him from the ground up. Other than the cooking and cleaning, which the young man seemed to take to as naturally as Franklin took to looking after livestock, Tory had no experience running a subsistent homestead.

He had learned fast, Franklin conceded as a grin crept over his face. The stretch of his skin around his horseshoe mustache felt strange while he waited for what could possibly be his execution. Did he like the young man so much that he'd smile just from the thought of him, alone in a gloomy jail cell? He supposed he'd hungered for companionship, more than he'd realized. Yet Wicasha, as much as he valued his friendship, had never been able to alleviate the pressing loneliness the way Tory had.

A fart from the deputy startled him. The man let loose another fart, grunted, and then began snoring anew. Franklin would have found it all funny if his life weren't in the hands of a bunch of drunken deadbeats.

He lay back down on the dingy cot, his ankles crossed, his one hand resting over his belly. His fate had never loomed more uncertain. Even when he had found himself lame in an Army hospital with no arm, his life had never teetered so off balance. Perhaps the ignorance of youth had shielded him then. Encroaching middle age made life's punches more stinging.

The moon must have descended lower over the western peaks, for the blue haze and shadows in his cell faded. Darkness covered him like a wet wool blanket. His isolation took on a new, tangible form.

Alone and weary, he calculated his chances of acquittal. There were some decent citizens in Spiketrout he could count on. The young Lutheran minister, Reverend Jacob Dahlbeck, and his new bride, Matilda, were considerate and mannered. They tried to rehabilitate the whores and drunken gamblers of Spiketrout. Yet they'd never looked down on their charges like some of the other missionaries. They even intervened on Madame Lafourchette's behalf whenever a customer became excessively violent toward the whores. Reverend Dahlbeck was a lot more considerate than that self-righteous Father Peter Fisk, who often did Bilodeaux's dirty work on his behalf, all in the name of God. Franklin had found it difficult to cleave to his tongue in the padre's presence.

Doc Albrecht, widowed at fifty and never remarried, was a good man. He'd moved to town a little more than a year ago and made a fast friend of Franklin. He not only kept the drunks and opium addicts alive as best he could by giving them vitamins and tonics, he tended to those with genuine ailments, like cholera and whooping cough. His ego wasn't so large that it prevented him from tending to even the area's livestock and pets when they needed it. Madame Lafourchette's adored cat, Beau Belle, had even been the recipient of his solicitous attentions.

And there were the taxidermist and butcher, Clarence and Walter Grishin, brothers who worked in the same shop on the north side of town. Franklin often sold his deer kill and jerky to them for a fair recompense. They were known for their politeness and quickness to rush out of their shop, their knives raised, whenever they heard a ruckus on the street and thought someone might be in harm's way. And the Chinese family, the Tangs, who ran the laundry, always minded their own business but were known to stand their ground against ruffians. Franklin, who brought them much business, might expect their support.

Would any of those kind folks intervene on his behalf? Even if they did, what influence could they wield over a town full of nefarious drunks, all clamoring for whatever gold lay in the creek pool on Franklin's homestead?

He had never wanted help from people before. Had never needed it except for his stint at the Army hospital in Maryland. Helpless and battered, he could barely move for weeks. But that did not count. If it weren't for ruthless people, he'd never have spent an entire month in a hospital in the first place. Now, he had no choice but to hope for his fellow man's help.

Wicasha had little sway with the men of Spiketrout, but it was nice for him to have rushed to his side when he needed it. He had always cherished his friendship. And Tory? He barely knew him. But he'd proven just as loyal. It was astute of him to go after Wicasha. He nearly chuckled aloud remembering how Tory had dared to fight with the rowdy men while the marshal had hauled him into jail. Feisty, for sure. And sharp.

He saw Tory in his mind, standing stoically beside him while the town hurled unfounded accusations. Tory's hair falling from under his rawhide hat in golden waves and his crystal-blue eyes sparkling in the sun....

HE AWOKE to a much brighter cell than when he had fallen asleep. What sounded like thousands of finches chirped in the ponderosa grove behind the jailhouse. Stunned that he had actually slept at all on the lumpy stinking cot, he rubbed his eyes and gazed about the grungy cell. It looked worse than the day before.

Chattering from the front office roused him. He pressed his head against the iron bars and peered toward where Deputy Ostrem had spent most of the night snoring and farting. The deputy had moved, but Franklin recognized his voice coming from somewhere in the office. He sounded as if he were speaking with someone but Franklin heard no responses. Then Franklin figured he must be talking on that strange audio transmission apparatus that had first come into existence ten years prior. Workers had strung the wires for it from Spiketrout to Deadwood and into Rapid City on towering creosote-soaked pine poles a year before. Wicasha had been one of the laborers.

"Yes, sir.... It's already been taken care of.... No problem.... I reckon we can do that...."

It was difficult to gauge the details of Deputy Ostrem's conversation, but Franklin had little trouble guessing *who* the subject was about.

"All right. I'll see to it. ... Right away. ... Yes, sir. ... See you then. ... Good-bye."

With the click of the apparatus, Franklin shouted down the short hallway toward the deputy, "Can a man freshen up some?"

Deputy Ostrem sauntered down the hall, his ring of keys rattling. Franklin had always had a difficult time judging the deputy's true age. Fine lines streaked over his weathered brown face, and the skin around his taut mouth sagged. But the rest of him looked no older than a twelve-year-old boy.

"You don't expect me to use that bucket, Ray," Franklin said once the deputy faced him.

"You promise to get right back in here?"

"I'd be stupid to face the whole town hunting me down."

"All right." Deputy Ostrem unlocked the cell door and escorted Franklin to the back. A few paces beyond sat the outhouse, sparkling with morning dew. When Franklin emerged a few minutes later, Deputy Ostrem was waiting for him.

Just as the deputy slammed the cell door on Franklin, he heard the grating, shuffling gait of Marshal Reinhardt, followed by his gruff voice calling for Ostrem. Like an obedient serf, the deputy double-checked the lock and rushed to the front office. Franklin cocked his ear toward their voices.

"I just got off the telephone with the Deadwood judge," Deputy Ostrem told the marshal. "He said he'll be here by eleven for the trial. He's taking the eight thirty stage. He's agreed to use the Gold Dust Inn for a courtroom. He said he wants a room for the night."

Franklin relaxed at knowing a little more of what was to come. So they had already arranged for a judge from Deadwood to preside over his trial. He wondered which one. Franklin was familiar with a few of the Black Hills judges. Some had better reputations than others. At least he would be in friendly environs. Madame Lafourchette would see to it that nobody got out of line.

The marshal murmured something. A minute later he shuffled over to Franklin's cell. "All right, Frank, I'm telling you right now, don't give me any trouble this morning."

"I want to know more about this judge you got coming here," Franklin said, his eyebrows squeezed together to emphasize his concern. "What's his name?"

"You don't need to worry about that, Ausmus. Just be glad you'll be getting one. We're making sure you get all your rights and due process and whatnot that you're entitled to."

"If you were concerned about all that, you never would've locked me up in the first place. You know I didn't kill that Johnson."

"I don't know anything." The marshal narrowed deep brown eyes at Franklin. "That's why we'll be holding a trial, all nice and legal and constitutional. Now just sit tight and don't give me no headaches. We'll let you know when it's time to head over to Madame Lafourchette's." He tipped his hat and walked back to the front.

"This is a big waste of everyone's time, Reinhardt," Franklin shouted after him, his hand clenched on a bar to his cage. "Any reasonable man knows I done nothing wrong." He wanted to taunt him for never taking off his hat, even indoors, knowing good and well how sensitive the marshal was about his thinning hair, but he held back from rubbing him any rawer. He was about to reaffirm his innocence when the Reverend Dahlbeck and his wife, Matilda, walked into the jailhouse. Matilda, carrying a tray covered with a tea towel, bypassed the men and headed straight for Franklin's cell.

The men's heavy voices traveled back to them as Matilda uncovered the tray and slid it into the slot on Franklin's cell door. "I made a nice breakfast for you, Franklin. Fried eggs, ham, toast, and some hot coffee."

"You're an angel, Matilda." The sight and aroma of the food sent Franklin's stomach grinding. The first thing he grabbed was the mug of coffee. He took one large swig. "That's the best coffee I've had in a long time."

"I didn't expect these boys to know any better to treat you to something to eat."

"Thanks for thinking about me, Matilda." He carried the tray to his cot and finished off the black coffee. He had halfway finished his breakfast when Matilda winked at him and excused herself as her husband and the marshal came to his cell.

"The reverend wants to talk with you, Ausmus," the marshal said, as if annoyed.

Franklin waited for Reinhardt to leave before setting his tray aside and meeting Reverend Dahlbeck at the iron bars.

"Did you give Johnson a send-off, Reverend?" Franklin whispered.

"Johnson was a Catholic," Reverend Dahlbeck said, matching Franklin's low voice. "Father Fisk attended to his soul's needs." The reverend leaned in closer to the bars. "Be thankful they're giving you a speedy trial, Frank."

Franklin did not feel like being thankful, but he supposed the reverend had a point. He shouted toward the marshal, who was speaking with his deputy. "I want some representation. I've got a constitutional right."

"He's right, Marshal," Reverend Dahlbeck said in his defense. "There'll be a mistrial unless he's got a proper advocate."

Reinhardt, poker-faced, stood at the end of the hallway. "And who do you think that might be? We haven't had an advocate in town since the gold started drying up."

"Send a telegram to Deadwood," Franklin said. "Or use that talking contraption. Have one come over on the stage with the judge."

"The territorial courts will accuse you of fraud, Marshal," Reverend Dahlbeck said. "You're just wasting your time unless you oblige him."

"I'll represent him."

Franklin pushed his forehead against the bars until it hurt so he could see who had just spoken. Doc Albrecht was standing just inside the jailhouse, his black derby clenched in his fingertips. He was smirking in his usual nonchalant way.

"You?" the marshal said, turning to the doctor. "What makes you think you know anything about the law?"

"I know a great deal," the doctor said, focusing his smiling eyes on Franklin. "I used to practice law before going to medical school. I vowed I never would step foot inside a courtroom again after I witnessed a fiasco of a trial a score and five years ago, during which time an innocent man who I represented was found guilty in absentia, then hunted down like an animal and subsequently hanged. But I'm willing to push that all aside now. On behalf of my friend, Franklin Ausmus."

Franklin's mouth remained straight, but he could feel his heart lighten with a warm gladness. His friends *were* coming to his aid.

"You got a license to practice?" Reinhardt asked.

"I have passed the bar in four states."

"Is that all right with you, Ausmus?" the marshal asked, looking at him from under the brim of his hat. "You want the doc to be your advocate at the trial?"

"Suits me fine." Franklin allowed his grin to show fully. "Suits me fine, indeed."

"All right, then," Marshal Reinhardt grunted. "We're all square with the law and the constitution. Everyone happy?"

"Not quite," Franklin said.

"What now?" The marshal sighed.

Franklin set tapered eyes on Reinhardt from between the iron bars. "I still shouldn't even have to face trial," he said. "Bilodeaux has orchestrated this whole subterfuge."

"I'm certain Bilodeaux's behind it too." Reverend Dahlbeck spoke with his chin held firm.

"Well, if that's so," the marshal said, "then it'll all come out at trial. I'm sure the doc will be able to help you with your laments. In the meantime, let's clear out. This ain't no meeting house."

# CHAPTER
# TWENTY

THE town bell rang for Franklin's trial. By the time the ringing had stopped, the makeshift courthouse was packed with as many people the town of eight hundred could squeeze in. Curiosity seekers streamed into the streets and blocked both sides of the boardwalk. Anyone wishing to get past by foot or horse had no choice but to wait out the trial if they did not wish to climb the surrounding mountains to circumvent the herd.

Tory, alongside Wicasha, ached to stand with Franklin. Only when they had come to town to see Franklin had they learned the trial was to take place that morning. Packed in by the growing throng, Wicasha took Tory by the arm and pushed and shoved to the back of the Gold Dust Inn. Wicasha led Tory to the little-known kitchen entrance. Madame Lafourchette, her "crowning glory" exploding with sugar curls and her face decked out in more paint than Tory had ever seen on any woman, spied them. With her wide bustled burgundy skirt and overpowering jasmine perfume, she squeezed them through the spectators as her "special guests." Two heavyset men who barricaded the bar stepped aside when the madam scooted Tory and Wicasha in for a grand view of the entire proceedings.

Franklin was seated at a poker table near the other end of the bar. So helpless he looked. Tory yearned to rush to him. Flashes of Joseph van Werckhoven lying dead on the sidewalk streaked across his mind. He had had no way to save Joseph. Was there a way to rescue Franklin from the humiliation and injustice? And a possible hanging?

"Who's that man with Franklin?" Tory asked Wicasha, his heart quickening.

"That's Doc Albrecht," he said. "Reckon he's acting as Frank's advocate."

The thought eased Tory's mind, but only slightly.

Marshal Reinhardt and his deputy sat adjacent to Franklin at another poker table. Tory had never seen the marshal without his hat on. His receding hairline reached near to the back of his head. In a court of law, even one that was temporarily established inside a hurdy-gurdy house, no man dared show disrespect by wearing a hat during the proceedings. The marshal's stringy hair fell past his shoulders and seemed to accentuate his baldness.

Looking about the throbbing crowd, Tory was surprised that many of the men held foaming beer mugs and other alcoholic drinks. Madame Lafourchette must have wanted to cash in on the huge gathering. The booze flowed as if it were a typical Wednesday.

A group of five men descended from upstairs. The herd quieted, but only momentarily. In the ebb of the clamor, Wicasha whispered to Tory that the five men were likely the jury. They sat in ladder-back chairs arranged in a tidy row by the staircase. Through the haze of cigar and pipe smoke, Tory inspected each juror's face.

"I know all but one," Wicasha said. "They're pretty fair men. The guy on the far right is Walter Grishin. He's the town's butcher. You can count on him to vote in Franklin's favor. At least we can expect a hung jury if the others don't follow."

"What about the marshal?" Tory scrutinized him sitting at the table. He reflected on how yesterday Marshal Reinhardt had yanked Franklin into the jailhouse with little concern for his rights.

"He's a glorified gunman, that's all," Wicasha said. "Most likely not as much on Bilodeaux's side as the Canadian might like to think. He just don't like Frank much. They always butted heads. I suspect in the end, he'll do what the judge and jury tells him."

Wicasha pointed out a man wearing a dark pinstripe suit and rose cravat. Wicasha explained he was Spiketrout's Mayor Winters, the first man elected to hold that post. To Tory, he seemed delighted, even overjoyed, as if he were about to watch a play staged for his benefit.

The atmosphere was charged like an Edison bulb. Pulsing heat and energy traveled from one gawker to the next. Everyone—including the madame's girls—wanted to see a grand spectacle. Franklin was their lead performer, or sacrificial offering, depending on how one might look at it. Implacable lust for excitement seized the crowd and kindled their souls.

Tory's worries escalated when Henri Bilodeaux strolled onto the floor from upstairs, a lancero cigar clenched between his teeth. He elbowed his way among the pressing crowd. The men, most far taller than him, allowed him passage. He stood undetected just askew behind Franklin in his typical cavalier fashion, arms crossed, head held high, and an obnoxious leer cut into his dark face.

Looking at Bilodeaux and the giddy crowd behind him, Tory fretted that few people, if any, would be able to aid Franklin, despite Wicasha's assurances.

A short, plump middle-aged man parted the crowd from the street, demanding in a strained falsetto for the crowd to allow him entrance. The marshal hurried over to the man's aid. They spoke into each other's ears, their freshly shaved faces screwed up with gravity. Wicasha told Tory he recognized the man as Adam J. Gevelinger, a judge from Deadwood. He reassured Tory that he was known for his reasonableness.

Whispers flared around them as the onlookers took notice of the official-looking man in the dark suit and black top hat. Annoyed and weary-looking, the judge approached the bar, which apparently would make due as his bench. He sat on a stool on the bartender's side and laid aside is hat.

"I need a gavel," he said, spinning around on the stool as if looking for one.

A man to his left, most likely the bartender, who had maintained his post, brandished from under the counter a quarter-empty whiskey bottle. The judge rolled his eyes, then snatched the yellowing bottle from the bartender. Thrusting out his chin, he banged on the counter with the bottle, the amber liquid sloshing inside. "Court's in session. Court's in session. Quiet. Let's have quiet."

Voices muffled and quieted. All eyes were riveted on the judge.

"All right," the judge began, his voice squeaky yet powerful. "Let's figure out who's who. Will the defendant rise."

Franklin and Doc Albrecht stood.

Judge Gevelinger asked Franklin to state his full name. Franklin obliged him, and the judge said, "Mr. Ausmus, are you fully aware of the reason why you've been brought before this court?"

Franklin looked ready to spit out a string of laments, but Doc Albrecht grabbed his stump and whispered into his ear. Pursing his lips, Franklin said, "Yes, Your Honor, I am."

"Please sit, then. Whoever brought the charges against this man, please rise."

Marshal Reinhardt obeyed the judge's request, his eyes wide and nose upturned. He kept scratching his head as if wanting to conceal his receding hairline with his hand. "That would be me, Your Honor. Marshal Peter S. Reinhardt."

"And why have you brought charges against the defendant, Franklin T. Ausmus?"

"The shooting death of longtime Spiketrout resident, Clayton R. Johnson." The mention of the deceased's name and Franklin's alleged deed brought a wave of chatter from the crowd. Judge Gevelinger banged the counter with the whiskey bottle.

"Quiet," he shouted. "No more outbursts." He set the bottle aside and turned back to Franklin. "How do you plead?"

This time, Doc Albrecht spoke on his behalf. "Not guilty, Your Honor," he said without hesitation.

Again, the judge had to bang the bar with the bottle to settle the gapers. "Any more outbursts and I'll clear this saloon... I mean, courtroom." Turning to Franklin, he asked, "Do you stand by your attorney?"

"Yes, Your Honor," Franklin murmured.

"All right. Now let's get the proceedings underway."

Marshal Reinhardt presented his arguments first, explaining, with little exaggeration, how Franklin had hauled in Johnson's body after "allegedly" discovering it at Moonlight Gulch. There were a few grunts of displeasure during the lawman's speech. Franklin chewed on his lips. Doc Albrecht kept a steady gaze on the bar, his smile one of confidence.

"It is my belief that the defendant misled us into thinking that he found the body on his property already dead," the marshal said, anchoring his speech, "in hopes of exculpating himself as the gunman."

Franklin stood with a fury. "Bilodeaux shot Johnson, wanting to pin it on me. He wants me in prison or hanged so he'd get to sweep in on my land and scoop up the gold. Everybody knows it's what he's after."

Doc Albrecht pulled him down. After the doc whispered in his ear, Franklin calmed.

"He speaks nonsense," Bilodeaux said. Puffs of blue cigar smoke shot from his toothy grin. "I have plenty of gold. Why would I arrange such an elaborate prank for more?"

"'Cause you, like so many others in this town, are addicted to gold," Franklin said, peering at Bilodeaux with fiery eyes. "You're addicted to it like opium, and now you're craving more since it's all drying up. You can't get enough. And when you can't get your grubby hands on it, you act like lunatics."

"Order," the judge said in his squeaky voice to calm the uproar that accompanied Franklin's outburst. "Let's have order." Judge Gevelinger let the silence seep in before proceeding. "Is there any hard evidence to support your claims against the defendant, Marshal?"

Marshal Reinhardt leaned into the table. "My deputy went to the scene and found a rifle belonging to the defendant that matched the shell casing the defendant said he found at the scene of the murder."

"That doesn't prove a thing," Franklin shouted above the hubbub that trailed the marshal's proclamation. "Half the men in Spiketrout have rifles with the same caliber as mine. You could find any one of them that matches that casing."

The judge silenced Franklin with the whiskey bottle. Doc Albrecht calmly pulled Franklin to his seat. He whispered something in his ear, and Franklin, squaring his shoulders with a grimace, slumped in his chair, his lips tighter than piano wire.

"Do you have this rifle?" the judge asked.

"I do, Your Honor." Marshal Reinhardt took the rifle from his deputy and handed it to the judge, who studied it a good minute.

While the judge examined the rifle, Tory whispered to Wicasha, "How do you think he got that gun? I'm sure you or I would've heard anyone sneaking around the homestead. Especially you, since you were sleeping outside. Unless they came while I was out hunting for you."

Wicasha said, "He probably got it from their own collection. Like Franklin said, every man in this room has a rifle that could match that shell. They're just using it as a ruse."

The judge placed the rifle next to him on the bar.

Doc Albrecht stood. "Deputy, did you obtain a search warrant before you looted through Frank Ausmus's private property?"

The deputy looked flabbergasted. "Well... I...."

Marshal Reinhardt spoke for him, his eyes downcast. The gas-lit chandelier hanging above the room reflected off his shiny forehead. "No, he did not."

"Your Honor," Doc Albrecht said, turning to the judge, "the deputy disregarded one of the fundamental rights found in the fourth amendment of our constitution, and that's the right against undue searches and seizures. Deputy Ostrem trespassed on Frank Ausmus's land without even his presence and withdrew private property."

"That's not true," the deputy stated. "There were people present. An Indian and that blond boy over there." He pointed to them. All eyes followed. Tory flushed. He sensed Wicasha's muscles tense.

"Were they aware of your presence on the property, deputy?" the judge asked.

"Well... I... umm. I suppose they were."

"We were not," Tory shouted. The sound of his voice resonating in the saloon surprised even him. His cheeks heated, and he shrank back behind Wicasha. But then he realized the importance of his outburst, and he stepped more fully into view and thrust out his chest. "Neither one of us were ever aware of the deputy's presence at the homestead," he reiterated with conviction.

"May I look at the weapon in question, Your Honor?" Doc Albrecht asked.

"If you feel the need." The judge handed the rifle, butt-side first, to Doc Albrecht. He walked the gun over to Franklin.

"Is this your rifle?" he asked.

Franklin scanned the length of the weapon. "No, I'm certain it's not. I'd know my own Winchester. This one looks too clean. I've had mine since 1880, and this one doesn't have the newer lock barrel. I'd guess this one is at least fifteen years old."

Doc Albrecht turned to the judge. "Your Honor, not only have the prosecution, in this case the marshal and his deputy, insinuated that they stole property without a proper search warrant, but they have committed a far worse grievance." He turned to face the marshal directly. "They have planted evidence."

A thunderous uproar erupted from the crowd. Judge Gevelinger wasted no time quieting them. He stopped banging against the counter only when, from the way he peered at the bottle, he worried it might shatter. "Keep quiet, or I'll clear out this courtroom."

"It's his word against ours," the marshal said.

"That's right," Doc Albrecht rejoined. "And you, Marshal, carry the burden of proof to show this man's guilt. His words are weightier than yours, according to law."

"That's absurd," someone shouted from the gallery near Tory and Wicasha. Tory turned to spy the accuser but saw only the same red faces, twisted with the thrill of the spectacle. About the only disinterested party in the entire proceeding was a yellow cat preening itself under the bar.

"What does any of this legal mumbo jumbo mean anyway?" another observer shouted from closer to the street windows. "Did Ausmus shoot Johnson fair and square one way or the other?"

The crowd exploded with agreement.

"Mr. Ausmus," Doc Albrecht said, smirking off the crowd's impatience, "given that you are one armed, how often do you rely on a rifle for your shooting?"

"Not often at all," Franklin said, sitting up fuller in his chair while the crowd around him settled with expectancy. "I can shoot one, I'd readily admit, but I most often use my Smith & Wesson revolver when game hunting, which gives me a better shot."

"Would you say that you find it difficult to fire a rifle at a long distance target?"

Franklin nodded. "Yes, I'd admit so. I can shoot maybe forty yards without worrying about losing aim."

"Could you demonstrate for the court how you might use a rifle, if Your Honor permits?"

Judge Gevelinger sighed. "Go ahead."

Franklin stood with the rifle in his left hand. Doc Albrecht encouraged him on with a nod. Franklin moved hesitantly at first, but then, as if understanding the value of the demonstration, he proceeded as if he were preparing to shoot one of his hogs. He held the stock between his knees, cocked the rifle with his left hand, and, using his stump, steadied the barrel while taking aim at the large mirror behind the bar. To maintain a steady posture, he had to pivot his waist left, away from the target, and crane his neck to look down the barrel, an awkward position for anyone.

"And I'm a natural right hander, too," Franklin said, bringing the rifle to his side.

"Thank you, Mr. Ausmus." Doc Albrecht took the rifle from Franklin and rested it on the table. "Your Honor, the victim was found with the bullet still wedged in his brain, directly between the eyes. That would mean that he had to have been shot by a man with the skill of hitting his targets from a range much farther than forty yards, a man with two arms. You can see from the demonstration that the defendant could not have committed this murder."

The crowd unleashed more howls. "I want order," the judge squealed as the crowd's eruptions intensified, "or I'll hold everyone in this courtroom in contempt. Now keep your mouths shut."

Tory observed Bilodeaux, who had folded his arms and clenched a smoldering cigar between his puckered lips. His expression never changed. A confident arrogance creased the dark lines on his forehead and around his grin. Under the thick contour of his brow, his eyes, blue like sapphires, barely blinked. He snatched the cigar with his stubby fingers and stepped forward. Tory braced Wicasha's arm.

"Despite what the defense alleges," Bilodeaux said to the judge, "I attest that I heard the accused threaten the deceased, and the Indian and the blond boy heard it too."

"And who are you?"

"My name is Henri Thibault Bilodeaux, Your Honor. I own the ranch north of town. I was present on the defendant's property about two weeks ago, where I witnessed him lodge murderous threats at the deceased, and the Indian and blond boy were present."

"Where are this Indian and blond boy everyone keeps referencing?" The judge glanced around, planting his eyes on Wicasha, the sole Indian in the room. "I say it's about time we hear their side, since they seem so relevant to this story."

Tory flinched. He could feel the blood pumping in Wicasha's arm quicken. The silence that surrounded them grew as stagnant as swamp gas.

"Step to the bar… I mean, the bench," the judge ordered.

Shakily, Tory followed behind Wicasha, hat tight in his hands. A reassuring gesture from Madame Lafourchette failed to ameliorate Tory's nerves. Standing by the judge, he was able to see Franklin clearer. A sudden rush of warmth settled his trembling limbs. Franklin's eyes glistened like jade under the chandelier. Tory couldn't help but smile at him. Frank nodded lightly in his direction, but his mouth remained firm.

"State your names," the judge ordered once they were fully before him.

"I am Wicasha, decorated veteran of the U.S. Army."

"And you, son?"

"I'm…. I'm Tory—" Suddenly, Tory's words were like musket balls. He couldn't recall if he'd mentioned his surname to Franklin in any of his letters. Would it somehow give him away? Standing before a court of law, he had no choice but to reveal the truth. His knees began to buckle. "I'm… I'm Tory Pilkvist."

"And what connection do you two have with the defendant?"

"I am his long-time friend," Wicasha said, "and this is his hired hand."

"Were you both present during the incident that this Frenchman has mentioned?"

Both hesitated. The judge pushed them for a response.

"We were," Wicasha answered.

"And did you hear the defendant make threats of death to the deceased?"

Wicasha nodded, his eyes downcast.

"And you, young man?"

Tory's head felt as if it were made of cement. Slowly, he nodded. But then a realization lightened his anguish. "I also heard the Frenchman here, Henri Bilodeaux, threaten the deceased," he said, looking straight at Bilodeaux with self-assurance. "He said that he would shoot him between the eyes, and in fact, that's just how the victim was discovered. With a bullet hole right between his eyes."

The crowd exploded. Tory looked over at Franklin. A soft smile emerged over his tanned face. Tory beamed back.

Bilodeaux's cocky grin changed in an instant. He glared at Tory. The strength that surged inside Tory at that moment gave him the sense that he could move mountains. Unfazed, he returned Bilodeaux's sneer. Yet the outcome of Franklin's trial still lurked unknown.

The judge was beating his fist on the counter, leaving the bottle to rattle next to him. "Silence! Silence!"

"He's one-armed, have mercy," a man shouted, defying the judge's command.

"He's a veteran of the Civil War, on the Union side," another said. "He done to Johnson what he done to a hundred men, all asking for it."

One man, a Confederate sympathizer, shouted, "The Yanks were criminal bandits. They took land that wasn't theirs. They burned down our homes, our cities, left us to starve and perish while hoodlums raped our women and beat our men. Ausmus is one of them, a traitor to his own people." Fellow traducers on the Confederacy's side joined in shouting down any support for Franklin and the Yankees. Tory hoped such strong emotions did not smolder with the jurors and shift Franklin's fate to hanging.

The judge banged on the countertop with the whiskey bottle. "Order. Silence. We're not here to rehash the Civil War, for Pete's sake. If a man were convicted purely from what he did during the war, we'd all be in jail."

The crowd broke into laughter. The judge pounded the counter once more. "All right," he said after everyone settled. He turned to Tory. "Young man, this Bilodeaux is not the man on trial."

"Your Honor," Doc Albrecht broke in, standing tall with his fingertips pressed against the poker table, "illustrating the possibility that others may have motive in Clayton Johnson's death is paramount to my client's defense. It could very well prove his innocence beyond a reasonable doubt. If these proceedings come down to merely one man's word against another, then we all might as well be put on trial. Each man here has a rifle similar to the defendant's, each man has motive likely in one form or another. The deceased, on more than a handful of occasions, riled most everyone in town with his drunken antics. Bilodeaux's known more than anyone to have harassed the sot. Besides, we've already proven the defendant, being one-armed, could not fire a rifle at the range required to lodge a bullet between a man's eyes."

Judge Gevelinger seemed annoyed with Doc Albrecht's legal technicalities. He knitted his bushy eyebrows and glared down at the bar top. "I see no point carrying this out any longer. I've heard enough chatter, from both sides. Let the jury deliberate. Any objections?" Neither the defense nor Marshal Reinhardt (nor the crowd) objected to the motion. The judge dismissed the jury with a casual wave of his chubby hand.

After one of Madame Lafourchette's working girls led the five jurors upstairs, Tory and Wicasha rushed to Franklin's side.

"This whole trial is a farce," Tory said through his teeth.

"Calm down, I think it'll turn out in our favor," Doc Albrecht said. "They have very little on Frank that can prove his guilt, we've clearly established that."

Only fifteen minutes passed before the jurors stepped back downstairs.

"That's a good sign," Doc Albrecht whispered.

A penetrating hush washed over the crowd. The swilling halted. Beer mugs and glasses froze in midmotion. Tory stepped aside with Wicasha. He was certain he could see the verdict written on the jurors' faces. Tension paralyzed him.

"Have you reached a verdict?" the judge said once the men took their seats.

The man Wicasha had pointed out as Walter Grishin stood. "Yes, sir, Your Honor."

"Go ahead. What is it?"

"Not guilty," he declared in a robust voice.

Shouts and cries ruptured from the crowd. Beer mugs clashed in toasts. Foam sprayed over everyone's heads. Men patted the bustled bottoms of the madame's working girls. Yet others bemoaned. They scoffed and kicked at the floor and pushed their chairs. Tory's soul lifted to the heavens. He glanced toward the chandelier and mouthed, "Thank you."

Dozens of men from the gallery swarmed Franklin with back slaps and sturdy handshakes. Madame Lafourchette left a bright cherry-red lip print on his flushed cheek.

Bilodeaux pinched the cigar from his mouth and marched up to Franklin. "I have done what I can to be fair with you, Ausmus. I have offered you a decent price for your land. On too many occasions you have given us no other choice but to use other tactics."

"Us? Who is this *us*?" Franklin, still grinning from all the congratulations, peered at Bilodeaux through the hands that reached out to pat his shoulders. "A jury handpicked to represent the town acquitted me of your crime, Bilodeaux," he said. "They're not all fooled by your tricks. You can't really expect them to fall for your fraudulent bleeding heart scheme that your lust for my land has anything to do with anyone's good but your own. It's power and greed that motivate you, Bilodeaux, nothing more."

"This is not over. Trust me." Bilodeaux dashed his cigar to the floor with a burst of sparks. His eyes blazing, he shouldered his way out to the street. Franklin's supporters pointed and laughed after Bilodeaux's heavy footsteps.

More drinks flowed around them. The bartender could barely keep up with the demand as the men pushed against the bar. Tory glanced at the judge, who was still seated at the counter, rubbing his temples. He eyed his improvised gavel, shrugged, popped the cork, and, bringing the mouth of the quarter-full whiskey bottle to his lips, drained it.

# CHAPTER
# TWENTY-ONE

"I STILL think that if they put you in jail and forced you to stand trial with so little evidence, then they should've arrested Bilodeaux right there on the spot once they acquitted you," Tory said back at Moonlight Gulch as the sun crested the western peaks. He, Franklin, Wicasha, and Doc Albrecht were sitting outside the cabin at the plank table, the first real chill in the early October air nipping at them. They were still buzzing about the past twenty-four hours. "It's just not fair."

"It would've been our word against his," Doc Albrecht said. "It didn't work for Reinhardt and Bilodeaux; it wouldn't have worked for us. Besides, the marshal won't want Bilodeaux behind bars. He's too much money to him. He's gotten immunity plenty of times in the past."

"It's a crime what they did to you, Franklin. All of them should be locked up." Tory could not stop stewing about the entire ordeal. He was relieved that the jury had cleared Franklin's name, yet each time he rehashed the episode in his mind, from when Marshal Reinhardt had first dragged Franklin to jail to Franklin sitting at the poker table ready to stand trial, he chewed on his bitterness like rawhide.

"What do you call those people in the city who steal right from you under your nose?" Franklin asked Tory.

"Pickpockets?"

"I was thinking more like politicians."

Tory chuckled. "Oh, well, yes, we have plenty of those in Chicago. Most of them are connected with crime syndicates, but then so are the people who vote for them."

"We have the same problem out here," Franklin said, shrugging. "The more power a person in the Hills has, the more they seem connected with bandits. The marshal isn't much different." He patted his holster. "At least he gave me my handgun back."

"All communities have their share of good guys and bad guys," Doc Albrecht said, lowering his cup of coffee from his lips. "From Boston to New Orleans, from California to right here in the Black Hills, I've seen them all."

"I guess there's no way of getting rid of nefarious men," Wicasha said.

"Nope, but at least they keep men like us occupied," the doctor said.

Their talk worried Tory. Bilodeaux's lingering threat to Franklin still echoed in his ears. *This is not over*. What gall Bilodeaux had. If he exhibited such disrespect for the laws of man in a courtroom, then what would prevent him from eschewing even more profound laws, such as those of common decency? Most everyone insisted he had murdered Johnson, even many of his cohorts. If he went to such lengths, there would be no stopping him. Tory loathed him more and more; he also feared him with mounting dread.

But to see Franklin surrounded by his friends, joyful and at peace, comforted Tory. For now, Bilodeaux had been subdued. The town had shifted allegiances. The embracing of justice had replaced the hunger for gold. Like the winds that rushed from the nighttime mountains, the town's sympathies had changed direction and now rested with Franklin, at least for the time being. Tory understood the mentality of mobs. He'd seen it in Chicago, when labor disputes transformed kindly family men into savages ready to tear into comrades and neighbors. But for now, Franklin had freedom and loyalty. And Tory had Franklin back at Moonlight Gulch.

The doctor stood. "I best be off before it gets too dark. My old scrub of a horse is sluggish enough as it is."

"Why don't you shack up here tonight, Doc?" Franklin said. "I can sleep in my bedroll in the barn, and you can have the feather bed."

"No thanks, Frank. I'll be needed in town tonight. There'll be a lot of drinking and whatnot after all that's gone on with your trial today. The town's frenzied. No telling how many broken bones and alcohol poisonings I'll have to deal with the next few days."

Franklin assisted him in getting his horse from the livestock pen. Tory watched Franklin place a few bills in the doctor's palm, probably much deserved recompense for advocating on Franklin's behalf. They shook hands, patted each other on the back. Doc Albrecht's staunch alliance with Franklin kindled Tory's heart.

Wicasha stretched upright when Franklin approached them. "I'll be getting back to my camp too," he said. He and Frank clutched each other's shoulders.

"Thanks for all your help, Wicasha."

"I'm glad things turned out good, Frank." Wicasha glanced at Tory over Franklin's shoulder. He flashed him that same strange slick grin Tory had grown accustomed to. Wicasha was always snickering under his breath, cracking toothy grins, as if he held a deep dark secret. Wicasha chuckled and made his way along his usual trail, the setting sun highlighting his quivering shoulders.

Dismissing it from his mind, Tory kicked back at the table. Franklin leaned against a tree stump, pulled his knees up to his chest. Cool, gentle solitude.

"I guess you don't want a fire?" Franklin grinned. His teeth glowed white in the encroaching twilight.

Tory winced. "I don't mind a small one. It's just those bonfires are a bit unsettling."

"Where did you pick up a fear of fire?"

"I don't know. Maybe it has to do with the Chicago Fire. I was only about five when it happened, but I remember sensing the alarm emanating from everyone. I was too young to put it into words, but I could feel it. I guess that's why I have a fear. Who knows?"

Franklin shrugged. "I reckon that could be. Sounds reasonable, in any case."

"You think I'm foolish?"

"No, I suppose we all got our fears. You don't mind if I light a torch? It'll keep the bugs away."

"No, of course not. That won't bother me much."

Franklin lit a torch and set it into the ground in a hole dug for such purposes. He resumed his position against the tree stump, his hat pushed back high on his head.

"Do you have any?" Tory ventured to say, probing Franklin's mind under the deepening denim-blue sky. "Fears, that is."

Only heavy breathing lifted Franklin's chest. Tory waited. He wondered if he had wounded him. Should he ask such pressing questions after his agonizing torment—overnight in a jail and a murder trial? The torchlight danced off Franklin's face, twisted in serious contemplation. Just as Tory was about to redirect his question, Franklin cleared his throat and spoke.

"If I had to pick what I fear the most, I guess I'd have to say it's dying alone."

Franklin's candid response surprised Tory. He had not expected him to expose his vulnerabilities. In a way, Franklin's confession provoked Tory to yearn to embrace him now more than when he had first spotted him at the trial.

"It's strange, because I like living alone," Franklin went on, studying the ground by his feet. "I reckon my whole life I was trying to find my Moonlight Gulch. Now that I have it, I think about sharing it with someone. The notion of dying out here, or growing old and sick, without anyone to care for me, well…."

"I suppose anyone would fear that," Tory said, eager to erase any embarrassment caused by Franklin's confiding in him.

Franklin fluttered a laugh. "I used to have a dog, a yellow retriever named Ash. She was a good companion. Then she just up and died one day, and I never got another one. I liked having her around. Guess I just didn't want to deal with another dog dying on me. Maybe it's best I'm alone. If I couldn't even handle the death of a dog…."

"Isn't there anyone for you to fall in love with?" Tory maintained a casual tone, though his insides churned with longing—accompanied by an eclipsing sense of despair.

"Not out here," Franklin said toward his knees. "Most of the women are whores. The good ones come out married. No decent woman would travel to the Black Hills alone and single, unless invited. Did I ever mention to you about the girl I once corresponded with?"

Blood drained from Tory's face. He heard himself gasp. Or had the booming thump of his heart reverberated in his ears? A cold silence swarmed him. In the stretching darkness, Tory could barely make himself answer. "No," he said, unable to hear his own words over his pounding heart, "you never told me."

"I met her from one of those nonsensical matchmaker periodicals." When Franklin mentioned Torsten P.'s name and that she lived in Chicago, Tory thought he might fall off the bench. The reality of his charade engulfed him like the deepening night. Franklin had inadvertently forced him to face a mirror, and what he saw horrified him. Deception and selfishness gaped back at him.

"I reckon I was desperate." Franklin sighed self-effacingly. In the flickering torchlight, Tory watched Franklin shake his head and smirk. "I was a fool to think it could amount to anything."

Tory did not want to face Franklin, not even in the dim glow of the torchlight that flickered in the breeze. Yet sorrow forced him to gaze at him. He noticed the lines on Franklin's face move in odd directions, the caverns deep and rugged. His horseshoe mustache cast a dark shadow across the left side of his face.

"I never even told Wicasha about her," Franklin went on, his eyes faraway and moist. Crickets began to awaken as the last vestige of evening twilight dissolved. "Not sure why I'm even telling you. Reckon you're easy to talk with."

As the crickets joined the night birds in their avian chorus, Franklin recounted the story Tory knew all too well. Hearing Franklin's voice rise and fall with emotion with the details of why he'd decided to submit an advertisement to *Matrimonial News*, his thoughts after reading Torsten's first letter, and the utter disappointment that he had endured after she had stopped corresponding with him out of the blue, Tory remained frozen, his eyes unblinking. Shame, regret, and sympathy paralyzed him.

He observed the top of Franklin's Stetson as Franklin poked a twig at the dirt. Apparently Tory's silence had smothered Franklin's candor. His cheeks flushed with what seemed bashfulness.

Wanting to foster Franklin's confidence in him again, Tory said, "I guess you sometimes never know why people do the things they do."

"Women are a fickle animal, that's for sure," Franklin chuckling. "Queerer than three-dollar bills. Could never figure them out."

"I suppose we're all like that, in a sense."

"You never told me if you got a girl back home," Franklin said. The tone of his voice, rich and thoughtful, forced Tory to look toward the darkening sky, absent from time and place, where the first bright stars glittered from billions of miles away.

"No," he said under his breath. "I don't have a girl."

"No one at all?"

He wanted to share his experience meeting Joseph, and how he too thought he'd met someone special, only to have it thwarted by calamity. But he knew revealing anything so blunt would shock if not horrify Franklin. Yet the drive to keep the deepening connection between him and Franklin could not be subdued.

"I was in love once," he said, sitting up on the bench and wrapping his arms around his shins as the cool breezes off the mountain peaks increased. He rested his chin in the cleft of his joined knees. His entire relationship with Joseph van Werckhoven played out in his mind like a stage play. "It wasn't that long ago," he said. "We had a wonderful short time together."

"What happened?"

How could Tory phrase it so that Franklin would think he was talking about a woman? "An untimely death," he said, hoping that would be adequate. Franklin's thoughtful repose proved it was.

"I guess you're young enough," he said. "You'll meet someone new. Me, well, I'm getting up there. Almost forty. My time has most likely run out. That advertisement was my last-ditch effort."

Tory thanked the heavens for the cover of night so that Franklin would not see the tears fall down his cheeks, along with the shame and craving that polarized him, convulsing the muscles around his mouth. He looked back at the infinite sky. Iridescent stars overhead appeared brighter, like millions of tiny candles. Their harmony failed to mollify the conflicting emotions burrowing under his skin.

Tory needed Franklin to know. Needed to convince him that someone had loved him, even if it meant preserving the deception. "I'm sure Torsten loved you," he said. "I'm sure of it. How could she not? Her father must have interfered with her correspondence with you. Did you ever think of that?"

Chirping crickets filled the ensuing silence. "I did," Franklin breathed. "When she stopped replying to my letters, I thought about hunting her down in Chicago, if only to make sure she was safe and unharmed. I worried she had fallen ill. But then I realized I'd be chasing after a mirage. I really didn't know her. I had no idea what she looked like or even what her family's name was. She gave me some mysterious initial."

Brazen remorse overwhelmed Tory, but also relief. He hadn't mentioned in any of his letters to Franklin his surname, after all. Yet nowhere could he escape from the torment of what he'd done to Franklin Ausmus. He craved to somehow ameliorate his pain.

"You had a girl during the Civil War, didn't you?" he said. "Wasn't she there waiting for you when you returned home?"

Franklin chuckled. "I was just fourteen when I joined with the Union," he said. "My girl was nothing but a schoolboy crush. She'd fallen in love with another fellow while I was away at battle. We were young, not likely things would've worked out one way or the other, with or without war." He paused a moment and joined Tory's gaze heavenward, reflecting on the shimmering stars, perhaps reliving scenes from the war, past interludes, a faraway life. He shrugged and looked back to earth. "After I realized my old girl and I weren't meant to be, well, I just hit the road. I was a war veteran out making my own way before I turned eighteen."

"All that must've been difficult," Tory said. "Especially with your injury."

"Stuff happens," Franklin said. "You gotta do what you gotta do."

"At least the war had ended," Tory said. "I can't imagine how horrible that must've been."

"Most people never know how such things get started," Franklin said. "It's like a storm that blows in over the mountains. It comes, and you hunker down and wait for it to pass. We had no use with worrying over whether it was horrible or not."

"I guess I grew up spoiled. I've never experienced a war."

Franklin chortled. "You will, don't worry. There's always a war around the corner somewhere."

Tory shivered. "You think that Bilodeaux will come back here?" He had to learn what Franklin thought about the issue. Sleep would never come without some reassurance. Franklin failed to provide it.

"He'll be back," he said flatly. "He might keep himself scarce for a while. But he'll be back."

"What will you do when he does?"

The implications of Franklin's extended pause loomed as clearly as the surrounding night. Franklin had no need to express his thoughts. He would resort to killing Bilodeaux if he must. If Bilodeaux didn't kill him first.

Franklin fiddled more with the stick, chucked it away. Tory felt as if Franklin had tossed him across the yard.

"Why does he have to bother you so much?" he said. "Why can't he just mind his own business?"

"He's just that way, like a lot of folks." Franklin wiggled his mustache. "Maybe I should just pan the gold, if that's what the world wants from me."

Shudders coursed through Tory. At first he thought he was shivering from the chilly winds coming off the mountains. Then he understood that a new fear had seized him and was shaking him like a cougar would its prey.

"Don't, Franklin," he said, almost in a cry. He sat up straight, the soles of his boots flat on the earth. "Please don't pan for the gold."

Franklin gazed at him under the brim of his hat in the jitter of torchlight. "Why so adamant?"

Recollections of all the people he'd come across since he'd first stepped onto the stagecoach in Cheyenne City rumbled in Tory's mind. So many of his fellow travelers had looked leery, suspicious, with greed seeping from their hearts like oil. He remembered the old silver miner on the stage north of Chugwater talking about how he hadn't even wanted the silver but that it had come so easily, he couldn't resist. Eventually, he'd become subservient to it. He'd wandered the country like a man sleepwalking, looking for more and more. Many in the town of Spiketrout had proved little different.

The night before, Tory had told Wicasha that he wished Franklin would pan the gold and toss it to whoever wanted it for no reason other than to get everyone off his back. Now, he realized the folly of his proposition. Franklin would never be able to give people enough. Gold enslaved men. Turned them into savages. Men would kill just for the chance of procuring it, as Bilodeaux had proved when he'd killed Old Man Johnson. Tory could not bear the slightest possibility that gold might seduce Franklin in a similar way.

He thought it curious how in nearly every language that he knew the words for gold and God were similar. In Swedish, "guld," and "Gud" echoed the English words "gold" and "God." The French called kings "roi," akin to their word for gold, "or." Was it all a mere coincidence? Or had humans long ago created a connection between gold and gods that had bled even into their languages, their very souls?

Tory would rather face off the raiders than risk Franklin becoming like them. He wanted to state his concerns without pretense. "I'm afraid," he said. "I'm afraid the gold might change you, like when people drink they sometimes act differently, some even violently. Don't pan for the gold, Franklin. Don't ever think of it again. Please, promise me you won't. Promise me you won't let the gold take hold of you."

A strong breeze came down from the rock face as Franklin opened his mouth to speak. "The evil of the Black Hills placer gold isn't the gold itself," he said, pronouncing each syllable, as if to make Tory understand the precise meaning of his words, "it's that it brings wealth too easily. That's what turns men into savages. When riches come to them like in a dream, effortlessly, without the need for using their minds or bodies, they become beasts who cannot stop wanting more. I've seen it happen to better men than me. Just look at the town of Spiketrout. Look around—who's decent and who isn't? The deadbeats want whatever comes trouble-free, whatever someone else got."

"Then you agree," Tory said, sitting straighter, his fingers clasped firmly around the bench. "You understand how evil it is. Please, please, Franklin. Don't pan for the gold. Tell me you won't."

Franklin cracked a smile. "You like the way I am, huh?"

The air shifted. Static charges rode on the back of the increasing wind. The tiny hairs on the nape of Tory's neck stood stiff. An animal scavenged near the woodpile. Wordlessness lingered for many seconds.

"I like the way you are, Franklin," Tory said unflinchingly. "You're just about the most perfect person on earth, one arm and all. There's more wealth in your shunning the gold than all the gold in the world."

The whites of Franklin's eyes reflected the light of the torch as he gazed at Tory. He seemed to mull over Tory's tribute. Chuckling, he shook his head and picked at the dirt on the ground. "I'm not all that," he said. "I'm just a hog farmer from Tennessee trying to mind his own business."

"And that's exactly what makes you heroic."

A gentle silence descended upon them. They remained like that a good ten minutes, listening to the night birds and the crack of twigs from the nocturnal rodents foraging under the shelter of night, until

Franklin, inhaling, stood and stretched. "I best get to bed. Been a long day."

With his one arm, Franklin snubbed the torch flame in the cold fire pit until gray smoke snaked toward the incandescent constellations. He left the extinguished torch sticking out of the pit like a lance.

Inside the cabin, Franklin lit a lantern. He held it to his face. The green of his irises sparkled like emeralds. "You sure that cot's doing all right for you?"

"Yes, I'm sure." Tory had just slipped off his boots and day clothes and was climbing into bed in his union suit.

"I feel badly making you sleep there," Franklin said. "But it's all I got."

"It's more than enough. Really."

"Maybe I'll craft another bed. Been thinking of doing it."

"You don't need to do so much. You've already given me an opportunity to live and work on your homestead. That's more than any man should ask for."

"It's been no trouble. Well, reckon I'll be turning in. If you need anything, just let me know."

"All right."

"Good night, then."

"Good night."


TORY had no idea how long he'd been asleep—five minutes, an hour, half the night?—when he thought he was freefalling in a dream. Then he realized he was awake, struggling as someone reached for him. Half-dazed, he thought whoever it might be was trying to suffocate him. The interloper groped, squeezed, choked him, twisted his arms, pinched his waist, grunting and moaning. Sour breath blasted heavy in his face. Someone was trying to force him off the cot. He gasped for air. His undergarments were pulled and yanked. He wanted to scream, but his tongue cleaved to his dry palate each time he tried to yell. Suddenly, he felt the sensation of someone lifting him and carrying him away.

# Chapter
# TWENTY-TWO

FRANKLIN had been lying in bed awake, unable to sleep after such a chaotic day, when the heated blood had begun to pound in his ears. At first, he had thought the intensity of the trial had prevented him from sleeping. But the preceding events had not been what raced inside his mind while he'd tossed about in his feather bed, his hand like a clamp over his head.

He'd been picturing Tory sleeping in the cot just on the other side of the wooden partition. He'd remembered back to when they'd bathed in the creek pool. He couldn't have helped but notice his figure. So subtle, yet firm and masculine. Like the granite rocks smoothed by the gentle flow of the creek.

And his words from a few hours ago. So sweet. He really did care for Franklin in a way Franklin had never thought anyone might. He had referred to him as *heroic*. The heat that had begun in his cheeks had spread like a wildfire throughout his entire body.

What thoughts had traipsed through his mind?

He'd clutched the bottom sheet with his hand, willing down the spasms. Squeezing his eyes shut, he'd hoped to rid himself of such images. Then that spicy boy from Richmond had appeared in his mind's eye. While on furlough in the South's capital, he had paid the boy for sex. The boy had been flirty, pushy, his intentions without pretense. Franklin had not needed the renter to have fooled him. He knew what he had been doing with him in the alley behind the tavern. He knew what they both had wanted.

Franklin's body had twisted like a torqued chain ready to unwind with a snap as he squirmed atop his bed. Heat had built in his groin to the point of pain. His top sheets had lain in a knot by his feet from his having kicked at them. Smoldering breathlessness had compressed his chest. His mind had gone swirling in heated blindness like a sizzling summer thunderstorm.

He had wandered to the side of Tory's cot as if in a spell, unable to contain the mounting force. He couldn't recall how long he'd stood there, staring down at the young man and watching his chest rise and fall rhythmically under the sheet. He had noticed Tory was aroused, and had ogled him, wanting to reach for him. When he finally had, it had been as if someone had moved his arm for him. Now, with Tory's muted yelps muffled in his ears, he found himself carrying Tory, fumbling with him in his one arm, determined to keep him tight to his chest.

He already had Tory's union suit stripped down to his waist by the time he tossed him onto his feather bed. How he had accomplished it without dropping Tory to the wood floor, he could not answer. Tory tore at Franklin's undergarments, struggling, twisting, punching, kicking. Shaking and frightened. Franklin could feel his own heat rising from under the cotton fabric as his skin was exposed to Tory's touch.

His senses in the dark weakened. He smelled, heard, saw almost nothing. But the sensation of touch intensified. The feel of flesh was like bee stings striking raw nerves. Suddenly, Tory's struggles abated. His muscles slackened. No doubt he understood fully what was happening to him, and he no longer fought to get away. He longed for it as much as Franklin.

Tory was allowing it. Wanting it. Demanding it.

The rest of their undergarments fell in a combined pile on the floor. They rolled on top of each other, kneading each other's flesh. Tory submitted to Franklin, melding with his body. Franklin's heart raced with a fury he feared might bring him near death. Yet he cared little. He needed, wanted Tory then and there. Damn the consequences. Tory was giving himself to him. And he was going to take him, determinedly and without reservation.

His tongue explored Tory's neck, ears, nose, mouth. Tory bit on Franklin's nipples and roved his tongue over his chest, then licked down to his navel. Franklin writhed, thrusting his belly upward. Defeated by desire, he rolled Tory onto his stomach, onto his back, onto his side, repeating his movements over and over, tossing him about as if he were an extension of Franklin's body, a new arm sprouting from his stump.

Tory whispered words in Franklin's ears that sent him into overflowing passion. He was telling him what he wanted. Telling him what he needed. Flipping him onto his back, Franklin spread Tory's legs with his thighs and pushed down into him; Tory pulled him closer. His stump, muscled with two decades of use, balanced him against his left arm while he went wild with Tory's submission. Invincibility and power propelled Franklin. Tory's moans and movements exclaimed that he wanted more. He pulled Franklin in tighter, demanding that Franklin follow through.

The earth rocked with the rhythm of their bodies. Pounding and thrusting, reaching and pulling. Tory chewed on Franklin's horseshoe mustache; Franklin met his bites with his tongue. Ecstatic shivers coursed through his blood. Tory's feet traced the length of Franklin's legs. Franklin wrapped Tory with his arm, pushing onto him with his weight. The release of anger, tension, apprehension, fear, and hunger carried him into another consciousness.

They ended with a final biting spasm, Franklin's back arched in a moment frozen in forever.

He collapsed on top of him. They remained motionless. Residual vibrations seemed to pitch the feather bed. Exhausted and drained, Franklin rested his head on Tory's chest. He had never needed release so badly. But it was more than the stress of imprisonment and the trial. Burning desire for Tory sleeping mere steps from his bed had controlled his movements. Tory felt good in his one arm, under him, beside him, against him. Tory's legs wrapped tight around his hips long after they had emptied themselves.

They did not speak. Heavy breathing lingered. Restless sleep overtook them. They dozed, twisting and sighing, pawing for each other in their dreams. During the night, feeling each other's heated bodies near, they made love three, four more times, sleepily, dreamlike. Their open mouths tracing along their necks and ears. Their hands grabbing in the fog of their fatigue, yet propelled by a profound hunger. Franklin taking Tory more and more, deeper and deeper.

Finally, Franklin lay depleted. With the expanding morning light, he could see Tory more clearly in the blue glow as it descended over them like a solicitous mother pulling back the blanket of darkness. Tory had fallen into a full sleep. Wavy blond hair splashed over the pillow.

Soft curls were matted to his moist forehead. His chest rose with each breath, still labored from their lovemaking.

Tory's body had grown harder since Franklin had first seen him in the buff while bathing in the creek. Two weeks of rugged subsistence work had tightened his muscles. Franklin had felt it beneath his initial resistance. He gazed at the smooth lines, the subtle hairless and taut flesh that crested over mounds of muscle and bone.

He thought back to their lovemaking. He had been greedy, drunk for Tory. And during their second, third time making love, when he'd thought he wouldn't survive, Tory had done something Franklin had never imagined a man would do for another, not even a renter. Tory had taken Franklin into his mouth. Completely and willingly. The sensation of his hot, moist tongue was like a million expressions of love, caring, desire. The ultimate submission. He grew aroused again.

Yet he left Tory undisturbed. He was in deep slumber, Franklin could tell. His eyes were closed like a porcelain doll's, twitching as if in rapturous dreams. And so Franklin also lay beside him as if in a dream.

A mellow pink flush seeped from the window as twilight acquiesced to dawn. He could see the mountains awash in a salmon-colored glow. Groggy, he draped his arm over Tory's pelvis and rested his head on his chest, listening to his drumming heartbeat, like the galloping of an approaching horse.

Franklin failed to realize it before it was too late, but blending with Tory's heartbeat *was* the galloping of an approaching horse. He struggled to lift his heavy head to see who had come onto the homestead. But it was too late. To his astonishment, Bilodeaux stood staring down at him and Tory as they lay naked on the feather bed. Franklin froze in disbelief. Bilodeaux, his sidearm in hand, looked on unblinkingly. The smell of whiskey swept down from his flaring nostrils. Amid the emergence of a subtle sneer, he turned away, sans words, before Franklin could react. The sound of his stallion's hooves faded.

# CHAPTER
# TWENTY-THREE

WHY had Bilodeaux shown up at Moonlight Gulch at the crack of dawn? What had he wanted? Had he come for some final attack after failing to accomplish his scheme to frame Franklin for Johnson's murder? What would he do now that he'd seen him and Tory in bed together, their naked, tangled bodies plainly depleted after a night of voracious lovemaking?

These were the thoughts that had churned inside Franklin's mind since he'd stirred to find Bilodeaux staring down at him and Tory in bed four mornings ago. Few answers surfaced. He needed a confidant. But how much could he reveal to his best friend, Wicasha? They were close, but both men had kept their personal lives mostly to themselves. Each appreciated the other's lack of curiosity. Franklin had not even told Wicasha about the silly advertisement he'd placed in *Matrimonial News* what seemed like ages ago.

He needed to feel Wicasha out about what Bilodeaux might do, while giving away as little as possible about him and Tory's relationship. The impulse to confide in Wicasha proved too overpowering to ignore.

He and Wicasha were building a barbwire fence that Franklin had ordered from Chicago back in July, which he'd stored in the barn, hoping he wouldn't have to use it. After Bilodeaux's latest antics trying to implicate him for murder (and especially since his barging in on him and Tory), Franklin realized he had no choice but to erect it. They had started two days ago and were on the final segment. He had no idea how effective the fence would be, but he had to do something. The October sun was hot, and both men were building a healthy sweat.

Wiping his forehead under the brim of his hat with the back of his hand, Franklin said, "What do you think Bilodeaux might have next up his sleeve, Wicasha?"

He had phrased the question simply and directly. Wicasha, Franklin knew, appreciated such manner of phrase. Speaking equally straightforwardly, he said, "He has something planned, there's no doubt. You can expect him to act ruthlessly. He's desperate. Like a fox caught in a trap, he's predictable only in that you can expect him to lash out in some unpredictable way."

"Have you any thoughts of what that might be?"

Wicasha held a wooden post in place while Franklin, with his one arm, skillfully hammered it into the hole they had dug in the black soil. Both men had to spread their legs wide to balance themselves against the slope of earth. Franklin's mule, Carlotta, snorted and swatted black flies with her tail while she waited to pull the cart loaded with the posts and barbwire. Wicasha delayed answering until Franklin finished hammering.

"He killed a man, Frank," he said. "He shot him between the eyes in cold blood for no reason other than to frame you for it and get the untapped gold on your land. If I know mankind well enough, his violence will only get dirtier, much like how it works with war."

They moved to the next foot-deep hole, one of about eighty they had already dug around the perimeter of the property. Carlotta followed with the cart, aware of her responsibility after already spending two days under the hot autumn sun. Most of the inserted posts had barbwire attached, and they had installed a small gate for Wicasha to come and go between his camp and the homestead and another larger one across the Spiketrout trail. They usually hammered five or six of the posts in place before backtracking and attaching the barbwire.

Franklin squinted into the sun, took a deep breath, and inspected a cut from the barbwire where his long-sleeved shirt and canvas glove had failed to protect his skin. "That worries me," he said, disregarding the itchy abrasion on his wrist and reaching for a post. "I wonder in this war that he's chosen to wage against me just which one of us will show the most violence."

"Man can be pushed to defend himself to great lengths," Wicasha said as he aided Franklin in securing the post.

They toiled in silence, Franklin ruminating on Wicasha's blatant warning. Carlotta nickered as she followed the men. Eventually, they came to an even part of earth where, nine years before, Franklin had cultivated the soil for his field. He had chosen the site near a dense spruce grove that abutted the granite rock face, wanting to take advantage of the winds that came off the higher elevations. Whenever toiling in the field long hours, he always appreciated the invigorating breeze on his weary limbs, especially on harvest moon nights.

Franklin had to tread carefully with Wicasha. He did not wish to reveal the new development in his and Tory's relationship. Yet he worried what ammunition Bilodeaux might unleash now that he'd discovered him and Tory in bed. "Do you think if Bilodeaux knew something about me… a secret that he thought might cause me trouble, that he'd use it against me?"

Franklin noticed only a fleeting flicker of curiosity flash in Wicasha's black eyes when he lifted his head toward the cooling breeze off the rock face. Turning back to his work, Wicasha said, "He would use anything he could. He's getting more desperate. To him, all is fair in war. The French have a saying: Le vainqueur rafle la mise."

"What does that mean?"

"To the victor go the spoils."

Franklin considered this. Wicasha was right. Bilodeaux had no scruples. Anything was just to a nefarious bandit like Bilodeaux if he thought it would carry him closer to his aims.

Should he warn Wicasha of the calamity that might come? He could risk losing the Lakota as a faithful friend if he confessed to him what even Bilodeaux now knew. At the moment, revealing his relationship with Tory seemed unwise. Best to keep the truth cached away, like his cured bacon and root vegetables in the storage barn.

A few posts later, with thoughts of Bilodeaux still banging inside his head, Franklin chose to ask Wicasha a question that had stewed in his mind for almost as long as he'd known him. Why he thought to ask at that precise moment, while they strapped wire to a series of wooden posts, when so many other worries splintered his brain, he was uncertain. Perhaps he was digging for something. The barbwire signified a shutting out of the world, more than even Franklin had wanted. A subconscious balance would be to open up to one another. Since Franklin was unprepared to reveal the truth about him and Tory, perhaps the alternative was to pry buried truths out of Wicasha.

"Wicasha," he said, "why did you go against your own people and fight alongside the cavalry during the Indian wars?"

Wicasha stretched to his full five-ten frame. After a quick reprieve, he bent back to aiding Franklin. "It's a long complicated story," he said. "Not sure how or where to begin."

"You don't got to tell me," Franklin said. "I guess the question just slipped out. It's none of my business."

"I figured you'd been wondering all these years. You should probably know. We're good friends." He had stated the last three words more like a question. Franklin jumped in to confirm.

"Yes." He nodded while wiping sweat from his forehead. "Yes, of course, Wicasha. We are the best of friends."

Wicasha rested his sweaty forearms atop a post that Franklin had just secured with soil. "Then I will tell you the story."

Franklin took a respite from his toil and gazed at his friend with expectation. Carlotta seemed to sense a break had come, and she began nibbling on the grass that grew in a swath next to the field, her ears folded back.

"Have you ever heard of a winkte?" Wicasha asked him.

Franklin eyed Wicasha. "No. I haven't."

Wicasha seemed to chew on his words before speaking, as if he wanted to express himself precisely without pretense, as was the Lakota custom. He motioned for them to continue working. Franklin followed along.

"A winkte is a Lakota word that means 'third sex'," Wicasha said as they went about placing more posts. "A man who is a third sex is said to be attracted to other men in a way that most men are attracted to women."

Franklin stiffened. Had Wicasha read his mind? He tried to steady his arm so that Wicasha would not think he was so utterly shocked he would hold back from telling him more. Yet the astonishment on Franklin's face at what Wicasha might be alluding to could not be lost to the sharp Lakota.

Wicasha chuckled. "Yes, Frank. I'm a winkte," he said. "I'm attracted to my own sex." He hesitated, as if waiting for Franklin to speak, gauging his face. When Franklin remained mute, he looked away and continued. "I've known I was a winkte since I was a little boy, no taller than a pine marten standing on hind legs. In my band, a winkte was not frowned upon as the white man sometimes does. There were those Sioux who laughed, sneered, even taunted, but mostly it was tolerated. It was thought to have a purpose, a part of the balance of nature. And so, when I was sixteen, I was brought before our chief, and he decided to make me part of his large group of wives. That is just how things are with my people. I had no choice but to obey."

Franklin worked in a trance. He brought the face of the sledgehammer against the post, but he no longer felt the vibration travel through his arm and across his shoulders and down his back. The sensation of Wicasha's words was all that shook him.

"Do you want me to go on, Frank?" Wicasha asked.

"Yes." Franklin swallowed. "Yes, please. Go on."

Wicasha continued his story with only minor pauses between for their work. "I did not like living as someone's concubine. The chief ruled the village. We obeyed his orders. The chief had asked for me, and I had to stay with him. For the next two years, I lived as his companion. Then I began to grow. I was a late bloomer, you might say, like the lupine that waits to blossom until fall, when all the other flowers have mostly faded. I grew tall, and my muscles expanded. I thought then that the chief would ask me to leave his harem since I had become larger than even him. I was wrong. He actually began to ask for me to sleep with him inside his lodge more often. His other wives grew to dislike me. They were jealous."

They had almost reached one of the many narrow trails that wound toward the creek. Franklin was near sapped of strength listening to Wicasha. He could hardly believe his ears. Wicasha was—what had he called it?—a winkte. A man who liked other men in the same way most men liked women.

Rumors that the High Plains Indian chiefs took on spouses of both sexes had reached his ears in the past, but never had he heard it straight from a tribe member's own mouth. Until now. It explained why Wicasha kept mostly to himself. And why he'd never frequented the Gold Dust Inn, where Madame Lafourchette took customers of any race or creed, as long as they carried plenty of greenbacks or gold dust. Negros, Indians, Chinamen, white men—they all frequented the whores. Even Franklin had, a handful of times. But never Wicasha.

Did Franklin have needs like Wicasha? Was it possible that he might be a winkte too, at least in part? For the past several nights, he had made love to another man, drunk only from passion, unlike that time with the renter in Richmond, when whiskey had taken him by the hand. He hardly identified with Wicasha's history of his attraction to the same sex. Franklin had only felt such urges a handful of times, and only twice—that was, only with two men—had he acted upon them—the renter when he was sixteen and Tory Pilkvist, whom he had made love to at least a dozen times since their first time together four days ago.

Tory was different from the Richmond renter, of course. Franklin had already admitted that to himself. Uncertainty still poked around in his mind. Had desperation for affection—for love—forced him to turn to the closest human being in his life at that moment? Transforming himself into something he wasn't? Had Tory evolved into a mere stress reliever from another war, the war waged between him and Henri Bilodeaux?

Were his feelings for Tory the same as the Lakota chief's were for the young Wicasha?

Carlotta bellowed. They left her grazing by the trailhead while they carried armfuls of posts into the grove and filled the holes they had dug leading to the creek's bank. This time, Wicasha took the sledgehammer while Franklin held the posts in place with his hand and feet. Between posts, Wicasha continued with his riveting story.

"As I grew with strength and confidence," Wicasha said, "I began to wander more on my own. I would travel for days, taking old trails into Paha Sapa, the Black Hills, which the Sioux had taken from the Crow many generations before. I would follow the ravens and see what they wanted to show me. Sometimes I would find them guiding me eastward to the Badlands, where I'd fast for several days and listen to the spirits tell me my future. I valued my time alone. The chief knew about my wanderings, and he'd said he understood. Yet he had cautioned me to remain nearby the village. Winkte were given more liberty than the women of the village; some were even honored as shamans. We are men, after all. Not really a 'third sex', as the Sioux like to call us. Mostly, it's just a term to explain the aberration.

"It was during one of my wanderings west of our village, north of what is now Spiketrout, many years before the white man had discovered gold in the Hills, when I ran into a fellow roving spirit. He was a Crow, about my age. We spied each other over the next few weeks but kept our distances. Our bands were instinctive enemies, yet I sensed we did not fear each other. Both of us pretended like we hadn't seen each other. After a while, it was as if we were putting on a show for the other to see. I would do something to demonstrate my strength, and he would, in turn, do something to show his skills in skinning or trapping. I reckoned we were observing each other to see if we were friend or foe, despite our peoples' heritage of warfare.

"Eventually, he was bold enough to approach me while I skinned the fox I had been tracking. I actually skinned it much like I had observed him doing on previous days. He cut along the hind legs and up into the rectum, causing less blood spill, something I had never seen in my village. For many hours we found ourselves talking in French, and sometimes in English, the only two languages we had in common. Often we used sign language to communicate when we stumbled over our words. The sky grew dark, so we decided it best to stay put until daybreak. We lay down on the earth by the boulders that had absorbed the day's sun to provide us warmth. We kept a good distance from each other. But during the night, we rolled closer and closer. Soon, we were within arm's reach. After many sleepless hours, we proved what we both must have suspected during our many days of scouting out each other. We were winkte."

Franklin could not help but think of himself and Tory. The same scenario had transpired between them. Almost exactly. It had been at night, the darkness lessening his inhibitions, when Franklin had found himself staring down at Tory on his cot, so close that all he needed to do was reach out and lift him to his beating chest.

"We became lovers after that night," Wicasha said, as if he were recounting the story of Franklin and Tory. "He was my soul mate, I was certain. We both agreed the spirits had brought us together and sanctioned our love. For many months, we would rendezvous between our two villages that sat many miles apart. The Lakota chief grew suspicious and one day had me followed. His scouts reported back to him that they had seen me with another man and that we had laid down together as man and wife by the boulders. When the Lakota chief learned of it, he banished me from his group of wives and said I was never to step foot inside his lodge. He permitted me to remain in the village, but no one could speak to me. The entire village shunned me, including my parents and siblings, of which I had at least ten.

"Unable to stand being around those who ignored me, I eventually found myself living in the backcountry, where me and my lover could spend more time together. When he learned of my predicament, he took me home with him to his village near Wyoming. I was delighted to see him night and day. But soon after I moved in with him, a Sioux raid on their village resulted in his capture, along with dozens of Crow women and children. I never forgave my people for taking him from me."

For the first time, the need to respond to Wicasha's narrative loosened Franklin's throat, if only to lessen the pain that appeared in Wicasha's dark face while he described his lover's capture. "What was the name of your Crow, Wicasha?" he asked in a hoarse voice.

Wicasha stiffened. He seemed unsure about Franklin's sudden bluntness but then composed himself. He lifted a post that had fallen and put it back into place. "Bua Ishte."

"What does that mean?"

"Means Fish Eyes in his native Crow. He had wide, gazing black eyes like a fish. It was the first feature you would notice about him." Wicasha seemed to reflect. He stopped momentarily from bringing the sledgehammer down onto the post. Resting the handle over his broad shoulder, he looked northwest toward the mountains, where beyond the granite peaks lay the Crow tribal lands of his former lover.

"I miss him," Wicasha said as if he were answering the question of an unseen spirit. "But he's living another life, most likely still a concubine of a Sioux chief after he was kidnapped by them, living in another world. If we met again today, we would not know each other. Life changes people. We take different paths, and those paths are what make a man who he is. We are not the same as when we had first met by the boulders."

"So that's why you took to scouting for the U.S. Army?" Franklin said. "Revenge for Bua Ishte?"

With his broad chest heaving and wide shoulders shaking, Wicasha laughed. "I reckon I answered your original question after all. Yes, that's the reason. At least in part. After Bua Ishte was kidnapped, I still remained with his band. I became fluent in the Crow language, and eventually, I began scouting for the white man like most of my new brothers. We made très bon scouts, as the French would say. I had hoped by scouting that I might find Bua Ishte and take him back home with me, but I never did locate him."

Wicasha and he had more in common than Franklin had ever considered, he realized, while tender images of Tory constricted his throat. Yet the notion of confessing to Wicasha about his and Tory's own "rendezvous" still came with difficulty. What exactly would he be revealing?

He and Tory had shared a bed since that first time they'd made love; did that mean they had become lovers, like Wicasha and Bua Ishte?

Weighing Wicasha's forthright words, Franklin retrieved the remaining barbwire from the cart. Each time he thought about confiding in Wicasha, the words failed to rise past his parched lips. As they continued to labor, Franklin remained silent.

Their three hands worked diligently, and before the sun had the chance to dip closer to the western peaks and turn the granite rock face pink, they had completed the fence around the perimeter of Franklin's deeded land. Yet as he walked about his property with Wicasha by his side and inspected the newly constructed fence, he realized the makeshift barricade would do little in keeping out a determined and, as Wicasha had called him, ruthless man like Bilodeaux.

In deep thought, he made his way to the cabin, with Wicasha following. A column of smoke carrying the aroma of Tory's fish stew, from the brown trout he'd caught in the creek that morning, only slightly lifted Franklin's drooping spirits. Just before reaching the cabin, Wicasha placed his large hand on Franklin's shoulder and held him from going farther.

Franklin turned and eyed him. The sun washed over Wicasha's dark face, his forehead tight with wrinkles.

"There's something else you should know about my past as a winkte," Wicasha said gravely.

Franklin gaped. What could be so dire that he would need to tell him right then and there? How many more secrets must he unleash? Franklin could hardly take any more. "Yes, what is it, Wicasha?"

"Bilodeaux and I were once lovers." He said it flatly, without emotion. A simple truth, spouted for Franklin's ears and the animals eavesdropping in the surrounding forest.

"You and him?" Difficult for Franklin to imagine. "You and Bilodeaux were together the way you and Bua Ishte had?"

"No." Wicasha's face grew gray and menacing. He dropped his arm to his side and formed a fist. His black eyebrows knitted. "We were nothing like that. Although at first I thought we might be. For a short time, I was in love with him, and I assumed he was in love with me. It was after you and I left the quartz mine and we went our separate ways. Bilodeaux and I met in Spiketrout after I returned from Washington to receive my medal of honor for scouting on the Army's behalf. He had remained in the Hills far longer than most, before Custer spurred the gold strike. He was one of the few white men of French descent still lingering after the U.S. Army came in."

"What happened between you?"

"He promised to take me to France," Wicasha continued, his eyes filling with red hatred, "where we would live on land he said his family still owned near Calais. We were together only a few weeks. I soon realized his promises, like his amorous attentions, were only meant to get what he wanted from me. He wanted me for the same reason he would go to the Gold Dust Inn for the whores. To men like Bilodeaux, everything is for his taking to satisfy his needs. He has no feeling.

"After I learned of his deceitful ways, I left him. He tried to double-cross me by turning me over as a wayward Indian to the U.S. government for a measly fifty-dollar reward. But when the Army realized I was a decorated war veteran, they let me go in peace. I suppose his large ego made it impossible for him to accept that I was the one to leave him before he could leave me. It was the same with the Lakota chief. Men like them like to be loved but are incapable of returning love. Since then, hating Bilodeaux comes as easily to me as it does to you."

Franklin's mind raced back to when Bilodeaux had stood by the side of his feather bed, staring down at him and Tory, naked and defenseless. He had feared Bilodeaux might use the discovery against him somehow to acquire his land by telling the locals of what he had seen, turning them all against him. Wicasha's confession had not eased those qualms. They had compounded them.

New fears rose inside him like the smoke from the chimney. On the other end of that chimney, Tory cooked at the stove, preparing supper like he had for the past three weeks. He had never informed Tory about Bilodeaux's discovering them in bed. Unwitting, he had gone about his life as Franklin's lover, thinking their relationship was a secret between only him and Franklin.

Franklin understood the gravity of their situation now more than ever. He recalled how Bilodeaux had always looked at Tory: eyes narrow, sharp, penetrating. He lusted after him. No doubt. Bilodeaux's awareness of his and Tory's fledgling romance would not pacify Bilodeaux. Jealousy and lust, two emotions perhaps more powerful than greed, now simmered inside Bilodeaux, waiting to erupt into fiery action.

Franklin was about to rush to Tory when Wicasha spoke. "I sometimes feel responsible for having brought Bilodeaux into your life," he said, his eyes narrowed with regret.

Wicasha's words straightened Franklin's spine. For an instant, he worried only for his friend. "But why, Wicasha? How could you have anything to do with it?"

"I would talk about you with Bilodeaux, about our friendship, about how we knew each other at the quartz mine. I boasted proudly about learning how you sat on mounds of gold without wanting it and how honored I was to be your friend. This was before I knew Bilodeaux's true nature. I must have sparked something evil inside him, unleashing him upon you like a thunderbird. I hope you'll forgive me."

Franklin shook his head. Now it was his turn to place a hand on Wicasha's shoulder. "Wicasha, you have nothing to do with Bilodeaux's gold lust. That evil lurked inside him long before you came across his path. From this moment on, I want you to never blame yourself."

Wicasha smiled and nodded, but his shoulders slumped. They continued walking toward the cabin and the fish stew Tory was preparing. Worries accumulated, making Franklin's steps heavy and cumbersome. If not for his hand still resting on Wicasha's shoulder, he feared he might topple.

Despite all that Wicasha had revealed to him, he would wait to share his truth about Tory. Too many secrets had been disclosed for one day already. Neither one would be able to shoulder more.

And as he glanced back at the barbed wire fence that now surrounded his land, he understood again that the three days of hard labor that he and Wicasha had exhausted installing it had mostly likely been for naught.

# CHAPTER
# TWENTY-FOUR

FRANKLIN thought back to Torsten P. whom he had corresponded with in Chicago. He had long since concluded she had rejected him. His concerns that she might have become ill and could no longer write had blown away in the wind weeks ago. He supposed Torsten used men like many Spiketrout residents used liquor or opium.

The women of the Black Hills were like Torsten: amusement-seekers gambling with their wily affections the way the men gambled with their gold. Women like Torsten used men to carry out their ego-driven games. He recollected his mother and two younger sisters. They were not like Torsten P. And most of the women back home in Knox County were not like her—except for maybe his old girl, who had left him because of his disfigurement. Or so he assumed.

He often wondered—if his old girl hadn't run off with the Confederate veteran, if the Black Hills weren't swimming with whores (nine out of ten worked as prostitutes, according to Marshal Reinhardt), if Torsten hadn't cast him off, would he find himself giving all his affections to a man, a boy in many respects, a nineteen-year-old nearly twenty years younger than him?

He peered at Tory over by the windmill. Tory had lowered the galvanized tower on the rotary axis and was removing branches wedged between the fan blades that had torn from trees in a heavy overnight gust. He was useful, that was for sure, Franklin thought as he went back to fixing two of Lulu's shoes in the livestock pen. He balanced her left fetlock on his knee and used his stump to steady her leg. Tory did his fair share, worked diligently, never complained. And he was loyal. The most loyal companion he'd ever known. Even more dependable than Wicasha.

As Franklin began to notice Tory in a strange, unique way, he contemplated…. Was Tory a winkte? The renter in Richmond had only sought to make money to survive the grind of war. Sure, he had clearly enjoyed himself, but how much of his means of making an income had accompanied superficial pleasure? Did Tory see Franklin in a similar fashion—a landlord with benefits?

Tory had shown desire for him each night they'd lain down in his feather bed. The things he would say to Franklin when they'd make love—things a woman had never whispered in his ears—no man would say those things unless he was born as a winkte, like Wicasha. Nature's balance, Wicasha had said of his aberration so casually the day they'd erected the barbwire fence. Tory's feelings must derive from more than desperation for survival or physical longing.

Since that first night five days ago, they had never spoken about their feelings or shown any overt affection—that is, until after they had doused all the lanterns, spread the wood in the stove, and bolted the door for the night (to keep out Bilodeaux). When they'd climbed into the feather bed they now shared, only in the dark would they reach for each other and become fused.

In the mornings, after they'd made love, Franklin would kiss Tory as the ascending sun cast a soft pink across his luminescent skin, then he'd rise, ready for the hectic schedule of subsistence living. At breakfast, they'd discuss matters pertinent to the homestead, like any two homesteaders might. During the day, the two men focused on whatever tasks needed completing. Whenever side by side, they never uttered a word about their passions from the previous nights. No one would suspect they shared a bed if they happened upon them during the day.

Even when Tory had treated Franklin's nicks from erecting the barbwire fence, they had exchanged minimal words. Yes, Franklin had gazed down on Tory's blond hair while he'd lubricated the small cuts with pine sap, resisting a swelling surge of sentiment. Tory had worked his hands firmly, yet, like during their lovemaking, so gently. But Tory had dressed the wounds swiftly, and afterward they'd gone back to their chores with few words.

At night, they were a different animal. In the morning, either he or Tory would have to fetch the sheets that they had kicked and tossed about during a night of lovemaking. Franklin remembered stories of the ancient Greeks, how they had often lived with each other in partnerships, like a husband and wife. And so had Wicasha, a winkte, lived with his Lakota chief as a wife. Were Tory and he any different? He grinned, recalling how Tory would do that thing to him with his mouth that felt so good.

It all seemed strange to Franklin, but at the same time, so wonderful. As the days passed, he found himself eager for winter to set in. He'd eye the sun more and more, eager for it to settle over the mountains earlier each day so that he could wash, go back into the cabin, eat the supper Tory had prepared, douse the lights, and climb into bed alongside Tory, where all the emotions that had built up during the daylight could be unleashed with a blistering passion.

"Frank, did I upset you with my truth?" Wicasha had asked before leaving for his campsite the day he had revealed his secret about living as a winkte.

"No, Wicasha," Franklin had said. "No, you didn't upset me with your truth."

And he had been honest. Wicasha's plainspoken words had long settled in his mind, like the mountain dandelion seeds netted in the pines, and they no longer disconcerted him. How could they? He and Tory were living a life much like the one Wicasha had described.

He flushed, picturing him and Tory sharing his feather bed.

ONE afternoon a week after their first lovemaking, their relationship underwent yet another change. They were raking soiled hay from the barn when the dairy cow kicked Tory in the stomach. He fell limply to the ground. Franklin raced to him. Holding his head under his stump, he beseeched him to open his eyes. Finally, bright blue began to shimmer through fluttering eyelids. Fully conscious, Tory gazed into Franklin's face.

"Are you okay?" Franklin swept the damp blond strands of hair from his ashen face. "Talk to me."

"I'm… I'm okay. She just bumped me a little. I don't even hurt."

"You need some cool water."

Tory remained dazed, yet he held onto Franklin's arm with uncanny strength. "Don't go. I don't need any water." His voice was shallow but full of conviction. "I only need you, Franklin Ausmus."

As if he were handling the most precious porcelain, Franklin carried Tory to the creek pool where he undressed him and bathed him in the cool water. His skin radiated with what looked like flecks of gold. Color returned to his cheeks. Franklin led him naked into the cabin and dried him with a fresh cotton towel and then rested him on the bed. Franklin slowly removed his own clothes and climbed into bed beside him.

"Is this really what you want from me?" Franklin asked Tory, his eyes tacked to the ceiling beams.

"Yes." Tory's voice came hushed but resonated in Franklin's ears. "This is all that I've ever wanted from you."

For the first time, they deserted the veil of darkness and expressed their affections in full daylight. Exposed to each other, a new intensity seeped into their relationship. With the autumn sunrays pouring from the windows, Franklin used his thighs to position Tory as he often did, and he entered him.


FRANKLIN'S shadow preceded him out of the cabin, where he stood and watched the western sky transform from sapphire to oil black. Dressed in his union suit, he gazed about his Moonlight Gulch. He could see the vague clumps of the trees and stumps and rocks and, through the ponderosa pines, the creek, black like a mirror, reflecting the white stars. And the barn, silhouetted against the rock face like a specter, stood as testimony to Franklin's one-armed carpentry skills. The windmill turned slowly yet with unyielding purpose. The cooling breeze carried the ripe odor of the pigpen under his nose. In an odd way, he felt as if he were beholding his homestead for the first time— or, did it seem, like the last?

Silver smoke from the cabin billowed skyward. Inside, Tory was warming last night's Swedish stew, which he'd called kalops. A warm yellow glow from the fire and lanterns danced behind the windows.

How long had they remained in bed? Four hours? He flushed thinking of it.

Recalling his heated moments with Tory, Franklin could not prevent his mind from roving back to Bilodeaux when he had walked in on Franklin and Tory that first night after they'd made love. The question remained—why had he come? What had made Bilodeaux enter his cabin without knocking (Franklin hadn't heard a knock, anyway) and brandish a gun at such an early hour? Of all the times Bilodeaux had charged onto Moonlight Gulch, he'd always remained outside, shouting for Franklin to appear. Save for a few occasions, he'd never even bothered to dismount from his stallion. Had Bilodeaux come to the homestead to murder Franklin in cold blood like he had Clayton Johnson?

Franklin heard the creek gurgle in the distance, a gentle fiddle-like music. Eyes glowed by a tree stump. A raccoon. The same one that had ventured close to the cabin in autumn for the past three years. Franklin had dubbed him "Green Eyes" for the way his irises shone in the darkness. Tory had said Franklin's own eyes glowed like a raccoon's at night. Franklin hadn't received so many compliments in ages. He sighed.

Wicasha had said Bilodeaux was predictable only in that he could be expected to lash out in some unpredictable way. What more surprises might he have in store?

Little reason to let his anxieties develop into a far worse adversary than Bilodeaux, Franklin concluded. The weight of worry alone might beat him down. For now, life continued. Inhaling, he stepped back inside the cabin to the zesty aroma of stewing venison.

"I WASN'T sure at first, but now I know." Wicasha chuckled. "Your eyes can no longer lie."

"What're you babbling about?" Franklin glared at Wicasha from under the brim of his hat. They were sitting by the blazing fire pit, enjoying what might be the last temperate evening of the season while shucking green beans. Wicasha sat at the plank table, Franklin leaned against a tree stump. Flames cast oscillating shadows on Wicasha's crinkling face as his chuckles turned to solid laughter that seemed to shake the last of the remaining leaves from the aspens and birches.

His broad shoulders quaking, Wicasha continued to shuck. "At first, I thought you might've been attracted to him for the same reason Bilodeaux or the big chief was to me," he said. "Just for your pleasure, just to have a body next to you. But now I can see I was wrong."

Franklin, his face heating, turned back to his bowl of beans. He snapped each one as easily with one hand as Wicasha did with two. "What do you mean?"

"Don't hide the truth from me, Frank. Not after all I've told you. For one thing, your cot has been folded and stored for days." He snickered again. "Where's the chikala wasichu been sleeping? With Carlotta?" He laughed harder.

Hot blood seared Franklin's cheeks. He removed his Stetson, hooked it on his stump, and combed his hand through his hair, which Tory had recently trimmed and was still wet after his kettle bath. Replacing his hat on his head, he said, "That's enough from you, Wicasha. There's nothing to poke fun of here."

"I'm not poking fun, Frank. Me of all people wouldn't do that. You know my history, about me being a winkte."

Franklin fell silent. This was all so strange to him. It was one thing for Wicasha to reveal his true self, but to have to talk about it openly? "Then why are you giggling like a drunken hurdy-gurdy girl?" he said under his breath with his bowl of green beans balanced on his lap.

"I just never imagined you with another man, that's all." Wicasha's tone was more level. "But I can understand why. That Tory, he's not bad. A good friend. He found my camp all alone after you were hauled to jail for Johnson's murder. He said that he had used the aid of raven guides to find it, then followed my stream. I wonder how a city boy could be so swift learning things."

They sat silently. Franklin gazed at the fire, the flames sweeping away the hard discomfort of Wicasha's candid words. His lover—it seemed so strange to call him that now—had a reasonable mind. Other than his fear of fire, he was as rational as a young man could be. Franklin wondered if he was frightened now, alone in the cabin, staying clear of the bonfire. Tory had said he had chores to do. Franklin wanted to stay with him, comfort him. Wicasha's company was embraced as usual—an entire week had passed since he'd last seen him. But Tory... he belonged to him and no one else. The thought thrilled him. Wicasha must've detected his subtle shiver.

"The way you feel, Frank... it's not so bad."

Franklin pondered for a moment, the beans snapping under his fingertips. "Am I a winkte?"

"Do you feel like one?"

"No, not really. I see Tory as, well, as someone whose company I like a lot." He flushed. "That's all. I'm not looking at other men the way... the way that you might."

"I would say you're not a winkte." Wicasha paused, then continued. "You wouldn't be the first man to seek another man's affections, Frank. I saw it even in the cavalry when two soldiers, far from home, isolated from any good women, would find themselves drawn to each other. They would pretend like it wasn't happening. But I could see it as clearly as if they were waltzing together in the middle of camp. Tory is a looker with a gentle spirit. No surprise you would fall in love with him in a place as lonely as Paha Sapa."

Wicasha was right. Franklin had fallen for Tory. He couldn't say when it had happened. Perhaps at the trial, when Tory had stood so bravely before the judge and defended him. Or maybe much earlier, when, the morning after he'd found him in the barn loft, he'd awakened to the smell of frying bacon and brewing coffee. His wonderful coffee that he always cracked an egg in, Swedish style.

Franklin felt something with Tory. As profound as what he'd experienced with his former girl back in Tennessee, the one who'd recoiled from his stump and run off with a Confederate soldier.

At times, Franklin missed his aloneness in the woods, but over the years his bachelorhood had grown heavy. Tory, a wistful, wonderful breeze, brought scents of comfort to his small parcel of earth. With him, he had the best of both worlds.

Occasionally, he fantasized about the feel of a woman, but the image of her lying beneath him would be fleeting. Tory would inevitably replace her. To his own pensive surprise, his arousal would magnify.

No, Franklin was not like Bilodeaux or the Lakota chief, who had both taken Wicasha as their concubine. Franklin respected Tory. He was not a mere plaything. He had not used him to release the stress from a needless murder trial. Deep inside, he knew. Tory meant more to him than Wicasha had meant to Bilodeaux or his chief.

The emotions were real, as real as at any other time in his life, as were the aching yearnings. And he resented Wicasha for having mocked him for it.

The spit of sparks from the fire seemed enough to express Franklin's angst. He settled back against the tree stump and brought his feet closer to his haunches. "You knew all along, didn't you, Wicasha?" Franklin grimaced. "You told me all that stuff while we were putting up the barbwire fence already knowing about the two of us."

The sides of Wicasha's mouth curled upward. Franklin snorted, shook his head.

Wicasha chuckled. "I had suspected you had laid down together for pleasure," he said, "but nothing like what I see now. You surprise even me with the love you two have for each other. I'm envious."

With the snap of the beans and the crack of the fire, they kept to their task in silence. Finally, Franklin rested his hand in the bowl and gazed into the fire. "What's it supposed to feel like to love a man?" he asked, almost to himself, or to the spirits that might be hovering above the shadowy mountain peaks.

Wicasha peered at Franklin, dark eyes wide and gleaming in the flames. "Same as a woman, I reckon," he said. He turned back to his beans. "Maybe harder. Men can be competitive with each other." Then a wide grin thinned his lips. "But maybe it's better. You don't have to worry about reading a man's mind. Even Lakota women gripe when her husband or beau fails to know her wants before she does."

The first real levity in many months tickled Franklin. In that instant, he realized—why worry over what brought him so much pleasure and joy? He needed to embrace his relationship with Tory in the same fashion he embraced Tory himself.

Yet concerns still nagged him. Henri Bilodeaux. Franklin could not think of his and Tory's relationship without images of his adversary haunting him. Bilodeaux was a vicious animal, capable of taking and devouring everything in sight. He stalked the forest like a rogue, without any fear of consequences for his dastardly actions. And Franklin knew the bastard had eyes for Tory.

# Chapter
# TWENTY-FIVE

FLUFFY, wet snow spilled over the Black Hills, covering Moonlight Gulch. A gentle calm accompanied the colder months that Franklin had always loved. Tory knew this from one of the letters Franklin had sent him. He had written that winter in the Hills was like "a massive white dove enveloping one with its wings." Franklin had also stated he liked that the cold locked the gold in the creek pool and "temporarily froze the greed in men's souls."

Tory cherished the colder months in the Black Hills too. Confined with Franklin in the cabin, he sensed a new, broader domesticity linking them. He and Franklin Ausmus truly were sharing a life together. Like a fawn appearing on the edge of the forest, nudging the snow in search of pinecones and moss, their union filled him with a sense of magic.

The approaching winter also meant Wicasha went missing from the homestead more and more. Tory worried he had chased him out. Franklin assured him that Wicasha, like a bear, often hibernated in the winter inside his teepee, wrapped in buffalo skins, emerging only to eat, drink, and whatever else living creatures do.

One of the few appearances Wicasha made in November was during Thanksgiving. He and Franklin had made it a tradition to feast on the holiday together. Ever since Abraham Lincoln had declared it a holiday in 1863, Franklin had said he'd taken Thanksgiving rather seriously. Tory cooked a lavish spread of goose, kalops, carrots with fried onions, baked potatoes, pickled green beans, buttered biscuits, mulberry pie, and Tory's special baked Swedish treats. They had devoured the feast without leaving a morsel for the forest creatures. Tory's first Thanksgiving was one he'd never forget.

Tory had already learned from Franklin that Wicasha was a winkte. He'd heard in Chicago that some Indian tribes openly practiced same-sex love, but he had never invested much time considering what that might be like for them. Whenever the three of them were together, Wicasha never spoke about it. What was there to talk about? They were all comfortable with one another's kinship, and they needed to express few intimate words.

Winter's arrival did not spare Tory and Franklin from outdoor work. They still had to pile hay for the livestock (which entailed shaking it free from frost), slop the hogs, feed the hens (although their egg production in winter dropped by half), chop extra wood, and keep a snow-free path from the cabin to the barn and outhouse.

But the fallow field and shorter daylight hours allowed for extra time together indoors, just the two of them, alone. Franklin stitched rugs and crafted wooden bowls and spoons. Tory started keeping a journal. He wrote by lantern for hours at a stretch. Some occasions they spoke not a word. Domestic bliss filled the cabin, underscored by the warmth from the stove. Tory never tired of the sound of the crackling and hissing pinewood, as long as he didn't have to sit near the flames.

Franklin seemed to find Tory's strange habits and fears amusing. Without complaint, he'd load the wood into the stove and stoke the fire, something he had always done for many years, anyway. Tory's awe for Franklin intensified. He garnered strength watching him work with one arm. Eventually, Tory began to take his dexterity for granted.

At Christmas, Franklin surprised Tory with a buckskin jacket he'd sewn. Tory had watched him work on it since September when he'd first arrived at Moonlight Gulch but had never imagined he'd intended to give it to him. In exchange, Tory pulled from under the feather bed a shaving set that he'd bought in Spiketrout in October and had kept hidden since. Franklin's elongated smile proved Tory had made a smart purchase.

Often on cold, dark nights, Tory read aloud to Franklin from one of the four books he'd brought from Chicago or from one of Franklin's tattered ones, or he'd recite from memory favorite passages of Walt Whitman. Franklin always grinned whenever Tory read to him. The look on his face, rosy and cheery, radiated simple happiness. He seemed to enjoy hearing the sound of Tory's voice.

The best moments were when Franklin stood and stretched after long periods woodworking or sewing and wandered over to Tory and kissed his head for no apparent reason. A frisson of power and warmth would overcome Tory. He'd lay aside his stirring spoon or pencil or book and wrap his arms around his new beau.

Tory never tired submitting to Franklin's touch. Inhibitions no longer hindered their passion under the glow of lanterns or the ambient light of a snowy day. They searched each other with their hands and tongues, whispering their hearts' longings, exposed and unrestrained.

One time, while Tory poured hot water into Franklin's kettle bath by the stove, Franklin simply stood, lifted Tory, and, leaving wet footprints across the cabin floor, laid Tory out on the bed. To the crackling of the wood fire, they made love until a chill reminded them that the embers needed feeding.

"Does it seem odd to you to lay with a man the way men are meant to with women?" Tory dared ask while Franklin stoked the fire. Tory lay sprawled on the bed, naked and spent. "Do you miss the touch of a woman, Franklin?"

Franklin remained quiet, contemplating. His brown skin had faded during the winter, and Tory found the faint freckles on his nose and cheeks delightful. Flames from the fire reflected in his eyes like tiny green orbs. Franklin's answer? He strutted to the bed, climbed on top of Tory, and pecked him with many kisses until Tory's giggles left him coughing.

Franklin's lifting Tory off his cot and tossing him onto his bed that hot and muggy October night after the murder trial hadn't really surprised Tory. He had sensed the stirrings inside Franklin, as he often did with men. If anything, Tory was shocked that Franklin had acted so quickly and with so little self-scorn afterward. Franklin's steadfastness had reaffirmed what Tory had guessed from the first time he'd read his advertisement in the *Matrimonial News*: Franklin harbored a strong, strident masculinity—so potent he was like the lone bull sitting upon a hill, dauntless in his desires.

Once Tory had realized who had carried him off, he had relented to Franklin's power. To feel his body pressing into him, melding with his, had swathed him in a surreal fervor. He had whispered into his ears, begging Franklin to do as he pleased, to take him fully. The days that followed carried the suggestion that Tory had another grasp at romance. He and Franklin Ausmus had become lovers. Not even nature dared to question it. Bachelorhood might not loom in Tory's destiny after all.

Guilt for having written Franklin those letters chafed him at times, usually when Tory was studying Franklin from across the cabin while he focused on a task. He'd see the workings of his mind comingle with the movement of his hand and knees that he often used as second and third hands, and realize that, along with his unwavering strength, Franklin was a gentle lamb—a man who kept to his own business and had harmed few in his life outside of the mandates of war. At times, Tory found himself on the verge of confessing his deed, his lips puckered, the words poised on his dry tongue. Franklin, annoyed with Tory's staring, would finally ask, "Speak your mind, Chicagoan." Tory answered only with flushes and chuckles. He never could reveal the truth.

Could Franklin accept that it was Tory—and not Torsten P.—who had written to him seeking to be his mail-order bride?

In February, they celebrated Tory's twentieth birthday. With the snowshoes Franklin had crafted from buckskin and pine, they hiked along the creek. Tory, wearing one of Franklin's hefty bear-fur coats, stood over the frozen creek pool and tried to see down to the bottom. Air pockets resembling diamonds obscured his view. The crunch of snow and frozen twigs joined their light chatter as they tracked a snowshoe hare to the barbwire fence but never found him. Melting icicles hung from the pine branches. The hazy sun warmed their exposed faces.

Tory lamented the first tangible sign of the lengthening days. Winter, sheathing them in solitude, had safeguarded them from all the tribulations of the world, walling off the pillagers. He enjoyed being stuck in the cabin with Franklin, when all he had to do was stand, turn his head, or utter a sigh, and Franklin would glance up with a smile or press his bushy mustache firmly against his mouth.

Yet spring released the fragrances and sounds that tickled Tory. Fever for adventure and exercise, to spread his arms to the Black Hills, lifted him early from bed each morning along with the sun and ushered him out the door. In those moments he missed Chicago the most. He'd reflect on his time with his comrades and their springtime baseball games or strolling the busy avenues where he would watch people and all the commotion.

Tory was not alone with his restlessness. The spring also aroused more agitation from the animals, particularly the hogs. One early April day, when the last of the snow had melted, Tory stepped outside the cabin, wondering why the swine were fussing. Franklin, stomping around the pigpen, seemed beside himself.

"What's the matter with the pigs, Franklin?" Tory said, walking to the pen. "I can hear them squealing inside the cabin."

"They know it's that time of year."

"What time of year?"

"Slaughter season. Time for last year's pigs to become this year's bacon and ham."

Tory winced. He'd seen more animals shot, gutted, butchered, hung, and cured in his eight months at Moonlight Gulch than in his entire life. He'd read about (and often smelled) the stock yards back in Chicago; never had he seen so many large animals killed. The pigs, especially, exhibited a humanlike awareness. But he understood the realities of subsistence living.

"Don't shoot that one." Tory pointed to a three-hundred-pounder he'd named Grover after the portly president.

"He's not big enough yet." Frank grunted over the squeals. "He's got another year."

"I'll make sure to put him on a diet." Tory had grown fond of the pigs, despite the stench.

Franklin eyed Tory in his gray pinstripe suit, blue cravat, and felt derby. "What you so dressed up for?"

"I wanted to go into town to mail a letter. It's about time I inform my parents about my whereabouts."

"Is that what you been scribbling in the cabin the past few days?"

"It's unfair to keep them wondering about my whereabouts. I should've told them months ago. Besides, I'm itching to get into town and buy a few things we ran out of over the winter. I haven't been back there since October. That's half a year ago."

"Can't you wait for me? We can ride in together tomorrow. I sort of planned it."

"I'd rather leave the hog butchering to you, if that's okay."

"Just make sure you don't dillydally. You might as well trade some of the jerky at the mercantile for some rifle bullets while you're there. I was going to, but since you're going.... We used most of them last hunt."

Tory flushed. "Sorry, I suppose that's my fault." Franklin and Wicasha had been teaching him hunting skills, and his wayward shots wasted rounds.

"No worry, you're learning fast. Get a twenty-pack. We don't need many. And don't think about riding one of those farm chunks into Spiketrout."

"Why not?"

"Those horses are too big for you. Either hitch the wagon or ride Carlotta."

"Ride a mule into Spiketrout?"

"She's good for it. Done it myself a few times when the horses were tuckered out or lame."

"Well, I'm not for hitching the wagon, unless you want to."

"I'm up to my knickers in pig slop."

Tory chuckled. "I guess I'll ride Carlotta."

"Don't forget to lock the gate behind you." Franklin turned back to the hogs.

"I'll see you later this afternoon. I've already got supper cooking in the Dutch oven." Tory saddled Carlotta and made sure to stuff the large pockets of his buckskin jacket, the one Franklin had made for him for Christmas, with enough jerky to barter with Mr. Kenny at the mercantile. He also stuffed in a handful of oats for the mule in case she tired during the eighteen-mile round trip.

He relished the quiet ride into Spiketrout. Spring was fully awakening. The small waterfall had broken from winter's icy grip and frothed with a fresh exuberance of snow runoff, not yet full force, but growing. Added color dotted the perpetually lush landscape. Along the south-facing slopes, tiny blossoms struggled to bloom. Pasqueflowers had pushed aside the duff, revealing purple bulbs about to explode. Berries hung from the alders like tiny ornaments. The breeze off the higher elevations brought the smell of snow, but the sun-dappled forest radiated with warmth.

Tory was almost disappointed to see Spiketrout emerge under the canopy of trees two hours later. Main Street lay flat, like a dirty blanket. Mud puddles and fresh horse dung in the street sloshed under Carlotta's hooves. The wood structures smelled dank and mildewy. Yet most things remained how he'd remembered them. Shouts, laughter, and player piano music streamed from the Gold Dust Inn, where the town folks had probably wasted most of their winter nestled in booze and Madame Lafourchette's steam heat. A few stragglers hung out under the canopy of the barbershop. Two men leaning against a post ogled Tory on his mule.

First stop, the postal office. He needed to deliver his letter to his parents. He'd decided against sending them a telegram until after they'd responded to his first outreach. Then, maybe, if all went well, they could maintain a regular correspondence by more modern means. He hitched Carlotta and strolled inside. Jim, working behind the counter, greeted him with a smile. The postmaster had several pieces of mail for Franklin, including a parcel he had stowed in the back, but Tory said he wouldn't be able to carry them and that he and Franklin would fetch them in a few days. He handed Mr. Carson the letter to his parents and headed across the street.

Tory traded the shopkeeper, Mr. Kenny, jerky for a box of rounds and some herbs. Mr. Kenny said he was glad to get the jerky, since he had run out. "None of the folks in Spiketrout seem to do much hunting anymore," he said. "They are all too busy with their drinking and scrounging. If it wasn't for all us business owners and decent homesteaders like Franklin, we wouldn't have any honest customers."

Tory pocketed the twenty-pack of bullets and herbs in his jacket and thanked Mr. Kenny.

On the way back to the homestead, Tory grew troubled. Mr. Kenny's coarse words had conjured images of Henri Bilodeaux. He had not thought of the man since before Christmas. Like the other desperados in Spiketrout, he possessed one standout attribute—a keen insight into his own wants. Carlotta stirred too. She halted and fussed, wheezed and squealed. Maybe it was a bad idea to ride her for such a long journey, Tory thought. Inexperienced in horsemanship, Tory tried to use gentle words to coax her. He stopped for a short break and handfed her oats. A pleased palate seemed to motivate her. She settled down, and they got back on their way. Ribbons of sunlight brushed Tory's shoulders as Carlotta carried him along in an easy stride. The crunch of leaves and duff under her shoes filled the narrowing gulch. Tory thought he heard other snaps. He looked around. Perhaps it was the echo of Carlotta's steps.

An object ahead attracted his attention. As they neared, he could hardly believe his eyes. A man lay on the side of the trail, holding his stomach and moaning in pain. He spurred Carlotta to a trot and quickly dismounted.

"What's wrong?" Tory asked, squatting next to the man. "Are you all right? Can you speak?"

The last thing Tory remembered, he was reaching for the man's shoulder to shake him when a sharp pain spread across the back of his head.

# Chapter
# TWENTY-SIX

WORRY kept Franklin from concentrating on his chores. He put too much feed in the horse trough. He'd forgotten to collect the hens' eggs until their cackling reminded him. He left open the gate to the pigpen after the slaughter and wasted ten minutes rounding up a wayward hog. The sun was already setting beyond the western peaks. They should be sitting down to supper by now. What was keeping Tory?

He took the roast off the fire but had no intention of eating, despite how delicious it smelled. From the window, he saw Wicasha making his way along the field. Relief buoyed Franklin. He dashed outside to meet him.

"Wicasha, I'm glad you're here. Stay by the homestead, will you? I need to ride out to Spiketrout."

"This time of day? It'll be dark soon. What's going on?"

"Tory went into town to deliver a letter. He should've gotten back by now."

Franklin did not like the lines that creased the Lakota's face. Wicasha had made a handful of trips into Moonlight Gulch since mid-March, and he had regained most of the weight he'd lost over winter, thanks to Tory's cooking, but his face still sagged with skin. That skin now crinkled and flexed with what Franklin recognized as alarm.

"I'll stick by here and keep my eyes peeled, Frank," Wicasha said, his tone grave. "You can take my gelding."

"No, Tory took the mule. I'll be able to ride Lulu."

"Maybe the mule tired, and they're resting along the trail. You know how mules can be. Stubborn as mules."

Wicasha's shoddy attempt at levity failed to lessen Franklin's worries. He jogged off to the barn. Two minutes later, he came galloping out at top speed atop Lulu. He stopped long enough to shout to Wicasha to shut the gate behind him. He turned a sharp right, reached down with barely a pause to unhitch the gate, and raced off for Spiketrout.

Tory was nowhere along the trail. No sign of him at all. Franklin shouted for him. No response. The trail, soft from the melting snow, showed clear signs Carlotta had stomped by. He dismounted a few times to inspect the surrounding woods. Nothing conclusive.

The concern that had nudged him earlier evolved into a pawing fear.

Postmaster Jim noted the distress on Franklin's face when he stepped inside the postal office.

"What's the matter, Frank?"

"Have you seen Tory?"

Jim said that Tory had come into the office earlier that morning, dropped off his letter, then left. That was the last he'd seen of him. "Sorry, Frank. I don't know what else to tell you. What do you think became of him?"

Franklin did not want to answer.

Out on the street, Mr. Tang, owner of the Chinese laundry, said he had seen something fishy when he'd noticed two men leaning against a post watching Tory run about town with more interest than he'd thought normal. But he'd only recognized one of them, Ralph Burgermyer. After Tory stepped into the mercantile, Mr. Tang said, Burgermyer wandered down the street, and he hadn't seen him since.

Franklin knew Burgermyer was a close associate of Bilodeaux. He often worked on his ranch north of town. But before he headed there, he hastened to the marshal's office.

"I can't do nothing about a missing person until he's gone a good while," the Marshal declared. Deputy Ostrem stood by Reinhardt's side, scowling at Franklin. "You know how many people around here show up missing? I'd never get any sleep if I always went out looking for them all. He'll show up, don't worry."

"You got to do something."

Reinhardt shrugged. "Like I said, nothing I can do."

"Something's not right." Franklin turned to leave. "And I aim to find out just what."

"Don't cause any trouble in town," Marshal Reinhardt hollered after him, standing up to showcase is full six-foot height. "It's been a quiet winter for Spiketrout, and I'm in no mood for a ruckus."

"I'm not in the mood for no ruckus either, Reinhardt." Franklin disregarded the marshal's warning as he hurried down the boardwalk for the mercantile. The shopkeeper's adolescent son said he'd seen Tory come into the store and trade jerky for a box of shells and some spices.

"Did he seem odd, Scott, like he was doing something against his will?"

The boy narrowed his eyes and wrinkled his forehead. "No, Mr. Ausmus, can't say that he did. I can ask Pop once he gets back. He's home tending to a leaky roof."

"If you don't mind, thanks."

With new fears squeezing the pit of his stomach, Franklin rode Lulu five miles north of town to Bilodeaux's ranch, where pasture opened like a cleaved pork chop. He was unable to admire the expanse of lush grassland surrounded by the mountains. He'd seen the Black Hills from inside most of his ten years, rarely venturing beyond Spiketrout or his homestead. Massive peaks, the tallest between the Rockies and the Alps, jetted toward the sky, darkening as dusk neared.

"You have no business here," one of Bilodeaux's men proclaimed from the gate to his ranch once Franklin reined Lulu alongside it.

"Bilodeaux trespasses on my land when he sees fit, I suppose it wouldn't hurt if I look around his?"

"You'll look around from the pearly gates up in heaven, but that's about the only way."

"Listen, Dunne, I know Bilodeaux pays you good money, but you gotta clue me in. What's going on? Does he got Tory or not? Some in town said they spotted Burgermyer trailing him, and Burgermyer is known to do Bilodeaux's dirty work for him from time to time."

"I don't know anything about Bilodeaux's doings, or Burgermyer's," Dunne said, peering at Franklin under the brim of his Stetson with cutting brown eyes. "I stand guard here, that's it. That's what he pays me for."

"How long you been standing on your post?"

"He asked me to come over a few hours ago."

That sounded strange to Franklin. Something was up. His instincts never betrayed him. "Is Bilodeaux inside?"

"I don't know." Dunne stood firm. "Been on this spot since I got here. It was Vargas who come get me on Bilodeaux's orders."

"All right, Dunne. You just better hope nobody's running afoul here, or you'll be culpable."

"Head on back to your homestead, Ausmus."

Frustrated and angry, Franklin rode back into town. He stopped by the Gold Dust Inn and inquired with Madame Lafourchette and her girls, along with the other employees and the patrons. No one had seen Tory. He revisited the mercantile. Mr. Kenny had just arrived from home and reaffirmed his son's account of Tory's time in the store, but he hadn't seen him since.

On the trail back to Moonlight Gulch, Franklin roved his eyes through the thickening darkness. Still no trace of Tory. His only relief came when he imagined that, once he returned to the cabin, he'd find Tory reheating the roast and Wicasha sitting at the table eager for supper. Smoke rising from the chimney might be the most wonderful sight he'd ever laid his eyes upon.

But as he cleared the dense grove of aspen and spruce along the northern rock face and craned his neck in anticipation by the gate, no smoke flowed from the chimney. His heart slumped in his stomach. He climbed down from Lulu and walked her inside the gate, too dispirited to ride her in. Then, suddenly, his heart fluttered with gladness. Wicasha was leading Carlotta into the barn. Tory had returned. Franklin rushed to Wicasha with Lulu in tow, yet something on Wicasha's face stopped him.

"What is it, Wicasha?" Franklin whispered. "Where's Tory?"

"I found Carlotta squealing by the gate, still saddled," he said. "But I couldn't see or find Tory anywhere. I followed down the trail a mile, saw nothing. How about you? Anyone in town able to help?"

His mouth too dry to speak, Franklin shook his head. Lulu's reins fell from his hand. He jerked into action. "I got to find him. Somewhere, he's out there. I have to look deeper into the forest. I have to look now."

"I'll come with you. It'll be total darkness soon before the moon rises. We'll need torches."

"Is it Bilodeaux, Wicasha?" Franklin appealed to his friend with wide eyes. He already suspected the bandit, but Wicasha would confirm what his gut told him.

The taut-mouthed Lakota nodded. "Yes, I'm certain it is. This was the ruthless act I've feared."

Franklin continued to eye him. "He saw us, Wicasha. Bilodeaux saw Tory and me in bed together."

Wicasha licked his lips. "We best get moving."

Franklin wasted no time. He raced for the torches, packed his guns and ammunition and other supplies, and filled the canteens with water. "He can have Moonlight Gulch, if that's what he wants," Franklin said, a lit torch searing the side of his face. "Let him have it. Let them all have it."

"Don't worry, Frank," Wicasha said. "I don't think Bilodeaux's plan is to plunder your land while you hunt for Tory. He has something craftier in store."

"Like what, Wicasha?"

"I guess we'll have to find out."

# CHAPTER
# TWENTY-SEVEN

TORY awoke with a pummeling headache. He rubbed his head, stretched to sit upright, fell back down onto something hard. Nothing soft like the feather bed he shared with Franklin. It was pitch dark. And cold. But not freezing cold. More like the damp daytime April temperatures.

Instinct told him it was not daytime but not as late as the darkness indicated. What time was it? He lifted his pocket watch to his eyes, then to his ear. No ticking. He tilted the watch, trying to get a better look into the face. It had been smashed. He tucked the watch back inside his pocket and sat upright slowly, biting his lower lip to push down the ache in his head.

He reached for the back of his noggin. There was something sticky. The dark on his fingertips glistened when he brought his hand closer to his eyes. Blood. Tasted like blood too. Something had hit him. Maybe a heavy branch had fallen while he rode the trail. That sometimes happened. It had even killed a man traveling on horseback from Deadwood to Rapid City, he'd once heard.

But where was he? Indoors somewhere, although it didn't feel like he was indoors. Didn't feel like he was outdoors, either. He tried to piece together all that had happened. For a moment, he used logic to deduce that he and Franklin had gone camping to get away from the heavy spring cleaning and repair work around the homestead. He must be inside a trapper's cabin. But where was Franklin? He wanted to call out his name, but something told him to stay quiet.

What had they done the past twenty-four hours? He and Franklin had worked around the cabin and the barn. Franklin was preparing to butcher the hogs. Tory had itched to get out. He'd been riding Carlotta. He'd mailed a letter in Spiketrout, bartered something at the mercantile.

Then he remembered.

He'd been heading back to Moonlight Gulch when he had noticed a man lying on the side of the trail, moaning in pain. Then what? Hadn't he stopped to see if the man needed help? Yes, he'd raced ahead and perched near the man, inquiring if he was injured. He couldn't remember anything else. That must've been when something struck him. Perhaps by a branch or....

Perhaps by a person. The same bandit who had attacked the poor man he'd found writhing along the trail. Made sense.

But something about that man he found curious. He'd looked familiar. He had seen him in town just a few hours before when he rode in on Carlotta. Where *was* Carlotta?

He peered around, searching for a window. He heard dripping. Dripping that echoed.

That was when he realized—he was in a cave.

His ears tuned to the low, steady hum of wind from the tiny crevices. He could make out only a faint light emanating from above about twenty yards ahead. The lone visible light. Instinctively, he went to move toward the light. But the sharp pain in his head forced him back.

Something in his pocket poked him in the side. He reached for what felt like a box—the shells he'd bartered for at the mercantile, along with the bags of coriander, oregano, and dill. They were in his pocket too, on top of the box. He had hoped to surprise Franklin with the spices for supper.

A stir somewhere in the cave.

Alert, he peered into the darkness. The hard rock underneath him cut off the circulation in his backside. He shifted his weight. Someone coughed. Were there others in the same predicament as he? The poor man he'd found along the trail, perhaps? Were they held against their wills? But what for?

"Is there anyone there?" Tory called.

He heard the clearing of a throat, then the advancing steps of someone in boots. "How you doing, youngster?" a raspy-voiced man said.

Tory stared, confused. Blurry images wavered in his mind. He squinted toward the voice as if to cut into the darkness. "Who are you?"

"I seen you in town," the man said. "Perfect opportunity to beat you out on the trail before you headed back. You thought I was hurt, didn't you?" The man snickered. "Stupid fool. Gullible as a lamb."

Tory's eyes adjusted to the dark, and he noticed the man wearing his derby. "You're... you're that man from the trail, the one I stopped to help."

"You felled for it too." The man chuckled. "While I was moaning and groaning and rolling about, my partner leaped from behind a tree and conked you on the head with a rifle butt. Guess no good recompense can come from helping out your fellow man." The man laughed so hard the echo pierced Tory's already splitting head.

"Where am I?" Tory whispered, wishing to have inflicted more strength into his voice.

"You're in a cave somewhere. There're hundreds of them in the Black Hills. No one is going to find you. So you might as well settle down and get comfortable."

"What do you want with me?"

"You don't need to worry yourself over that. Just sit back. If you want some water, to your left is a puddle. You can drink it up. Nice and cool and clean."

"What happened to my mule? Where is she?"

"Don't fuss none over that longears, she'll find her way back home. I gave her a good swift kick in her hindquarters to get her moving."

"I don't have any gold, if that's what you're after."

The man chortled. "It ain't *your* gold we're after."

"We? What do you mean by *we*? Who else is here? Your partner, is he here, too?"

The man's laughter grew fainter as he wandered back from where he came. A moment later, a small flickering light ascended from the ground. Smoke rose into the small opening where Tory had first noticed a dim light, what he now guessed must be from the flickering moon.

Soon he could smell cooking, and his stomach grumbled. Must be past suppertime, perhaps seven o'clock, based on the lack of light coming from the crevice. He had no food, only the herbs in his pocket. He wished he had saved some of those oats he'd fed Carlotta.

He glanced behind him. Deeper blackness met his gaze. The opening to the cave must be closer to where the man had started the fire. If he could get to the fire, snatch some of it, perhaps he could use it as a torch and find his way out. But how would he avoid that man? Or his partner, if he lingered somewhere hidden?

Was he trying to talk himself out of getting near fire?

He wrapped his arms around his stomach. The dampness seeped into his bones. He wanted to sleep, but he feared he might never wake. He could use a drink. Despite himself, he felt his way to his left, where the man had said a small puddle was located. Finding it, he cupped some of the cold water and sipped. The water, dribbling through his fingers and down his chin, revitalized him.

After five or six handfuls, he scuffled back to his spot, his eyes fixed on the fire. Other than his pounding heart, it was the only sign of life in the dank cave. Then an idea came to him.

"Would you like to add spice to your meal?" he called to his kidnapper, hoping his voice remained steady. He heard movement. The man was stirring. He had succeeded in grabbing his attention. "I've got some spices you can use. I'd hate to see them go to waste."

Footsteps echoed closer. "Spices? Where you got spices?" The man blocked Tory's view of the fire.

Tory gazed at his murky form. "In my pocket. Dill, coriander, and some oregano. I bought some while in Spiketrout. I can put some on whatever it is you're cooking. I'm sure it'll improve the taste, whatever it is."

The man breathed. "I already fingered your pockets."

"You must've missed," Tory said, his tone genial. He reached into his jacket and held out the three small bags of spices.

With a snort, the man squatted in front of Tory and yanked the herbs from his hand.

Tory could see he had lifted the bags to his face and was smelling the scents. "Thanks, boy," the man said, his voice full of mirth. "These'll make my beans tastier, you can bet. Too bad you won't be having none." Snickering, he stomped back toward the fire.

Tory mentally kicked himself for failing to carry out his plan. At least the man had missed finding the box of rifle shells whenever he'd "fingered" his pockets. Good thing Franklin had made them extra deep. Too bad Tory had no rifle to use the bullets in.

He worried for Franklin. Whatever nightmare Tory had gotten himself into, he hoped that Franklin wasn't in a worse predicament.

# CHAPTER
# TWENTY-EIGHT

FRANKLIN cursed himself for his stupidity permitting Tory to travel into town alone unarmed. Winter had made him soft, forgetful, less mindful of his worries. He had become passive. Tucked away in the gulch in the warm cabin with Tory, he'd lost sight of the dangers that lurked all around them.

He should've known as soon as the first buds had emerged on the aspens and birches, Bilodeaux, too, would be awakening—awakening to his greedy deceptions and manipulations.

The sun seeped inside from the back windows. The brightness left Franklin empty, like a hot air balloon released of its helium. He and Wicasha had slept not a wink. Their overnight hunt for Tory had been futile. The nighttime forest had coughed up no tracks, no sign of Tory. Not even the skilled scout Wicasha had located clues that might lead them to Tory's whereabouts.

Once they'd returned, they had sat awake through the rest of the night. Four lanterns had burned until the pink glow of dawn stole away the blue twilight. Wicasha had encouraged him by saying that morning would chase away the fears and the uncertainty. He had been wrong. Franklin paced. Wicasha sat at the table, his arms frozen across the top, his eyes on his half-eaten breakfast of cold roast and carrots.

Franklin kicked a dust pail across the floor. The sound reverberated in the small cabin, empty and chilly.

"Obviously Bilodeaux wanted me to know about Tory," Franklin said, stomping back and forth. "Why else would he have let Carlotta wander back home? He wanted us to find her and to despair."

Before speaking, Wicasha allowed Franklin to throw another tantrum, this time chucking a broom into the corner of his sleeping area. "Her showing without her rider is a message, you can be sure,"

Wicasha said sympathetically. "A message that he's ready to play a game with you."

"What can we do? Reinhardt didn't give a flying pig's rump when I told him Tory's missing."

"The others will keep their eyes peeled," Wicasha tried to assure him. "Doc Albrecht, Madame Lafourchette, Reverend Dahlbeck and his wife, the Tangs. Many others have shown concern for Tory."

"What if it's too late?"

"It's not too late, Frank. Do you think Bilodeaux took Tory for no reason? He will use him as ransom. He wants your gold, not to harm Tory."

Franklin recalled the stares the bandit had given Tory. Lustful, hungry ogling. He cringed. Perhaps Wicasha was wrong, like he had been about morning driving off the troublesome thoughts. Bilodeaux might want to hurt Tory. But would he...? Could he? Franklin tossed aside the wooden spoon he'd been fondling to curb his frustration. "I'll give him my gold. I'm sick of fighting them. It's not worth it if Bilodeaux or anyone else harms Tory."

"You must love the chikala wasichu very much," Wicasha said, his eyes following Franklin around the cabin.

Thoughts of his love for Tory softened Franklin. He almost chuckled, realizing how much Tory had stolen his heart. How could it be? How had it happened? Had he stewed in the backwoods of the Black Hills for so long that he would fall for the first human being who showed him the slightest tender care, even a man? Or, he considered, allowing truth to reach from his gut and grasp onto his mind, perhaps he had always searched for Tory. Perhaps the renter in Richmond had not been so much of an anomaly. Had he, Franklin Ausmus, been the one who had left his girl in Knox County, and not the reverse?

Shaking himself, he realized none of that mattered now. He must find Tory. Yet Wicasha insisted they stay put.

"Bilodeaux will come," he said, making the Lakota hand sign for calm, both hands raised, flapping up and down at the wrists like a bird's wings. "He will let you fret, then he will send a message somehow. There is nothing to do now but wait. Trust me. Bilodeaux must make the next move, and then you will have Tory back in your life."

# CHAPTER
# TWENTY-NINE

IT HAD to be morning. A brighter light fell from the overhead crevice used for the chimney. Tory's stomach had stopped grumbling. He had gone without food for so long that his body's hunger cravings had ceased demanding satisfaction.

He rubbed his eyes and stretched his arms. He noticed an added ache to match the one in his head—his back. His buckskin jacket had proved a poor excuse for a mattress on the hard cave floor. His cravat, having choked him during much of the night, lay unfastened next to him. Clammy chill nipped at him. He slipped on his jacket and blew hot breath into his cupped hands.

Presently, Tory could make out shapes and shadows in the cave more clearly than the previous night. The cave appeared medium in size, with no noticeable openings or climbable shelves. Flowstone and columns spread around him. He detected no means of escape on his side of the fire, which still flickered with feeble flames. Two men stood on the fringe. Bilodeaux's thick accent suddenly reached his ears. He and the other man were arguing.

"I want my recompense," the man grunted.

"You will get it, Burgermyer." Bilodeaux sounded perturbed, impatient.

"When?"

"As soon as we get the deed to his land. You will be paid in gold, like the rest of us. Lots of it."

"You think Ausmus will give up his land, with all that gold on it, just for some youngster?"

"Trust me," Bilodeaux said with an odd lilt to his cunning voice. "He will not want anything to happen to that one."

"I don't get it."

"You do not have to. Just shut up and keep watch over the entrance."

"Listen, Bilodeaux. If not for me, you wouldn't even know about this cave. You owe me a bit more respect."

"I owe you nothing," Bilodeaux barked. "Now, where is that boy?"

The man Bilodeaux had called Burgermyer must have pointed, for Tory did not hear a response. Footsteps receded as he obeyed Bilodeaux and went to keep watch outside. Soon, another set of footsteps approached Tory. A few seconds later, Bilodeaux looked down at him.

"Comfortable?"

"I knew you lurked behind this." Tory had no use for inane pleasantries with Bilodeaux. He was ready to butt heads with him if he must. "I never heard of anything so desperate. Tricking Franklin into signing over his deed in exchange for me?"

"Your Franklin gave me no other choice, mon ami." Bilodeaux dropped to a squat and dragged his finger along the cave floor. Tory, unable to distinguish any subtle facial expressions, watched Bilodeaux's teeth and eyes shine bright and penetrating. "All he had to do was relinquish his gold," Bilodeaux went on. "He could have kept his land. Could have kept you. But it is his greed that prevents things from running smoothly."

"But it's his land. How can someone be greedy for what belongs to them? Greedy people take from others. Franklin can do what he wants with his own property. You have no rights to it."

Bilodeaux laughed, throwing his head back in the way Tory had become accustomed to seeing with the bandit. "Rights? What does the word *rights* mean, anyway?" Bilodeaux said. "You want to hear about one's rights?"

Tory sat straighter, alert to the change that had come over Bilodeaux's tone. Severe, piercing, yet faraway.

"My father left my mother and me when I was no older than two," Bilodeaux said, his gaze on the rigid cave floor. "Left us penniless, with absolutely nothing. He took even the dishes. I watched my mother struggle. I grew up hungry, angry, wondering how I could protect her yet knowing I was as helpless as she. It reached a point she would do anything for a pence." He stood and walked to his right staring off away from Tory. His voice became muffled.

"I vowed I would never live in poverty again," he said. "When I think about men like your beau sitting on so much wealth, it sickens me. Rights? I have rights too. Rights to live a life that men like your Franklin Ausmus cheated me out of. Rights to sanctify my mother, who endured unthinkable misery merely to feed her son one measly meal a day."

"Franklin isn't responsible for your father leaving you and your mother."

"He is more responsible than you realize, mon petit chéri. It is men like him who want only for themselves, like my father, leaving nothing for anyone else, not even crumbs to scrape off the floor."

"Your unfortunate past is no excuse for criminal behavior."

"Criminal behavior?" Bilodeaux's voice strengthened. He had turned back to face Tory. Tory could almost feel his blue eyes cutting into him. "What do you understand of criminal behavior? You think I am a criminal?" He laughed again. "You have no idea what a real criminal is capable of. You are living like a prince in my company. If I did to you what the real criminals of the world do, like what the Tories in Quebec did to my mother, treating her like a slave to do what they wished with her until they used her up like filthy rags, you would scream bloody horror."

Despite the chill, sweat broke out above Tory's brow and dribbled down his temples. Bilodeaux's meaning eluded him. The man was mad. The longer he was forced to remain in his presence, the more Tory feared for himself and Franklin.

"Don't you have enough money?" he spewed, tears salting his eyes.

"There is no such thing as *enough money*." Bilodeaux snorted. "Money is like water. You do not pour one cup, drink it, and be satisfied for the rest of your life. You must have more. De plus en plus. More each day, until you die."

"Why don't you leave Franklin alone?" Tory snapped.

"It is not so simple." Bilodeaux stepped closer. "Beyond wanting the gold in the creek pool that sits on his land, all for the good of the people of Spiketrout, of course, your Franklin represents a man who, well… he is the worst of all men. The idea that he does not pan for the gold on his land when others suffer... it is more than unnatural. It is cruel. Men like him should be punished. There should be laws against his kind of selfishness."

"What difference is it to you?"

Bilodeaux thrust out his chest. "He wastes a colossal resource that could benefit many."

"If he refused to farm his land, would you bother him then too? There's soil on it, rich soil. No law says he must cultivate it."

"Laws are not always designed for justice." Bilodeaux's voice softened into something akin to a cat yelping for its meal. "If he refused to harvest a bountiful crop, ten thousand acres worth of ripe green corn, then, yes, I would say that I would bother him."

"That's a ridiculous analogy. It's not the same thing, and you know it. Gold is just a rock."

"It is a rock that has ruled the entire planet since before the white man stepped foot in the New World, from Tenochtitlan to Constantinople."

A tear dropped from Tory's eye and chilled his cheek. "You're nothing but a bully, that's all. A rotten bully."

"Ah, you like to protect your man, do you not?" Bilodeaux chuckled.

Tory remained quiet, brooding. He sniffled. "What do you mean?"

"I know about the two of you," he said. His words came at Tory like chucked pickaxes. "The night after his murder trial, I saw you lying in bed together, as if you and he had employed very little time sleeping." He snickered.

Tory stiffened. He didn't recall Bilodeaux intruding on them. He must have been out cold, exhausted and drained. Did Franklin know about this? Conjuring as much courage as he could, Tory said, "I don't care what you think."

"Do not be ashamed." Bilodeaux again squatted near Tory. His breath was hot and bitter and reeked of cigars. "I can understand what Franklin sees in you."

Tory flinched when Bilodeaux stroked his cheek with his broad thumb. He tilted his head, shaking off the bandit's cold touch. Bewilderment and disgust sealed his lips.

"Do you know why I came into Franklin's cabin that morning, hmm?" Bilodeaux stood and peered over Tory's head toward the darkest recesses of the cave, the whites of his eyes like shards of crystal. "The boys in town talked me into standing up for myself. Ausmus had humiliated me in front of the entire town. I had thought drink goaded me. I rode out. My stallion knew the way, even in the dark." He paused, reflecting. Then he blurted, "My intent was to shoot your Franklin between the eyes."

Tory recoiled as if Bilodeaux had struck him. No words came to Tory's quivering mouth. The cave grew smaller, suffocating him. He wanted to flee. But how might he make his escape?

Bilodeaux remained fixed, staring into the bowels of the cave.

"Yes, murder," he said, snapping back to the present and gazing down at Tory. "Just like with that old sot, Johnson. After I blew Ausmus's brains out, my plan was to burn his entire cabin with him in it. When I saw you lying in bed beside him, I sobered fast." Bilodeaux waited, calculating, breathing heavy.

"You saved his life, ma pépite d'or," he continued. "Because you had lain in bed with him, because you had given yourself to him as a woman might, you spared him. Did you ever think your lovemaking might prove so powerful?" He chuckled. "Your love for Franklin infuses me with power, as well, mon garçon. With you, I am certain your beau will give me everything I demand, so long as he can have you back in his bed. I know, I saw it in his eyes even in the dull light of dawn when I looked down at the two of you entangled like bougainvillea. He would rather lose his one remaining arm than lose you. Every man has a price. For your Franklin, that price is you."

The impact of Bilodeaux's words terrified Tory. No doubting his intentions. The bandit's wrath derived from more than hunger for gold or that he thought Franklin "unnatural" for not lusting for it as most men did. Something more sinister and primitive prevailed. Bilodeaux saw Franklin as the epitome of the man he could never become, all that he could never achieve. His hatred for mankind had somehow coalesced into one target—Franklin Ausmus. Bilodeaux had used gold only as a pretext for his crusade. He wanted blood. Franklin's blood.

And Tory, somehow, had to find a way to stop him.

# CHAPTER THIRTY

A SICKLY sound brought Franklin to his feet. Screaming and squealing, underlined by a grunt and a dull thump. With a lit lantern in hand, he rushed outside barefoot. Wicasha, who had slept in the barn the past few nights, was the first on the scene. He was already staring down the trail, where the sound of horses' hooves faded into the pre-dawn. Franklin rushed over.

"Who was it?" he asked, observing that someone had left the gate open.

"I believe we've received Bilodeaux's message."

"What?"

"Over there."

Franklin followed Wicasha's pointing finger with his eyes. His mouth dry and his heart racing, he scurried over to the pigpen. In the glare of his small lantern, a gruesome sight froze him. One of the piglets lay dead outside the pen. Someone had cut its throat from ear to ear and left the knife plunged into its back.

A piece of paper, soaked in blood, was attached by the implanted blade. Trembling, Franklin lowered the lantern over the piglet's carcass and read the note. *Your boy is alive, but it is up to you if he ends up like your piglet. If you choose to involve any officials, you will not like the consequences. More instruction to come.*

Franklin dropped the lantern. Wicasha, who had chased after him, fell to his knees and snuffed out the small flames that had jumped onto the grass. He lifted the lantern as it flickered back to life. Franklin buried his head in his hand.

"That Bilodeaux," Franklin whispered into his palm. "There's no doubt now. I can spot that strange French-style script. I'll kill him. I won't let him get away with this. I'll kill him. One way or the other, I'll kill him."

"Keep your mind straight," Wicasha warned. "Don't let him get you tangled. We'll find Tory. Don't worry. But for Tory's and your sake, keep yourself thinking rational. If you go loony, you'll fall right into Bilodeaux's hands."

"I can't wait any longer, Wicasha." Franklin gazed toward the trail where the pig-killer had escaped. "We have to do something."

Wicasha brought the lantern to his side, away from his eyes. He looked into the cobalt sky, where tiny stars were fading and the Great Bear had shifted over the western mountains. Screwing up his eyes, he said, "Perhaps I'm the one who should do something."

"What? You?"

"Yes." Wicasha's gaze locked onto the darkness. "I have scores to settle with Bilodeaux as well." He turned to Franklin. "But you must stay here and wait for Bilodeaux's next message, like his horrible note says. If he suspects you've left and gone for the authorities, he might stretch his scheme out for days. I can sneak away. He would not be so interested in me. I also know where he likes to hide out in the backwoods. He used to take me to certain spots when we were... before I realized what kind of man he was."

Franklin still hesitated. "But Tory belongs to me," he said without restraint. "I'm the one who should find him."

"No time for you to play hero, Frank. The best thing for you to do is wait here." Wicasha made to move. "I'll need a sack with some supplies, the field glasses, a canteen of water, and three guns. A revolver, a rifle, and a shotgun, fully loaded."

Despite his apprehension, Franklin rushed to gather the supplies Wicasha needed for his scouting trip. Once he collected everything, he handed the sack to Wicasha, who had dressed in his heavy buckskin outfit.

"I'll be back, don't worry," he said. "We will find Tory safe. In the meantime, you keep still, Frank. I won't be gone long. I will try to circle outward, then spiral back in. I'll return back to Moonlight Gulch with or without Tory by tomorrow afternoon. If you're not here, I'll know that Bilodeaux has called for you, and I'll wait for your return. Remember, stand your ground here."

"Aren't you taking a horse?"

"No, I'll want to get through the thicker groves more easily. Best I scout on foot, like I used to when I was with the Army."

"Take this." Franklin thrust out the lantern he held.

"It'll only burden me," Wicasha said, raising his hand. "It'll be light soon enough. Now remember all I told you. Keep your head." He left without looking back.

Helpless and angry, Franklin watched him disappear into the dark.

# Chapter
# THIRTY-ONE

"YOU won't get away with this, Bilodeaux," Tory hollered, feeling bolder in front of the bandit after his second night in the cave. "They'll hang you or put you behind bars for good. The law will catch up with you."

Tory was eating beans the man Burgermyer had baked. Currently, Burgermyer was on his way to Moonlight Gulch to deliver a message, the second mission Bilodeaux had sent him on since last night. He had left late yesterday at Bilodeaux's bidding, but Tory had failed to learn where to or for what purpose. Tory winced. Burgermyer had used too much of the spices he had swiped from Tory, and the beans tasted bitter. At least Bilodeaux had permitted him to eat.

"What law?" Bilodeaux shouted over his shoulder, his back to Tory where he sat by the fire. "I will have everything all legal. Franklin will sign over the deed to his land to me, and then, like each time before, if he accuses me of wrongdoing, it will be his word against mine."

"I won't let Franklin give up his land."

"You are not the one to make that decision."

"You believe Franklin will do anything to save me because of his love for me? Well, I, too, would do anything for Franklin out of love."

"Even sacrifice your life?" Bilodeaux turned to Tory. Ominous shadows masked his face. Only the enamel of his teeth, from what must be one of his sneers, was visible.

"Yes," Tory said, shivering. "Even my life."

Bilodeaux turned his back to him. Smoke curled toward the small gap where scant sunlight cut through. "That may be. But your beau still has time. Burgermyer will give him word. If he longs for you as much as I suspect, within a few hours, the gold will belong to me to do what I wish with it—including allocate some to the unfortunates in the community—and you and Franklin can run off together and live like wolves."

Tory dropped his spoon in the tin plate with a resonant clink. "Please, promise me you won't hurt him. Just promise me that."

"It will be up to your Franklin to decide how much harm will be done." Bilodeaux turned around to face Tory again. He lifted a twig with a small flame on the end to illuminate his face. His contorted features belied no secrets. The oscillating flame revealed the anger, the desperation, the sickness eating away at his heart.

Dispirited, Tory slumped back, away from his empty plate, away from Bilodeaux. All the gold in the world would not quench the fiery hatred in Bilodeaux's soul. Tory knew that. Bilodeaux would haunt Franklin until one of them or both died.

With his knees tight against his chest, Tory rested his forehead in the crook of his arm. Bilodeaux had outfoxed them. There was no way to save Franklin's homestead. The law would rest on Bilodeaux's side, like always. He bore the power and the money the bureaucrats in Spiketrout envied. Even Mayor Winters had sided with Bilodeaux in the past.

Just like in Chicago. Gangsters and politicians. They always stood shoulder to shoulder.

Tired and weak, Tory leaned against a mound of flowstone, wincing in pain. Those darn shotgun cartridges. He wanted to take them out of his coat pocket and chuck them, but Bilodeaux might grow angry that he had carried them.

Suddenly, a notion pushed him upright.

Tory knew that without him, Bilodeaux's plans could not succeed. If he could only find a way to escape. Was it possible? But what if Bilodeaux had ordered guards to stand watch outside while Burgermyer was on his latest mission? Many men had formed allegiances with Bilodeaux for no good reason other than to get their greedy hands on Franklin's gold.

Tory needed to find out.

"Is there a chance I might have some fresh air?" he said.

Bilodeaux's laughter echoed off the cave walls. "Surely you do not think I am that stupid, mon tout beau garçon."

"I only would like some fresh air to breathe, if for only a minute, to clean out my stinging lungs from the soot." He faked a cough into his fist. "I'm sure I'll be unable to get away, what with your henchmen all about guarding the entrance."

"Ah, so you do think I am a simpleton." He snorted. "I have no henchmen. The fewer people involved the better. People have a tendency to talk. I have selected the most loyal of the Spiketrout rowdies to have at my beck and call. Only you, Burgermyer, Parker, I, and your beau know about our doings here. You are as good as disappeared, my young friend."

"I suppose I have underestimated your intellect." Tory shuddered with relief. The cave entrance was unprotected. Now he could consummate the second half of his design. He hoped Bilodeaux would bite as easily.

Coughing and kicking at the ground to distract Bilodeaux from any noise he might make, Tory reached into his pocket, took out the shell box, and carefully placed a handful of bullets back into his pocket as soundlessly as possible. The remaining few shells he left in the box and tucked behind a stalagmite.

With his hand clenched around the bullets in his pocket, he hollered toward Bilodeaux. "You won't mind if I at least sit closer to the fire to get warm. The dampness of this cave is causing my bones to ache."

"Your lungs sting, your bones ache. Any other ailments bothering you?"

"I won't be much good to you sick or dead."

Silence hovered over them. "All right. All right." Bilodeaux grunted. "Come on over. Perhaps we can keep each other warm." He scooted over as if to make room by his side when Tory, his hands thrust deep in his pockets, edged closer to the fire.

Tory gathered confidence in his voice. "That will never happen, Bilodeaux. One thing is certain, if you touch me, I'll make sure Franklin hears about it. Whatever happens with his gold or land, you lay one finger on me, and I doubt he'll let you live to make any good use of it."

The silence that followed Bilodeaux's awkward chuckles indicated that he'd conceded to Tory's warning.

Sitting across from Bilodeaux, Tory measured his next move. The flames leaped, flickered, snapped at him. He swallowed. He must remain calm. He inhaled, his right arm tight around his bent knees, his left hand still in his pocket, clenched around the shells. His fear of fire must in no way keep him from his one and only attempt to rescue himself, to rescue Franklin.

With his free hand, he reached for a small branch sticking out from the fire. Casually, he toyed with it, not wanting to draw Bilodeaux's suspicions. Bilodeaux observed him only for a second. Grunting, he turned back to the fire. Tory lifted the branch, a flame dancing on the end, and grasped it in a tight fist.

Balancing in a subtle squat, he licked his lips. Bilodeaux seemed focused on the flames, lulled into a trance by the way they cracked like whips. Tory squeezed the small torch, his fingernails cutting into his palm. The metallic shells began to itch against his sweaty hand. Coalescing his energy, he took a deep breath.

In one fluid motion, he tossed the bullets into the fire, rolled backward, rushed to his feet, and fled for the cave's opening.

A rush of explosions like from a string of dynamite ricocheted off the cave walls behind him. He stumbled, cut himself on a stalagmite, scurried to right himself, and charged ahead. The small torch barely lit his path. Sheer luck prevented him from gouging his head on the stalactites hanging from the rocks overhead. Gunshots whizzed by his ear. He heard Bilodeaux on his tail, cursing him in French, ordering him to halt. He found himself scurrying up an incline, slipping, rushing forward on his hands and the tips of his toes.

Light appeared. A steep climb of about three feet awaited him. He tossed the torch aside and leaped with all his power, tearing the knee of his trousers on landing. The brightness of the sun blinded him after his confinement in the dark for so long, but he kept running. He had little time to fuss with Bilodeaux's gray stallion, which was hitched near the cave entrance. He bushwhacked through the alders and thickets, zigzagging to keep Bilodeaux off his heels. He wasted no effort glancing back. He gritted his teeth and kept running.

He heard twigs crunch and snap behind him. Bilodeaux must be fast on his trail. He skidded down some duff along a steep slope. He tripped and twisted his ankle on a fallen aspen covered in duff. He discerned the sound of heavy breathing. Bilodeaux—and he was coming down on him like a hound after a fox. He must keep moving, despite his ankle. Which way was Moonlight Gulch? He had no idea where Bilodeaux had held him captive.

He observed the moss growing on the north-facing side of the tree trunks. Both Wicasha and Franklin had taught him, while they'd hiked the forest surrounding Moonlight Gulch, that moss grew on tree trunks away from direct sunlight. Parker and Burgermyer had ambushed him on the trail about five miles north of the homestead. Surely they hadn't taken him south of Franklin's land. He must be still north of there, closer to Spiketrout.

He hoisted himself up with the trunk of a tree and, wincing in pain, ran straight down the slope until it leveled off in a small dell full of early-blooming pink pasqueflowers. Finding the sun flickering from the crowns of the pines and birches, he squinted as he made his way south.

But he didn't get far.

A shadowy figure lurked between the alder bushes at the edge of a ponderosa grove abutting the dell. Bilodeaux must have found him again. Limping from his twisted ankle, Tory dropped to his knees. He crawled behind a birch tree and peeked out. Bilodeaux had gone. But where? Tory held his breath, waiting....

A heavy hand clasped his forearm, covering most of it from his elbow to his wrist. Tory's heart deflated.

"I've been scouting for you."

Tory jerked up. Wicasha's wide, dark eyes gazed down at him. Exhilaration enfeebled Tory. He almost fell over like a doll when he tried to stand. Wicasha steadied him.

"Wicasha, I thought you... I thought you were Bilodeaux."

"I don't see him around. But we'll have to keep going if he's trailing you."

"I've sprained my ankle."

"No matter." Wicasha lifted Tory as effortlessly as if he were a sack of goose feathers. "The trail is just over the next incline. We'll be home soon." After flinging Tory over his broad shoulders, Wicasha carried him toward the trail and on to Moonlight Gulch.

# Chapter
# THIRTY-TWO

RALPH BURGERMYER faced down Franklin like a general with an army of ten thousand men behind him. He clutched Franklin's revolver, which he had swiped from him after Franklin had rushed out of the cabin to check who had blasted onto his land. Franklin had hoped Wicasha had returned with Tory. Bile had burned his throat when he'd seen the no-good Burgermyer galloping in on his crowbait of a pinto.

"Don't make any moves, just listen to what I got to say," Burgermyer said. The muzzle of Franklin's Smith & Wesson brushed Franklin's mustache. "We're gonna go inside your cabin and you're going to get your deed to your land, then we're going to go for a little trip. Just do as you're told and that boy won't get hurt. Not sure why you care, he's nothing but a ranch hand, but Bilodeaux seems to have it in him you'll give up your life for that brat."

"You're awful brave-acting, Burgermyer." Franklin stood face to face with the outlaw. He wanted to strike him, but he held back in case Burgermyer possessed a slippery trigger finger.

Burgermyer nudged the barrel into Franklin's chest. "Let's go. Move it."

They were about to go inside when the sound of galloping hooves made both men turn in the direction of the gate, still ajar from when Burgermyer had entered.

But Henri Bilodeaux did not bother to slow and walk his stallion through the gap. Instead, he rushed the gate full speed. His gray stallion cleared the top wire by at least six inches.

"What's he doing here?" Burgermyer scrunched up his nose. "He's supposed to wait at the cave for me to bring you back, along with the deed to your land."

Franklin winced when he heard the word "cave." They had been holding poor Tory in a damp, dark cave for more than two days. Scolding bitterness clutched his throat.

Bilodeaux dismounted before his stallion came to a complete halt. Next to the lanky Burgermyer, he stood chin-high. Like his cohort, his clothes were covered in dirt and soot. "I got your boy, Ausmus," he said, breathless. "He is safe, for now. You can have him as long as you sign over your deed all nice and legal. No need to make this any more complicated. Go easy and no one will get hurt."

"I want to see him now." Franklin stepped closer to Bilodeaux. He scowled at him, his nose pointing to the top of Bilodeaux's hat.

"There is no time. I told you he is safe. You sign your deed with me now—Burgermyer here standing in as witness—and afterward I will escort you to your boy."

"I thought you wanted me to bring Ausmus to you," Burgermyer said, kicking at the dirt. "I had him all ready to go. He was all scared and whimpering. What gives, Bilodeaux?"

"Shut up, you idiot." Bilodeaux kept his eyes on Franklin, his rifle pointed at Franklin's face. "We will get your deed, you will sign it over to me, and then we will take a ride to see your Tory. Everything will be nice and sweet. But we must hurry."

Franklin eyed the rifle staring him down. The gun, close enough he could make out the rifling grooves inside the barrel, reeked of grease and sulfur. Bilodeaux had discharged it recently. His mind whirled with what to do. He realized the most important action was whatever would carry him quicker to Tory.

"The deed is in my war trunk next to my bed," he said flatly. "You won't miss it."

Bilodeaux gestured with the gun to Burgermyer. "Get it. And grab something to write with."

Burgermyer darted for the cabin.

"You really think you can get away with this, Bilodeaux?" Franklin said, fending off his resentment and anxiety with a snicker.

"You gave me no other choice, Ausmus. You speak of your rights, you and that boy of yours. Well, all mankind possesses rights. Rights to what will bring him riches, a better life. Your sitting on this land refusing to pan for gold—that is the true crime. You gave me no other option how to get it. Most others will agree. Even the marshal."

"So the end justifies the means, is that it?"

Bilodeaux had no time to answer. Burgermyer jogged out of the cabin waving a piece of paper and one of Franklin's graphite pencils. "I got it. I got it. Here it is."

Bilodeaux ordered the lanky man to hold his pistol steady on Franklin while he yanked the paper from his hand. After unfolding the document and scanning it, he grabbed the pencil from Burgermyer. "Sign it over to me," he commanded Franklin, shoving the pencil and deed at his chest.

"How can I be certain you haven't harmed Tory?"

"You have my word. Now do as you are told. You sign, then I give you back your boy, unharmed."

"We ain't harmed him none," Burgermyer asserted. "That's the truth, other than a small knock on his—"

"Burgermyer," Bilodeaux fumed through clenched teeth, "will you keep your mouth shut!"

"I'm supposed to trust the likes of you two?" Franklin eyed the deed pressed against his chest, hesitating, assessing.

"So you harbor less fondness for the boy than I assumed, Ausmus," Bilodeaux said, a sinister grin stretching above his turquoise ascot. "My mistake. You do not care for him, after all."

Burgermyer crinkled his nose, his gun still trained on Franklin. He scratched under his hat. He scanned from Franklin to his boss. Everything around Franklin seemed to converge into the bandits' blaring eyes. He grabbed the deed from Bilodeaux with a defiant brutality and tucked it under his stump. "Give me the damn pencil."

He snatched the pencil and was about to sign when shouting from the gate froze his hand.

"Stop! Stop!"

Franklin turned to see Wicasha waving his arms over his head. Tory, leaning against him, hobbled on one foot.

"He doesn't have Tory," Wicasha hollered. "I got him right here. Don't sign away the homestead. Tory knows Bilodeaux's scheme. He wants you to sign the deed. Don't do it. Tory's free and safe."

From the corner of his left eye, Franklin gauged Bilodeaux's reaction. Bilodeaux, his blue eyes blazing, lifted his rifle, but before he could fire, a shot rang out and the rifle flew from his hands. Franklin acted fast. He punched Bilodeaux full in the face, snapping the pencil in half in the process, and simultaneously kicked Burgermyer in his gut with his left foot. Both went down. Wicasha, with Tory gathered in his arms, raced to them, his rifle smoking.

Franklin grabbed their guns and stared down at the two sprawled bodies. "Get some rope. Let's tie them up before they come to, so we can cart them into town."

THE sight of the two men bound like wayward hogs in the back of Franklin's wagon grabbed nearly all of Spiketrout's attention, including those indoors. Nobody wanted to miss the spectacle of the men bouncing down Main Street. Bilodeaux's gray stallion and Burgermyer's pinto, tethered to the back, wheezed and snorted. Franklin pulled alongside the jailhouse.

Marshal Reinhardt stepped onto the boardwalk, shaking his head. "You bring in more bodies in that wagon of yours than any man in the Hills, Ausmus," he said, peering into the back of the wagon.

"Don't worry, Marshal," Franklin said. Relief still quivered his bones after finding Tory safe and sound. "These two are alive and kicking."

During the drive into town, the two had come to consciousness about the same time. They had fussed to find their hands bound and their ankles tied with a third rope yoking their hands and feet behind their backs. They had cursed up a storm most of the way.

"He has kidnapped us," Bilodeaux shouted. He twisted and squirmed, vainly trying to release his ropes. His hat rolled beside him. His bushy hair fell into his eyes. Dried blood was caked under his nose where Franklin had socked him. Some folks snickered; others stared in shock.

"Now, Henri," the marshal said, scratching under his Stetson, "even I can't be expected to believe Ausmus tied you up for no good reason. Especially since he hauled you into town for anyone who cares to gawk."

Bilodeaux tried to sit upright. He arched his back like a snake and set his eyes on Franklin. "If you people only knew what a deviant this man in your midst is, you would not be so quick to stand here and listen to him."

Wicasha stepped between them. He peered at Bilodeaux with squinty eyes. Bilodeaux's face fell, and he kept his mouth taut. Franklin understood the exchange. Bilodeaux, having once courted Wicasha as his lover, was hardly one to accuse someone of "deviant" behavior.

"What they done, Ausmus?" one man with cavernous black eyes asked.

"Yeah, Frank," another said, reeking of whiskey. "What's going on this time?"

"It's a long story, one best told before a judge and jury," Franklin said. "The short of it is, he kidnapped Tory, tried to use him as ransom to get me to sign over my land so he can get the gold in the creek."

"He is a liar," Bilodeaux shot. "He is the one who abducted us."

"Stop your lying, Bilodeaux," Burgermyer said, his head shaking back and forth and his moist eyes downcast.

"Shut up, you imbecile."

"Aw, you shut up for once, Bilodeaux. I shoulda known all along we ain't gonna get away with your scheme. I'm ready to confess if it means I can get an easy sentence. Jack Parker was in on it too. He's the one who hit the boy on his head."

Bilodeaux's dark-blue eyes simmered purple with fury.

Deputy Ostrem grabbed Burgermyer and untied his leg restraints. "You'll get whatever the jury and judge decide. Come on."

Reinhardt dragged Bilodeaux closer to the edge of the wagon and began untying most of the ropes save for those on his wrists, which eliminated the need for handcuffs. "Let's get you to your feet," he said. "You got yourself in it way up to your head this time, Bilodeaux. Not much anyone's going to be able to do to help you out. Kidnapping? That ain't gonna look good to a jury and judge."

"I want an advocate," Bilodeaux cried, jerking from the marshal's hold.

"You'll get all your rights coming to you, don't you worry. Go easy along with me, we'll take care of you. We got an empty cell, nice and clean, ready for you and Burgermyer."

"I refuse to be confined in the same cell with that cretin," Bilodeaux protested, glowering at Burgermyer.

"We'll put Burgermyer in the other cell with Bloom, Doughty, and Carlyle."

"Fine by me," Burgermyer said, kicking out his liberated feet. "I don't wanna be near Frenchy none, either."

"This is not the end, Ausmus," Bilodeaux spewed at Franklin as Reinhardt poked him toward the jailhouse. "This humiliation will not go unchallenged. You hear me?"

Franklin shrugged off the bandit's threats. He sighed, glad Reinhardt and Ostrem had hauled off the two men to jail and out of his sight. But he wanted Doc Albrecht to examine Tory's injuries, which he had already tended the best he could back at Moonlight Gulch. The doctor, who was standing around with the other gawkers, kindly escorted the three to his office. Tory's prognosis looked good.

"His vision is clear, no apparent trauma. Scrapes and cuts should be fine with the iodine. Ankle's a bit swollen, but if he keeps off of it the rest of the night, shouldn't cause trouble. He'll be back to work on your homestead in no time, Frank."

"Good to know, Doc, thanks."

"I'm hungry," Tory said. "They gave me only beans to eat, and sparingly. I'm sorry, Franklin, they took the herbs I bought for you as a surprise."

Everyone chuckled but Franklin. During the ride into town, he had marveled over Tory's account of his ordeal held captive in a cave for forty-eight hours. Franklin had barely spoken the entire nine-mile trip as he'd listened, other than to turn around and command Bilodeaux and Burgermyer to shut their traps. A strange fury had whirled inside him, mixed with a gentle happiness that everything had ended well. Still, he smarted over the entire ordeal.

"Told you he was in good shape," the doctor said. "Any man with an appetite can't be sick."

Franklin glanced out the window. "It'll be dark before long. I wasn't savvy enough to bring along some lanterns for the ride back."

"You had a lot on your mind," the doc said.

"Let's stay in town," Tory said. "We can get a room at Madame Lafourchette's."

"The Gold Dust? You sure?"

"Why not, it'll be sort of a vacation."

Wicasha gave one of his all-knowing chuckles. "Go ahead, Frank. I'll head back to the homestead by foot. You won't have to worry about things there. I'll take care of the animals. I can find my way along in the dark, done it hundreds of times."

Feeling safer in Spiketrout than at any other time now that Bilodeaux was locked behind bars, Franklin said, "Well, if that's what you both want. Sure. Let's get a good steak and afterward shack up at the inn. You at least join us for supper, Wicasha?"

"That I can do."

"How about you, Doc?"

"Sure, why not?"

MADAME LAFOURCHETTE personally served the four men. She cleared aside a table used for poker, kicked out two earsplitting drunks, and had the finest-looking of her girls help cater to their needs, so they might enjoy a well-deserved "classy meal."

"We'll treat you like kings," she trumpeted. "I'll do my best to get your orders fast. My head cook got himself in some trouble over in Deadwood. He was sneaking around with a married woman. Ain't that something! He's surrounded by my girls, has the pick of the litter, and he has to go find trouble with a married woman. Isn't that just like a man." She shook her head. "Now the fool's holed up in Deadwood with two broken legs, six bruised ribs, and I got a half-wit cook doing the work of two."

"We're in no hurry," Tory said.

"Steaks all around?" she asked.

They all agreed, and the madame hustled into the kitchen. Two of her hurdy-gurdy girls carried over four mugs of beer overflowing with thick froth. Doc Albrecht raised his mug for a toast.

"To finally putting Bilodeaux where he belongs," he said.

"Hear, hear." They tapped their mugs and took long swills.

"I know it sounds a bit odd after I just toasted Bilodeaux's incarceration," the doc said, setting down his beer and wiping the foam from his mustache, "but the man's going to need representation, and no one else in town is capable. Hope you fellows won't get upset if I defend him."

"What?" Tory sat up straight. The beer clenched in his fingers sloshed inside the mug. "How could you do that?"

"Settle down, Tory. Let the man speak." Franklin set his eyes on the doctor. "Defend that deadbeat? What for, Doc?"

"A man has a right to an advocate, whether he's a scoundrel or not," the doctor said. "Innocent until proven guilty. That's what our Bill of Rights provides. Don't worry, I'll just make sure his constitutional rights are upheld, I'm not going to go after your characters or try to fudge his to look good, if that's even possible."

"I doubt Bilodeaux will trust you enough," Wicasha said.

"He won't have a choice, as far as I see it," Doc Albrecht said. "He can defend himself if he wishes, but just wanted to let you know, I'll offer him my services and defend him if he sees fit that I do."

Tory still stewed. Franklin patted his shoulder and tried to laugh off the unpleasantness. "I got another toast," he said, fisting his raised mug tightly. The others joined him, including Tory, although he raised his mug slower and less high than the others. "To constitutional rights."

"To constitutional rights," the others chimed in with chuckles. Tory mumbled the toast but brightened as their mirth grew contagious.

Twenty minutes and many laughs later, Madame Lafourchette brought their steaks, thick and steaming on a large platter. Onions and mushrooms were piled high, and baked potatoes as big as a man's fist (Franklin boasted they might be his, since he often sold some of his potatoes to Madame Lafourchette), lathered in whipped butter, rolled on the side.

"Madame, you've outdone yourself," the doc said, eyeing the plate set before him. "We might have to make another toast." He hoisted his second beer. "To Madame Lafourchette and the Gold Dust Inn."

"Hear, hear."

Madame Lafourchette's blush barely burned through her powdered cheeks. "You fellows enjoy your steaks now," she said, waving her hands at them. "If you need anything, holler at me or one of my girls."

Franklin cut into his steak using the way he'd accomplished the task since losing his right arm: cutting downward with enough pressure to keep the plate from sliding, ensuring he pulled the knife toward him so the plate would rest against his chest for extra resistance. He grinned, noticing Tory watch him with admiration in his eyes.

Not since waking in a tent on a battlefield outside of Petersburg, Virginia, and realizing he was alive after someone had shot him, had Franklin known such relief. Good friends, good food, good conversation. He smiled wider when Tory sneaked a piece of meat under the table for Belle Beau, Madame Lafourchette's yellow housecat. To Franklin, life couldn't get any better.

# Chapter
# THIRTY-THREE

"YOU got any rooms left for me and Tory, Madame?" Franklin inquired at the bar. The others were still sitting around the table, rubbing their full bellies. Coffee and brandy helped with the digestion.

"You want two rooms?"

"Umm… one might be best. Someone should keep an eye on Tory, since he was hit in the head, don't you think?"

"You're a good friend, Frank. I got three open rooms, but none of them have more than one bed." She winked. "In my place, not too many people request two beds."

"No matter," Franklin said, heating a bit under the collar. "I can sleep in a chair." He figured a woman like Madame Lafourchette wouldn't care if two men *did* sleep in the same bed. She'd probably seen everything.

"Nice you guys reconnected," Madame Lafourchette said, reaching under the counter.

"Yep, I sure thought he was gone for good. Worried awful what Bilodeaux might have done to him."

"I meant before that."

"What do you mean, before that?"

"Aren't you two old friends from somewhere? I just assumed, since he queried about you when he first came into town last year. Strolled right up to me fresh off the stage from Deadwood, asked which direction your homestead was in. Said you two knew each other but you probably wouldn't remember him."

"Are you sure about that?"

"Sure as I'm looking at you. Followed you into the inn but ran out before greeting you."

Franklin wracked his brain. He had no recollection of meeting anyone in the past who resembled Tory Pilkvist. He played back his days working in Kentucky at the lumberyard, then on the steamer in Quincy, Illinois, followed by the quartz mine a few years later. Tory's face failed to materialize. Besides, Tory would have been a mere lad in those days, barely out of diapers for most of it. *Odd*, Franklin thought.

"Not sure why he told you that." He shrugged. "I never seen him before he came to my homestead, I'm certain."

"Well," the madame said, "guess he thought you were somebody else. People mix each other up sometimes."

"Sure, that's probably it."

She handed Franklin a room key, and he returned to the table, where Doc Albrecht was in the midst of describing his Idaho Territory days, tales Franklin had heard many times since the doc's moving to town last year.

"Frank, you're missing my exciting yarn about when I practiced medicine in the Bitterroot."

"Not the one where, using your medical expertise, you saved a big mining company ten thousand dollars from a lawsuit filed by six grieving widows who claimed their husbands died from dyspnea?" Franklin chuckled as he sat at the table. He understood how Doc Albrecht regretted that undertaking against the widows, especially since, according to the doctor, miners could slowly suffocate from working long arduous hours after many years—although it was difficult to prove, as Doc Albrecht stated on behalf of the mining company.

"I thought I'd spare them that tale," the doctor said, his face souring. "That would be a bit hard on the old digestion."

"That it would," Franklin agreed.

"Well...." The doctor stood and stretched. He extended a hand to each of the men around the table. "I've got to get some sleep. I'll have a busy day tomorrow. More scoundrels to defend." He wished everyone luck at the upcoming trial and apologized again for defending Bilodeaux, Burgermyer, and Parker. Wicasha readied to take his leave too, promising to look after Franklin's homestead until Franklin and Tory returned the next day.

"There're still some greedy bandits wanting the gold in your creek pool," he warned. "They might be riled now that Bilodeaux's out of the picture."

"I'm not fretting over it," Franklin said. "Tonight, no worries. But thanks for all your vigilance, Wicasha."

Once they were alone in their room upstairs, the exhaustion set in. The murmur from downstairs seeped through the floorboards, but it hummed a gentle tune. A current of tranquility flowed around Franklin. In the bathing room down the hall, he and Tory bathed together. The warm water, like a wash of respite, soothed his mind and body. They refrained from kissing and kept their three hands busy with washing before the water turned cold. Yet once they had again undressed and climbed into bed, they reached for each other with unbridled craving.

Under the canopy of haze drifting from the bar, Tory did things Franklin had never imagined. He started by doing that wonderful, warm move with his mouth. Then he roved his tongue down farther between his legs, and a new sensation lit Franklin's body like a torch. He moaned. Bit the pillow. Wanted to push him off, but the tantalizing tingle forced him to give in to Tory's nibbles.

Learning from this novel move, he tossed Tory onto his stomach and reciprocated. Tory writhed, whimpered, groaned. Franklin lifted him by his waist, pulled him closer to his mouth. Blood rushed from his head. For fear of fainting, Franklin stopped, panting. Yet Tory couldn't get enough of him. He quivered like an aspen branch under Franklin's touch. Tory, his blue eyes shimmering in the electric lanterns, rolled to his back and gave himself completely to Franklin.

Raw breath mixed with earthy, riotous sweat, propelled Franklin deeper and faster, until their tongues and bodies combined into one flesh. As he worked Tory, he kissed his cuts and bruises and whispered how he'd agonized he might have lost him forever. He grunted between pecks on Tory's chin and neck that he could no longer imagine life at Moonlight Gulch without him. Tory responded by grabbing onto him tighter, forcing him into him deeper, demanding Franklin brand him with his imprint.

"Always belong to you," Tory breathed in his ear. "Always belong to you."

But Franklin's last release did not mean they had finished. Offering himself in a way he'd never conceived of, Franklin flipped onto his back and, his eyes locked on Tory's, brought his knees to his chest. Tory stared at him, questioning. Without words, Franklin guided Tory toward him, wanting to complete their perfect union. Tory, eyes dazed, followed Franklin's silent command. He moved gently at first, slowly. Franklin winced and moaned. Tory's gaze rained into his eyes until Tory arched his back and tossed back his head.

Next morning, they awoke, three arms entwined. The orange sun penetrated the flimsy lace curtains. Franklin estimated the time to be close to eight thirty by the position of the sun. He hadn't slept so late since his stint at the Army hospital in Maryland. Tory, rubbing his eyes, wrapped his legs around Franklin's waist. Both men were aroused and ready. They made love for another half hour. Franklin had had no idea he could take anyone in so many different positions.

Stretching with a wide satisfied grin, Tory said he was hungry. Franklin marveled at his appetite. It must've been trying spending two nights in a dank cave against his will with so little to eat.

After a hearty breakfast of hotcakes with globs of maple syrup and butter, mounds of bacon, and plenty of steaming coffee, they retrieved Lulu from Doc Albrecht's, where the kind doctor had allowed Franklin to stable her free of charge. While Franklin hitched her to the wagon, Tory dropped in at the mercantile to replace the shells and herbs lost during his abduction. Franklin decided to check for mail with Postmaster Jim.

"Hi, Jim," he said, stepping inside the small office.

"Hi, Franklin. Heard about the ruckus last night. Bilodeaux's behind bars, huh? It's about time, if you ask me."

"Let's hope he stays there. I get any mail?"

"Quite a bit. Haven't seen you since last year." He handed Franklin about fifteen pieces of mail.

"Thanks, Jim." He glanced through the stack, mostly advertisements for farming implements, political flyers, and one letter from his mother in Tennessee. Tucking the mail in his coat pocket, he said, "I guess I'll be seeing you back in town sooner rather than later, what with Bilodeaux's trial coming up."

"I'll be there to cheer you on this time, Frank. Take care of yourself until then."

Outside, Franklin dropped the letters onto the bench of the wagon and climbed in after them. Tory had yet to return. Instinct insisted he worry, but relief welled in him when he pictured Bilodeaux behind iron bars. The scoundrel's night surely hadn't passed as pleasurably as Franklin's, he reflected, snickering to himself. He grew heated, remembering his and Tory's lovemaking. Especially the spontaneous moment when Franklin had—

"Oh, Frank!"

Franklin looked up. Postmaster Jim ran toward him, carrying a parcel. He reached the wagon and caught his breath. "I darn plum forgot. You got a delivery back in March, but I stowed it in the back since I didn't know when you'd get into town. I meant to give it to Tory before all of Bilodeaux's antics, but he had no room on him. Guess it was a good thing. Might've gotten lost or stolen. It's postmarked from Chicago."

He handed Franklin the parcel. Franklin gazed at it wonderingly. He hadn't ordered anything from the big Chicago mail ordering houses since last summer. The package sounded solid when he shook it. He did not recognize the name or address of the sender.

Franklin thanked Jim, and the postman returned to his office. His mind racing with curiosity, Franklin opened the package with his pocketknife. He found several envelopes bound together with twine. Cutting the string, he counted four letters, each one postmarked last summer and still sealed. His confusion intensified when he recognized his own name and address as the sender. And the name and address of the recipient—Torsten P.

The unanswered letters he had written to the girl he had corresponded with from *Matrimonial News*.

Had Torsten sent them back to him unread after all this time?

An open-faced note on top explained.


*March 15, 1887*

*Dear Franklin Ausmus,*

*My name is Thomas Persson. I am a postman for the city of Chicago. You may not remember me, but I will get to that in a moment. A while back, I was delivering letters to the addressee on the four enclosed letters, which I am certain were sent by you. I was instructed by the recipient's father to burn the letters as they arrived. I am not sure why, but, feeling compelled to abide by my customer's wishes, I consented that I would. However, federal law prevents me from destroying or tampering with U.S. Mail, so I stowed the enclosed letters in my apartment. I worried over them for many weeks, wondering what should be done with them. I had considered returning to sender, but for some reason I held onto them. By the arrival of autumn, I had concluded to return them to Torsten, your intended recipient, despite the wishes of Mr. Pilkvist, since that was the legal and moral decision; but fate had sent Torsten away from Chicago before I could turn over the letters. The Pilkvists had no idea where Torsten had gone and held no address where I might forward the letters.*

*Guilt prevented me from discarding them or forwarding them, since I had held onto them for so many months. Giving them to Torsten's parents seemed unwise. I again tucked them away in my apartment only to forget that I had ever come upon them. It wasn't until the arrival of March this year, when my wife embarked on much-needed spring cleaning, encountered the letters and reminded me of them. I had forgotten they were there. A new and ponderous culpability possessed me. For many days, I would take them out of the cupboard where I had stowed them and stare at them, wondering just what to do. I had determined to finally burn them, like Mr. Pilkvist had originally wanted, when suddenly my wife pointed out your name as the sender. How odd, to have read the envelopes so often only to recognize the name upon my wife's mentioning it.*

*I believe that you and I fought alongside each other in the Civil War, a stage of my life which I have chronicled for my dear wife in detail, including my acquaintance with you, which is why she had recognized your name even before I had. I was in the 6th Infantry Illinois Volunteers. Under the great leadership of Gens. Logan and Grant, we charged through the western front of Tennessee. If you are the Franklin Ausmus of Knox County, who had fought in the 11th Regiment Tennessee Volunteer Infantry, which I am near certain you are, then you and I fought bravely, shoulder to shoulder, like brothers, during the Battles of Fort Henry and Fort Donelson.*

*Shortly after those powerfully fought battles, which God saw fit, as you know, for the land to fall into Yankee hands, shrapnel from a well-pitched exchange of cannon fire in Kentucky devoured part of my left foot. The injury, as you might assume, ended my military endeavors. I recall how bravely you and your regiment fought, and the pleasure we had to spend time with you in camp, where song and jokes lifted our spirits. We Illinois boys were rather stunned at the steadfast devotion to the Union shown by you boys from eastern Tennessee. Even while I convalesced in the hospital, my remembrance of our time*

*together spurred me to a quicker recovery, for which I will always be
grateful.*

*A mutual comrade, Skaggs Yardley, who I had the great pleasure
to run across here in Chicago several years ago, had mentioned your
name, and in so doing stated that he had heard from another good
friend who bravely fought on the western front that you had settled in
the Black Hills of Dakota Territory. Because of that, I am certain you
are the Frank Ausmus from our fighting days. History united us as
brothers in arms; therefore, I am obligated and committed to ensuring
that I do nothing that would cause you grief. I am prompted to forward
you the letters, since I believe you might regard them with the utmost
importance, with the hope that you accept my sincere apology for
failing to deliver them to your intended recipient. Torsten had
expressed concern you had, apparently, stopped corresponding. I do
hope the letters find you in peace and prosperity. Again, forgive me if
my failing to deliver them has somehow caused you undue distress.*

*Your brother,*

*Thomas R. Persson*

*Postman, United States Postal Service*

*Chicago, Illinois*

The note fell from Franklin's shaking fingertips into his lap. His
mind whirled. He remembered young Thomas Persson. They had
joined the fighting at about the same age, mere teenagers. Persson had
affirmed himself a solid soldier and comrade, like most of the boys
from the Illinois regiments. Always quick with a fun story to lessen the
stress of war, Persson had reminded Franklin of his older brother, who
had died from scarlet fever at age thirteen. In some ways, Persson's
quips had proved stronger medicine than the opium that had passed
from hand to hand in camp to combat scurvy, dysentery, body lice, and
other maddening ailments.

Franklin held the bundle close to his heart. Torsten, the girl from
Chicago, hadn't rebuked him after all. A smile stretched his face. She
hadn't meant to end their correspondence. Her father, the horrible Mr.
Pilkvist, had stood between them. Like Tory had once suggested.

What might he do now?

He sat taller. Pilkvist? Where had he heard that name recently?
Tory had given his name to the judge during his murder trial. He was

certain Pilkvist was the name he'd used. And hadn't he heard him mention his family's name a few times since? Tory? Torsten? His mind spun. What was it that Madame Lafourchette had said last night? Tory had come to town asking for him? Could it be? Impossible.

There were probably many Swedes who lived in Chicago, all sharing the same surname.

Franklin passed his hand over his face, resting it over his horseshoe mustache, where he allowed the rough bristles to poke his fingers (the same bristles that had often left Tory's lips red and swollen). He bit his palm. The wagon seemed to pivot. Massaging his mustache, he tried to compose his erratic thoughts.

Tory, carrying a sack, stepped out of the mercantile and made his way down the boardwalk with a smile. His toothy grin slowly faded as he approached the wagon. Franklin could not conceal the bitter horror that he knew plastered his face like a death mask. Tory stood by the horse, his hands clutching his sack of purchases. Franklin remained motionless save for the quivering of his hand.

"Franklin, what's wrong?"

"Your full name," Franklin whispered into his palm.

"What?"

Franklin kept his eyes straight ahead, as if Tory were still in the mercantile. He brought his hand to his side and licked his lips. "Tell me your full name."

"T-Tory Pilk... Pilkvist."

"Are you not Torsten Pilkvist from 12416 Chicago Avenue?"

Only when Tory's face went white and he dropped the sack did Franklin no longer doubt his suspicions. Tears stung his eyes. How could he? Why had Tory played him for such a fool? He'd never experienced such raging humiliation. Even Henri Bilodeaux had never devised such a dirty trick against him.

Franklin glowered at Tory. "How could anyone stoop to such subterfuge?"

"Franklin... I...."

"I should've left you at Madame Lafourchette's when I brought you into town last year."

"Please, let me explain—"

"You can rot here in Spiketrout with the other deadbeats, for all I care. I don't want to ever set eyes on your face again. Don't you think about trespassing on my property like last time, or I'll treat you like I did Bilodeaux."

"Franklin, please—"

Tossing the parcel of letters into the back of the wagon, Franklin pulled the reins to get Lulu to galloping speed. The mare squealed, unaccustomed to the harsh snapping.

# CHAPTER
# THIRTY-FOUR

ON THE drive home, Franklin tried to organize his stormy, muddled thoughts. Tory came from Chicago. Of Swedish ancestry. His parents owned a boarding house and a bakery. Walt Whitman was his favorite poet. And the last name. No getting around that one. All the same as Torsten P.'s.

Madame Lafourchette had said Tory had inquired about him even before they had set eyes on each other. Too much for a coincidence.

At the cabin, Franklin retrieved the letters Torsten P. had written him, which he still kept stowed in his old Army trunk. Next, he dug among Tory's belongings in a chest of drawers and uncovered the journal he'd kept throughout the winter. Tory's handwriting and Torsten P.'s were identical. Straightforward and unembellished.

Everything coalesced into concrete recognition. Doubt no longer lingered. Tory showing up unexpectedly at the homestead. His lack of curiosity of Franklin's life because he already knew so much about him from reading his letters.

And, of course, Tory, in his silence after Franklin had confronted him in Spiketrout, had admitted to his scheme.

Tory Pilkvist and Torsten P. were the same person.

Sickness gurgled inside him, worse than when Army doctors cut off his arm. Now, something far greater had been severed from him.

What worthless solace came from realizing that Torsten P. had not rejected him. She had never existed. And, in some appalling way, neither had Tory.

Impostors like Tory were the reason why he'd hidden himself away in the mountains. He'd exposed his soul in those letters to Torsten. Yet he had received nothing in return but pain. Tory had played him like a hand at a faro table. And it was Franklin who had lost.

To think he had given himself to Tory at the Gold Dust Inn in a way that no man would ever consider. How could he have been so gullible? So desperate to allow a demon to lure him into his den?

He clenched Tory's journal, about to chuck it into the still smoldering oven, but he shoved it into Tory's satchel instead, followed by his other belongings. Fuming, he stomped to the gate and, with a solid one-handed windup, heaved the bag over the barbwire.

Wicasha watched Franklin from the barn, where he looked to be currying his gelding. Franklin refrained from making any eye contact with him. Wicasha, astute enough to find his way in the pitch darkness without the aid of a torch, knew better than to bother Franklin in his present state.

Yet the remainder of the day, Wicasha lingered at the homestead, as if discerning he needed to stand guard by his friend. The notion both irritated and reassured Franklin. Wicasha remained silent, only speaking when necessary. But later that night, as they sat at the cabin table eating leftover stew that Tory had made (how bitter it tasted), Wicasha finally asked Franklin why he had abandoned Tory among the people of Spiketrout.

"There is no Tory. There is no Torsten," Franklin said, the food tasteless and dry in his mouth.

"Frank, speak plainly with me."

Franklin stood with a harsh skid of his chair on the wood floor. He traipsed behind the wood partition. A few seconds later, he returned with the letters sent to him by Thomas Persson and the other ones Torsten P. had written him, and slapped them on the table.

"There. Go ahead. Read them."

Wicasha eyed the letters, his face smooth and calm. Slowly, he reached for them. One by one, he thumbed through the letters, his expression passive and thoughtful. Eventually, he began to read, skipping every other two or three.

Franklin turned his back to him. "I placed an advertisement," he said, his voice low and hoarse, "in one of those foolish matchmaker periodicals. I didn't want you to know. Didn't want anyone to know. I was looking for a mail-order bride, I confess. I thought I had found one. We wrote back and forth for months, all during the spring and most of the summer. I fell in love with her through those letters. Then they suddenly stopped. I waited and waited, rode back and forth to Spiketrout four times a week like an idiot to check at the postal office. You must remember how often I was going into town, Wicasha. Well, that's why. I did it for her." He began to pace. "Turns out, Torsten, the girl from Chicago to whom I had given my heart, doesn't exist. She was a joke concocted by Tory. Yes, that's right. Tory was the one who had written me from Chicago the entire time, proclaiming those things I had assumed came from a woman named Torsten. To further his hoax, he traveled all the way from Chicago to Spiketrout just to ridicule me. Remember how you found him in the barn loft? There he waited for discovery so he could trick me, needle his way into my life, string me along like a jackass. And how he succeeded."

Franklin, panting with anguish, stopped pacing and faced a barren corner of the cabin. Suddenly ashamed Wicasha had learned the truth, he formed a tight fist and froze in disgust. The rumple of Wicasha turning the pages of the letters sounded like chalk dragging against a blackboard. But didn't Franklin deserve the humiliation? Appropriate punishment for entrusting his future to a periodical? Franklin wandered to a chair by the door, where he sat, slumped, clenching his fist between his quaking legs. Wicasha finally placed the last letter on top of the others and nudged them aside.

"I'm sorry, Frank."

His words were enough to send a shock through Franklin's system. The reality of his calamity descended over him like a thick rain, drenching him in despair. He hunched forward until his knuckles touched the floor. The misery no longer perched solely in his mind. He had shared his dark secret with another. Wicasha's knowledge of the whole affair solidified his disgrace and hopelessness.

He stood, rigid, and pushed the chair over. Heat burning his ears and eyes, he stormed from the cabin and headed into the far reaches of his land, past the storage barn and the field where the irrigation ditches still needed a good cleaning, to a hillock, where he stood on top and peered around his homestead under the cloudy afternoon sky. He heard the hogs jostle and squeal in the pen. The hens rattled. Wind parted the alfalfa growing along the edge of the field. What had at one time brought him joy now brought him gloom. He loathed his homestead. Loathed every inch of it, barbwire and all. The entire Black Hills had turned against him.

Later that night when Franklin lay alone in his feather bed, sleep taunted him. He kicked at the sheets, clutched the mattress, fumed at the ceiling in his misery. He could smell Tory (or should he refer to him as Torsten?) enmeshed in the bed sheets. He balled his sheets and threw them into a corner. He cursed heaven for mocking him.

He jumped from bed and paced the cabin, the wood floor cold and callous beneath his bare feet. Under a flickering gas lantern, he forced himself to reread the letters Thomas Persson had sent him—the ones Franklin had sent Torsten P. He had wanted to toss the bundle at Tory while he had sat in his wagon in Spiketrout, accusing the lying rascal of his crime. But why let him have the satisfaction of reading them? His tender expressions were meant for someone who had never breathed life, never walked the earth. And he had wanted to marry that illusion? Even worse, he had wanted to share a bed with Tory, the master of that falsehood, for the remainder of his life.

A duplicitous villain had deceived him—Tory Pilkvist and Torsten P. One creature, cloven in half, had achieved the destructive undertaking of two.

He screamed, bellowed into the night, revealing to the world his anguish in one continuous heartfelt roar. And after he stopped, his cry lingered, carrying over the Hills far and wide, riding on the wind rushing off the mountain peaks. Then he realized—no echo chased after his screams. Somewhere near Moonlight Gulch, a lone wolf was howling at the world. Franklin cried out again. His and the wolf's sorrows formed into one vortex of agony.

If Tory had shot him, the pain would have proved less severe.

"I know how you feel," Franklin shouted at the wolf howling into the night. "I know. I know." Sobs stole away his voice. He broke down, his body convulsing. He wondered if he might die from the relentless spasms. He wouldn't care if he did.

TWO days after the horrible revelation, Wicasha informed Franklin that Bilodeaux and Burgermyer's trial was set for Friday. When the day came, Franklin traveled with Wicasha to the Gold Dust Inn, where the trial was to be held. He shuddered at thinking he'd have to face Tory. During the trial, he did his best to avoid his crystal-blue eyes. In a moment of weakness, he glanced at him. He regretted the rash move as soon as he noticed his red, swollen eyes. Only briefly did he wonder where he'd been staying, what he'd been doing. Three hours of agonizing deliberations passed before the jury declared Bilodeaux, Burgermyer, and the third accomplice, Jack Parker, guilty of kidnapping, extortion, and bodily assault. The verdict failed to lift the desolation cemented in Franklin's soul. Judge Blanchard sentenced Bilodeaux, Burgermyer, and Parker to the maximum—seven years at the territorial prison in Bismarck.

Franklin left immediately after the judge uttered the sentence. He resented Wicasha when he told him on the drive home that he had already visited Tory on two occasions and had carried his satchel to him. When Wicasha tried to relay to Franklin that Tory meant no harm in coming to the Black Hills, Franklin silenced him.

As the days passed, Franklin transformed his anger into energy to focus on his homestead. It was spring. Much work was needed to keep the homestead functioning. Wicasha, as usual for the time of year, stopped by regularly to help with the new crop of carrots, onions, potatoes, and green beans. At last, they cleaned the mud and debris from the irrigation ditches. Together they repaired the hole the heavy winter snowfall had left in the roof of the barn.

Wicasha remained silent about Tory while they toiled side by side, even when Franklin had known he'd traveled back to Spiketrout after the trial, most likely to meet with the Chicagoan again. The stillness covered them like an itchy blanket. Days of choring left Franklin exhausted. He relished his burning muscles and knotted neck. But his bitterness toward Tory never waned.

A grazing mule deer seemed somehow sinister with its large dark eyes. A rare black bear emerged from the woods like a demon from hell. Franklin got no satisfaction from cultivating the land, refurbishing the barn, henhouse, and pigpen after the long winter. He was sickened by the squeal of the newly born piglets and the sight of their greedy, ravenous suckling.

Franklin resented Tory for snatching his awe for nature from him.

He now even considered panning for the gold in the creek pool. What a joke that would be on Bilodeaux! Now that the bandit was imprisoned, Franklin would do what the greedy French Canadian had long wanted. What did it matter to Franklin if he succumbed to the greed, the wanting of more and more until it transformed him into a drunken beast who lived only for more easy-gotten loot?

A part of his humanity had already deserted him anyway.

He reread the letters Torsten had written him last spring and summer for no reason other than to see if he had missed something. Had Torsten's mastery of deception blinded him from realizing the letters had been written by the hand of a male prankster? Through one letter after the next, all seven of them, he failed to distinguish between Torsten P., the woman, and Tory, the man who had robbed him of dignity. They even smelled like Tory.

Seething, he kicked the letters across the room, where they lay scattered like leaves churned in a wind.

He fumed, remembering how he had rejected the other responses to his advertisement. Dozens of others had written him. He wondered how different his life might be if he had responded to one of their letters instead of Torsten's. A tear fell hot against his cold cheek. He wanted to toss the letters into the fire, but he held back.

Why couldn't he burn them? Why couldn't he end that terrible chapter in his life and simply toss them into the fire and incinerate all his pain?

TEN days after Franklin abandoned Tory in Spiketrout, Wicasha finally spoke to Franklin in his familiar straightforward manner. They were sitting outside by the fire under the nighttime sky after a hard day working the field. Franklin, leaning against a tree stump, whittled a spoon out of a fallen pine branch, while Wicasha sipped coffee at the roughhewn table.

"Frank," he said, setting down his coffee, "you once asked me why I turned against my own people in the war against the Sioux. I gave you my best answer. I was angry they had tossed me aside like an outsider and stole away my lover, Bua Ishte. Why did *you* turn against your people in the Civil War?"

"My people?"

"Southerners like you. Southern states surrounded you, yet you went against them, defended the Union."

"In Knox County, most of us sought secession," Franklin said into the fire. The flames burned his eyes, but he welcomed the gritty sensation. "We despised the Democrats and their pro-slavery. If you opposed us, we considered *you* a traitor." He glanced at the dark, starless sky and chuckled. "I guess even among outcasts, there are outcasts."

"But you were still surrounded by states loaded with people loyal to the Confederacy. Even the majority of Tennesseans loathed your Republican loyalties. You understand what it's like to face scorn," Wicasha said. "We both do. You have to remember that when you try to understand why Tory did what he did. A man like Tory will always live in an environment where he is an outsider, surrounded by those who detest him. He'll always be peering in at the world from behind bushes. Where most people find each other out in the open, Tory must search in secret places."

"There never was anyone named Tory." Franklin spit into the fire. A fierce hiss lashed back at him. "Or Torsten, for that matter."

"Frank, my point is, for Tory, growing up the way he is, well, there aren't many ways for him to find true love." Wicasha gripped his coffee cup, his eyes transfixed on the liquid. "You can find physical needs about anywhere—hurdy-gurdy houses, desperate soldiers, or cowboys lonely for women. It's not unusual to come by. But love? That's another thing altogether. For men like me and Tory, it's a treasure rarer than opal stone."

They were quiet, gazing into the flames, listening to the whisper of the smoldering spruce logs, as if they held some secret to tell. A rush of wind off the eastern mountain peaks brought the lingering chill of a departed winter. The flames darted, cowered, reemerged stronger.

"I know where he's staying and what he's doing," Wicasha said on the tail end of the gust.

Franklin sat up straight, his shoulders squared and rigid. "I don't care," he said. "It's no matter to me."

"He's working as a cook at Madame Lafourchette's," Wicasha went on as if he hadn't heard Franklin's protest, which even to Franklin had reverberated in his ears as hollow and insincere. "He's unhappy, Frank. More despondent than you are. Mostly because he fears he's made you unhappy. I talk to him when I'm in town. You're the only person he asks about. He only wants a chance to explain why he did what he did. I can get word to him, if you want."

"No," Franklin snapped. "He's no longer any of my concern."

"Frank, I saw you flinch when I mentioned he works at Madame Lafourchette's. You still care about the chikala wasichu. You want him back by your side."

"Don't put thoughts into my head, Wicasha."

"I'd give anything to stand in your boots." Wicasha stared beyond the fire, through the ponderosa bordering the creek, where the sound of gurgling water pierced the breeze. "To have a chance at love again," he whispered to the wind. "What a joy that would be. Don't ruin this for yourself, Franklin Ausmus."

Franklin snapped the wooden spoon in two with his one hand and dashed it to the ground. "Don't you understand English no more, Indian? I told you, mind your own damn business."

Wicasha set down his tin cup on the table and stood with a crack of his large bones. "Suit yourself, Frank. But I have to say, you've become lousy company since you've left Tory in Spiketrout."

# CHAPTER
# THIRTY-FIVE

HOT grease leaped at Tory and stung his cheek. He jumped back, unaccustomed to the endless steamy work even after two weeks on the job. As he flipped the pork chops over on the grill and listened to the sizzle, his persistent worries hardened—he had lost Franklin. And yet, he believed, he most likely deserved the desolation residing in his heart.

His father had spoken the truth. Walt Whitman, yearning for love by the moaning of poetry, was nothing but "Amerikanskt skräp." Tory would die on the prairie alone, like so many before him who had ventured west for romantic and aimless dreams. Alone and, if he walked away from a job he found more intolerable each day, penniless.

Madame Lafourchette paid him room and board. A stuffy old room in the basement, with only one window too high to look out or let in much light, and a cot that provided far less comfort than Franklin's had. The only consolation was the two finches that nested by the window, waking him each morning with naïve chirping. He'd take the scraps he'd saved from the kitchen, climb on a chair, open the window ajar, and feed the birds like he had the pigeons back in Chicago. Little else lifted Tory's spirits.

Looking back at the past several months, Tory marveled that Franklin hadn't learned the truth about him sooner. So often Tory had slipped with information only Torsten P. would know. He had lived half a year with his lies undetected—as precariously as Joseph when he'd perched himself on the twelfth-floor windowsill before his fatal fall—longer than he deserved.

How horrible to mislead Franklin merely for his own selfish aim to lessen his loneliness. He'd chased Franklin for the same reason he had sought men at the cabaret on 35th Street in Chicago, only with higher stakes and a more elaborate scheme. Traveling one thousand miles by train and stagecoach, Tory had set Franklin up to fall into his hands. He had never imagined Franklin would fall in love with him, but hadn't he done all he could to ensure he might?

Tory did love him, loved him with all the power his body could contain. He wanted to tell Franklin he had meant his words in those letters, and that the subsequent sharing of their lives since September was as real to him as life itself. Another letter to him explaining himself, conveyed away by Wicasha, would only add a sarcastic insult to Franklin's grieving.

Wicasha's visits were minimal comfort. He had tried to talk Tory into coming back with him to Franklin's homestead. Tory wanted to, but the thought of facing Franklin's wrath stymied his determination.

"Does he want me back?" Tory had asked during Wicasha's latest visit, his eyes probing.

Wicasha's downturned head and silence had said enough. Franklin was still fuming over Tory's wicked stunt. He never wished to see Tory again.

And Tory could not blame him.

What he had done was inexcusable.

Tory hated himself too.

Working at the hurdy-gurdy house (a place he never even would have considered stepping inside seven months ago, much less work and live in), surrounded by foul-mouthed and nefarious men and women, seemed fitting for Tory. Just punishment for his actions. He took to his chores as a prisoner in a chain gang, living out his sentence.

Madame Lafourchette, pleased Tory's cooking had increased her business, kept him busy in the kitchen. "I actually got people stopping by just for the food," she had said, laughing, a few days before. "Some don't even look at my girls."

She had whispered something else to him, alluded to a proposition. "Just between you and me, honey. I've had a couple of the men ask about you. They seem interested in making a deal with me like most do with the girls."

Had the madame insinuated she wanted Tory to become a renter? He had tolerated the renters in the cabaret on 35th Street. Never did he want to become like them. Madame Lafourchette's proposal had filled Tory with horror.

"They think you're awful pretty," she had gone on. "It's a steady income and comes with fringe benefits between you and your suitor. I won't say anything more, I'll just let you stew on it, and you can tell me what you think when you're ready."

After nights of tossing and turning, Tory had considered consenting to Madame Lafourchette's offer. But did Tory hate himself enough, after everything, to stoop to such a degrading means to earn income? He detested knowing such a practice even took place under his nose. But where else was he to go?

As the pork chops hissed and spit at him with greasy rancor, he pondered if perhaps his destiny might not be to work as the lone male renter in a hurdy-gurdy house. Perhaps he should accept Madame Lafourchette's proposal. What difference would it make? He was already enmeshed among whores and gamblers and drunks. Working as one of them, after all, might be proper punishment for his ugly betrayal of Franklin.

# CHAPTER
# THIRTY-SIX

FINALLY, the spasms stopped. In their place emerged a complacent calm. A strange tranquility settled in his veins. Good feelings shivered down his spine and constricted his throat. Listening to the rain patter the roof as he lay in bed, his head cleared. The night became retiring, gentler.

What had happened? Where had his misery gone? Had the rain washed it away, down the gully and into the creek?

Franklin understood. His agonizing sorrows had reached so low, there remained nowhere for his emotions to carry him but out of the abyss. On the wings of rising emotions, soft considerations began to bloom. Had he meant his words when he'd cursed Tory for wronging him worse than Bilodeaux? Was it "subterfuge" that had propelled Tory's actions?

Wicasha had said Tory existed in a world of desperate loneliness. Perhaps he'd had no choice but to masquerade himself as Torsten P. Wasn't it loneliness that had driven Franklin to take out a silly advertisement in that matchmaker periodical in the first place?

And hadn't Torsten P.'s words been the same as Tory's? If Torsten's letters had moved Franklin, then in reality, Tory's words had moved him, too.

Somewhere in his unclogging mind, an understanding took hold. As the rainy night caressed him, he kept still, allowing the new sensation to seize him. He lay helpless, yet contented. A supple light began to fill his deadened soul.

Tory had whispered during their lovemaking at the Gold Dust Inn, "Always belong to you." Had he uttered mere words during a moment of unquenchable lust, a sinister extension of Tory's game? Or had Tory affirmed his commitment to Franklin that night, a commitment that might have sprouted from his first correspondence?

Franklin had submitted himself to Tory, permitting him to do what Franklin had never imagined. The sensation of Tory penetrating him had been painful, but he'd relished the closeness, the intensity of melding with Tory's body. What had it meant? Had an unusual, mystical marriage taken place between him and Tory at Madame Lafourchette's inn that night?

Tory had broken from his captivity in a cold, dank cave and rushed out of the darkness to search for Franklin at Moonlight Gulch. Franklin now also observed a light emerging, beckoning him. Pushing him to seek Tory. Yet he balked.

*Always belong to you.* Did Tory ever belong to him in the same vein that his homestead, and everything else on it, belonged to him? Had Tory woven his way into his existence much like how the creek curled its way through his land?

He moaned with one final spasm, unleashed against a withering pain of need, fear, loneliness.

Franklin climbed out of bed and retrieved Tory's letters from his old Army trunk. He read them again, each one, by the residual light of the stove. He detected his mustache lifting, tickling his nose. He was smiling.

Wicasha had said Tory was working at Madame Lafourchette's as a cook. Wicasha knew Franklin well. Franklin detested the idea of his being at a hurdy-gurdy house. He never did want him to work there, even that day when he'd driven Tory into town after his first night at the homestead. Something about Tory had made Franklin want to protect him from the rowdies. Since Wicasha had mentioned Tory's whereabouts, an added irritation had compounded Franklin's misery.

Shouldn't he at least listen to what Tory had to say? Didn't he deserve that much? Surely he hadn't staged all the love and attention he'd shown Franklin since last September. The caring for his wounds from working the homestead, the gentle touch of his hands when he'd trimmed his hair. All that wasn't subterfuge. Was it?

And Tory was certainly no gold digger. Franklin had no doubts of Tory's sincerity when he'd pleaded with him to never pan for the gold amassed in the creek pool.

*He'll always be peering in at the world from behind bushes.* Wicasha's words brushed his mind and released a sharp odor, like the crushing of the leaves of the stinkweed. Too much had passed between him and Tory for Franklin to let him float from his life like dandelion seeds. He should at least hear him out. He owed Tory that much.

He had decided. He would drive into Spiketrout next morning and finally have a face to face with Tory.

The night sighed. Franklin crawled back under the bedcovers. Sleep inched over him. Like the warm wash of a kettle bath over his achy limbs, wispy dreams swallowed his torment.

BUOYED with fresh optimism, Franklin rode the muddy trail into town dressed in his Sunday best, rehearsing over and over in his mind just what he would say to Tory once they'd meet for the first time since he'd abandoned him in Spiketrout more than two weeks before. He would maintain a distant air, but allow Tory to speak his mind. They would find a remote table away from the rowdies. He'd sit opposite him with an unmoved expression. According to Wicasha, Tory would be glad to see him under any circumstance.

Franklin would listen to Tory's explanation of why he'd answered his advertisement and what had induced him to come to the Black Hills. While listening, Franklin would pretend to mull Tory's words over in his mind, although he'd already determined his intentions. Standing casually, he would offer to allow Tory to return to Moonlight Gulch where he may continue as Franklin's hired hand. But they must maintain a proper distance, of course.

Would Tory take Franklin's fancy dress as a sign that he was desperate for him to return as his lover?

Once in town, Franklin hitched Lulu next to the Gold Dust Inn and asked one of the girls fanning herself outside for Tory. He was surprised when Madame Lafourchette approached him a few minutes later with a worn expression.

"He's gone," she said.

"What?"

"Tory left this morning on the six thirty stage for Rapid City. Went to catch the new train line to Dakota Junction. Sorry to see him go. He was bringing in more money for me just with his cooking than some of my best girls with their affections."

Franklin had to work the spit in his mouth to speak. "You know what his final destination might be?"

Madame Lafourchette drew back her lips, painted the same burgundy red as the goose feathers in her chignon hairpiece. "He left so unexpectedly. Never even mentioned he was leaving until this morning. All he said was he had to go. I figure he's heading back to Chicago. Poor sweet thing. Seemed so lost and hurt. Whatever did come between you two, anyhow? He never would cough up about it."

Franklin barely heard her. Her jasmine perfume suffocated him. He glanced past Madame Lafourchette's fluffy shoulder to the grandfather clock against the wall. It was ten thirty. Four hours had passed since the stage had left town carrying Torsten Pilkvist. He'd be halfway to Rapid City by now.

He considered chasing after him, but by the time he reached Rapid City, Tory would be aboard the train heading to Dakota Junction. Maybe he could rush a telegram to the Rapid City train depot. But then he deflated, realizing it was over. Torsten Pilkvist had left his world as unexpectedly as he had entered. He had no reason to go after him.

The light-green leaves of the aspens and the wildflowers parting the duff in the dells failed to inspire Franklin the way they normally would when he rode the trail back to Moonlight Gulch. Sapped of any hope, of any feeling, he found the ruckus of the birds no more joyful than the clamor of drunks and gamblers at the Gold Dust Inn. Mere noise. Empty clatter.

Tory had been an illusion after all.

# CHAPTER
# THIRTY-SEVEN

THE stagecoach pitched and swayed over the hilly terrain south of Deadwood. The rain from the night before had muddied the trail and caused delays. Tory should've arrived in Rapid City three hours ago for the new North-Western railroad spur to Omaha, and then onward to Chicago. He hoped they would have a later train.

Despite the annoying delays, it was a good idea to leave the Black Hills after everything that had happened between him and Franklin. Besides, the people at the Gold Dust Inn were crazy. He could never endure working as a renter. Ludicrous idea. He had no business there. So why was the pit of his stomach expanding with each lumpy, mud-covered mile the stage crossed?

Two prospectors climbed aboard at Lead, filling the stage to capacity. Tory had no interest in striking up a conversation with any of his fellow passengers. He gazed out the window, disinterested in the lush mountain scenery that had at one time captivated him.

"Placer gold's all snatched up," one of the old prospectors with thinning gray hair said. "Dry as a bone. Not a thing left, except perhaps in far-flung places no one with sense would go. People trying to scam each other with brass shavings."

"There's some gold left in the rock," his red-haired companion said.

Tory glared at them, irritated. He was sick of talk of gold. He turned back to the soggy landscape, beaten and tired.

"No one wants to put that kind of backbreaking work into getting gold," the gray head said. "It ain't worth it. Yep, the streams are all played out. Not one left that someone hasn't sifted through and sucked dry."

"Word is there's a stream south of Spiketrout untouched," the one with red hair said. "On someone's homestead."

"Who's that?"

"Frank Ausmus."

Hearing Franklin's name, Tory jerked his head toward the two prospectors. His mouth lopped open. He cocked his head, needing to hear more.

"I heard about that dude," the gray-haired man said. "He's sitting on all that potential gold but don't want to pan for it. Crazy fellow. Whoever heard of such a thing?"

"He's the one who got Henri Bilodeaux locked up for scamming to get his hands on his land."

"Serves him right," the gray-haired man said with bitterness. "I've heard about that deadbeat's exploits. He's got no right to Ausmus's land. Even if he is dumb enough to not pan for gold on his own homestead."

"It's more than just plain dumb, it's plain unnatural." The prospector scratched his red hair under his hat. "Especially when people are going around starving and without decent clothes."

"You mean gamblers, drunks, and opium addicts?" His silver-haired travel companion snickered.

"They ain't all like that. Bilodeaux wants the gold for the good of the community, I hear. He talks about using it to build a hospital and an orphanage and other community whatnots that folks could use. Maybe even build a park for kids."

"That crooked Frenchman ain't got no notion to do any of that. If that was the plan, he and some others would've used their own gold for that a long time ago. Why is it people only get generous when they use other folks' money? He just wants his hands on it for himself. He should be hung for what he's trying to do. A man has a right to his own property."

"I think the people have a right to it, if it could help them."

"That's nonsense. People act like vultures on a carcass sometimes."

"Bilodeaux's got a whole plan going," the redhead said. "Word is he's got the deputy of Spiketrout in on it."

"You talking about the same Bilodeaux jailed for kidnapping and extortion? He got some seven years, I heard."

"Yep, that's the same dude."

"He sure is planning well into the future, then. He got some notion to get revenge once he gets out? Won't he ever let the poor homesteader rest?"

"Not that far into the future." The redhead smirked. "He got out a few days ago. Some scheme cooked up by him and the Spiketrout deputy. Walked out of the territorial prison in Bismarck as free as you and me."

"Wasn't there some other men who got locked up along with Bilodeaux for the same crime? Burgermeister and Parker or something like that?"

"Ralph Burgermyer and Jack Parker. And they ain't going nowhere. The law don't help those with no friends or money."

"How do you know all this?"

"I heard it from a buddy who just got out of jail for shooting an unarmed bandit. But he was on his land, trying to get at his claim. Jury was crooked." He scoffed. "Was in the same cell as Bilodeaux for a few days before they moved him. Then he had to shack up with that sourpuss Burgermyer."

"What do you know? So what's Bilodeaux got planned for Ausmus?"

"Gonna waylay him right off his land, saying something like he gonna torch the place and take all the placer gold he can get. Saying it's all for the good of the community."

"You don't say." The gray-haired man shook his head. "I sure hope that Ausmus is ready for him."

"Won't bother me none," the other man said. "Ausmus got it coming to him. The dude's wasting all that wealth. He deserves whatever harm he gets."

The silver-haired man shrugged, his mouth turned down. "I still say a man's got a right to do what he wants with his own property."

"Not when it's hurting others."

It was a good minute before the two prospectors' words penetrated Tory's mind. When they finally did, he jumped up in the stage, nearly striking the padded ceiling. His fellow passengers gaped at him. Tory's heart leaped into his ears, pounding until he was near deaf.

"Stop the stage! Stop the stage!" he screamed toward the driver with his head out the window. "You've got to stop the stage."

The driver pulled the horse team to a halt. "What's going on back there?"

Tory hopped out. "When does the next stage head this way back to Deadwood?"

The driver checked his pocket watch. "In about two hours, I'd say. No telling, though. With all the rain last night, a bunch of the stages are backed up. I got a telegram this morning two stages are delayed an hour at least."

"I can't wait that long."

"Wait for what?"

"Never mind. Please, get my bag. I have to head back."

"This some kind of trick?" the shotgun messenger asked, his rifle poised.

"No, please. My bag."

"You going to walk?" The driver narrowed his eyes.

"I have no choice. My bag. Please, hurry."

With his satchel in hand, Tory ran as fast as he could down the trail, slipping on the mud in a few spots. Half an hour later, muddied and panting, he spotted a man fixing a wheel to a wagon full of caged hens that faced the direction of Deadwood. Tory dashed over to him.

"Can you drive me into Spiketrout?" he asked, gulping for breath.

The man stared at him from his squat position, his arms frozen over the fresh wheel. "I'm only going as far as Deadwood."

"Then take me there."

"I got two lady passengers in front." The man stood, wiped his hands on his breeches. "There'll be no room for you."

"I'll pay you ten dollars. Please. I'll ride in the back with your hens."

"Ten dollars? Hop on up, son." And the man gave him a hand into the wagon's box.

# CHAPTER
# THIRTY-EIGHT

FRANKLIN was clearing debris away from the front of the cabin when Wicasha raced to him on his gelding.

"I just got in from Spiketrout, Frank. I got some bad news."

"I already know, Wicasha. He's gone."

"He sure is. We better get ready."

"Get ready? Get ready for what? What are you talking about?"

"He's coming for us. It's going to be big this time, Frank. I can feel it in my bones. We're going to have a full-out battle."

Wicasha filled in Franklin with the news he'd heard about Bilodeaux's release from prison while he was in Spiketrout looking for summer work. Franklin listened in disbelief. So much had already happened, and now this. His melancholy transformed into action.

Over the next few hours, they prepared for the coming attack. They stockpiled whatever weapons they could get their hands on and cleaned them so that they would perform without flaw. They dragged out the wagon, cart, plow, and anything else large enough to duck behind. They piled hay as high as it would stand. Franklin insisted he wanted to play no further games with Bilodeaux.

"I can feel eyes on us, Frank," Wicasha said once they settled outside the cabin, the rifles, shotguns, and revolvers either on their persons or propped against the table or the makeshift covers. "He's got some men with him this time, more than a few simple-minded cohorts. Word in town was Ostrem's with him. Probably about five or six of them altogether."

"How long you think they've been stalking us from up there?"

"I've smelled their campsite for a few hours. They been staking us out for a while. Planning and waiting. Bilodeaux most likely got back into the area last night."

"What do you think they got in store?"

"Probably try to use force of some kind. I suspect they'll come in with guns blazing. Bilodeaux has nothing to lose this time."

"We'll be ready for him."

Both men kept their eyes peeled around the surrounding mountains and rock faces. They were as vigilant as eagles.

"That fence won't keep them back, I fear," Franklin said.

"No matter," Wicasha said. "We'll be ready for them either way." He eyed Franklin. "I'm sorry to hear about Tory. I heard from some others in town he left for good."

"There's no use for sorrow. It's over. All in the past. Wasn't thinking straight much with him around, anyway. I was in a war with Bilodeaux. War makes men do crazy stuff. Things'll right themselves. Who knows? Maybe I'll even find a nice woman and settle down."

For the first time in many weeks, Franklin grew annoyed with Wicasha's silence. He wanted the Lakota to agree with him. Yet even Franklin could not fool himself into believing he'd want anyone other than Torsten Pilkvist. The young man who had entered into his life last summer and the woman he had corresponded with in Chicago—he wanted them both. Knowing that they were one and the same, he no longer cringed with regret and shame for having loved them. But what good were such feelings now? Tory had left. Franklin would never set eyes on him again.

And as he gazed around his land, with pistols and rifles cleaned and ready, he realized Tory's abrupt departure was for the best. If he did love Tory as much as his guts told him, then bringing him into a war zone would be unwise. Best to let him return to Chicago, or wherever he wandered next, out of the way of whatever danger lurked ahead. The young man had his whole life before him. Good thing he was gone from the Black Hills, where war clung to the mountains like pungent wood smoke in the air.

"I got a plan, Wicasha," he said. "Grab those field glasses from inside, then climb up on the windmill and keep a keen eye on things. Now don't fret any once you see what I've got in store. You keep your eyes peeled up in the mountains. Pretend like you don't even notice me."

While Wicasha climbed the windmill with his sidearm and two rifles, Franklin ran inside the barn. He hadn't thought of his purchase from last summer in a while.

Where was it? He dug about, kicked aside sacks, livestock feed, empty crates. Then he saw it. In the back against the wall. He had ordered it from Denver and had it delivered to the Spiketrout mercantile, figuring it might come in handy. The violence that surrounded him required effective protection. The crate of dynamite.

He traipsed for the creek with the twelve dynamite sticks and other supplies in a burlap sack, shrugging off what he knew must be Wicasha's skeptical sideways gaze from the windmill tower. By the creek bank, he prepared the dynamite (inserting the caps and stringing the wire connecting each), stripped naked, and dove into the pool with the sack of sticks. He placed each stick strategically in the fashion he'd learned while working at the quartz mine. Beneath the water, he wedged the dynamite between the boulders or in deep crevices, using his hand and both feet. With the lead wire in hand, he rushed to the surface and gasped for oxygen. He swam for the bank, waded ashore, and connected the wire to the blasting machine. Stepping behind a hefty ponderosa pine, he waited no time clicking the blaster.

The first stick exploded, spraying frothy water and boulder shrapnel for a dozen yards. Then another explosion. Soon they were popping off so quickly Franklin lost count. The boulders roiled, rocked, splintered. The accumulated shockwaves sent Franklin reeling back. Vinegar-like nitroglycerine fumes coated the air. Sitting upright on his elbow and stump, he could see chunks of shiny yellow rock flow down creek.

Gold nuggets blasted onto the bank. He kicked them into the gushing pool, which was losing volume by the minute, and tossed in more of what he could find. Dead fish washed up by his feet as he pushed the sandy bank toward the pool and whatever gold dust or nuggets might be trapped in it. He was glad to see it go.

Water rushed over, where for perhaps a thousand years it had remained a tranquil pool corralled by the boulders. Bilodeaux might claim Franklin's life, but Franklin would have the final victory. The gold deposits would be harder to get at. Thousands of dollars had already washed down creek. The spring runoff whisked them away faster than the wind carried the dust. The sound was like an enormous waterfall. Then it subsided. The pool was gone.

He glanced at Wicasha above the pines and spruces. The Lakota stood tall on the windmill. He had seen it all, magnified by the field glasses. Dripping wet, Franklin dressed and headed toward the cabin. Wicasha lowered the field glasses and raised his rifle high into the air. He had understood. Franklin smiled at him.

The explosions would bring Bilodeaux and his men barreling down the mountain at any moment, fueled by confusion and anger at what he assumed they had already realized he'd done. He hoped that the barbwire might slow them. So far, it had done little to prevent outsiders from penetrating his world.

Now, he must take his own position. He grabbed a .45 and, with his bare feet, cocked a Winchester between his legs, ready to fire both weapons.

A handful of minutes later, Wicasha lowered the field glasses and waved from the windmill. "Bilodeaux and his men are coming," he cried.

"How many men they got?"

"About four or five. They even got Deputy Ostrem with them, like I heard."

A multitude of galloping hooves descended from the north-facing slope. Within minutes, the raiders appeared in the grove. Franklin noted that Bilodeaux had not even the courage to lead. Deputy Ostrem took the first charge into Moonlight Gulch. He scaled the barbwire fence with minimal effort. The others followed. Franklin's pains building the fence had not even slowed them. In fact, it might have shot them farther ahead with the horses' wide leaps.

The horsemen filed in line before Franklin. He was certain by the way they eyed only him that they had yet to spot Wicasha atop the windmill.

"You have no business coming back here," Franklin snapped. "You belong in prison, Bilodeaux, with your fellow convicts."

"We're here for the gold," Bilodeaux said. "Like I promised you."

"There're people hungry in Spiketrout, and beyond," Deputy Ostrem said.

Franklin grunted at them. "You mean the men who gamble away their wages and buy whores?"

"People have a right to a good time," Ostrem said. "Ain't their fault they can't eat."

"Where is it written a man minding his own business on his own land must take care of people he ain't even laid eyes on before?"

"What about the women and children?" Bilodeaux said. "Good people, people with families."

"The people. The people. You're always going on about the people." Franklin spat at him. "You could care less about any of them, Bilodeaux. You only want more money and power for yourself. Quit using the lame excuse that you want to save mankind. I'm not stupid. I can see through your specious games, bandit. There ain't nothing left for you or anyone else, anyway. I blasted away the creek pool."

Bilodeaux whispered to one of his men, someone whom Franklin did not recognize, and he rode down to the creek, where dust from the exploded boulders was still settling. A minute later he galloped back. "He's right," he said. "It's what we heard right. He shifted the entire creek. The pool's gone."

"We'll take care of you," Bilodeaux said between clenched teeth. "Get him!"

Franklin rolled to the side of the cabin. Guns fired. Dirt and duff blasted from missed shots. Sparks rained from barrels of guns and rifles. In a flash, he caught sight of Wicasha on the windmill. The men did not know he was there. Franklin scurried backward behind the hay pile. Straw snapped and sprayed from gunfire. One of the bandits fell off his horse and clutched his bloodied arm. He'd been shot by either Franklin or Wicasha, or perhaps his own men by mistake. Wicasha fired off several shots but missed his targets. Franklin grabbed another revolver from the table, dashed behind the wagon, and fired off shot after shot. More rounds rang out from the bandits. They were aiming at Wicasha. They'd spotted him. The field glasses fell from Wicasha's hands, followed by Wicasha himself. Franklin, wheezing from the dust, ran for him, but shots by his feet forced him to take cover behind the plow. With his attention diverted over his dear friend's calamitous fall, Bilodeaux's men surrounded Franklin at gunpoint. Trapped, he had nowhere to run.

# CHAPTER
# THIRTY-NINE

TORY saw the Spearfish-Deadwood stage leaving. He jumped off the wagon and raced to catch it, but he realized the slow-moving stage would take too long. He'd already wasted a good hour riding with a wagonload of squawking hens. He saw a saddled horse hitched to a post, its owner's rifle and bag wedged in the saddle straps. He looked around. Someone was getting a drink from a well. He must be the horseman.

A powerful surge overtook Tory. He had lost Joseph van Werckhoven in a tragic fall without any way to save him. He was not going to allow Franklin Ausmus reach a similar demise, whether the man still loathed him or not.

He dropped his satchel, containing nothing but clothes and toiletries, and mounted the horse. Grabbing onto the horse as tight as possible, he slapped and spurred the horse to a full gallop. Hesitant to obey an unfamiliar rider, the horse faltered. But Tory's urgent spurring propelled the mare onward. The man by the well cried after him, his mouth gurgling with water. Tory detoured into the nearby woods to keep the law off his tail, but he made sure to turn back onto the trail heading to Spiketrout once he was far enough away from town. He checked the trees for moss growing on the north-facing trunks, just as Franklin had taught him, to maintain the correct course.

"Please, just keep moving," he implored the confused horse. "Trust me. Please."

He rode the horse high and hard. The mare soon melded with his motions, focused on the pressing mission as much as Tory. Mud splattered onto his travel clothes. He wiped his eyes clear of sweat. An hour later, he came into the muddy streets of Spiketrout.

He galloped down Main Street, shouting without stopping as if he were Paul Revere warning Concord residents of the approaching

British. "Help. Anyone. Help. It's Bilodeaux. He's out to get Franklin Ausmus. Please, help. He needs help at his homestead."

Without checking to see if anyone heeded his call, he headed straight for the trail to Moonlight Gulch. He could feel the pull of Franklin's homestead. He was certain others would come along soon. The sun beamed down from the west. Blinding curtains of sunrays draped across the trail.

He did not realize that the horseman had most likely run his mare half the day until she could go on no more. She slumped forward, and Tory slid off the saddle that had loosened during the strenuous gallop. A thick lather coated the horse's hide. Once the mare fell to her side, rendering her crow bait, Tory, without hesitation, gathered the rifle, strapped it to his back, and raced down the trail.

Using his flair for speed, he ran as fast as he could the remainder of the way. "Locomotive," the sobriquet his old friends back in Chicago had given him, could gallop faster than a spent horse. His city boots rubbed his feet raw, but he continued on unfettered.

As his muscles heated, he gained speed. The weighty iron rifle strapped to his side failed to hold him back. Sprays of mud and duff kicked up into his face. No time to spare. The sense of doom lay over his head like the sun that rained from the branches of the spruces and birches.

But even Tory had limits. He had to rest, if only for a moment. Blood drummed in his ears. His lungs felt like knives were piercing him. Bent over, he gulped as much oxygen as his lungs could take, and then he raced on.

# CHAPTER
# FORTY

"HOW you feeling, Wicasha?" Franklin whispered.

The bandits had bound Franklin and Wicasha together back to back inside the cabin. Their hands were tied and their legs had been roped like a wayward pig's. Franklin could feel something wet on his shoulder. Wicasha was bleeding on him.

"Wicasha, can you hear me?"

A moan, faint, but something.

"Don't... don't worry... holding up."

Franklin knew by Wicasha's voice he was languishing. And languishing fast. He had to find a way to untie the ropes, rush Wicasha to Doc Albrecht. Did the others in town know about Bilodeaux's scheme? Would they rush to their rescue?

He had never needed his friends more than now.

"Shut up." Jeff McIntosh, a middle-aged man Franklin had seen a few times in Spiketrout, had been left to sit watch over them while the others raided his homestead. He was much older than his fellow bandits, yet surliness oozed from his yellow eyes. "You keep your mouths shut or I'll shut them for you."

Franklin could feel his friend's body growing colder. He was losing blood. He needed urgent medical attention.

McIntosh rolled a cigarette, sealed it with a swipe against his tongue, and lit it with a match struck against the table. Blowing out a cloud of smoke, he said, "It's over for you, Ausmus. Your Indian friend is already dead. You won't be far behind. Quit struggling and let God take you. We don't need you down here no more, anyway."

Franklin was about to speak, but the sound of squealing and screaming from the horses and other animals paralyzed his voice. Bilodeaux and his bandits were slaughtering Franklin's livestock, shooting them, and, from the sound of their gurgling wails, slashing their throats, most likely solely for the feel of warm, gushing blood.

He smelled smoke, could hear the crack of lapping flames. Bilodeaux was burning down his barn. Burning everything. Franklin craned his neck to look out the window, but from the floor where they had tied them, he could only see smoke curl to the distant mountain peaks.

If only he could get the old man away so he could squirm and loosen the ropes. Bilodeaux's men had tied them haphazardly over his one arm. He could wiggle his fingers.

"They're going to leave you in here to die without a speck of gold, McIntosh," Franklin spat at the old man, hoping his plan might work. He had no other choice. He needed to get McIntosh out of the cabin.

McIntosh stood, his grip on his rifle tightening, the cigarette clenched between his stained teeth. Franklin could see his knuckles go white. "I said, shut your face."

"Don't want to hear the truth, huh? They're keeping you in here while they scoop up all the gold. I hid most of it in the barn, you know. They've found it by now." He'd gotten the crusty man's attention, all right. His forehead corrugated with deep wrinkles, his lips puckered like he was sucking on a lemon. "I panned it a long time ago," Franklin went on. "Didn't want anyone to know. You didn't really think I'd blow up my creek pool without taking the gold out first, did you?" He faked a snicker. "They're probably getting ready to load up the saddlebags, probably even fill my wagon with all the gold I got stored, while leaving you behind, with nothing."

"You a lying sack of cheese, Ausmus."

"If you say so, McIntosh."

More squealing. Dozens of rifle and pistol blasts. Wicasha's body went limp against him. The weight of his large frame pushed Franklin forward, complicating maneuvering his hand. Any more time wasted surely meant death—to them both.

"Sounds like they got your steed that time, McIntosh."

McIntosh shuffled to the window. "I don't see nothing." He raced to the side window that looked toward the barn. "It's all burning down. Everything," he said once he turned back to Franklin, grinning.

"Including your horse, McIntosh. They're going to leave you high and dry. I know those outlaws. They'll leave you in here."

McIntosh's entire face puckered. Red inched its way along the loose skin on his neck and into his wizened cheeks. He spit out the cigarette. He peered out the window again. "Where the hell is that steed of mine? What those bastards doing? I just take a look-see what's going on. You best keep still." He went for the door. As soon as he was gone, Franklin went into action. He twisted, squirmed, carrying the weight of Wicasha's body. Finally, he loosened the ties on his wrist. Wicasha's ties remained firm, but now Frank had the leverage to work them loose. He dug his fingernails into the rope, tried to work his way between the grooves.

"Stay with me, Wicasha. We'll get out of here."

Outside, he could hear cursing. Bilodeaux barking orders. French and English thrown above the crack of flames. He kept focused on the second rifle on the table. He had to get to it before McIntosh returned.

He was within arm's length, but the gun lay to his right. For the first time in many years, he resented having one arm. No way could he get to it with his stump. If only he could will it to grow.

Then he saw another shot of flame. He thought the flames were coming from the barn and pigpen. But the heads of two men rushed by the window, screaming and shouting and chortling, carrying torches. Bilodeaux's men were setting fire to the cabin. McIntosh cursed him from outside. "You lying sack of horse turd, Ausmus. You'll get yours. You think you can fool me? You'll get yours. Who's the fool now?"

"I have been dreaming of this day for many years," came Bilodeaux's hoarse voice above the rise of flames and smoke. "Finally, I get my revenge for your vile humiliations."

Franklin jerked up, tried to rouse his friend. "Wicasha, wake up. Wake up, Wicasha. They're torching the cabin. We got to get out of here."

The Lakota no longer moved. His cold, hard body, as if his blood was frozen in his veins, grew heavier and heavier against Franklin's back.

Smoke oozed inside from the crevices in the wood and under the floorboards. Franklin wiggled, squirmed, kicked, cursed, prayed. He was helpless. Nothing more he could do. Soon, he'd be as dead as his friend. At least they would ascend together.

The flames climbed the walls, torched logs fell into his sleeping area, igniting the floorboards like bales of hay. Fire engulfed the feather bed.

Suddenly, Wicasha no longer felt heavy. As if he had left the world, taking with him the weighty worries of the material earth. Franklin gave one last cry before the roof began to rattle and break.

# Chapter
# FORTY-ONE

TORY, clutching the horseman's rifle, had been waiting in the thick alders by the rock face near where the fence once stood. He had come across the barrage of wild men and needed to collect his breath and thoughts before choosing how to act. He had witnessed everything. The barn, henhouse, pigpen, storage barn, and much of the grass along the hillside had all been engulfed in flames. The outhouse had exploded like dynamite, sending one of the marauders to his probable death. He had watched in horror as the men kicked asunder part of the barbwire fence. And in their sickening rage, he had seen them butcher and waste the animals, including Carlotta. But only when the gang set fire to the cabin, which he knew from the men's gleeful and twisted shouts that Franklin and Wicasha were trapped inside, had he jumped into action.

He came out firing the first volley, his limbs shaking violently, screaming for God's mercy upon him and his friends. Franklin and Wicasha had taught him enough about shooting that he hoped he'd get good enough aim, despite the constant muscle spasms. The men, drunk with their orgy of destruction and wild shooting, had not noticed Tory coming at them. One of Tory's bullets struck a man in the neck, sending him flying off his charger. Another shot lamed Bilodeaux's gray stallion. It ran off toward the creek before tumbling and falling over. Shots whizzed by Tory's ears once the men noticed him. He volleyed back, striking Bilodeaux himself, the ringleader of the carnage. Once the fourth man saw Bilodeaux and his accomplices lay either dead or dying, he took off on his horse down the trail.

Horrified of the fire around him, Tory froze. A few yards away, Bilodeaux lay by his writhing stallion. The man was still alive but struggling. He had dragged himself across the clearing. A blood trail streaked the grass. Tory could see the fury still smoldering in Bilodeaux's dark blue eyes.

Strident snapping jerked Tory's attention. The back wall of the cabin had caved in. He must get to Franklin and Wicasha. Bilodeaux, too, had flicked his head in the direction of the discordant snap of wood and coiling flames. Tory fired another shot. Bilodeaux jumped, arched his back, then slackened. Veiled in the smoke, he and his stallion merged into one beast.

Tory only allowed himself a second to coddle his fear of fire. Picturing Franklin trapped inside, he shouldered his dread like he did his rifle. Inhaling, he rushed in, forearms covering his face from the raging inferno.

"Franklin!" Gray smoke concealed his view. He coughed, gagged. Heat wrapped around him like searing tentacles. He saw movement of limbs. Frank and Wicasha were tied together back to back on the floor. Tory fell to his knees and fought to loosen the ropes. Rafters began to split and fall. Wood hissed like venomous snakes. Fighting his fears, the fears he had carried with him since he was five years old, Tory screamed and shouted as he pushed and pulled on the bonds.

Mustering all his strength, he yanked the men toward the door. By then, Franklin had kicked free the loosened ropes on his ankles. Heaving Wicasha onto his back, he rushed through the door with Tory close behind. Outside, they fell to the earth and coughed, spitting phlegm. Franklin shook the last of the ropes from him. Wicasha collapsed to his side. No coughs, no tears came from his still form.

Through the haze of smoke, Tory crawled to Franklin and, dropping the rifle, wrapped his arms around him. Tears of fear, relief, and love poured down his cheeks. "I'm so glad I came back for you. I'm so glad you're all right." He sobbed like a boy.

Flames engulfed the cabin in a final sweep.

"Franklin, we got to get out of here."

Franklin did not want to leave his friend's side. But Tory's tugging forced him to his feet.

"There's nothing you can do for Wicasha. We need to get into Spiketrout."

Tory pulled Franklin upwind from the smoke and flames, encouraging him to move faster away from the flying sparks. Bloody and covered in soot and soil, Franklin held onto Tory and pressed his head onto his shoulder. They slipped and limped toward the dismantled gate, coughing and wheezing.

A rifle shot echoed through the gulch above the crack of flames and falling timber, then another, and another. Both Tory and Franklin jerked up. Bilodeaux stood by the side of the flaming cabin about twenty yards off, his wide open eyes leering at them. He appeared frozen, like a statue, his rifle pointing straight at them. His eyes gaped. Something inhuman and unworldly emanated from his fiery irises.

Tory braced himself for the pain, the agony. He turned away from Franklin. He could not bear to watch one more man he loved expire before his eyes.

But neither fell. Slowly, Franklin and Tory turned to gaze into each other's eyes. Against the soot and sweat and his singed horseshoe mustache, Franklin's eyes sparkled with green fire. Full of abundant life.

Still clutching his rifle, Bilodeaux fell forward, propped up by the gun. In an instant, he fell completely over and lay lifeless.

Wicasha, his dark eyes fluttering from where he lay trembling on the ground, held onto the rifle Tory had dropped by his side. A thin ribbon of smoke wafted from the muzzle.

# CHAPTER
# FORTY-TWO

OUTSIDE their temporary cabin tent, the kind used by the cavalry, Tory stirred the pot over the open fire. He no longer recoiled from the flames. Franklin kissed him full on the mouth and carried his plate of stew to the makeshift table he'd fashioned from fallen logs. A minute later, Tory joined him.

"Torsten Pilkvist, you make some brain-slapping good food." Franklin stared at Tory, his expression comically severe. Then a slow smile crept above his taut jaw line. His horseshoe mustache, trimmed after the singeing a week before, lifted to near his ears.

"That's why you want me to stick around, for my cooking?"

Franklin shrugged. "I don't see any harm having a good cook around, do you?"

Tory simpered. The love pumping his blood at that moment was like nothing he had ever experienced. More full-blown than a steam locomotive crashing into his body.

"I guess we can count our blessings," Tory said, glancing around at the few items they had salvaged from the fire, including the stewpot. A growing pile of logs, recently felled by Franklin and Tory, spread near where the cabin once stood. They were set to start rebuilding by the end of summer, after the logs had a chance to cure. "Lucky all this happened in the spring and not the autumn. We'd be freezing our tails off about now."

"That's what I like about you," Franklin said, "always looking on the bright side."

"No matter, at least that Bilodeaux is out of our lives. I still can't believe it sometimes. I cringe, expecting to see him riding in on his gray stallion."

"Don't need to worry about that no more," Franklin said, his cheeks bulging with stew. "He's gone for good. He's the devil's trouble now."

They were both relieved to have put the entire ordeal with Bilodeaux behind them. The bandit was dead. Two shots in his back by Wicasha's painfully steadied hand just as Bilodeaux was about to shoot Tory and Franklin had ended any more of his enraged greed. One last shot, just as Bilodeaux had turned in surprise to see where the bullets had come from, had finalized the already done deal.

Many men from Spiketrout, including a few women, had heeded Tory's call for help during his charge down Main Street that afternoon. They had gathered quickly, and, as Doc Albrecht had later described, met the lone survivor escaping on horseback down the trail head-on. Like Bilodeaux, Jason Wozniacki posed few worries for Tory and Franklin now. Tried a day after his capture, a Deadwood judge had given him a fifteen-year sentence. He never made it. In the jail wagon heading to Bismarck, vigilantes overtook them and shot Wozniacki in the heart. Turned out the killers were paying him back on another score, no connection with Franklin whatsoever.

The man killed by the exploding outhouse turned out to be Deputy Ostrem. Tory's shot had taken out the man who had kept watch over Franklin and Wicasha inside the cabin, Jeff McIntosh.

Having killed a man left a dull perforation on Tory's soul. But the stakes had been too high. He had done what circumstance had ordained. For the love of Franklin. For the love of Moonlight Gulch, which he had grown to consider a part of him. The homestead represented more than a mere place to live. The lush gulch stood as a symbol of defiance against raiders. McIntosh got what he'd deserved, whether he had expired by Tory's hands or someone else's.

Despite the horror of Bilodeaux's schemes being over and done with, they still had to face the long resurrection of Moonlight Gulch. The only remaining structures—the chimney and the sturdy steel windmill Franklin had ordered by mail from Chicago years ago—were triumphant reminders that the homestead could be reborn. Most of the barbwire fence lay twisted and useless. Franklin had said they didn't need a fence any longer, anyway.

Salvageable debris from the pillaged site was used for kindling and fertilizer for the crops, where the ashes would nourish the soil much the way forest fires did. The alfalfa, bursting with yellow daisy-like blooms, already grew taller, sturdier, the blooms more firm and robust. The field was left undamaged from the pillage, and, with the irrigation ditches cleaned of soot, they still had carrots, onions, potatoes, and green beans to look forward to come harvest. Venison, thanks to a recent hunt, provided them ample meat. Curing hides and jerky draped from several ponderosa branches.

Tory washed down some of the venison stew with a sip of coffee. "This must remind you of your old days back when you were wandering the Black Hills looking for a homestead," he said. "Camping out with nothing but you, the mountains, and the sky."

"How do you feel about it?" Franklin said, shoveling stew into his hungry mouth. "You never lived this rugged before. You up for two months in a tent?"

"With you, I'd live in a cave."

Franklin shook his head. "Don't mention talk of living in caves. Not after what happened with you going off to Spiketrout alone."

Tory shrugged and chuckled. "After everything that's happened to us, living in a tent will be like a vacation, I guess."

"It was awful nice of Doc Albrecht to invite us to stay at his place, though," Franklin said.

"I'd rather stay close to the homestead," Tory said. "We still have the crop to tend to."

"I reckon the crop and good friends are a few more blessings we can count on," Franklin said. "One thing about all this nonsense with Bilodeaux—we sure did learn who our real friends are."

And by August, when the logs cured and they were ready to erect the cabin, their real friends lent use of their hands. Doc Albrecht, Clarence and Walter Grishin, Postmaster Jim, Mr. Tang, Reverend Dahlbeck, along with a half-dozen others, offered their sweat.

Even Marshal Reinhardt, an old adversary of Franklin's (wracked with guilt that his own deputy helped trigger the destruction of Moonlight Gulch), had given his best effort to rebuild. Unfortunately, the marshal lived only a few days after they christened the new cabin and outhouse. A long-forgotten rival shot him in the back of the head while he lifted a mug of beer to his lips at the Gold Dust Inn. He spied the gunman in the large mirror behind the bar a split second too late. The shooter, the brother of a man Reinhardt had killed while he worked as a sheriff in a Texas panhandle town known for rough cattle rustlers, was apprehended by none other than Madame Lafourchette. Within two days of the killing, authorities promptly tried and hanged him.

Many called for Franklin to wear the marshal's badge, but Franklin refused to have anything to do with living in town. Instead, Mayor Winters, always far enough from the action but still close enough to maintain control of important town affairs, recommended an old friend, known throughout Utah for his fast draw, for the post. A week after Reinhardt's interment (a few paces from Henri Thibault Bilodeaux's tombstone), the men, with an 87-36 vote, elected Booth Jorgensen as the new marshal. He was scheduled to ride into town in two weeks. The town hadn't gone without a marshal in many years, but after all the hubbub with Franklin's homestead and Henri Bilodeaux, the rowdies knew better than to get too far out of line.

Spiketrout still struggled, yet a new dawn had risen over the old gold rush town nestled in the lush gulch. A nascent tourism, indeed, seemed to awaken, just like Madame Lafourchette had predicted a year before when Tory rode the stage into town. With the opening of the new railroads, Easterners came to see for themselves the romantic west they had read of in dime novels or glimpsed during Wild West shows. Mr. and Mrs. Pilkvist, who now corresponded with their son regularly through mail and telegrams (they no longer held a grudge against Tory for having left so rashly last summer), had even mentioned they'd like to see America's grand western peaks.

Each day, Moonlight Gulch grew bigger and better. "Like Chicago after the Great Fire," Franklin said. Franklin had crafted much of the furniture during the summer while they had waited for the wood to cure. They filled their new cabin with a log sofa, tables, chairs, and a brand new feather bed. With the little money Tory had left over from his four hundred dollars, plus what Franklin had at the bank, they purchased a stove and cushions, much of it ordered from Chicago mail-order companies. Reverend Dahlbeck's wife, Matilda, sewed them curtains for the new windows. Franklin told Tory he'd never even considered curtains for his old cabin, but now, with someone to share his life with, curtains seemed a perfect fit. Madame Lafourchette, always helpful in her assertive way, gave them a set of sheets that smelled of her jasmine perfume for weeks after.

No one ever questioned why Tory and Franklin chose to live together. Why should anyone? With the dearth of marriageable women, many bachelors shared cabins and labored as partners on homesteads across the west. It was the practical thing to do. The extra bedroom they'd added to the new cabin put to rest any suspicions anyone might've had about their relationship existing beyond business.

They had hoped Wicasha, who had needed most of the summer to recover from the gunshot to his stomach and a broken leg from his fall off the windmill, might want to move into the smaller bedroom. He insisted he preferred his teepee beyond the hillocks. Wicasha regretted his inability to help with the building of the cabin, but Tory and Franklin reassured him that by next summer, they would welcome his hands when erecting the barn.

A small pile of lumber was already in the makings near the old barn site. By next June, Franklin hoped to have the barn erected and ready to fill with livestock, which they would acquire slowly over the course of time. Franklin hoped to purchase hogs and a new dairy cow by next spring. In the meantime, they hadn't the need to buy any new horses. Lulu and Wicasha's gelding had both, by chance, escaped the flames and the bandits' gunfire. They had showed a few days after the pillage, grazing in the hillocks behind the field as if nothing had happened. Franklin and Tory kept Lulu tethered near the site of her old pen, and Doc Albrecht currently stabled Wicasha's gelding, close to where he convalesced.

Tory and Franklin visited Wicasha often during the three months he recuperated at the Gold Dust Inn under Doc Albrecht's care. It was strange for Tory to watch Wicasha limp around with the assistance of a cane. But Wicasha quipped that it seemed unfair that he should have a third leg while Frank still had only one arm. A former soldier of Custer's Seventh Cavalry, who had managed to conceal his deafness during the entire seven-year campaign by his uncanny ability to read lips even from great distances, helped nurse him to health. Sean Brennan, often hired by Doc Albrecht to administer care to the sick, supplemented his lip reading with Indian sign language.

Yet even after the doc gave Wicasha the thumbs-up to return to his camp, the two remained inseparable. Franklin and Tory never spoke of Sean to Wicasha, since Wicasha preferred his privacy. But whenever Tory and Franklin watched Wicasha and his new friend amble over the hillocks toward Wicasha's camp after a day of visiting, they turned their heads and smiled at each other. On some days, the new lovers didn't even bother to wait until they cleared the first hillock before reaching for each other's hand.

Joy filled Tory's heart to see Wicasha find a new love. Like Wicasha, who had lost Bua Ishte to the marauding Sioux, Tory had lost Joseph van Werckhoven to unexpected tragedy. After overcoming their grief, both had a second chance at love. The fears Tory had had that he would forever wear the heavy cloak of bachelorhood had vanished along with the smoke from the fires that had engulfed Moonlight Gulch.

He thought of Joseph often. Like a rose flattened between the leaves of a heavy book, Joseph, though out of sight, was never far from Tory's mind. In many ways, Joseph had lit the spark that had led Tory to find happiness at Moonlight Gulch. Joseph's love—a love so rare that even Tory still wondered if he had imagined it—had spurred him to demand more from life. Joseph, in the way he had expressed his love for Tory, had spoiled him, in a sense. Tory would wear that precious love for the remainder of his life, like a figurative charm around his neck.

The days following the cabin's completion passed as if the fires had never consumed the homestead. Tory and Franklin went about life, harvesting, hunting, building, and living a quiet domestic life together. Slowly, they mended the pieces of their land. The cabin tent, now used as cover for the logs curing for the barn, reminded Tory how far they'd come in only a few months. Who knew how glorious next year would be? But Tory felt he had already accumulated enough good fortune to last him a hundred lives.

Tory and Franklin never did pan for gold in the creek. Even after Franklin blasted away the natural pool, they knew some gold deposits most likely remained. Once, while bathing in the creek on a warm autumn day, Tory came across a nugget the size of a baseball wedged at the bottom between two pieces of boulder. Tory and Franklin looked at each other over the surface of the water a long time. The gold itself, as Franklin had said many times, wasn't evil. The evil was that it came too easily. Just like back in Chicago while playing ball with his comrades, Tory pitched the pricy nugget down creek as far as he could.

Baseball Gulch, Tory sometimes referred to the homestead as a quip afterward.

To Tory's relief—and also a little to his embarrassment—his letters to Franklin (and the letters Franklin had written to Torsten that Postman Persson had returned) had survived the blaze. Spared inside Franklin's sturdy leather war trunk, Tory did not know about Postman Persson's parcel until many months after he'd sent them, weeks after they'd completed the cabin. Wicasha during his many visits to Spiketrout had refrained from telling Tory the details of how Franklin had learned the truth. Tory had always assumed Franklin had pieced together the lies.

They were sitting outside by a blazing yet innocuous bonfire when Franklin, without explanation, handed the bundles to him. Tory held them for a time, as if weighing their frailty. Inhaling, he began to read them, one by one, by firelight. He sobbed, he chuckled. He sat up straight, then fell limp with sentiment. It was like finding himself transported back to his parents' row house on Chicago Avenue, upstairs, concealed behind his bedroom door, reading Franklin's letters for the first time.

He considered it a treat to read letters he thought Mr. Persson had destroyed by fire. Franklin's words had intensified with each postmark, as Tory had expected. When he read the letters that he had written Franklin, a strange sensation burned his eyes. For Tory, the letters still represented deception, yet also a genuine desire for love.

After Tory laid the last letter aside, three hours later, Franklin, as if he had been waiting for him to finish, wrapped his arm around him. His stump lay across Tory's shoulder. Tory reached up and held onto it. Blood pulsed inside the veins in a frenzied rush, as if still seeking to fill a limb that hadn't existed in twenty years.

"The letters I wrote you weren't fake, Franklin," Tory said. "I meant every word of them. You must understand. I meant every word."

Franklin never asked Tory to explain why he'd responded to his advertisement in *Matrimonial News*. Whenever Tory tried to, like now, Franklin always placed his hand over Tory's mouth and gently shook his head. Tory knew to say nothing more.

"I'm glad you answered my advertisement," was all Franklin would say about the matter.

SHELTER SOMERSET enjoys writing about the lives of people who live off the land, whether they be the Amish, nineteenth-century pioneers, or modern-day idealists seeking to live apart from the crowd. Shelter's fascination with the rustic, aesthetic lifestyle began as a child with family camping trips into the Blue Ridge Mountains. When not back home in Illinois writing, Shelter continues to explore America's expansive backcountry and rural communities. Shelter's philosophy is best summed up by the actor John Wayne: "Courage is being scared to death but saddling up anyway."

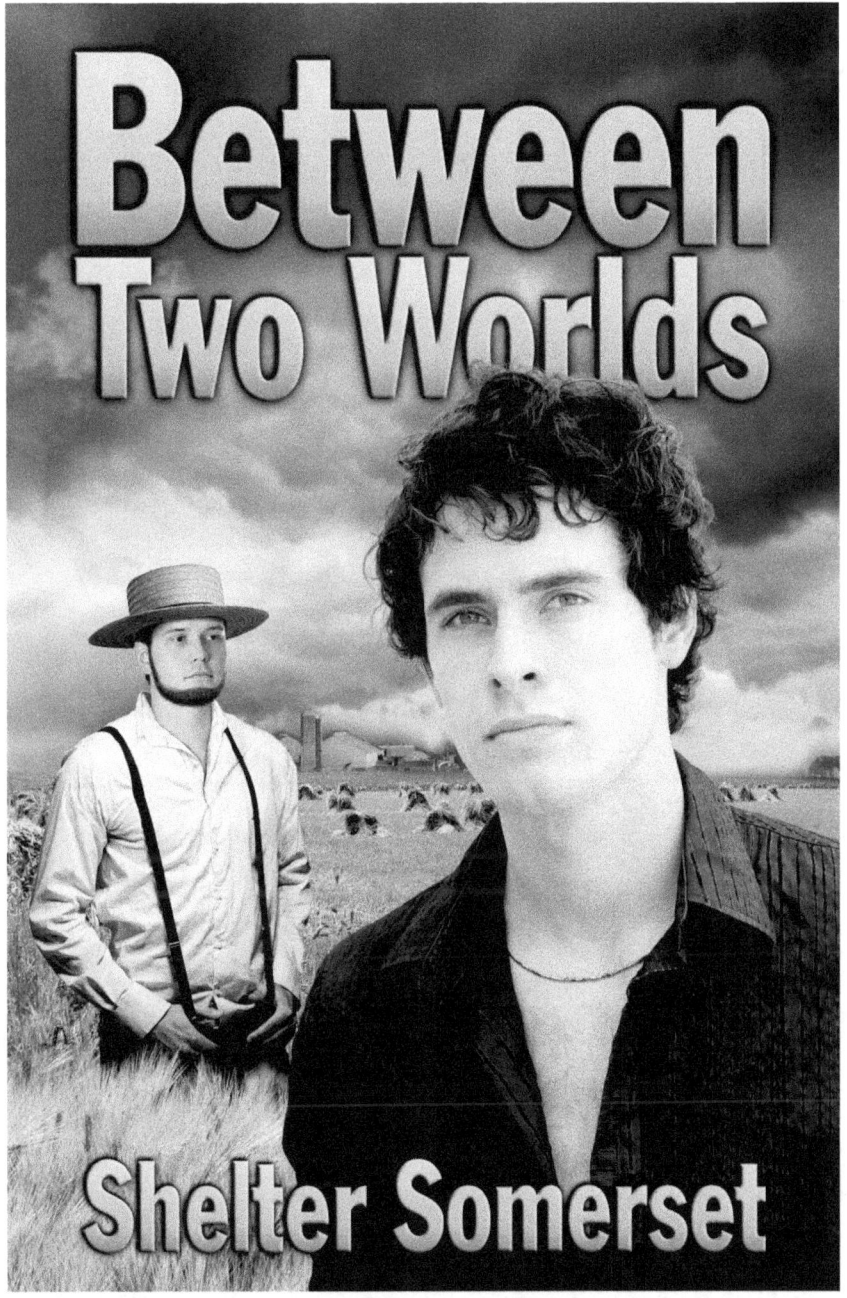

Between Two Worlds

Shelter Somerset

http://www.dreamspinnerpress.com

## Also from DREAMSPINNER PRESS

http://www.dreamspinnerpress.com

www.ingramcontent.com/pod-product-compliance
Lightning Source LLC
Chambersburg PA
CBHW070048030726
47506CB00002B/395